About the Author

After reading thousands of books which later in life focused on the paranormal genre, E. M. Sorensen decided to try his hand at writing. He drew on his experiences in the army in the early 1960s, then as a race car mechanic, factory-trained Porsche mechanic, gunsmith, and private investigator. Now an author. With each novel E. M. Sorensen writes, his storytelling skills improve in giant strides. Though his stories are related, they do not have to be read in any specific order.

The Unusual Life of Paulie Zahn

E. M. Sorensen

The Unusual Life of Paulie Zahn

Olympia Publishers
London

www.olympiapublishers.com
OLYMPIA PAPERBACK EDITION

A CIP catalogue record for this title is
available from the British Library.

ISBN: 978-1-80439-267-6

This is a work of fiction.
Names, characters, places and incidents originate from the writer's
imagination. Any resemblance to actual persons, living or dead, is
purely coincidental.

First Published in 2022

Olympia Publishers
Tallis House
2 Tallis Street
London
EC4Y 0AB

Printed in Great Britain

Acknowledgements

But not in any special order are: Lisa Ruth, Alesha Escobar, Paulette Zander, Chip Roach, Karan Oliver, and others that have pre-read my manuscripts and given sage advice to the stories.

AUTHOR'S LEAD INTO HIS SOMEWHAT ODD WORLD

You are about to start on a journey through the suburban paranormal world. One that is different enough that it could just be possible. I have not knowingly or without permission used the names of any real persons. For any scene descriptions that don't seem to be accurate, please remember this is a work of fiction and I claim my right under the 29th Amendment of the Constitution: authors shall have the right to make up silly stuff. Find a comfortable place to sit or lay and start reading. If you read past the first sixty or seventy pages, you won't want to put it down till you have finished.

15 NOVEMBER 2016 – 1745 HOURS

It was starting into winter in Seattle, but the weather had remained mild and the trademark daily rain hadn't started yet.

I pulled out of the employee parking lot near the Boeing Museum, onto Marginal Way, and headed north toward downtown Seattle. Took the right-hand fork onto 1st and in just a few blocks, I was backing my bike into the curb in front of Slim's Last Chance.

I was there for the Wednesday night special which consisted of a pint of beer and a bowl of chili with meat for $5.00. Not that cowboy vegan crap with just beans, but robust, very spicy chili with chunks of beef instead of ground. Wednesday nights were no-band nights. Just come and eat cheap.

The fun part of my arrival was when the wanna-be bikers that hung out in front saw that I was a woman. Cue the catcalls.

"Hey, string-bean, watcha doing on your ole man's bike?" one would call out.

"How bout I teach you how to ride that thing?" That from Scruffy No#2.

Or, "That's a fine-looking machine you got there, hun. Any time you want someone to ride with, you just say the word and I'll take you around and introduce you to the real bikers around here."

Same shit chat, different night. I got my chain and lock out of my saddlebag and ran it through my front rim and frame and around the Motorcycle Parking Only signpost to slow a possible theft. Shit, a van could roar up, three guys jump out and physically pick up the bike and shove it in the back, and roar off in fifteen seconds or less. The chain and the odd mix of the crowd outside the front door were my only real preventatives. That and a .357 Magnum which may be up for acquisition later.

I walked in and took a seat at the bar. I ordered the special and the barmaid drew a mug of beer and turned my chili order in.

I had been to Slim's at least a dozen times now. The ambiance is quite the kaleidoscope of sights where your eyes never stop looking at the decorations… and the patrons. Quite the cross-section of humanity. Rarely a suit, but a lot of inked-up ladies and gents. Most everyone is here to enjoy the food, music, and good company. Most of the guys have been in many times before and watch their manners. It is the occasional newbie wannabe biker who wants to make an impression and usually gets up in the wrong dude's face.

I usually get several requests to dance or offers of a beer or a shot. I politely thank them, turn down the dance card request, but not the drinks. I will give a few minutes of lip service to the ones who buy me a drink but make it clear that I would not be going home with any of them later in the evening.

So far, all of the guys trying to get my favors have been well mannered and respected my aloofness. I'm not a snob, I just have no interest in getting involved right now.

Today was almost like the others except some scuzzball didn't seem to get it through his little pea brain that I wasn't available. It was the middle of the workweek and I had no intention of staying very late so somewhere between eight and nine p.m., I settled my tab and headed out.

I was almost onto my bike when someone grabbed me by the arm. Well, the wonder of wonders if it isn't Mr. Scuzzball himself! I started to rip my arm out of his grasp, but he was unbelievably strong. Within a heartbeat, he had pulled me into the alleyway.

"Oh! A fighter. I'm gonna enjoy getting a taste of you, my little chickie," he snarled.

This was not going well. And what exactly did he mean by 'a taste'? He pulled me in close and bit me. *What the shit is this, biting?* I got an arm free and clocked him straight in the face, which got a snarl out of him. Then he punched back.

I heard and felt my jaw bone or bones cracking. I was in serious trouble. As I was starting to lose consciousness, I felt him clamp his foul mouth down tight on my neck.

Everything was serious pain and flashing colors. I thought I heard someone shout and felt the weight of Scuzzy lifting off me before everything went black.

THE EARLY YEARS – STARTING IN 2008

My name is Paulie (Paulette) Zahn and I have been living and working in the Seattle area for four or five months now. I had rented a studio that was converted from a separate garage behind a beach-type cottage in the Alki Beach district of southwest Seattle. I had moved here from Truckee, California, which had been my home since I could remember.

My dad raised me. No one ever told anything about my mother and by the time I was in high school, I no longer had any thoughts about having one. I spent all of my time after school helping Dad in his auto repair shop. He taught me how to use tools and helped me build my motorcycle. It's the same one I have now.

I bought the used 2000 Harley FXR4 in the summer of 2005 and rode it through my school years, except in the winter. Winters in Truckee brought snow up to the roof of our house, making riding difficult, to say the least. The two winters before I graduated from school were filled with working on the bike. I dissembled it completely and rebuilt it with some changes, including camshafts, re-worked cylinder heads, S&S Carburetor, and Vance & Heinz exhaust. Keeping the displacement to the original 80 Cubic Inches made for a very reliable motor. 80 spoke rims front and rear. Everything I did was for strength and reliability as I believed that I was going to have it for many years.

After graduation in 2008 just short of my eighteenth birthday, I started thinking about what I was going to do next. I had taken a few days to ride down off the mountains and into Reno and I was browsing through the dozens and dozens of clothing stores when I passed a U.S. Army Recruiting Office. There were pictures of men AND women in uniform. Some were in tanks, some riding in Humvees, and there on the far wall was the picture of a woman in fatigues with her arm inside the gearbox of an Apache attack helicopter. That was it. That was what I wanted to do. I sat with the recruiter and told him what I wanted to be trained in.

Sgt Sign-em-Up was excited to get me enlisted. He started me with the basic Armed Forces Qualification Test to see if I was even smart enough to enter the army. "You will have forty-five minutes to finish. Take your time and finish as many questions as you can."

Something was wrong. It was only twenty minutes into the exam and I had finished everything. Maybe there were more pages that he forgot to give me.

"Excuse me, Mr. Sergeant, I think I am missing some pages."

He came over and picked up the questions booklet. "This is the entire test, ma'am. What was the last question that you finished?"

"The one on the bottom of the last page."

"Maybe you missed some of the middle pages. Look over your answer sheet to see where there is a group of unanswered questions."

"No unanswered questions, Sergeant, I marked every question."

He looked at the answer sheet and then at his watch, verifying the time by the clock on the wall. He took the answer sheet and went back to his desk where he took out the answer overlay and placed it over my answer sheet. I just sat in the chair in the testing area and watched him. He looked over the exam first with the answer overlay, and then he looked up at me.

"Young lady, how many times have you taken this test before?"

He was looking a little red above his collar. And he seemed to have become rather stiff with me.

"Never, I haven't even been into any recruiter's office before, anywhere. Never have seen that test before this morning. Why? Is there something wrong?"

"I have been a recruiter here for the past three years. In that time, I have never had anyone finish the test that fast and have never, ever had anyone get 100 percent. You got 100 percent, and you did it in record time. I want to sign you up as fast as possible, but I want to warn you about something. When you go to basic training, there is a battery of assessment tests they give everyone to see what they are best qualified to do in the service. Those tests are different and harder than this one and if those test results are, let's say, in the lowest percentile, it will suggest that you knew the answers to this test before you took it. At that moment, you would be tossed out."

I nodded understanding. "Sergeant, I want to do that," and I pointed at the girl helicopter mechanic.

"Ms. Zahn, I can get you signed up now, but you have to wait till your eighteenth birthday to be sworn in, which is not for another three weeks.

And that is when I joined the army. By May of 2009, I had finished the advanced repair and maintenance courses at the head of the classes. That got me a prized assignment to Bagram Air Base. A real Garden of Eden.

20 APRIL 2016 – 1400 HOURS

The maintenance and repair unit I was attached to in my first tour was composed of 60 percent women mechanics. That made this unit desirable for the women in uniform. The sexual innuendos were fewer and the actual sex attacks were a lot rarer in this unit as compared with the rest of the army posts in Afghanistan. I didn't give it much thought during my first ten-month tour, but my second tour demonstrated the advantages of a woman-dominated unit. A sexual assault attack by a male officer during that tour starkly highlighted the situation and left me with little interest in the male species. I was still heterosexual, but decidedly uninterested in dating.

The attack probably left me even more aloof than I was used to normally, and maybe a little more hesitant than usual to bow to the egomaniac men who ranked above me. I was incredibly good at my job and had made it to Specialist E-6 several times, but I was somewhat of a non-conformist when it came to jumping up and saluting some officers.

One time, I was working upside down in the pilot's cockpit, hands deep up in the main control panel when this newbie lieutenant who was just out of the academy climbed up and looked in.

After a minute or two, he growled out in a voice that was supposed to intimidate enlisted personnel, "Don't you come to attention when an officer is in the room?"

"Hand me the wire strippers," I responded.

"What was that you said?"

"Please hand me the pliers… sir," I said.

"Trooper, get out here and come to attention," commanded Lt. Butthole.

The helicopter I was working on was on a 'RUSH' status and now, thanks to the self-important lieutenant, it was not going to be ready on time. The lieutenant then dressed me down in front of everyone in the hangar and sent me to the barracks until my hearing on Monday morning when my company commander Captain Brown returned from a strategy and planning session.

Monday morning came and I got into a clean set of camos and went to the Headquarters Quonset Hut for my 'hearing.' Lieutenant Iron Pants was in the front office. No question, he was waiting for me.

"The captain wants to see you right now, Trooper," he said.

That was all he said before turning and marching (ramrod stiff) down the hall to the captain's office.

~ ~ ~ ~

"Sergeant Zahn reporting as directed, sir," I said as I came to attention and saluted. And I did it quite smartly I might add.

"At ease, Sergeant." Captain Brown said. "What is this about, Lieutenant?"

"Captain, I have brought charges against Sergeant Zahn for insubordination and disobeying a direct order."

"I read your report yesterday morning. I also contacted several of the other mechanics that were working in the hangar at the time of the incident. I have already pulled the sergeant's personnel file and the work requests for the bird she was working on at the time," said the captain.

"Before I ask any questions to either of you, is there anything else that you would like me to know about, Lieutenant?"

"No, sir, I stand by my report," smirked the lieutenant.

Turning to me, the captain asked, "Sergeant Zahn, what were you doing at the moment lieutenant approached the helio you were working on, and what was the bird's status?"

"Sir, I was upside down in the pilot's seat with my arms up under the instrument panel. I was working on replacing the primary fire direction control module. I neither saw nor heard the lieutenant approach. I heard a voice and asked that person to hand me a pair of wire strippers.

"The next thing I know is the lieutenant became quite agitated and ordered me to quit what I was doing, come out from the aircraft, and come to attention. He dressed me down in front of the entire maintenance crew and ordered me out of the hangar bay until this could be heard in a court-martial setting, and here I am… sir."

"What happened to the helio? Did it make it out for the Friday night assignment? The 'assignment' was a special operation against the enemy that had taken several months of planning and meetings to coordinate?" the captain asked.

"No, sir. It missed the assignment. As I was the only technician fully trained and certified to repair and re-calibrate the main combat controller, my absence meant the bird didn't fly."

The captain opened one of his desk's drawers and pulled out a small folder. Pulled out some form from the folder and put the folder back. He wrote on the paper and then pulled out some rubber stamp and impressed some mark over his signature.

"Sergeant Zahn," he said as he handed me the slip, "take this to the first sergeant and have him make all the arrangements. You are dismissed and I don't want to see you for a week."

I snapped to attention, saluted, and said, "Thank you, sir."

I closed the captain's door as I left to see the first sergeant. But something said to just sit tight for a moment. I bent down to re-tie my boot laces while I listened.

I didn't exactly have to strain my ears because the yelling from behind the door was easy to hear.

"Lieutenant, do you have any understanding of what all the troops in this country are here to do? We, which includes both me and you and all the troops here, have a job to do. The protocol is secondary to performance. You are no different than all the other West Point grads that come with a cob stuck up their buts. It usually takes a good two years before you academy grads realize that whipping your subordinates into shape by threat or coercion will get you a very poor performing unit.

"This is a combat unit in a combat zone. Polished belt buckles and buttoned pocket flaps are NO longer important. Saluting and coming to attention every time an officer is passed is no longer the standard. You have caused a major offensive to be canceled because of the lack of the nighttime-enabled attack helicopter to cover the ground troops. Several million dollars went into organizing this offensive and it is all a waste and will have to be re-spent. Not to mention the dozens if not hundreds of ground troops that went without critical air coverage during this operation. Your actions were so book correct, but so wrong. I will be entering a full statement of this activity on your part with a strong recommendation that you are sent to the rear and are never allowed a combat command again.

"Next time you are in the hangar, roll up your sleeves and get down on the floor with the people that know what they are doing. Hand them tools they ask for, make sure they have a supply of mechanics wiping rags. In general, make yourself useful and forget about the difference between an enlisted person and an officer. We are all here to do a dangerous job and a stiff backside will just get you shot. If I hear of you making like Little Lord Fauntleroy again, I will put you in charge of the clean garbage can detail, which if you know anything about compounds in war zones, is operated by local civilians that you have no authority over. You're dismissed."

I shot out to the sergeant's desk and was handing him the note from the captain when the lieutenant went past on his way out the door. The temperature in the office rose to volcanic levels as he passed behind me. The only sound was that of the front door being slamming open and then shut.

21 APRIL 2016 – 1830 HOURS

Aviano, Italy, is the most desirable air base that the USAF has in Europe. It is simply beautiful. The weather is usually cloudy, but the temperatures are mild because of the proximity to the Dolomite mountains. Vineyards and small villages surround the airbase.

The R & R barracks were like a civilian resort. The mess there was more like dining out at an upscale restaurant than chow at a military base. Waiters and waitresses took your orders, brought the food, and cleared the dishes away. You sat wherever you wanted and if invited, you could dine with strangers at your table. No one wore rank insignias, so you could be having a sit down with a major or a private or anything in between. And the men have a meal with women at the same table. Gender-based biases and the co-mingling of officers and enlisted were gone. Everyone at this retreat had seen or had been the recipient of the horrors of war first hand, making everything else unimportant. For the first time, I felt like we were all comrades-in-arms and I was proud.

It was the second day there and hadn't gone off the base yet. The R & R facility was complete with every indulgence one would expect from a four-star resort. How would I know what is available with a four-star resort? Until my evening meal, I hadn't even considered going into the nearby villages.

When I entered the dining area, I was given a table for two, but I was the only one there. I ordered a mojito and was reading the menu when another person approached and asked if it would be okay to share the table.

I'm usually very aware of my surroundings and to have anyone get this close without me being aware of their presence is rare. My spidey senses must have let me down this time.

I looked her over as she took the seat opposite me. She was easily as tall as me. Exactly how tall I couldn't be sure as the 4" spike heels took her well above the magical six-foot number. Not that I own any fancy spikey heels. She seemed to flow like liquid mercury. It was a piece of moving art to watch her melt into the chair. Simply put, I was awed by her presence.

I have never been one to take notice or interest in the physical appearance of another woman. Being tall wasn't what had me dwelling on her presence. It was the entire HER. She exuded a commanding presence. At Bagram Airbase, there would be the occasional VIP coming through, like senior generals, Secretary of the Army, VIPs of that status. Not one I ever saw had the command of presence like this woman did.

I'm not attracted to women; I mean I'm not interested in being buds with or hanging around with the girls. I'm just not one to spend the day shopping or getting a pedicure. But this person had my attention.

"Thank you for sharing your table. My name is Lisa Connor and am on respite from my job," and she held out her hand for me to shake.

That was a firm handshake. Not a grip like she was trying to impress me with her strength, just firm. And warm.

I do not have any lack of muscle that's for sure. I would have played high school football if they had let girls on the teams. By the time I finished 5th grade, I had beaten up every boy in my grade and half the boys in 6th grade. Ms.

Congeniality I wasn't.

I knew by her handshake that she was probably stronger than me.

"How do you do. I'm Lisa Connor."

"Hello, I'm Paulie Zahn."

She smiled but added nothing and neither did I. Mealtime consisted of some very short mention of the different menu choices. Other than a few grunts and hums, there wasn't any chit chat which was all right with me.

Toward the end of the meal, Lisa Connor displayed her warm smile again and said, "I'm going to stop at the lounge after we finish, for a nightcap, and to wait for the late afternoon news feeds from the States. I would like it if you joined me."

"I think I would like that," I responded, half surprising myself.

~ ~ ~ ~

This lounge was not like the ones at Bagram. There they were separated by military rank. Here in Aviano, there was no segregation at all. You could tell the combat harden soldiers from the rest.

Like the group of the ten men and two women that were huddled together on the far side of the room. They had encircled themselves with chairs and tables as a barrier against the rest of us, closing ranks. They were loud and rough around the edges. Every fourth word wasn't printable and the rest was from the trough that bred these case-hardened souls. I knew these people. No, not personally or by name. I knew them because I drank nightly with them and felt the horrors they had gone through. Remembering the many, many comrades that have given everything they could give for their country.

Lisa picked a separate table right by the main bar. Fast service and a perfect view of the gigantatron TV. Not much interesting was on.

"Your heart is beating a mile a minute," Lisa commented. "Relax, my friend. There is nothing to do so just hunker down and live your life for yourself."

True, so very true, I thought to myself. Sitting there with her, I unconsciously changed gears and let the tension leave my arms and legs. The creases in my brow started to dissolve. This woman had some strange ability to reach into my mind and prop me up.

Contrary to my normal personality, I blurted, "We haven't said very much so far and we haven't discussed our past or our future, but there is something about you that makes me comfortable. I feel like I could trust you with my life. I have never even come close to another person that I trust like I think I may trust you. Why is that? Who are you? Where have you come from?"

I sat back in my chair a little horrified by my outburst. I told myself it was the alcohol talking, but I knew that wasn't true. I had only the one drink at dinner and the one that I just started here at this table. But here I was, blubbering and gushing over a strange woman I had known for about an hour.

"I work for a military contractor, Newmark Industries." She explained, "I am here to troubleshoot some reported irregularities in the equipment we supply. I troubleshoot and correct or help correct any deficiencies. It is all fieldwork in the heart of the conflicted areas of Afghanistan and I have to get out and back into civilization just to decompress. I'm here for two weeks just relaxing."

"I've never heard of Newmark Industries," I said.

"You would be surprised to know how many of our products are used by your helio unit."

I could feel a tingling sensation running up my spine. "How did you know that's what I work on? I don't even recall telling you that I am in the army, let alone what my job is or where I am stationed." I was getting a little tense about talking with this woman.

"It's my business to know. My security clearances equal or exceed those for most of the generals in this theater of operation. I would never have sat down with you at dinner or for drinks unless I knew it was safe to have contact with you. I rarely fraternize with anyone. On those rare occasions when I choose to socialize with anyone, I pre-screen them. I get a background clearance on all of those I am in contact with so I am fully prepared for any interaction."

"How could you have possibly done any background on me?" I asked skeptically. "I mean, I haven't spoken to anyone since I arrived outside of the employees here, and you, whom I haven't met before."

"I was in the main lobby when you checked in. I could see that your physical makeup is similar to mine, that you are also an attractive person and I could tell that you are independent and positive. Those things caught my attention."

The whole thing made no sense and I was increasingly uncomfortable. I started to gather up anything of mine that was out on the table.

Lisa put her hand on my arm, again displaying a smile. "Hold on for a minute," she said. "You are certainly attractive, but I'm not hitting on you, I'm straight too. I just enjoy the company of smart, talented people, and I recognized these particular characteristics in you when I saw you in the lobby. You make quite an impression. After you left the check-in desk, I requested a copy of the information on the hotel registry. Then, for me, it only takes me an hour or two to receive a copy of your military file."

I was tingly all over. In all my time in the military, I had never heard of anything like this. "How did you get them to give you my registration information?"

"My credentials will get me most anything I ask for without any red tape getting in the way. The bottom line is, I'm in Italy to relax and I am very selective about the company I keep. Know that I would like to spend the next week exploring Italy with you."

"Why?"

"I don't wait around for things to happen. I want to have a traveling companion, but I want it to be the right one. One that I know can take care of themselves in strange situations. Don't want to babysit. You, I already believe, are more than capable and I would like to spend my downtime with you or someone like you. I say, 'one like you,' but I doubt that I could find your replacement. I am just finishing up on forty straight hours of work and travel and am going to my room for some much-needed sleep. If you think you would want to do some sightseeing with me, be here for a late breakfast at around nine a.m."

With that, she reached out and gave my hand a warm AND STRONG squeeze.

And then I was alone.

22 APRIL 2016 – 0845 HOURS

The next morning, I woke up as the sun rose. Six years in the military and you get into a routine that is hard to break. The room I was in was furnished like the Ritz. Maybe not that fancy, but my comparison is between this room and my room back in Afghanistan. Then there was the bed. Even my bed back home in Truckee was not nearly as comfortable as this one. I decided that the next day I would ignore the urge to get up early.

The room had its private bath with this most luxurious shower with five shower heads that all come on at once. For the past six years, I had a communal shower and the toilets were lined up with no dividers let alone a door. One never really gets used to the lack of privacy.

I had left the base to catch the air transportation in a rush. I just had time to grab my backpack and cram some clothes and toiletries in it and dash for the airstrip. My civilian wardrobe consisted of jeans, shorts, an assortment of rock concert T's, and my Converse sneakers. I was thinking that I should go down to the commissary and get some new duds. I was just about to leave the room when the room phone rang.

"Hello."

"Good morning, Paulie. I have a rental car and want to drive down the coastline toward Venice. It is close to this wonderful beach called Lido di Jesolo. May stay overnight or two in the area. There is also a castle that I want to see. I would love to have you accompany me. It is a really pretty drive through the wine country before we near Venice or the beach communities. I took the chance that you would say yes, and I reserved two rooms at the hotel, Al Ponte Antico."

I was caught short. I didn't know what to think. "It sounds lovely, but I think a hotel in Venice is a little out of my reach and besides I don't have anything appropriate to wear. I will be wearing the same today that I had on last night. I will probably buy some new clothes from the commissary later today."

"Don't worry about the rooms, they are paid for by my company. For clothes, maybe you should wait till we go through some of the towns and villages on the way to Venice. This is Wednesday and trade will be slow as the best times for merchants are the weekends. Today, you can barter and get some great deals."

"I don't know why I am doing this, but okay, I'm on for the trip. When do you want to leave?"

"Right after we have had some breakfast. Meet me in the dining room."

~ ~ ~ ~

The dining room was full, unlike the lounge last night, and I had some difficulty finding Lisa.

"Good morning, Paulie," she said from behind me.

I mean right behind. I was startled because I should have seen, heard, or felt her approaching. "*Err*, yes, good morning. I didn't hear you approaching me and was a little taken aback. I just got here a moment ago and haven't put my name in for a table. It looks like we will have a little wait. I want to grab a cup of coffee; do you want me to get you one?"

I turned to look at her to see what she wanted to do. She

was waving to someone. It was the restaurant manager, I think. Gray slacks, a white jacket, and a look on his face made me feel like I was the most important person in the room.

It was Lisa that garnered his attention.

"Good morning, Ms. Connor, are you and your friend ready to be seated?" asked the maitre d'.

She turned to me and asked, "I'm ready to sit, are you?"

"I'm ready," I said. "But I don't see any tables available."

The maitre d' turned to me and said, "It isn't a problem. This way please." And off he went...

He stepped out quite smartly and we followed. Halfway through the dining hall, he turned and headed to the left side of the room through arches that were like little alcoves. Right inside the faux alcove were a set of doors. When he opened them up, we walked out onto a small private patio with a table set for two.

"It is good to have you with us again, Ms. Connor. Your waitress will be here in just a moment. And of course, if there is anything special you want, please let me know."

"Thank you, this will be perfect, Vito."

I sat. This was just too beautiful. The tablecloth was bright white clean. And real glass glasses and they were spotless. No sand on the table or anywhere for that matter. And I won't have to go get my meal on a tray, waiting in line with a bunch of hot sweaty, dog-tired GIs.

"Is there a menu?" I asked Lisa.

"The choices are a coffee made any way you want it, and a collection of items from the bakery. The rolls, if you want to call them that, have Italian names but are better recognized for their French names. We are going to get a basket of assorted items to pick from," she told me.

The waitress came and deposited a large covered wicker basket along with some orange juice and endless butter.

"What beverage can I bring you, madam?" she asked.

"A double cappuccino, please."

"I'll have the same," Lisa said.

For the next ten minutes or so, I let my mind relax and enjoy the moment. The croissants were right out of the ovens. They tasted different than what I had expected, but it was a delicious surprise. Later on, while on the trip with Lisa, she would correct me and explained that the dough used for the cornetti, which is the Italian word for a croissant, is made with a different mixture than its French cousin. Croissant—cornets whatever you want to call them, there is nothing like this in Afghanistan. I was inhaling them until I realized I looked like a pig.

"I'm sorry," I said, "I'm not sharing very nicely. I haven't had anything this good since, well, since probably before I joined the army. Several years of playing shoot and duck have brought out my crude and uncouth side."

Lisa looked at me in a curious but pleased manner.

"Don't worry about taking breakfast away from me. There is a lot of depth to this kitchen."

"Lisa, I'm having some second thoughts on just taking off with you. I know nothing about you and to drive off into the countryside in a place far from home and far from my unit in Afghanistan is leaving me a bit nervous.

"To be serious, I have been with you for less than six or eight hours. All you have said is that you have all these special credentials that let you access information on me that I didn't think anyone outside of the military could get to. Like there are warning flags that I should be paying attention to. How often do you do this, pick up a stranger and drive off into the countryside of a foreign country?"

Lisa looked down at her plate. I could tell she wasn't seeing anything in particular. She was in serious contemplation for a few moments.

"Paulette, I do understand what may be going through your mind. If the roles were reversed, I would be heading for the hills right now. I already like the thought of doing things with you. I honestly think I would enjoy your company. Now for the other shoe…

"I haven't lied to you but there is a whole lot more to our meeting. It was not by accident," Lisa said.

I wasn't shocked, no, but now I was curious. I wanted to hear her out before I just got up and went my own way. "Okay, so can you sort this out and help me decide to stay in or not?"

"I do work for Newmark Industries. Newmark is a large aerospace engineering and manufacturing firm that develops and sells a myriad of hardware items to the United States military. Newmark Industries designed and built the fire direction control used on your helicopters. You have been instrumental in making some improvements because of the suggestions you have forwarded up through your chain of command. We know that your term of enlistment is coming up in about five months and I was tasked with making contact with you and making an offer."

"This R&R time off was a sudden surprise to me. I had no plans of being here three days ago. How did you make contact so quickly?"

"I had landed at Bagram only to find that you had just left in a military transport headed to Aviano. My company aircraft is a lot faster than the prop-driven transport you left in. I landed in

Aviano just ahead of you," Lisa told me.

"That's all very interesting, ya know, about how you have the wherewithal to keep up with me especially since I wasn't all that sure of where I was going myself. And that doesn't begin to give me a clear picture of 'why.' I think that I want to know that before I make my decision. You know, to go or not to go."

"That is more than fair. I was hoping to talk this out with you while we were on the road. Sort of a captive environment, just the two of us in a car driving through strange territory. But maybe it is better to get this part over with before we go anywhere. As I said, Newmark was already aware of you from your reports. I wanted time alone with you to make an offer of employment for when your current enlistment is up. It would also give me the proper amount of time to answer all possible questions you may have and even answers to questions you don't ask.

"There is the bonus of you being a girl after my own heart. I think we feel the same on a lot of different subjects. That is pretty much the whole story. One other thing before I forget; I have a very open expense account and you do not have to worry about some of the cost of our travels."

That had me feeling a lot more comfortable about going with her. The carrot of a job offer was also interesting so I said, "Okay, let's go."

"Go get what you want to bring. Don't worry about clothes because we can stop in the nearby village that has some good shops for everyday clothes. If you don't see anything you like here, we are going to be able to stop at a lot of places before we get to Venice and there are great clothing stores in Venice.

"Meet me in an hour outside the front door of the main lobby."

~ ~ ~ ~ ~

My nervousness had been eased by what she explained about the job prospect and about how she knew about me from my helio work. I was so elated that I flew to my room and threw undies, a change of shorts, and my one other T-shirt and toiletries into my backpack and I was out the door and down to the lobby.

As I walked out the front doors to the drop-off area, the only car I saw was this dark blue convertible. Not any convertible but a BMW. I know cars and this was a 650i series. Ooo! I could see myself driving through Italy in that car. All I needed was some big round sunglasses and a white headscarf.

And just hold that thought because here came Lisa with big round sunglasses and a white scarf over her head and around her neck, a black short-sleeved blouse, and a short black skirt. She certainly had long legs. I was gawking like she was on the runway of a movie premiere.

She held her hand out and I saw her press the button on a key fob and the trunk of the 650 popped open. *Sweet Jesus, this is where my job interview is going to be conducted. What world have I just gotten myself onto?*

Ever since I joined the army, I had always sent half my pay home. My dad didn't need the money as the repair shop always did well. I figured that he was stashing it in a savings account for when I return home. The other half was for me to take care of my personal care items and a night out now and then. After the first four years of my enlistment, the pay increases left me with extra at the end of each pay period and I had started a savings account. I never drew any of the money out as my social exploits were slim to none so I had close to $6,000 in the account. Maybe this was the time to draw down on it for this trip. I already doubted that I would have this opportunity again, ever.

"I want to make a stop at the bank here on the base," I said. "I need some running around money."

Lisa didn't say anything and motioned for me to get in. I did and eased down into the plush leather seat that seemed to wrap me in a cocoon. When I was in high school, I got to drive a wide range of cars while I was working in my dad's repair shop but never had been in a high-end luxury car of this caliber before. I closed my door, buckled up, and off we drove.

I took $2000 out of my account in euros. That should set my spending limit. The one problem was doing the mental gymnastics to match the U.S. dollars with the wad of euros I now had in my wallet. *Wait a minute, this is probably the grandest vacation I would ever have so I should let my hair down,* I thought.

I turned and watched Lisa as she drove. She was beautiful is all I can think to say. She exuded a level of confidence I don't think I had ever experienced. She was so completely relaxed behind the wheel that at first, you thought she wasn't paying attention to the traffic or anything. I sort of held onto that feeling until later on in the trip when I realized that she was alert and focused on the job of driving without showing any strain.

In a few more moments, we were leaving the base and heading right into the village of Aviano.

ITALY

Aviano Air Base was second in size to Ramstein Air Base in Germany. While Ramstein had been expanded over the years, Aviano was restricted to its present size. There was only a limited number of on-base barracks and the majority of personnel stationed there lived in the village of Aviano.

Even though it was Wednesday, the town thronged with shoppers. They were a mix of locals and the personnel from the airbase. My neck was on a swivel taking in as much as I could. Lisa turned the car off the main road onto a less-traveled street.

"There is a clothing store back there that has just the things you will need for the trip."

She parked and raised the top. As we got out, she spotted a teenager sitting on his skateboard on the sidewalk in front of one of the stores. Lisa walked up to him and spoke to him in Italian. I didn't follow well; hell, I wasn't able to follow at all. English was pretty much the only language I understood. There was an exception, I had picked up enough Spanish, or rather Mexican to get by. It was acquired from almost eight years in the army. There are a lot of Hispanics in the service and one couldn't help but pick up some of the languages because it is as prevalent as English in the barracks or the field. As I listened to them talk, I realized that maybe Italian wasn't that different than the Mexican version of Spanish that I knew. The realization came before I could sort of follow what they were discussing.

"I have arranged with Vito here to keep his eye on our car

while we shop," Lisa said.

"You trust him?"

"In Italy, if you put something down and walk away, it won't be there when you get back. The difference here is that this lad relies on the personnel from the airbase to pay for his watchfulness. No one will bother the car while he is here. He needs this job." She turned and pointed down the street.

"Here, the shop I want is on the main street just around the corner."

The shop she indicated was a lot larger than I expected. The selection had something for most everyone's taste. I went to the racks and shelves of the type of clothes I would gravitate to. I leaned toward the sturdier items. Plain in design and color. Nothing flashy for me.

"Paulie, take those clothes back to the racks. I'm going to pick out some things for you. We are on vacation, we are in Italy, we have no one to answer to but ourselves."

She picked out several sundresses in various colors and patterns. She also picked out what looked to me like a cocktail dress. I had never dressed for cocktail hour, not ever. Never got invited to anything like that and didn't see the need to own a dress like that. I also got a peek at the price.

"Lisa, that dress costs a third of what I have in my wallet."

"Don't look at the prices. Wait till we are finished and see what the total comes to. Then let me talk to the salesperson and I will get you a deal you can't refuse."

So, I let my financial hair down and sorted through the racks and shelves until I had an impressive assortment piled on the front counter. It included two summer dresses of colorful cotton with flowing skirts and off the shoulder necklines, a pair of sandals, four-inch heels in a shade that went well with the cocktail dress, a colorfully printed cotton skirt, and two peasant blouses to go with the skirt, a black bikini of questionable coverage and some undergarments. While I was trying on the items, Lisa was picking up some things for herself, including an exact twin of my cocktail ensemble. I visualized the two of us walking into a bar or restaurant together in our matching outfits. I was sure that would turn a lot of heads.

I was just finishing up the search and heading for the counter when I saw the salesgirl packing everything in bags.

"Whoa, wait a minute. I have to see how much this will all cost," I said.

"*Scusa, senorita,*" she said. "Your new collection comes to €256.00."

There had to be an error. There simply was no way this pile of clothes came to that price. I turned to Lisa and saw a grin on her face. Something was up, this just did not smell right. I mentally ran through the tag prices in my head and it had to be worth more than half of what I had with me, which was about $2275 which included the $2000 I had just withdrawn from my bank account.

"Pay the lady, sister, and let's get the show on the road. No, wait, get into that peasant skirt and blouse first, you'll look great driving down the coast with the top down."

'Sister.' She called me sister. It made me feel pretty special at the moment. I looked at this woman as if she were a goddess and she was. And to have her sort of making me her equal or at least her partner in crime felt right on me. Little did I know at the time that 'partner in crime' would come to a lot closer to being real than I ever imagined. I paid the charges, ran back to the changing booth, and got into new undies and the blouse and skirt that Lisa pointed out and slipped into the small light sandals.

When I came out of the dressing room, Lisa was buying some sunscreen to go with everything else. We picked up our packages and went back to the car… yepper it was still there with Vito sitting on the rear trunk lid smoking a cigarette. He was like twelve years old and smoking. I don't smoke. Never have, but I am surrounded by smokers in the army. And I noticed that the number of smokers and how much they smoked rose dramatically when we were stationed in a war zone.

I saw her hand Vito a €10.00 note and he grinned and grinned till the corners of his mouth practically wrapped around his head. He jumped down and helped us load everything in the trunk and then he pulled out a water bottle and some rags and cleaned the windshield of every speck of dust there was.

We got in and as we buckled up, Lisa put the top down. She started the car and before she put it in gear, she handed me a small gift bag and a tube of sunscreen.

"Put lots of sunscreen on and then the other item. A small gift from me," she said.

I understand the sunscreen. Even though I've spent several years in the arid and constantly sunny days of Afghanistan, I wasn't there to sunbathe. The briefest my clothing attire ever got was camo pants and a beige T-shirt. In the field, we all used lots and lots of sunscreen on our arms, neck, and face but not on the rest of our bodies. Here I was with a scooping neckline and the skirt exposed an awful lot of leg. Lisa had started to drive while I pulled up my skirt and slathered sunscreen on my pale legs. That little chore was done, I reached into the little bag she had handed me. Inside was an exquisite silk headscarf.

"Lisa, this is beautiful," I said while getting the words stuck behind the lump in my throat. Since I have been in the army about the only thing anyone ever bought me was a beer from a horny GI that I never had any intentions of going out with.

I wear my hair short. Not butch short but short. Low maintenance. I wasn't going to have any hair blowing in my face. I decided to wear it around my neck like Grace Kelly in *To Catch a Thief*.

"Paulie, we are alike in many ways. Frankly, we share a physical beauty that sets us apart. I'm not conceited, it's just a fact that I have learned to accept over the years through many oglers and offers of marriage and the few who assumed that I could be had easily.

"Secondly, we are both physically fit, beyond the twice-a-week yoga crowd. If push came to shove, I am more than physically capable of taking care of myself in, shall I say, a dangerous situation? Your occupation has kept you physically fit and I'm quite sure you, too, can take care of yourself.

"We don't have the looks of a fashion model. Not by any means of comparison. Neither are we movie stars who wear lots and lots of make-up or indulge in Botox and whatever else. What we are is two very treetop tall, radiant, beautiful women that will hush the crowd when we enter a room."

I could feel my skin redden, not from the sun but at the slight embarrassment of her praise. The only other people who had ever expounded on my looks were my dad, who I thought was biased, and James Style, the high school football captain who only wanted to show me how to play 'hide the sausage.' Just so you know, I'm not a virgin, but I am select with whom I roll in the hay. I can honestly say that all the men or boys that I ever had a booty call with I can still call a friend.

I looked up to clear my head of everything that had

happened in the past twenty-four hours and noticed that we had cleared the outskirts of the village of Aviano and were plunged into the miles of wine grape vines planted in almost every field. The air was clear and hovering at eighty degrees. *What a day for a ride in the country with my best new friend.*

I couldn't believe I just thought that. I had only known this Lisa Connor for less than a day and here I was thinking I had just become one of the dynamic duo partners. Well, I was comfortable being on a trip to wherever with her.

Lisa had turned the radio on to a station. No opera, thank goodness, I couldn't take the yowling of an operatic aria sung by a four hundred pound Amazon dressed in leather battle armor. I was lost in my thoughts and must have missed going through the small villages and towns and into the country lanes through the wine fields. I suddenly realized that I was looking straight at the Adriatic Sea.

That got my attention and drew me back to the here and now. As we crested a small rise in the road, Lisa started taking several turns until we were following the beach. Couldn't see the sea much as the endless hotels pretty much blocked the view from the street. Lisa drove with the confidence you would expect from someone who had made this trip before.

"Ah, here we are," Lisa said. "This is the Hotel Beny. I have enjoyed staying here in the past. A few days here and you will forget that you are on vacation from the desert wars. A perfect place to decompress for a few days."

We pulled up to the loading portico and if you ever wondered what it was like to be a famous movie star, this was it. The bell boys (and a girl) surged toward us and with hardly a word from Lisa, started unloading our belongings onto a cart and whisked into the cool lobby.

The main desk was done in marble and polished woods. At one of the stations was a female receptionist seated behind a computer and standing right behind her was someone that I thought must be the person in charge. He was medium height and looked to be quite fit. A very full head of graying hair and nothing out of place.

"Welcome, Ms. Connor. We are pleased to have you back with us. I understand that this ravishing beauty with you is the traveling companion you mentioned. I have given your room key to the bell captain and he will follow you to your suite. And again, I welcome the two of you, and please do not hesitate to call down to get anything you want."

Lisa picked up the two keys to the? suite? and handed me one. I was getting a little nervous. One room? I did feel comfortable around Lisa, but I was wondering whether the rooming together thing would work. I mean, one minute I was in a court-martial hearing and two days later, I was getting a room in this posh sea-front luxury hotel with someone I had only known a day. Yes, only a day out of Afghanistan, and here I was. I followed her lead to the elevators. The bell captain took a different elevator because we had this one to ourselves. And now to the next surprise; Lisa put her card in a slot and pushed the button for the top floor.

As we exited the elevator, we stepped into a wide hallway that ran left and right and it appeared the hallway spanned the width of the hotel but there were only four room doors and they were all on one side, the seaside. Lisa turned right and went to the farthest door.

The double doors were recessed in a slight alcove and were white and filigreed in gold leaf. As Lisa reached with her key to unlock the door(s), I looked down at my matching key. It was cut out of bronze and gave the appearance of being an old fashion skeleton key except the notch pattern was much more complex. Not easily picked, I thought. She pushed the door(s) open and I walked into the lavish suite. I was standing in the main lounge or living room area which was furnished with couches in crushed red velvet, wing back chairs, a large coffee table between the couches, and a few more tables with straight back chairs around the room. Toward the back of the room, there was a formal dining table and beyond that a full kitchen. Back to the main room, it had a full bar, I mean an actual bar that one could go behind to mix drinks. The living room had windows on both sides, one facing the sea and the other south down the beach toward Venice. Going through the dining area and past the kitchen going down a hallway that must parallel the outside hallway, we headed toward the bedroom.

This is where my anxieties grew. We had not discussed the sleeping arrangements and though I am no shrinking violet, I was apprehensive about bringing up the issue. Lisa eased the tension as we approached the end of the hall, by asking which bedroom I preferred, the first one or the second.

"They're both pretty much identical, but one is closer to the living room bar."

Just at that moment, I heard the cart with our belongings arrive.

Lisa said something in Italian, which I interpreted as meaning something like, "We're down the hall by the bedrooms."

The cart appeared and stopped between the two bedrooms.

"I'll take this middle room if that is okay with you?"

"Perfect."

She spoke to the bell boy again in flawless Italian, and he picked up my backpack and the bags of clothes from the store and went into the bedroom that was now mine. As he was putting everything away in the dresser and closet for me, I fumbled through my wallet for a tip. Saved just in time. Lisa came into the room and gave me a stern look and shook her head 'No'.

After he finished with me and put Lisa's belongings away, he gave us a little bow and wished us a pleasant stay, and left.

Before I had a chance to swoon with delight, Lisa came into my room. She had already changed into what was left of a bathing suit somewhere. I don't know why I was gawking, the suit she had me buy was just as skimpy. She had on a wrap-around skirt that left an opening up to her waist. I remembered she had put a similar one on my pile of purchases back in Aviano.

"Suit up, Paulie, we have to get a space at the pool. It is time for something to tide us over till tonight which includes some serious libations. If the towel boys don't overwhelm us, we will have a chance to talk."

I got into the bikini and covered myself with the bottom and top of the diaphanous blue sarong skirt and top. I was still naked. If I was going to walk around in public wearing just these scraps of cloth, I needed not one but three libations. And if the bareness wasn't enough to make me nervous, I had the whiteness of my torso and legs. As I walked into the grand room, Lisa turned and looked me over from top to bottom. If that wasn't embarrassing enough, she let out a low wolf whistle.

She certainly was a morale booster.

"Just bring your room key," as she headed to the front door.

As we rode the elevator down, she explained that we tip the staff at the end of our stay.

"When we are on the hotel grounds, we need nothing other than our room key to purchase anything sold on the premises. This hotel has some excellent dining and I thought we could eat here tonight and tomorrow night we can start our off-campus pub crawl. If that is okay with you?"

"I'm in awe of everything. I think I will go along with whatever you create."

~~~~~

We were able to get a pair of recliners right at the pool's edge, with a table and an umbrella between us. I had just sat when a pool boy appeared at the foot of my lounge chair. He rattled off something in Italian to me and Lisa came to my aide.

"He wants to help you put on sunscreen and take your order for any drinks and food you might like. If you trust me, I can order for the both of us."

"Okay on the order, but a question about the sunscreen. He doesn't think he is going to get to rub his hands on my body, does he?"

"Well, yes, but it's all professional. I'll go first. If he seems to be too hands-on, you can tell him that you can take care of the chore yourself."

After a few words from Lisa in Italian, the pool boy started applying the lotion to Lisa's back first and then went to the back of her legs. It didn't look like anything was amiss, so I told her that I would like him to put the lotion on me too.

I'd never even had a massage in my life. Letting this *boy* rub me with lotion was… *er* well, interesting, I guess. Everything was fine until I thought he was spending too much time on my upper thighs. It a little too close to home base. I grabbed his hand and pulled it away. I was polite and thanked him, but indicated that I have enough lotion on now.

Lisa was smirking.

"What?"

"A little too friendly?"

"Just a little. I'm not keen on being fondled."

"Paulie, this is Italy. In the next few days, we will be
~~~~~

walking by a lot of shops, bars, and restaurants, and your butt will be pinched, patted, and caressed. The Italians—the men—will press up against you in the bars, in the crowded streets, and wherever they have the opportunity to cop a feel. It is Italy and it is expected. Normally, all it takes to get them to stop is grabbing their wrist, stare them in the eye, and say, 'No!' You know, like training a dog."

I was learning a whole new set of ground rules.

Moments later, he re-appeared with our drinks and a plate of assorted cheeses and crackers. Well, all was forgiven, I guess.

The drinks were automatically replaced as soon as they were empty and by the late afternoon, I wasn't thinking about anything at all.

"I planned to talk to you today about the reason I came into your life, but I am still tired from my recent travels. If you don't mind, I would like to wait and have that conversation tomorrow when I am fully refreshed. For today, I would like to have our evening meal here in the hotel and get to bed at an early hour."

She looked relaxed, but I could see that she was still tired.

That was okay with me. I was also a little more tired than normal, and a day of rest before whatever big discussion was coming made sense. We ended up ordering room service, and shortly after we finished eating I headed to my bedroom. I swear I must have been already asleep when I got up from the table as I can't remember walking down the short hall to my bedroom.

23 APRIL 2016 – 1200 HOURS

It was noon before we got our act together. Lisa took me out to the tourist shopping stores and we browsed and bought. We stopped at a few espresso bars as we meandered, working our way back to the hotel to change for the evening.

The sun was just going down when we parked near what I would call a restaurant row. I was wearing another one of my peasant blouse and skirt combos and carrying a light jacket I had found in one of the shops earlier that afternoon. Once the sun went down, it would get a little chilly. I smiled to myself, thinking what a fashionista I had become over the last few days.

We ended up at a small family-owned restaurant that was on an alley just off the main strip. It wasn't crowded probably because we were sitting for our evening meal two hours before most self-respecting Europeans would eat.

We both ordered osso buco with risotto. After we finished the main course, we each had a scoop of limoncello with a cappuccino. A perfect ending to the meal.

Being early diners, we had pretty much our choice of tables. Lisa had selected one that was in the back and had a divider between the tables. A bottle of wine appeared and the waiter poured some into each of our glasses. Then we were alone, pretty much.

"Paulie, this is a good time for me to explain how and why this getting together with you happened. I told you I work for Newmark Industries. Newmark's home base is in Seattle, but there are research and manufacturing plants all around the globe. A lot of our equipment is with the army in Afghanistan. One of our items that you have worked on is the Fire Direction Control system used in the Apache and also in the main battle tanks. There are many more different pieces of military hardware that use our products.

"You wrote a report describing a persistent problem with the F.D.C. units which your commanding officers sent on to us. What made your report different was that you told us about the problems that we were already aware of, but you also outlined a solution. Your solution is now in the production units and that upgrade is going out to the field this month.

"I was told that your enlistment term is coming up soon. Also, your tour is coming to an end soon and you will be rotated back to the U.S. just before it is time for your re-enlistment. I would like to meet with you before you report to your stateside assignment. I want to fly you up to our main facility which is in Seattle, Washington, and show you around and make you a firm job offer."

"I hadn't been thinking of getting out. Don't get me wrong, this may be the stimulus to get me to make the career change. What is the position?" I asked.

"You would be working in one of our R&D units with the rotary and fixed-wing facility that is in Seattle. I know that you are from Truckee, CA, which is similar in climate to Seattle except for the huge snowfall. You would be surrounded by the best in the business. Your pay and benefits package would be far above what you have now and above anything you could expect to reach while in the service," She paused and sipped the wine. "I also want to ask you about something in your report. There was something about an incident, something that happened that gave you the idea for the change. Could you tell me about that?"

"We had this one helio that every time it went out, the system malfunctioned and the pilot and gunner had to go to manual override. They sent me over to Kandahar Air Base where that particular Apache was operating. When I got there, I pulled the Target Acquisition Unit out and went through it. It checked out perfectly on the bench. I re-installed it and asked the crew to take it up and put it through its paces. This is where everything almost brought me the farm.

"The gunner/co-pilot asked if I would go instead of him. The thinking was to have the ace troubleshooter operating the equipment if and when it went wrong. I had been up in the front seat several times before on equipment checkouts so this wasn't unusual. Helicopter crews don't wear g-suits as a jet pilot does. Your standard fatigues are fine, and you need the full battle helmet that plugs into the FDC/TAG unit. You are supposed to calibrate the helmet's optical guidance system to be compatible with the wearers. Still, we weren't expecting to engage any enemy, so I put it on, climbed up into the co-pilot's seat, strapped down, turned the unit on, and started the pre-flight.

"Within fifteen minutes, we were soaring up, over and out of the city limits of Kandahar. There was a practice area, and as soon as we got over that area, we started simulated attack runs on ground objects.

"It is a great feeling to be flying above all the crap going below. You start to believe that the conflict was off in another world, and it was just you and the aircraft, oh yes, and the pilot too. Suddenly, the world seemed to come to an end.

"We took a hit. It wasn't a rocket or explosive round. It must have been larger than a .50 caliber, though, and it struck the pilot's windscreen at just the right angle to shatter it. As we were not on a regular mission into enemy territory, we both had our visors up, and the pilot took a lot of glass shards in the eyes. During my tours in Afghanistan as part of the repair team, I was allowed to ride in the front cockpit on check-out flights. It had become a regular event, a pilot taking me up with him on check-out-flights. They had started giving me instructions on flying, including letting me take the controls. I had amassed enough unofficial time at the controls to qualify me for my pilot's license; 'bring the craft down to the ground level as quickly as possible to avoid the shooter.'

"Great idea, but Habib had something else in store for us. I hadn't known where the rounds were coming from and was only trying to hug the ground and head back to the base as fast as possible. The error was that I ended up flying right over where the shooter was hiding. And he saw an ample opportunity and let me have it with both barrels, or whatever. Anyway, a piece of shrapnel from somewhere came into my cockpit and got me in the thigh. It also hit something in the turbine or the rotor gearbox because it sounded like the coffee bean grinder at Starbucks.

"Thankfully, the pilot had kept a cool head and was on the radio calling in our Mayday and location. We had only traveled several hundred meters or so when I knew it was time to call it quits and land. No trees to worry about, just acres and acres of sand. And I plopped it down just as there was a loud CLANG, and the tail rotor quit, and it quit immediately. Had I still been in the air, we would have been spinning around. I hadn't learned how to cope with a problem like that.

"I popped the canopies and climbed around to help the pilot. We both ditched our helmets, and I grabbed the emergency first aid kit, the flare pistol, and a handful of flares. I didn't have a pistol or rifle with me, but the pilot had a sidearm. When we got on the ground, he pulled out this big beautiful Springfield 1911 .45 automatic. I expected to see the 9MM Beretta, but this pilot, like many, swapped their service issue for their own of a larger caliber. My dad has one and taught me how to shoot one as a kid.

"I put gauze squares over the pilot's eyes and wound a bandage around his head, mostly to keep sand away from his already injured eyes. With what bandage material I had left, I tied one end around his wrist, and I held the other end in my hand as I led him away from the aircraft, which was starting to smoke. Hopefully, it would burn up and not give the Taliban anything valuable.

"I knew that we had been headed toward the base, but I had no idea how far it was. I had to get moving, though, as I wasn't sure where my rascally little sand rat was or if he was even coming after us. We had traveled over and around half a dozen dunes, and I was starting to relax when gunfire rang out, and the sand around us was kicking up from the hits.

"Nope, he had tracked us and was trying to finish us off. We dropped to the sand, and I peered over the top of the dune to see if I had a shot. I spotted him about 150 meters out and did not have a shot with the pistol. As I was worrying, we heard the sound of rotors beating the air. When the sound was loud enough to think the rescue was just out of sight, I fired a red flare.

"I spotted an Apache up high. Then a Bell UH-1Y popped into view a dune and a half away. The first Apache was acting as a scout as a second one roared over my head, and I heard and felt it let loose with its chain gun, and I bet that was the end of the sand bogy.

"We got back to Kandahar Airbase safely. I think the pilot was going to get to go home. I didn't get to see him again. Me, I got the puncture in my leg cleaned, sewn, and patched and sent back to duty. I also got a Purple Heart.

"Where this ties into my report is that I was sure that the AMPEX connector between the control module and the airframe was at different angles. It was causing the cable to be stretched and bent too taut when the unit was bolted down. I've already seen that the connection socket location has been moved on the replacement units making them more reliable."

"That is a fascinating story, Paulie," Lisa said. "I am proud to have met you and maybe become your friend."

"Thanks."

That was all I could say. Other than when I filled out my report, I hadn't thought about the incident, and the retelling had made it all real again. It was a scary day, and I wanted to forget about it.

"Paulie, it's getting late, so we should head back to our room. Tomorrow, I am taking you to see a castle that I know. And tomorrow, I will tell you more about myself and more about Newmark if you are interested."

24 APRIL 2016 – 0745 HOURS

I awoke to a knock on my bedroom door.

"Paulie, I want to get some breakfast before we leave. I'm sorry to ruin your beauty sleep, but I have a destination I want to get to before noon."

"Be right there."

I was up, through the shower, dried, and in my clothes in less than ten minutes. I didn't have to dry my hair. Just shake it out.

"Tada, here I am," I said as I walked into the kitchen area.

Lisa had brewed fresh coffee, and there was a stack of pastries that must have come from the hotel kitchen. I grabbed a cuppa and two of the freshly baked treats and went out on the balcony to sit with her.

She had on a more substantial outfit for today, not the string bra and a skirt sarong wrap from yesterday but something similar to my peasant blouse and skirt. Breakfast was pleasant enough, but Lisa seemed to be on edge a little. It was hard to read how seriously she was concerned about something because I already knew enough about her to know that she was good at hiding her emotions. A trait I wish I had better control on. Instead, I have a fuze that seems to get lit up at the worst of times.

"We're driving to Castello di Miramare this morning. It is back the way we came from Aviano and beyond. We'll be on the road for about one and a half hours. Incredible scenery, and we will have time to talk and plenty of time for me to make a noon appointment."

We were on our way by nine a.m. She was trying to hug the coastline, which slowed our progress, but that was all right. I relaxed and enjoyed the scenery, and she started talking about herself.

"I've been with Newmark Industries for twenty years. These have been the happiest years of my life. I love my job, the company, and the other people that work there. Spartak Newmark, the company owner, has ensured that everyone working for him is companionable with all the other employees. I already know that you will fit in—that is, IF you take the job offer. I have to admit, and I know you will, it is too good of an opportunity for you to walk away. I know that you will see this the moment you meet some of the others.

"I'm originally from France. My parents were American ex-patriots that moved there after W.W. One. Dad had first come to France during the war, and after it was over, he went home and came back with my mom. They purchased a small farm in Southern France. He was a gentleman farmer as he had a substantial family fortune left to him, so they never really had to work. When the Germans came in the '40s, my parents didn't worry as the farm was in a very rural part of Southern France, known as Vichy France. They were established with the rest of the villagers. They toed the line for the French Fops that were governors of the district. They never had any trouble. The only significant limitation because of the German occupation was no foreign travel.

"When I was eighteen, my parents sent me to Cambridge, Massachusetts, to attend MIT. I graduated cum laude in mechanical engineering. I worked for several aircraft companies and ended up working for Newmark Industries. And here I am on a recruiting mission to hire you. It is a rare project for me to work on as my primary responsibility is troubleshooting defects or problems in the field. Sometimes, going out into a full-on combat zone to look at equipment problems. I have been working in the Middle East areas for the past seven years."

I was paying attention as her story was unique. It made me feel like a jerk for what little I had accomplished in my life. She has stopped talking, and I ran through the details of her story. I had a little tingling in the back of my mind and finally realized why.

"Lisa," I said, turning toward her. "How old are you?"

"Ooh! Now, Paulette, a woman never tells her age."

"If you went to college at eighteen and made it through in four years and have been with Newmark twenty years, that would make you over forty-two. But you don't look that much older than me."

"You're quite astute. I can explain how it seems that way, but this is not the time or place for further discussion on this subject. I will only tell you that you will have access to that information once you take a position with Newmark Industries and have been vetted and given clearance by the company."

"My dad would call that 'chumming the waters.'"

"You are due for rotation stateside this December. If you tell me that you are interested in interviewing and touring some of the facilities, I will make sure that your next stateside assignment will be to the Lewis-McChord Joint base in Washington State. About an hour from the home offices of Newmark.

"I would be there to meet you at the base and drive you up to the offices." Her tone lightened. "As for another teaser, I know some of the best restaurants in that area."

I had to think. I didn't get a good enough answer on the age thing, and my intuition told me something was just a little off-kilter.

I'm suspicious by nature, and she had put up a few flags that had me tingling. I didn't want to find a problem here because I enjoyed her company. We were very much alike—personality-wise. I should just take a deep breath and change the subject.

"Can you tell me anything about this castle you are taking me to?"

"It is quite special in the history of Italy. It is still in good repair, and I think you will enjoy the visit and tour."

~ ~ ~ ~

The Castello di Miramare was something to see. It wasn't like a fortified castle with a moat and stuff. It was more a stately stone Manor facing west over the Adriatic Sea on Italy's far eastern part that heads down toward Croatia.

There was a parking area for the tourists and tour busses. But Lisa drove past all that and up to the guard gate onto the grounds proper.

We stopped there, and the guard came out of the shed.

"Good day, Ms. Connor. Welcome." I was starting to be able to follow some of the Italian. The guard opened the gate to let us through.

We drove to a smaller parking area near the house. There were three other cars already there, two Ferraris and a Bentley convertible. I might have been intimidated. But we were riding in a top-of-the-line BMW, which allowed my nose to stick up in the air just as far as these other cars' owners. My association with Lisa had made me their equal, at least in thought and appearance, which was good enough for me.

As we walked toward the main building, a tall and very Italian handsome type came out of a side door.

I caught the "*Ciao Bella*, Lisa;" after that, the Italian was too rapid-fire for me to follow.

Lisa introduced me, and I received a firm hand and kisses on both cheeks. I know my cheeks got a little warm too. My new friend Lisa Connor had, in just a few short days, transported me to an alternate universe where I was part of the upper crust, the right side of the tracks. I decided that I was going to go with it. I would have to be declared mentally unwell to turn my back on this life. I was so awed that any thoughts about irregularities in the background story of Lisa's life faded. At least for now.

"Paulette Zahn, this is Mr. Quaranta. He is the curator here. I need to talk with him about a business matter. If you don't mind, I will get you inserted into the interior tour while I have my meeting. I will probably finish at the same time the tour ends, and I will meet you back here."

And I was led off toward the front doors to get into the tour group, and Lisa and Mr. Quaranta headed toward the side door that he had previously exited.

~~~~

The castle must have been quite splendid in its day. Now, however, though, the furnishings and artifacts had become musty and stale. About the only time I ooohed or awed was when we passed a window that looked out on the sea.
~~~~

"Does Mr. Quaranta live here on the property?" I asked the guide.

He looked at me a little funny and responded, "No one lives here on the grounds. The caretakers go to their own homes at night, and the only ones here after dark is the night guards. However, I don't know a Mr. Quaranta."

I shut my mouth. Strange. This whole vacation was a little, no, extraordinary. I decided I needed to have a talk with Lisa on the drive back.

Just as the tour finished by the main entrance, my cell phone buzzed—it was on vibrate. I pulled it out and looked to see who was calling. No caller I.D., and the call dropped. I only had one bar, and it was in and out. Hopefully, whoever called would try later.

~~~~

I parted ways with the rest of the tourists and headed to the side parking lot where we had left the car. I stepped foot on the tarmac just as the side door to the castle opened, and Lisa came out.

She was alone, and that was fine with me.

"Did you enjoy the tour?"

"The buildings are beautiful, but inside… well, the insides are a little too moldy for my taste. Are we leaving now?"

"Yes. We are going to head back and change for our evening meal. If we aren't too tired after that, I think we should try the local nightlife."

I had gone quiet, dealing with the carousel of thoughts running around and around in my mind. To be agreeable, I said, "That sounds fine with me." I didn't believe it, but maybe by
~~~~

the time we got back to the hotel, things would smooth out.

~ ~ ~ ~

As we neared the hotel, Lisa pulled into an off-street parking lot, and we went through the routine of putting the top up and locking the car down.

My curiosity over the incident at the castle and other irregularities in things Lisa had said were waning. I was back to the Dynamic-Duo mode again, enjoying her company and letting her lead me around.

I was glad we weren't driving with the top down any more. It was getting dark, and the temperature was dropping, and I hadn't brought a jacket. Lisa guided me into a bar. Well, it was more of a nightclub. It wasn't crowded, but the numbers were growing now that it was nightfall. The Italians transitioned seamlessly from jet skis and tanning to dancing and boozing.

My phone rang again and before I could answer, the call was dropped. Only one bar, again. The caller's I.D. did not come through.

We had taken a table back away from the dance *pit.* The place didn't have a band, but it did have a D.J. gearing up to make the place jump. Jump, do people say that any more?

I was on my second cocktail, and I noticed that Lisa was on her third. Maybe she was planning to make a short evening of it.

"You okay?" I asked

"Don't worry about me; I have a high tolerance for alcohol. I would not allow myself to get wasted while I am trying to interest you in a civilian job."

Just then, some lizard-looking guy walked up and grabbed Lisa's hand, trying to pull her out of her seat. I think he said,

"Come with me, we are going to dance."

In just a millisecond, a half a heartbeat, faster than a speeding slice of pizza, she had the guy's hand twisted around—fingers straight up and the guy letting out a growl. I can't remember ever seeing a defensive move that went that fast.

She was talking to him in a low voice and in a language I did not understand.

I was getting up to jump in with a punch or two if needed, but the guy stopped fighting Lisa and hung his head down. He was saying something in that other language to her. She released his hand and stood up tall and rigid in front of him. She had fire in her eyes.

Mr. Lizard dropped to one knee and reached out and took Lisa's hand. He bowed his head and touched his forehead to the back of her hand. She touched his head with her other hand, and that must have been some signal because he stood and backed away, bowing every step or two until he disappeared into the crowd.

"Holy shit. What was all of that? I have never seen anyone react as fast as you did. Then there is the bowing and scraping. He was treating you like royalty."

Just at that moment, my cell phone rang, and there was someone on the other end. Better reception now, I guess.

"Hello. Sergeant Zahn speaking," I said.

"Sergeant Zahn, this is your first sergeant. Something has come up, and we need you to return to the base as fast as possible. I have sent an emergency transport request on to flight operations on Aviano Air Base." They will get you on the very next flight going out, even if they have to cancel someone else's travel orders."

"Why...? How come?"

"It will be explained when you get here. How far away from the airbase are you?"

"Less than an hour, maybe forty-five minutes," I told him. Then I looked over at Lisa.

"Lisa... crap. I need to ask you a lot of questions, but everything has gone sideways. My sergeant just called, and I am on emergency orders to return to Bagram immediately."

"Why?" she asked.

"I have no idea, but the sergeant was very firm. I have to get back to Aviano as fast as I can. Do you think I can hire a cab to take me that far tonight?"

"You're not taking a cab. I will drive you. Let's get back to the hotel and gather up our belongings. I can get you there a lot faster than a cab can."

I was boarding C-130 Gun Ship an hour and forty minutes later. It is not a passenger aircraft. I was wedged into a jump seat between the racks of chain gun ammunition. I even had to wear an oxygen mask as we were flying at 15,000 feet, where the air is rare and God awful cold. When the ship landed at Bagram, it took me the full walk across the tarmac to the flight hut, just to warm up enough to let my fingers uncurl.

25 APRIL 2016 – 0545 HOURS
BAGRAM AIR BASE

Afghanistan marches to the beat of a different clock. It is one of the time zones that are half an hour off. When it is eleven p.m. in Aviano, Italy, it is one thirty a.m. in Afghanistan. Another useless factoid about this part of the world. I landed at Bagram Air Base, Afghanistan, at 0545 hours or 5.45 a.m.

As I let myself into the flight shack, I was practically tackled by some private.

"Sergeant Zahn," he said. "I have a Humvee outside waiting to take you back to company H.Q."

He reached out and took my backpack and asked if he could carry the bag that contained some of my new clothes. Most of the items had yet to be worn.

"What's going on?" I asked the private.

"Don't know anything, ma'am."

"I'm a sergeant, not an officer. You can just call me Sarge or Paulie. I'm not stuck up on ranks."

"Okay, Sarge, follow me."

My hangar and barracks were down the flight line, and it took almost ten minutes to get there.

He helped me carry stuff into the H.Q. building and left.

The duty N.C.O. was at the front desk. I walked up and handed him my I.D. I hadn't seen him before and didn't want to assume he knew me.

"Top is back in the captain's office. I already alerted them that you had arrived," he said.

F.Y.I.; Top is the customary slang title for the top or head N.C.O., first sergeant of the unit.

Before I could say or think anything, my first sergeant appeared and motioned for me to follow him down the hall. We were going to the captain's office.

"Come in, come in and take a seat, please, Sergeant," the captain said.

No standing at attention and saluting, just take a seat, which I did.

"Paulie, I have some bad news. I don't know how to say it any way other than right out. We received a Red Cross message saying that your father has passed away."

I was in shock. I didn't hear much else. The sergeant took my arm and eased me up out of the seat. He led me out to the primary office area. When I walked into the room, I saw my duffle bag with all my military gear and an additional canvas bag with all the extra things I had accumulated during this tour.

The next thing I know, Sarge was handing my military records file and a separate set of orders. I only heard a few words. He was thanking me for my service while under his command. He was expressing how sorry he was that my father had died. He said more, but I wasn't listening. Then he was escorting me out to where the Humvee was still sitting. The same private that was still the driver. He was out helping the duty N.C.O. lift my belongings into the back. Then the first sergeant took me into a hug. I had never seen or heard of him hugging anyone.

"Sergeant Paulette Zahn, I, along with most everyone in this unit, will miss you. God speed," he said, turned, and went back into the H.Q.

I didn't even look to see where I was being driven. I was having a real problem coming to grips thinking that my dad was gone.

It wasn't fair. I should have been there. I don't even know how my dad died. I had to get home.

"Private, where are you taking me?" I asked. I didn't want to be moved to another unit until I had worked out something for my dad. I am, or was, in a rear company away from the real heavy action, but we weren't without losses. Often one of our Apaches didn't return, and later we would learn that no one made it out. I knew those pilots, but they weren't my father. My dad was gone, and he wasn't even in a combat zone. I had to find out where I was being taken. I had to make arrangements to get home to take care of things back in Truckee, California.

"We're here, Sergeant. I'll help you get your things stowed aboard."

"We're here? Where are we here?" I asked, finally focusing out the windshield.

We had pulled up to a C-37-A jet, the military version of a Gulfstream private jet. It is the one the generals and admirals get to fly in. Was the army going to fly me home in this aircraft?

That's what was happening because a sergeant in a crisp, clean, tailored pair of fatigues came down the dropout stairway and right over to the Humvee.

"Good morning, Sergeant Zahn. Here, let me help you stow your things in the cargo space," he said. "I saw your orders and want to express my condolences for the loss. It is unusual for enlisted soldiers to get a general's jet to travel anywhere, let alone Seattle. I have been with this aircraft for three years, and this has never happened. You will be traveling with two other soldiers, two colonels, I believe. We are dropping them off in

Washington, D.C.

"I suggest that you keep a change of clothes out. Once we are airborne, you can give yourself a wash towel bath. You will have to keep your camos on till we let the two colonels out, then you can change to civies if you have them. We will stop to refuel in Halifax and then just a quick stop in D.C. and then off to the Reno-Stead Airport. Have you seen or even had a chance to read your orders?"

I just sort of nodded and grabbed a few things from my shopping bag and packed them in my backpack. Everything else went into the spare canvas bag, which then got stowed.

I lifted my dusty, worn backpack and dragged it up the stair and into the aircraft. All the seats were single file down each side of the cabin, and they all faced rearward except the last two that were up against the bulkhead for the bathroom. Not a full bathroom, no shower or bathtub, but it was a lot roomier than those toilets in commercial jets.

The two aforementioned colonels were seated across from each other in the same row. I went all the way to the back. I wanted to keep a space away from everyone else for this trip. I had a lot to think over.

I was barely buckled into my seat when the jets were started, and we rolled toward the end of the runway.

I pulled out my orders to see what was going on, where I was going, and when I had to report to my next duty station. I pulled the papers out of my backpack and laid them in my lap. I glanced at my watch and couldn't see it. It was blurred. The whole cabin was a blur. The world outside the porthole window was blurred. Tears were running down my face, and I was sick to my stomach. I probably wasn't breathing too well either. It was all set off when I looked at my watch. My dad had given me this watch when I was home for Christmas two years ago. It was my most prized possession, even dearer to me than my motorcycle. It was a Rolex GMT-Master II in gold and steel with the Batman Blue dial and Bezel. This would have cost me six months of my pay.

I couldn't focus my eyes on anything. I was thinking about home. My home where I lived with my dad when I was on leave. My whole life now was the army, but my home would always be my home, and Dad's death had me re-thinking where I wanted to go with my life.

"Excuse me, Sergeant. I want to ease by."

It was one of the colonels.

I started to jump up, but he put his hand on my shoulder and eased me back into my seat.

"Easy. Sit back and relax the best you can. We are not officers and enlisted on this plane. We are all just regular humans. We were told why you are on this flight. We are both sorry for the loss of a loved one. Nothing can compare. If you need to talk about it, either of us would be glad to sit with you."

He went into the lavatory, and I got lost in my thoughts. I didn't even remember him coming out or that the other colonel and one of the pilots came by to use the bathroom.

I didn't come out of it till we were halfway to Halifax, our refueling stop.

"Excuse me, ma'am. We have a fairly full bar, or beer or wine." It was the sergeant that helped me onboard. It suddenly dawned on me that this sergeant was the steward on the aircraft. He must know someone high up in the army or government to land such a cushy job.

"I will get changed first, thank you. Then I will take you up on a drink, Scotch neat, four fingers. Is there any food aboard? I haven't eaten since early last evening, and this has burnt up all my energy," I told him.

"Take your time. When you come out all clean and sparkling, I will have your drink and a menu of the few items I have in the galley. So that you know, I know the two colonels up front there. I have ferried them around quite often. Trust me. They are both the salt of the earth. You should sit near them. They won't bite your head off, and in this cabin, on these flights, the only superiors are the captain and her co-pilot."

Captain—her. That perked me up. I was always delighted to come across another woman in a unique position, such as the captain of this aircraft.

With that, I picked up my backpack and went into the lavatory. There were paper towels, but there were also cotton towels and washcloths. I stripped to my underwear and gave myself a sponge bath with what was available. My hair was getting a little dingy, but I didn't think I could give it a good wash here, so I wet it down and pulled a brush through it. Another one of the peasant blouses and skirts and the pair of flats that I hadn't had a chance to wear yet.

When I exited the loo, I grabbed my military file containing my new orders and walked up to the next row from the colonels.

One of them got up and asked, "Would you want to have a seat facing us? We would love to talk to you and express our condolences adequately."

"How are we going to face each other?"

"We can turn them around. Here, let me show you."

He stuck a foot under the side of the seat and must have stepped on a release lever because I heard a click as he spun the seat, so it was facing forward.

"If you are wondering, the rules say we have to have all the seats facing the rear when in a combat zone or when landing or taking off. The idea is that if there was a crash, it is better to be seated facing back instead of forward."

"Thanks," and I sat and pulled out my file just as my steward was bringing me my drink and the menu.

I had meant to take a sip but ended up gulping half down in a single swallow. I was hoping the alcohol would ease the anxiety I was feeling.

Now to read my orders. There were a lot of pages here. Orders for emergency leave or transfer to another duty station weren't this voluminous. What could all be here? I noticed that there were several separate items. The first two I understood. The next two sets had me almost falling out of my seat, lap belt, and all.

The first was Emergency Leave Authorization. I had probably forty-five days of accrued leave, and this order gave me thirty days. The second set was my orders transferring me to report to my new duty station at the Lewis-McChord base just south of Seattle.

The third set was what almost knocked me over. I was looking at the orders awarding me the AIR MEDAL with a V for Valor. That was unexpected. I knew why just never expected it. That outranked my Purple Heart. I didn't know I had been put in for this medal.

Fourth set. Holy Crap. I could not believe what I was reading. I had been awarded a DFC. A Distinguished Flying Cross. I had only seen a few of these, and they were on combat pilots. And here I was in the ranks of a flying combat soldier that has seen real action.

And I was crying all over again. I was thinking of how

proud my dad would have been. Why did he have to leave me now?

"What is it?" one of the colonels asked.

I handed him my two award orders. They shared them. Then they both stood up, or best they could in this low ceiling aircraft, came to attention, and saluted me, right there in the plane while it was in flight.

"Sergeant Zahn, we salute your service to our country." Their hands came down. "The two of us will always remember this day, remember you, and what you have unselfishly done for the country. Now we would like to buy you a drink if you will allow us?"

I started to stand, but they both motioned me to sit.

"I already have one, but I will need to freshen it up in a moment."

"You just sit there, ma'am. Hand me your glass. We have a private stash of some Johnny Walker Blue Label on board, and that is now your private bottle," said colonel no. 2.

They were addressing me as 'ma'am' as if I was an officer. That was a level of respect that I never had, never ever had experienced previously. I was so choked up I couldn't say anything. Shit, my eyes were so teary I couldn't see anything either.

~~~~

I didn't eat until we left Halifax. Sergeant Tidy, not his real name, had gotten off and returned just as the fueling was completed. He had a large box that contained assorted Chinese take-out containers, several Subway sandwiches, and a pizza. Where or how he had come up with all of that out here in the
~~~~

middle of the airfield tarmac was a puzzler.

"We radioed ahead and had it all delivered to the flight shack just as we landed. Fleet of foot am I, but that was beyond even my fastest day," he told us.

Good thing too. I was approaching twenty-four hours since my last meal, and with the Scotch I had been inhaling, I needed something to slow the adsorption. I noticed that the two colonels had relaxed some. They had probably taken on some of my angst. I finished some of the food, and the next thing I knew, the sergeant was nudging me awake. I had slept the rest of the way to Reagan National outside Washington, D.C. The aircraft was on final approach, and he wanted me buckled in.

The plane stopped, the cabin door was opened, with the engines still running. The two colonels got up and came over and shook my hand again. Then they were gone, and I was the only passenger left. As soon as the cabin door was shut and secured, we rolled out to get in the takeoff queue.

25 APRIL 2016 – 1645 HOURS

The jet was just touching down at the Reno – Lake Tahoe Airport, and the sergeant steward called out, "Last stop. All out."

I was feeling a little better, and his call did bring a weak smile to my face. When the aircraft came to a halt, and the engines wound down to a stop, I got up and grabbed my backpack. Before I got to the door, the pilot and co-pilot came back. They too came to attention and saluted me.

"Thanks" was all I could get out lest I choked up again.

They both hugged me, as did the sergeant, and I stepped down the ladder. The sergeant followed me off the aircraft. He opened a hatch in the rear fuselage and pulled out my other two items. A van from flight services pulled up, and we got my things loaded, and I rode to the private flight terminal.

I was chilled. Springtime, and there was still snow in the mountains. But the air smelled wonderful. The clean, crisp smell was a welcome change from the stale, dirty air in Afghanistan. Yes, Afghanistan smelled. The dense cluster of humanity, most of which didn't use any soap and water, and the vast amount of sheep shit piles that grew and grew.

Before I got out, I asked the driver where the closest car rental desk was.

"Here, let me take you to their lot so you won't have to haul these bags all over the place," he said. He drove out through the security gate and across to the car rental agencies area. "Do you have any preference for rental agencies?"

"No. I am traveling on orders, so my military credit card will work."

~ ~ ~ ~

It had been a while, but I still knew the route to my house. I didn't know what was ahead of me, and I only rented a sedan large enough to get my baggage in. In about forty-five minutes, I was pulling up in front of my dad's shop. The house was on the property behind the shop, and I changed direction and drove to the house. It was dark. Dark, silent, and lonely. I wondered how my dad's dog was doing. Had someone come by to feed her?

I went up to the front door and saw an envelope taped to it. I had my key, so I opened up and let myself in. The electricity was still on, and so was the heat, which felt nice. I looked around, and everything was pretty much like always. Everything was shipshape like he always kept it. I looked around, going through the downstairs rooms. I had all those lights on now, and before I steeled myself to go up to the bedrooms, I unloaded my stuff from the rental.

As I dragged the last duffel bag in, the phone rang.

It was Ms. Abdallah. She was a long, long-time friend of ours. I think she secretly fancied my dad, but he was a one-woman man.

"Paulie, I saw the lights come on and knew it was you. Can I come over? I can tell you everything. I am so so sorry. He was so young. I have your dog, and she is doing fine here," she said.

"Sure, that is okay, come on. I need to find out."

She didn't waste any time, and she let herself in. That was

okay; that was sort of how the Connor clan is.

It was all right to have her in the house. She prattled on about Dad, and I tuned much of it out. I wanted to avoid another cry session. Then she got down to the story. Dad must have been working late in the shop. A customer had come by in the morning to drop his car off for repairs, and he walked in to find my Dad slumped over his office desk. That was it. All of it. No trauma, no drama. It was like he had just put his head down on his desk and gone to sleep.

That eased my mind a little, knowing that he probably didn't suffer or it was too fast to feel anything.

"He's resting over at the Boyle Funeral Home. I can go with you to help you through making the arrangements."

"Thanks, Ms. Abdallah. I appreciate that. Would tomorrow morning at about nine thirty be a good time?

"That is a good time, and I will stop by and pick you up."

~ ~ ~ ~

The funeral was held on Saturday, 28. I had brought up images of all my medals and printed them off on a stiff piece of art paper. I placed it in the coffin before they closed it. That was it. A significant part of my life was gone, and I only had myself.

Over the next week, I went through everything and separated out the items I didn't want to let go of. I did receive some news that took some of the pressure off. Chipper Roach, the local real estate salesman, came by, paid his condolences, and said he had someone interested in buying the shop lock stock and tool bit. He told me that the same person wanted the house also. He was pretty spry for an old guy.

I had gotten everything in the will, and there were no debts to pay off. The house was free and clear. I had already moved all of Dad's money into my savings account with U.S.A.A. As for the offer on the shop and house, it was more than fair, so I took it. I signed all the papers, and Chip said that when the sales closed that he would have escrow send the proceeds to the same savings account.

I got the rental car returned and then loaded Dad's F-350 four-wheel-drive van with my belongings and the items I was keeping. I took some linens and blankets, and kitchen items. From the shop, I put together a set of tools and left the rest to the new shop owner. I hooked the motorcycle trailer on and got my Harley on, and fastened down.

It was the third week of my emergency leave, but I decided to report in early. I had many good memories about growing up in this town, but I didn't want to hang around to think of them now that my dad was gone. I had to drive over the mountains and connect up with Interstate 5. I made it to Portland and decided to stop at a motel.

Surprisingly, I rested that night and got up to a fair and early start. Drove to a Denny's, got breakfast with sausage, hash browns, and eggs over to start on my way. I reached Lewis-McChord before noon.

I walked into the first sergeant's office and introduced myself. I handed him my military file.

"See the corporal out front. He will show you to your billet. I do have some questions as I was noticed of your arrival. After you get squared away, see me. Tomorrow morning some time would be good. I can introduce you to the captain then also."

As I started putting my belongings away, I decided that I was not interested in the military any more. It had been good to me, but my head wasn't into it. I wanted a change.

Things ended up being a lot easier than one would believe. As scheduled, the next morning, I reported to the first sergeant, and he immediately took me in to meet the captain.

"Sergeant Zahn, welcome to the unit. I think there is something I want to do before I talk about this unit. If you would please step outside and come to attention in front of the company."

I had no idea what was up but being the good little trooper, I did as I was told.

The first sergeant came out and ordered everyone to come to attention. Then the captain came out.

Captain came to stand directly in front of me, and in a voice that had to carry a hundred yards or more, he said, "It is my distinct honor and pleasure to present Sergeant Paulette Zahn with the first of two medals. The first is the Air Medal with the V pin for Valor. It is in recognition of her actions that she saved a pilot from a burning helicopter while under enemy fire.

"This second award is the Distinguished Flying Cross for her bravery and actions that resulted in her bringing the helicopter safely to a landing and helping the pilot blinded with glass in his eyes. She got him out, shot at the one enemy that had shot them down until rescue teams could retrieve them."

The captain pinned the ribbons on, took a step back, and saluted me. I have never had so many officers saluting me first. I was starting to feel very important.

The first sergeant dismissed the troops and said to me, "Come back to the H.Q. room. We, the captain and myself, want a few words with you.

~~~~
~~~~

I followed the first sergeant through the H.Q. office and down the hallway to the captain's office. He didn't knock, just walked right in and motioned for me to sit. He sat in the chair next to me.

"Sergeant Zahn," the captain started, "we are glad to have you here in this unit. We also see that you are due to re-enlist if you are going to stay in. You have had some excellent reviews by most of your previous commanding officers. Your test scores are out of the park. I want you to consider going to O.C.S., Officers Candidate School. My first choice is that you re-up and stay in this unit. There are several avenues for you to go, and whatever you decide, we will back you up."

The first sergeant chimed in, "You have less than ninety days on your current enlistment. If you decide not to re-up, we could process your discharge papers right away, and you could be a civilian by next Friday, 9 June. That is if you decide on that today. You have had an impressive career, and we don't want to lose you."

"I have been thinking on this for the past week, and I was all ready to go ahead and put in my papers. I know that if I do take my discharge now that there is a time frame that I could sign up again without losing rank or anything. The army has been good to me, and I appreciate everything I have seen and learned. It won't be forgotten. I just want to see what life has to offer me outside of the military."

So, on the following Friday, I changed into jeans, a camo T-shirt (have lots of them), and my Converse and signed off the last of the papers and collected my final pay. It was quite a bit of money because they included unused leave time and travel pay. The travel pay was a curiosity as the military jet had transported me across the country. I didn't want to slow the exit process, and if there were a call for the return of some of the money, I would get it back to the finance branch if and when they send me a bill.

16 JUNE 2016 – 1600 HOURS

After leaving the base for the last time, I drove up I-5 to Seattle. I spent the next three days staying in a motel by the Sea-Tac Airport. Saturday and Sunday, I looked for a place to live.

I found what I was looking for late Sunday. The ad was by the owner who lived in the house on the front of the property, and the studio I rented was in the back. I spent all of Monday unpacking and running to the store for the household items and food that I hadn't brought with me.

Tuesday had me up early. Went to the nearest Starbucks for a triple venti latte, a blueberry scone, and the Seattle Times. Guess I had been away for too long because I quickly found the local newspaper was no longer a good source of classifieds. I had the help wanted section open, but there was little there.

"Excuse me, but are you looking for work?" asked a voice over my shoulder.

I looked up and saw a woman dressed in some sort of a blue-collar worker's uniform. She was close to my age, and I could tell that she wasn't being nosey and thought she could help.

"Hi, yes, I am," I said, motioning to the paper in front of me. "These classified ads are not very helpful. Is there another place to go to find work around here?

"I'm sorry, my name is Sarg—*er*, skip that, now I am just plain Paulie Zahn."

"My name is Billie. What did you do in the service, if I

may ask?"

I invited her to sit and told her that I had been a mechanic on army helicopters and specialized in electronic control systems. "I don't suppose there's much need for helicopter repair around here. But would you know of anything in that general ballpark?"

"I think this may be your lucky day. Believe it or not, I, too, am an A&P mechanic. I work just south of here at the Boeing Air Museum. It's less than a mile on East Marginal Way. We restore and maintain the exhibits. The museum just got several helicopters that came back from Iraq and Afghanistan. I saw them when they were trucked in, and the three of them looked like they had certainly seen action. I know personnel is actively looking for someone trained with these aircraft. If you can show that you have the training and experience, you will have no trouble getting the job. Well, you do have to go through an extensive background check."

The coincidence seemed almost too good to be accurate, but I was thrilled. "Billie, I am going to go there as soon as I finish my coffee. My clearances were all suspended when I left the service, but the files are current within the last forty-five days. I don't think there will be any problem getting it re-instated."

"Good. I hope to see you there. I am currently working on a project in the south hangar, so if you get to the museum, stop by."

She left me to my meal. As soon as I was finished, I got into the van and drove down to the museum to take a look.

My experience fit their needs because I got the job and was getting a temporary clearance and would be allowed to go right to work next Monday. Lots of details, but the crux was that I had a job using the skills I had learned in the army. My military file went a long way in both getting the job and having an I.D. indication that I was cleared. If they had any problems with the actual background investigation, I would be let go. I was pleased and comfortable. There wasn't any hitch that would come up. I was positive on that point.

The pay was way above what I was making in the service. Not as many perks, but it had full medical, and they started me at three weeks of vacation as I was used to thirty days a year.

And that takes me to the fateful night of 15 November 2016.

15 NOVEMBER 2016 – 2300 HOURS

I had been out cold, and I was just coming around. I heard noises and voices, and my vision was able to make out dim figures around me in… in what? Was this a hospital? What happened to me? As my faculties started to return, I felt the pain in my jaw then a raging, burning fire in my neck.

"Well, well, our girl is waking up." Sounded like a woman's voice, but I wasn't sure. My brain's synapses still weren't firing on all cylinders. And my whole head was in its own world of pain.

I had been hurt. Hurt badly enough to be in a hospital. So bad that I couldn't remember exactly what had happened to me.

Someone was hovering over my face. Someone was pulling my eyelids up and shining a very bright into one eye and the other. Ooo, that was fun.

Then that someone was poking around my mouth and jaw and down to the soreness on my neck. That was not any fun. I tried to say something, but only a moan came out. I couldn't say a word. I stopped trying because my jaw hurt. I tried to remember what had landed me here, and I vaguely recall some rube punching me.

Then Dr. Someone, or was it Nurse Someone, was mumbling something, and everything went black.

18 NOVEMBER 2016 – 1000 HOURS

My mind was floating up through a fog, I was back in the room with the fuzzy people, but things slowly started clearing. My vision cleared, and so did my pain tolerance. My jaw and neck were busy driving sharp pointy needles up through my brain, delivering pain at a level that I had never experienced in my entire life.

I tried to ask where I was and what was happening to me.

I was alert enough to know that what I wanted to say just came out pretty muffled. I tried to bring my hand up to my face, but it was held down somehow. That motion and my moans got someone's attention.

A face came into my view. It was a she and she was, well, she had a beautiful face.

"I'm glad to see you are coming around. You gave us quite a scare over the past couple of days."

Last couple of days? Again, I wondered where I was and what was happening. Forming words seemed useless, so I gave up.

"Don't struggle yet. It is going to be days until you recover your speaking ability. If you feel up to it, we will try to get you to write notes. Not today, hopefully, tomorrow.

"If you hear me, let's try to communicate by blinking your eyes. One blink for 'no' and two for 'yes.' Do you understand what I just said?"

Two blinks.

"Good. If you get tired, just close your eyes, and I will stop talking and let you rest.

"My name is Amelia Croyl. I was going into Slim's with my boyfriend, Eddie Vangh, when we saw the rogue pulling you into the alleyway.

"We were able to save you, and we had you brought to our company infirmary. We have the resources here to take care of you and monitor whether you received any, *er*, well, the person that attacked you could have infected you, and we are here to make sure you recover no matter what."

Rogue? What is she babbling on about? Now that my mind was clearing, I remembered it was just some drunk asshole surprising me and getting past my defenses. Was his name 'Rogue?' Figured if it was. But she made it sound like he was some kind of something else. I couldn't ask verbally, and my hand was not under enough control to write anything, and the whole thing was starting to make my head hurt more. Much more.

I tried looking around. My head wouldn't turn. It was in some rigid brace, so all I could see was what was visible to my eyeballs as I searched to the limits of their movement range. It looked like a hospital room. Instruments and carts and beeping monitors with oscilloscope screens with a lot of wiggly lines. I also saw more than one tree holding IV packs of blood and what was probably sugar water or some other nourishment since I wasn't able to eat.

"You were out cold by the time we got him off of you. He broke your jaw in two places, and while you were in the coma we had induced for your safety, the doctors went in and repaired your jaw bone, and you have a couple of shiny screws holding everything in place. You will have to be in the brace until the doc decides that the bones have knotted together enough to be on their own. The downside is that you will be on a liquid diet for some weeks. The good thing is that you will get a lot of ice cream, milkshakes, and sodas."

I fluttered my eyes and tried to say something.

"I suppose you may be wondering about the bite on your neck. Well, we are anxious about that little item as well. I can't tell you much more until we see how you are coming along and when you can communicate easier."

Amelia sat down to me and continued, "I can tell you this much; the being that attacked you has a particular pathogen in his blood. We want to make sure it didn't transfer into your body. This facility happens to the one best suited for this type of infection in the entire United States.

"I'll come by tomorrow with Eddie. As I said, he was with me when you were attacked, and it was mostly him that pulled the rogue off of you. There isn't anything you can do but let your body heal. You will get antsy to be up and about, but you must follow the doctors' orders. There is a great staff here, and every one of them has worked with this situation before. My best suggestion is to let the pain meds take over and get as much sleep as possible, even if you aren't tired. It will make the time pass faster, and it will help you heal more quickly."

And with that, she left.

~~~~

I slowly started to improve. By the next week, my speech was still somewhat garbled, but I was talking, and I was getting some answers. I met many new people, and they all fussed over me as if I were their long-lost sister.

I was having a hard time matching up their warmth with the reality that I was just someone they dragged in off the street.

About seven days in, I was visited by a very pretty, petite girl. She came in with a big fat file in her hands and sat down next to the head of my bed.
~~~~

"Hello there, Paulie Zahn. My name is Larisa Sykora, and I am the head of security for Newmark Industries."

My head snapped around, and I looked very intently into her eyes. *Newmark, I know that name.* I had to rummage around for a moment, and it came to me. That was the name of the company that Lisa Connors supposedly worked for.

To think that I was being treated in a Newmark facility, the same Newmark that Lisa worked for, was a coincidence gone too far.

"*Aah,* I see you recognize the name. That is a good step. We have notified Ms. Connor that you are here, and she is trying to re-arrange her schedule to come to see you. She had written a pretty in-depth report on what she thought of you. It wasn't all good…"

And she paused, for effect, I believe.

"It was better than good.

"We have your Harley in safekeeping, and there is a detail assigned to your studio apartment in Alki Beach. All your belongings are safe.

|Don't be stunned by what I know about you. We got your I.D. from your wallet when you were first brought in. Everything was sent to me to find out who you were. Amelia and Eddie didn't know anything, but I already had a complete file on you, including your entire military file and the clearance reports that are so classified that even you never get to see them. You were on our radar before you met Lisa because we wanted to get you to come to work for us.

"Your sudden departure from the army caught us off guard, and it took us a little time to catch up with you. We were in the process of having one of the upper staff contact you and re-open the job offer when your attack happened.

"The Boeing Museum has been informed that you had been in an accident and are in our hospital facility. We, no, I talked with the proper person there, and he knows that we are going to make an offer and has agreed to stand off and let it be your decision.

“You will get a formal offer from our firm just as soon as we know how you are and what position we want you to take. No matter what, our offer will be for considerably more than you were receiving at Boeing. I will make sure that you get to know a lot about us. I want you to make an informed choice.

“Eddie and Amelia have taken a deep interest in your health, and they will be stopping by more often. I, on the other hand, have my office on one of the floors below this. Any time you want to talk, any time twenty-four hours a day, you can leave a message on my iPhone. Your phone was smashed during the altercation. I have had a new phone prepared, and it contains all your contact information and some of the people here at Newmark, especially Amelia’s, Eddie’s, and mine. It also automatically defaults to encryption whenever you contact one of us or whenever we call or send you a message.

“You aren’t one of us, but you are so close that you are only a signature away. So, until you decide to take or not take our offer, you will have the full protection and resources of the company at your disposal.”

She leaned forward and smiled broadly. “Now you tell me that this hasn’t been the most exciting conversation you have had in a long time.”

She got up and reached out for my hand. She just held it for a moment staring into my soul, and then let go and left.

Good thing my jaw was wired shut, or it would have fallen open and bounced off the floor.

6 DECEMBER 2016 – 0815 HOURS

I had been sitting up for two weeks now. I was even getting out of bed to use the facilities all by myself. They had brought me a 15" laptop, and I was using it to learn things. Like who or what Newmark Industries was. Unfortunately, information was scarce. The only thing online was the founder's name, that it was heavily involved in the aerospace industries and that the company had offices around the globe. That was about it. No fancy show and tell of any of the product, no financials, no headcount, no specific locations of the other offices and plants.

There was a knock from the open door to my room. It was Amelia and Eddie, the dynamic duo that got me away from my attacker and to this facility. I owed them my life.

"Well, you look pretty chipper, Ms. Paulie," Amelia said.

"A lot better than when we first met you," Eddie said.

They were a beautiful couple. She, Amelia, looked to be as tall as Eddie, so it goes to reason that if they were at a dress-up affair, she would tower over him. Shit, she would probably tower over everyone in the room. They appeared to be close to my age.

Then it occurred to me that everyone I had met here was close to my age. From the little I had learned from searching the Internet, Newmark was not a new, young company. Although the specific date of establishment was not published, it appeared to have had been in business since before World War II. Maybe this branch or section was a newer one, and all of those working here were recently hired. Still, it seemed strange.

As much as I tried to start a conversation, my mouth still wasn't cooperating. I had to talk through my clenched teeth. The doctors had removed the exoskeleton brace from around my head and jaw, leaving only wires that held my jaw immobilized, still on the baby food diet, which was only bettered by many servings of ice cream sodas.

They had brought a wheelchair with them.

"Uuooo gize springing mme oot?" I mumbled.

"We're going to take a stroll around the facility. We think you should see where you are and maybe meet some of the others that work here. Nonmedical people for a change," Eddie explained as he maneuvered the chair closer to the bed.

"'Asst goood," I said, and I got my legs over the side and onto the floor. As I pulled my arm around, I hit my ice cup, and it headed for the floor. I reached out and snatched it before it hit. Without another thought, I set it up on the night table beside my bed.

As I looked up, Amelia and Eddie were looking at each other. I thought I saw concern in their expression, and as soon as they noticed me watching them, their faces went neutral. I know that they were hiding something. But they didn't let on.

They just reached out to help me get settled in the chair, and they even made me wear a safety belt.

"While we walk about with you, we want to ask a few questions about how you are feeling," Eddie said. "You are healing up perfectly, and we don't think you will be able to tell that you were scarred. You should be healed enough in two weeks or so to go home."

"'Asst goood," I said. Seemed I was a two-word conversationalist.

They wheeled me down to the elevators, and we rolled in. I immediately realized what a secure facility we were in. Instead of punching a floor button, Amelia held her eye up to an optic scanner and entered a series of numbers on the keypad that was next to the scanner. There was a chirp that came from a speaker next to the keypad. Then she pushed another floor button. I think it was two, but that was hard to tell because there were more numbers or floors than what I believed this building to have.

It was only a short drop to floor #2, and during that moment, Eddie handed me a security pass that had my picture (before the accident) and two letters in red, S and V.

"You are to keep that with you from now on. The S.V. identifies you as a visitor with secret clearance. Later, if you want to roam around on your own, you will be able to go to any area that is marked S or less. Later on, on this tour, we will be stopping in the security department to visit with Larisa, who will teach you and set up your access codes."

That was a lot of information to take in without being able to comment or ask questions very easily.

We went down a long hall to a door that had the same security optic scanner and keypad as was on the elevator. Amelia went through the routine again, and the lock clicked, and Eddie opened the door.

It opened up onto a walkway that went around three sides of a very large aircraft hangar. Very large. There was a Boeing 727 that took up most of the area, but there was a smaller jet, a Citation, a single-engine turboprop, and two helicopters of different capacities. I also saw my motorcycle sitting by the hangar floor office along with two others; another Harley and a BMW Adventure.

"Your bike is safe and sound. The other two are ours. Some day when you are all better and have some time, we can go for a ride," Amelia said.

They wheeled me from one end to the other. I was drooling by the time we got back to the door to the elevator hallway.

"Now we are going to take you down to the security unit," Eddie said.

Neither one said anything more. When we got into the elevator, they both had their retinas scanned, and they both punched codes in. They then had me face the console and held my pass up beside my face.

The speaker came to life, "Your passenger is authorized," and then the elevator moved. It moved down. And it moved long after it would have reached the first floor. Basement? No, this was lasting longer. When it stopped and opened, there was a large room in front of me with hundreds of monitors in front of dozens and dozens of operators. The room was lit just from the monitor screens, but that was more than enough for me to see everything.

They wheeled me into the room and past all the cubicles to a circular room in the center of all the workstations. It was glass all around with a desk that I would learn later is the security command center. And sitting at this desk was little Larisa.

As we neared the glass walls, a section slid aside, and I was wheeled right on in and up to Larisa's desk.

"It's about time you showed up. I have been sitting here for two weeks waiting for you to get out of bed and down here." Larisa grinned.

I looked up at my two hospital orderly hench-people, and they had some grins going on too.

"Here she is, Larisa. Be gentle on her. Remember, she is

just getting over the flu," Eddie said.

And he and Amelia left.

The glass portico slid shut, and then the glass went opaque. I couldn't hear any other sounds except the ones created here in this room. This room was probably soundproof.

"I have some sparkling water, a fresh Nespresso Expresso or Latte, or some juice or soda," Larisa offered.

"I have many things to cover with you, so you are in charge of telling me when you want a break.

"Newmark is a large company with over 15,000 employees in all parts of the globe. Seattle is where this is based. The founder lives just across the sound on Bainbridge Island, and you may be visiting there soon.

"I know you haven't seen much, but I want you to give serious thought to coming to work here. The hangar you just were in is only a small fraction of the aviation facilities the company has. We are thinking that you might want to head up a section that keeps all our helicopters flying. Just so you know, we have thirty or so, but they are scattered around. If you were to take that position, there would be a lot of traveling.

"The H.R. director for the Boeing Museum has agreed to keep your position open till you decide. We have a close working relationship with them."

That put my mind at ease, but there were still a lot of questions.

I reached out for the pad and a pen from her desk. Since my verbal skills were still all wired up, I decided to speed everything up.

I wrote, "What about my medical bills? Still have my V.A. privileges. That would have saved me a lot of money."

Larisa saw that she was reading upside down as I was

writing. When I finished that question, her hand reached out and took hold of my writing hand.

"You will not be receiving any bill for your care here. Not one cent for any part of it, including your bike storage upstairs and for the security detail watching your studio apartment," she said.

Before she could continue, I wrote, "Why?"

"There are several answers, so I will start going through them one at a time.

"You would have been contacted by someone from the company soon, but the incident accelerated that process. We had Lisa Connor's reports, and we already wanted to make you an offer. The incident also changed what your starting position would be. The new offer would be starting a few steps up from what we had intended to offer you initially.

"I am going to be setting up your access codes and show how to initiate the change in the daily encryption codes into the iPhone you were given earlier. Once that is done, you can go into or onto any of the Newmark properties. If your clearance level isn't enough for a particular area, you won't get in. Your accesses are limited because you aren't officially an employee yet, but we are all hoping that will change soon.

"Now I want to set up your clearance into the worldwide system. I will be getting a picture of both of your retinas and will have you set the secret ten-digit word that does not repeat any letter of the alphabet. I will be out of the room while you decide on the ten digits because you and only you will know what that phrase is."

She got up and pushed me around to a smaller console that was on her side desk.

"Put both hands on those plate glass panels. That will scan

your finger and full palm print into our system. Then get your eyes close to the two cameras that will photograph your retinas into the system too.

I did as she asked, and then she got up and walked to the sliding glass portico. It opened, and she turned and said, "I am going out of the room. It will close and go opaque so no one can see in. That is when I want you to make up your secret combination, type it on the keyboard, and hit enter. As soon as you push the enter key, the screen will go blank, and the room's glass will clear. That will alert me that you are done and that I can come back. I will have someone who wants to meet you with me when I return. Actually, I will have two someones with me."

As soon as the door closed, I stared at the keyboard. A word with ten unrepeated letters, or maybe a name or a short phrase that I would remember.

WALT DISNEY, or waltdisney. I entered it, and a moment later, the screen blanked, and the glass was starting to clear.

Larisa walked in, followed by this tall blonde, I mean severe model tall. And she was followed by Lisa Connor.

"Eesha, Eesha, Eesha," was all I could squeak out.

Lisa came over and got down beside my invalid's transporter and hugged me. "I am so glad to see you. We—I thought I had lost you. Twice. First, you disappeared because of your dad's death, and we had to play a little bit of catch-up. Then you got attacked. We were only a day or two behind when someone was going to contact you. I was hoping that I could have been here to be the one.

"You are going to have to pick a nicer crowd to hang out with." She turned to the tall woman with her.

"Paulie, this is Karan Newmark. The three of us are here to

explain a lot of things that are about to change your life."

"You gave us a scare." Karan took my hand, and instead of shaking it, she just held it.

"I want to extend my condolences on losing your father. I could only imagine how I would take it if I lost my dad."

I tightened my grip. It was all I could do to acknowledge her comment without starting to weep again. It had been around four months now, but every now and then, something or some person would trigger my memories of him.

"I want to talk to you about the position at the company. There is also another matter that is more sensitive than anything you have ever been exposed to that I want to discuss.

"I know that sounds ominous and I don't want to scare you, but other than the excellent job opportunity we are offering, we have some things to talk about that have come about because of the incident."

I had already pretty much decided to take the job offer. It did sound a little too good, but I was sure that I wanted to take the chance.

The 'other thing' they wanted to talk about had me a little nervous. I didn't have the foggiest idea of what it could be about. I actually had no nightmares from 'the incident.' I'd been knocked down before and got back up without missing a heartbeat. That attack, though, it did more damage to my body than I have ever had happen, still it was not a long-lasting memory. No flashbacks, no dreams, just nothing was following me about that night.

I shook my hands loose and reached for the paper and pen. I jotted down a few facts. "I am interested in the job, and second, the 'incident' didn't leave me with any long-term problem. I'll be fine as soon as I have my jaw unwired."

"Well, we will consider that the acceptance of the position even though you haven't had the requirements outlined. I know that whatever task is given to you, it will get accomplished. We don't have any pesky lieutenants here at Newmark to mess with you. In fact, your position could be equated to the rank of major or Lt. colonel. There will only be one other person between you and me, and that can always be skipped if you think talking to me directly is important," Karan Newmark said.

I wrote, "What is your position with the company?"

"I'm the president."

I just stared at her. Was I understanding her correctly? Nah, she must be the president of some division of Newmark. I knew from my little Internet research that this was a company of global proportions. And she appeared to be younger than me.

Larisa sensed that my mind was stuttering over the revelation. I think Lisa did too. They were both trying to talk at once.

Lisa won.

"This Karan Newmark is the president of the entire Newmark company. Every and all branches of Newmark Industries. Most people don't believe it either, that is until they sit down to discuss a contract or negotiate some deal with Newmark. Her dad, Spartak Newmark, is still Chairman of the Board but has left the running of the company's day-to-day affairs to her. She is here because the three of us are going to be telling you some things about yourself that you may have a problem accepting. Well, at first. One of either the three of us will be with you around the clock and until we know that you are all right."

They were scaring me more than the first time I was in a helio, and the pilot said, 'Paulie, take the stick.' There I was, eight thousand feet in the air and no safety net.

I looked to the side of the wheelchair and could see the floor. Didn't seem like far to fall. Don't see how I could get hurt.

I wrote, "Tell me."

Lisa chimed in, "We were worried about the bites on your neck. Your attacker's blood is different. His blood contains, or contained, some elements that if enough had gotten into your blood, you would have had some physiological changes to your system, to your body."

"Ooot 'ind of 'anges?"

"I want you to keep that thought for a little bit while I go through some things.

"Here, at this company, you will be in contact with other employees that have received this serum and, as a result, this change to their bodies. The changes can be a great thing to happen or a bad thing. The person that attacked you was one of those changed persons, but there is a difference. The people here at Newmark who survived the change to their system were mostly administered the serum under controlled conditions, and they were all volunteers. They knew what they were in for and were prepared to take measures to ensure that they didn't change to the dark side as it did at some time to your attacker.

"Your jaw was one thing, and that was easily cared for. The other item, the rogue's serum. We couldn't tell if you had received any at all or did you get some into your system. The doctor was fairly certain that you did receive some, but how much we couldn't tell. We had to give the serum enough time to settle into its new home to determine the extent that was there. You being the new home.

"Whatever the extent of change we believe you will have

remains to be seen. Here is what you must remember; the change that results from exposure to this serum can and will make you a stronger, healthier person for the rest of your life. The serum is not a bad thing. It is only bad if taken without a support team to ease you through the changes that happen to your body."

"Amm ei canging?"

"A little, yes. Normally, if there can be anything normal about it, a person would go through a complete and full change, and it takes about a week. You were attacked three weeks ago."

"'Aat meens eim alll canged."

"No, you aren't all changed.

"The staff caring for you have noticed some differences. Things that are not generally achieved by a regular Normal. We are going to refer to all of the population of the world that has never had any of this particular serum introduced into their bodies as Normals, or Norms as they are commonly called.

"We have another term for those that have gone through the full change. But, let's talk about your situation.

"You had two significant injuries, your jaw and the bite on your neck. You had your jaw bone broken in two spots. Your jaw was wired together and then wired shut.

"A jaw broken in the manner yours was would typically take a human being ten weeks to heal. You have been here for only three weeks. Tomorrow, you are going to the operating room to have the rest of the wires removed. Your bones have completely healed and knitted together. Your mouth and jaw will be a little sore for a week or so, but by the end of that time, no one will ever be able to tell.

"That was an indication that your body has accepted some of what the serum causes. There were other signs.

"We have been turning the lights in your room down. They were being controlled at the nurse's station. What was noticed was that the much-dimmed lights didn't hinder your sight at all. You won't be able to see in total darkness, but if there is even the slightest source of light, you will be able to see very well. We snuck that in on you.

"Then there was the incident this morning."

"Waaah inssaset?"

"Remember knocking your ice cup off of your nightstand and catching it before it hit the floor?"

"'Ees, uh-uh."

"Both of your friends, Eddie and Amelia, noticed. They know that no human could have reacted fast enough to catch the cup, but you did. Your reflexes are trigger fast."

Too much. I grabbed paper and pen, "So what am I now? Will I lose some other ability, or will I have to be kept away from the public? Have I changed into the person that attacked me? How long with this last? Does this mean that I won't be getting the job you offered?"

"Relax, or at least try to. You have no worries about the job. It is yours, and you can start as soon as the doc clears you.

"For the 'What am I now?' question, this is all we know. We don't know what you have become. It's the first time a partial change has been observed. You have not manifested all the traits usually associated with a change. Just some. We don't know if you will lose the changes or if they will continue till you are entirely changed, or if this is all that will happen to you.

"We can accept you in any form this takes. You are one of the Newmark Family now."

Lisa continued, "Paulie, that was not a normal person that attacked you. He wasn't even human."

I thought, I know he wasn't human. He was a deranged animal. If he hadn't gotten the blow to my jaw, I would have beaten his face to a bloody pulp.

Larisa chimed in then, "If Amelia and Eddie hadn't shown up just then, you would have died in that alleyway. What attacked you was not a human. He was a rogue. He will never bother you or anyone else again. Eddie and Amelia made sure of that."

I wrote, "Rogue what? A deranged human being."

Karan took the floor. "Paulie, this is where it gets difficult to explain things. I want to start with your present condition.

"I see you squirming around, but what we are getting ready to tell you is more significant than you imagined. So, try to relax and listen. Questions later, and it will take many weeks to tell and teach you everything you need to know about your new self.

"You were brought to this facility not because of the broken jaw but because you had been bitten. The 'thing' that bit you was not a human being. I already said that. But the not-human part is what this is all about. I will start with this. There are more than just human beings on the Earth. I'm not talking about animals, birds, rabbits, and elephants. I am talking about beings that look human but aren't. He belongs to a group we call vampires."

Ding ding ding, here comes the wagon. I'd seen the Twilight series of movies. There is a fan club in Afghanistan that were all 'True Blood' junkies. This wasn't a hospital I was in. It was a sanatorium for the mentally deranged. A sanatorium that has a colossal aircraft hangar attached to it. I think I wanted to see daylight. I mean, see daylight right now.

I wrote, "Can I go outside for a moment?"

Lisa said, "I'll take her. I will let her know that she is free to go any time and is not a freak or medical study doll."

She took a hold of my wheelchair, and we went to the elevator. She did the scan thing and keyboard entry, and the lift started. When the doors opened, I could see that we were in a central entry atrium. Not twenty-five feet away was sunlight and freedom. I took charge of my wheelchair and headed to the front doors. They were automatic, and I went through. There was a handicap ramp to the side, and I rolled down it. I heard the doors open again and turned to see Lisa standing there. She wasn't moving any further.

I turned toward the sounds and motion of the street. I was in the visitor's parking area. Concrete berms blocked the larger traffic from going through, but there were enough gaps that I could get through.

I didn't go through. I saw across the street was the northernmost building belonging to the Boeing Museum, which I used to work in.

The Newmark building was on Marginal Way. The back where the hangar was opened onto the runways for the airport. There were no barriers between me and the street. If I wanted to, I could wheel my way right on out there. In fact, there was a bus station right in front.

6 DECEMBER 2016 – 1445 HOURS

I must have sat there for an hour. I was trying to make sense of what had been said to me.

It didn't. It was science fiction.

If I hadn't been able to sit outside here with the illusion that I was free to go if I wanted to, I might have kept going.

They were leaving any decision up to me. I believed that they trusted me. I had no reason to disbelieve them except that the story was not believable. I shouldn't be upset it was; after all, it was just a story. A fun, made-up story. Something you tell your kids to scare them straight.

I turned my chair around, and Lisa was still standing outside the front entrance.

The sun goes down early in Seattle in the winter. It was fading now, and the day hadn't been very warm to start with. I had on my backward nightgown and a thin robe on. My teeth would have been chattering if they weren't tied together.

Life decision time.

I turned and started wheeling myself back toward the Newmark building.

Lisa didn't come to meet me. She just stood and watched as I wheeled back and up the handicap ramp to the front doors.

As I neared the front doors they automatically opened and Lisa stood to the side as I wheeled myself in. We passed the front desk, where two guards were standing behind a security checkpoint. They both just nodded to us, and we proceeded to the elevator door. When the door opened, I wheeled in, and Lisa followed.

The doors closed, and Lisa didn't do anything.

"'eesa" I gurgled out.

"Use your own eye and code set to get us entry to the security section. Here, let me have your phone."

I handed it to her, and she searched around and then showed it to me."

"Here is the Newmark App. Press it and enter your passcode you created earlier. Your phone will give you a code to use on the elevator keypad."

I followed her directions, and in a moment, we were on our way back to the security center.

~ ~ ~ ~

I wheeled myself back and into Larisa's crystal palace, her throne room.

Karan and Larisa were sitting, and when Lisa came in, she sat too. I didn't have to pick a seat. My seat was strapped to my butt.

The door slid shut, and the walls went opaque.

Karan spoke.

"We were going to wait until you had use of your mouth before we started this discussion, but things are going on that caused us to move the revelation of the World of the Others to you now.

"You came to this medical unit a little bit by luck—for you. You were kept here after the initial repairs to your jaw were done because we know what kind of creature bit you. Many times, nothing comes from one of these bites. Because your name was already in our databases as a unique person of interest, we kept you to ensure that the venom's characteristics in the creature's blood didn't infect you."

Paper and pen time. "Am I all right?"

"You are healthy. In fact, you are extra healthy. So, the answer is yes, you are fine."

---pregnant pause---

"When I said that you are fine, I meant it. You are perfectly fine for who and what you are. The other side of the coin is that you are now physically very different from you a month ago.

Sometimes, when the blood of a vampire enters the bloodstream of a human, it may change them. Are you now a vampire? The answer is that we don't know how deeply the virus infected you. You will be watched, and tests run periodically to see how much you have been affected by his bite.

"Most human doctors would not be able to explain how that was possible. Even a doctor that has is well versed in the physiology of vampires wouldn't have an explanation of a partial change phenomenon. I have looked at several ancient documents on this subject, but all I could get out of my research time was that there hadn't been a partial conversion in many hundreds of years.

"You are still a human, but there have been some changes to your body that have given you enhanced senses. That means your healing time is faster than any non-lethal injury. You will gain the ability to hear like an owl and see like an eagle, especially at night. There is a lot more, but we need to get you initiated to your new form so that you don't think about suicide. 80 percent or better of the humans unwillingly bitten by a vampire commit suicide within the first three months.

Paper-n-pen time. “Are you a vampire?”

“No, I am not. I am human. What I may become in the future remains hidden. But for you, I am all human. Larisa and Lisa here, however, are a different story. I have some matters to attend to elsewhere, and I think this discussion is at the stage that I can leave you with these two, and they can get you oriented.”

And Karan Newmark left. I was locked in here with two, *er*, two somethings. I wasn’t sure what to call them.

I was frustrated at not being to talk normally. I couldn’t write fast enough to get it all on paper. I would start a sentence, and my mind would jump to another question before I got the first one written out.

This wasn’t a high-security office in the basement of a building. It was in the belly of an intergalactic spaceship full of aliens. Any minute now, I expected to see them wheel out a huge black cauldron to cook me in.

I started regretting that I came back into the building. I was staring at my former friend Lisa. Yep, I could see it. She had wrinkles and crow’s feet by her eyes.

My body convulsed. I was feeling like I was going to be sick. That would be a disaster considering my jaw was still wired shut.

I wasn’t looking at either of them. I was staring into my hands that were in my lap. I was feeling sicker than I ever had in my life. Where the fuck was I?

I started to turn my wheelchair around toward the door. I just wanted to get to my room and shut everyone out.

Lisa got up and came around behind me. “Larisa, I’m going to get her back to her room. I think she needs some quiet time to herself.”

I was spaced out. So much so that I didn't remember the ride back to my cell. Elevators, doors, and long hallways. It all went by in a blur. I wasn't concentrating on anything in particular. I tried to listen to my mind, but all I could hear was white noise. Background static that was pounding away at my brain. I couldn't get a stable thought going.

Dad, Dad, Dad, why did you leave me? I had no one. My world was shattered into a million pieces, and there was no one to help put Humpty Dumpty back together again.

I was wheeled into a different room. This one had a large window facing the King County International Airport runway. It was a larger room also. There was a closet standing open, and I saw that it was filled with MY clothes. My shoes, my jackets. My stuff. I forgot. The VAMPIRES have access to my apartment. Access to everything I own, including my body and mind.

Suicide. I can see where that would come up with someone in my situation.

I could see out of my new window. I could even wheel myself back to the elevators, down, and out the front door again. If I could find my wallet, I might even have enough money to get on the bus and go... *er... er...* Fuck! I didn't know where I would or could go.

"Paulie."

It was Lisa speaking. She was the only one in the room. I had known her longer than anyone else with this company, the Newmark company. My world was gone. I was left here with someone I had liked and trusted, and she was all that there was that I could reach out to in an attempt to save my sanity.

But wait, she was part of the insanity. She had been following me for months and months now, just waiting to push me over the edge into the looney bin. There was no way I could trust her for anything, ever again.

I got out of the wheelchair and into the bed by myself.

"Paulie, If there were any way to undo what happened to you, I would have urged the staff to do just that. Purge this toxin from your body and make you Normal again.

"That is not possible, though. We, and I am referring to all of the Newmark employees and their families, have never found a way to reverse this type of change. I, at one time, right after the serum was introduced to my bloodstream and I started to feel the changes, had regrets about what I had gotten myself into. The process was all my own choice, and the regrets passed in a few days as I became aware of each of the improvements to my body. I changed my outlook and became eager to learn the extent of my new abilities.

"Had this not happened to you, you would have still been offered the job with Newmark. Then, as you became more and more involved with the company, you would have gently been introduced to the other people that you were working with who had gone through this change to their bodies. You would see that they appeared just as normal as you or anybody else in the population. Through a slow indoctrination, you would have been given a choice to have the change be administered or not. It wouldn't affect your position with Newmark.

"As time goes by, you will meet many of the upper-tier management from Newmark. Some will have been changed, and others are still Normals. You will see that we all work together regardless of what we are.

"We are a family. I want you to become a part of this family. I liked you from the minute I met you. After our time in Italy, I found myself thinking about you. LIKE A SISTER, before you go down the wrong thought path.

"I have no living relatives, and I don't fraternize outside of the Newmark circle. Life, at times, has been a lonely one.

"After our time together in Italy, I had dreams of getting together on different occasions and going on vacation trips. You would have been the first person that I have let get close to me on a personal level in a long, long time.

"I want you to work in this company. I want you to take the time to learn everything there is about what you have or are becoming. I want you to know the advantages of receiving these life enhancements.

"We have asked that Amelia and Eddie spend as much time as they can with you. They were both changed by this serum, and they will know best how to answer your questions. The significant advantage in talking to the two of them is that Amelia's change was voluntary while Eddie was not. Or not knowingly. He has a great story to tell if you give him a chance.

"I am going to sit by your side tonight. In the morning, they will take you to the operating room to remove all the wires in your jaw and mouth. When you are brought back to the room, I believe Amelia will be here.

"She will answer any questions that you may ask. That is, if it is a question she has an answer to. There will not be any questions that you could ask that we, any of us, would avoid answering. You are now a part of a wholly different sub-classifications of humans. We can't turn you back. Listen to and ask questions of Eddie and Amelia.

"I know that if you give them and all of us a chance to teach you about this life, you will come to embrace it and learn to use your newfound changes to advantage and for good in this world."

I closed my eyes. I squeezed them tight. Then I turned off my ears. I wanted to close the world out. I was trying to shut out everything and everyone around out of my mind for a while. Maybe I would go to sleep and wake up to the old world, a world without all this, *all this*… I realized that I didn't even understand what 'all this' really meant any more.

7 DECEMBER 2016 – 0600 HOURS

I was awoken by two orderlies and a nurse, all wearing scrubs. They wanted me to get up and go to the bathroom before they took me to the OR.

Lisa wasn't around. I hadn't spoken with her the night before, and I was so lost in my thoughts that I didn't know when she left. At first, I thought I had not slept, but not seeing Lisa leave and having my three new besties wake me up meant that I must have.

They had brought a gurney in, so I wasn't traveling in the wheelchair. Got to lie there and stare up at the fluorescent as they wheeled me down the hall. *Blink, rumble, rumble, blink, rumble, rumble,* and then I was at the OR.

The room was almost painfully bright. And there were several people attending. They were all masked up, so I couldn't see faces.

One of the masked bandits came to my side and started swabbing my arm with betadine solution. Then a heplock was inserted into the back of my hand. She, or he, then repeated the procedure for my other arm and hand.

"We will be giving you some fluids and blood if it is needed. The other side we will be using to administer the anesthetic. The doctor will also inject the jaw area with some pain killers for when we remove the wires. That will ease the slight pain you will have as the anesthetic wears off.

You should be waking up in your room in an hour or two."

I didn't say anything. I wasn't in the mood to talk to anyone just yet. And suddenly, I was out of it…

~ ~ ~ ~

Slowly I became aware of some light. Then I tried opening my eyes. Surprisingly, my vision was clear and sharp.

I was back in my room, and there was a fluid bag dripping into my heplock. I tried to sit up, but that was not going to be my next best trick. My body was feeling weaker than I expected. When I did make a move to sit up, I saw someone get up from the chair and come over.

"Well, lookie here, our new little ray of sunshine has returned to the land of the living."

It was Amelia. She used the control remote and raised the head of the bed. I felt momentary dizziness, but it also quit right away. I started to say thanks and realized that my mouth worked. My whole jaw and mouth felt numb, like when the dentist shoots you up with novocaine. Then you drool uncontrollably for the rest of the day.

Being able to open and close my mouth was worth all the embarrassing drool in the world.

Amelia took my hand, held it, and looked into my eyes.

I knew right then that I was glad she was here. I knew that she was now my official mentor and could explain away most if not all of my questions and concerns. I was ready to figure out my life, and she had answers.

"You're one of them," which I regretted saying right away. I saw it in her eyes. She was hurt by what I said. Before I could retract the statement, she spoke up.

"Paulette, it's okay. I'm here for you. I want to help you

understand what we are. Our life is different than the Normal person. We, on the other hand, are vampires."

I was startled by just the word. It just didn't seem like a real thing. They were for a fantasy world that didn't exist. But I was lying here with a person that was telling me that she was a real one. A vampire.

I unconsciously looked at her mouth. Seemed like a regular mouth to me. I wondered if the fangs retract or something. A grin spread across her face. Then she opened her mouth so I could see her upper canines. Same as mine.

"Common misinformation," she said. "Long time ago, vampires did have larger canine teeth. And yes, they would bite into the veins of human victims to get the human's blood into their system.

"That disappeared before I was born. I mean born as a normal human baby and then later when I was re-born or converted into a vampire. I have never gotten blood directly from a human.

"To help you understand, I will have to go into a long explanation. It will take some time. I think you need some liquids to sip on and if you are hungry, let me know, and I will have a meal brought in."

I nodded and then realized that maybe I could speak well enough to be understood. "Some juice would be good. I think I want to eat but don't have anything in mind."

Amelia got up and went out to the hall. I could hear her. I could hear everything she was saying, even though she was out of sight and probably down the hallway a little.

When she returned, she had a cart with several assorted sippy-bags of juice and yellow-green Jell-O and several packets of saltine crackers. Some people would grimace at the selection, but when your meals had consisted of pureed baby food through a straw, this offering was from heaven.

"You go ahead and eat. I will just start talking and explaining things to you.

"We are the New Age vampires. I just made that term up, so don't rely on it when talking to anyone else. Now about the blood thing. Humans' blood and that of a vampire are almost precisely the same, except there is a factor in a human's blood that a vampire does not have and can't produce on their own. Back whenever the vampire race started, it was discovered that to stay alive, a vampire had to get some human blood. It is a falsehood that a vampire can drink the blood like a glass of wine. A vampire has to get human blood by drawing it out with a hypodermic-type instrument. Vampire's canines were elongated and had a hollow capillary running down the center. To get pure human blood that hadn't been exposed to the air, they would bite into a human with their canines. Preferably biting directly into a major artery.

"The stories and movies go off on a totally wrong tangent. IF we were still getting the human blood by biting a human, the amount we ever need is less than a quarter of a pint or four fluid ounces. We have to repeat that amount, four liquid ounces between three and six weeks apart. It depends on our level of activity.

"Using me as an example, I am very physically active. I am either walking, running, riding a bicycle, or working out at the gym. I need to replenish the human factor every three to four weeks. If I don't get that human factor, I will become anemic and eventually fall into a coma and die.

"That is how much and how often. Now about now. In the early 1900s, the medical world discovered transfusions. Some vampires in England tried direct transfusions from humans into an artery in their arm. It worked, alleviating the threat of having a human reporting being attacked and bitten.

"Then in the middle of the century, hospitals started storing whole blood. That made it a lot easier to get our needed nourishment in the privacy of our own home. Over an amazingly short evolutionary period, our long prominent canines shrunk to almost average size. If you look closely at mine, you will see that they are only slightly larger than other people's.

"My canines never grew long. Sometimes when we have a party amongst ourselves, I will put in a glue-on pair. Sorry, that was silly. Just couldn't resist dropping it in there.

"At the time when we were starting to use stored whole blood to maintain our health, the European Vampires Council made it a law that all vampires were to use stored blood supplies and outlawed biting and drinking blood that way."

"Wait, Wait a minute. But why did the guy that attacked me bite me in the neck?" I asked. My mouth was working better. It was feeling a little achy, and the numbing agent must be wearing off.

"That has all of us worried. I was hoping to delay the answers to this part of your life till later, but maybe now would be a good time."

Before she got started, Eddie came into the room.

He was pretty darn cute… for a vampire, that is, I thought. And he belonged to Amelia, so that was a dead end.

"Well, our latest addition is up and looking chipper."

"That's enough, Eddy," she said. "Sit down. You are interrupting our discussion. Our lessons. Now, where was I?"

"Why was I bitten?"

"Though THE council outlawed it about seventy-five years ago, there have been rogue bands of vampires that believe that the old way is the only true way to exist. They are created with a bite and maintain that they must only nourish themselves by sucking the blood out of some unwilling human. The council does have a section whose responsibility it is to locate and eliminate these bands of rogues. There is a special reason for eliminating them. They have the habit of biting a human and making sure they give back some of their blood, infecting and converting that human into a vampire. Almost all of those unwilling converts die within a few months because no one was around to explain what had happened to them and show them how to nourish themselves and, more importantly, teach them what their new abilities are and how to use them properly.

"You were unfortunate enough to have been attacked by a rogue. That, and your attack, is the first one we have seen in a long time. Had you died that night, the rogue would have disposed of your body so that it wouldn't be discovered that they are present in this area.

"We are looking into this problem ourselves because we want to keep the European Council out of our hair. We also didn't notify them because they would have wanted to take you back to Europe to experiment on. They believe that if you are bit by a rogue that you will only want to get nourishment from biting into an artery of a human. We don't follow this thought."

Eddie spoke up, "You are not going to turn rogue. We don't even know for sure that you will reach the full conversion. You are a one of a kind."

"Shit, I must be the lucky one," I said.

"Yes, little one, you are very lucky," Amelia said. "You are now officially aligned with the strongest arm of the Vampire

Council. Spartak Newmark and several others who work for Newmark Industries are part of the thirteen that make up the council. Newmark is pretty much autonomous in policing the western part of the U.S. No other group in the world holds as many seats on the council. You have become part of the most politically influential and wealthiest group of all the vampires in the world."

It could not be helped. I unconsciously puffed up a little with pride. A month ago, I was doing just fine on my own. Today, I felt even finer—wrong English, correct feeling. Though I still had apprehensions and questions and needed to get more answers.

"I don't have any yearning for blood. Maybe I don't need blood. Maybe I'm not changing into anything at all."

"Paulie," Eddie said, "you are unusual in that there is only one like you in the whole world. You are different because we know that you have not become a full vampire. Never has there ever been anyone that only changed partway. We don't know if, in time, your change may go through to completion or if your system will flush out.

"It will take Amelia and myself many days to explain all the differences between a human and a vampire. And then, we will have to explain what changes have occurred to your body. It will take us time to explain and your time to absorb it all. We will be available to you around the clock till you are knowledgeable and confident enough to spread your wings."

"Do you want me to explain about her need for blood, or do you want to? It may be best if I did it as I think I can stay on subject instead of trying to explain the workings of the whole world," Amelia said.

"I'm hungry," I said.

"I see she is past the grunting state," said Eddie.

Thonk!

Amelia hit Eddie across the back of his head with a rolled-up magazine.

"Ow! That hurt."

"Don't worry, Paulie. His head is made of petrified wood. There isn't anything inside anyway."

I grew a little smile at that, And they saw it, and they both smiled also.

"Eddie, I'll explain about her blood needs. Please see what we can get for her to eat. I bet she would love a pizza, but maybe that much chewing would be too much today. See if you can get some pasta with plain sauce, no meatballs, or anything lumpy.

"While he is out being chased by the nurses, I will talk about blood. There is so much that has to be explained about everything, but I have to take the leap and get it all out.

"You have been monitored and had tests run on a periodical regimen since you arrived. The first blood tests showed slight traces of the toxin present. The doctors weren't sure if it was enough to convert you into a vampire or not. So, they added some other tests in. Sensitivity to light, noises, reaction times, general strength levels in your limbs and your sleep cycles."

"I don't remember any tests other than the blood draws."

"They snuck everything but the blood draws into your daily routine. For instance, the strength evaluation was done by handing you items that we added lead weights to, a little at a time. The water carafe that holds your drinking water is insulated but full, it weighs a pound or pound and a quarter. The one you have beside your bed now is weighted in the bottom to over six lbs. You have been handling it like a normal carafe. Go ahead and pick it up and try to guess its weight."

I did. I picked it right up. Nothing unusual about that. Then I moved it around from left to right in front of me. Then I noticed the weight. Not picking it up, but when I was swinging it back and forth, it took more effort to make a sharp change in direction. It wanted to keep going. It was the weight.

"You have been sitting in bed for several weeks now, enough that you should have lost some muscle tone. Instead, you are much stronger. You are a lot stronger than you ever were.

"The other test was the amount of light in your first room. You learned downstairs yesterday that the light level had been reduced over time until it was just dim lighting. You never had problems seeing anything or reading this magazine.

"The blood tests were our best indication. During the first two weeks you were here, the toxin level increased. Never to the level we usually mark as the amount that is necessary for a full conversion into a vampire. Your levels only got to the halfway mark, and there hasn't been any change, up or down, since.

"I'll be very, very honest with you. This is something we have never seen or heard about. None of the staff has a clue as to what way you will go. It is possible that you will remain right at this level. That isn't a bad thing at all. Things like being a little stronger than a comparable Normal, seeing in partially lighted or dim places, being able to hear a pin drop in the next room. Those are only some of the perks, and you seem to have a little of each one.

"But now I'm going back to the blood test results. They showed that you will need to take in some of the factors that are only in human blood. These are factors that our bodies can't produce. You are going to need transfusions of whole blood but not in the amounts nor as often as Eddie or I do. Or all the other vampires in the world. You will need about 100 cc's once every four to six weeks. You will need a little more if you are injured."

She saw me draw my knees up and the wry look on my face.

"We do have a way for you to get those human factors you need without having to get a transfusion. Three or four years ago, at the direction of Sparky Newmark, our laboratory was able to isolate the human factor we need from human blood supplies. The factor is a live organism, and the lab discovered that it could keep the organism in a freeze-dried state using cryogenics. This essence is then put into gelatin capsules that you can take in the place of transfusions. For you, it has been estimated that you will have to take one of these capsules just once a month or as your body lets you know that you need nourishment."

"Who is Sparky Newmark?" I asked.

"That's our pet name for Spartak Newmark, the head of Newmark Industries and Karan's father. About your eating habits, you/we have to eat. Regular everyday food. We are not un-dead like in the movies. We have to breathe air. We have to eat regular food, eat garlic, crosses and holy water don't affect us. No bat's wings either. It's a long list of what we are and aren't. There is no handbook, but you will have access to dozens of us that will always take time to educate you.

"Here are the last two tidbits to let you in on; your aging process has been slowed, and your metabolism is greatly increased. These two processes usually happen in tandem, but with us, they are going in opposite directions. Faster metabolism and slower aging. The increased metabolism will help you heal fast, and it can burn off alcoholic drinks rapidly.

The real big change is the slowing of your aging process. We, the doctors, haven't yet been able to determine how much slower you will age. Just accept the fact that your aging process has slowed."

"Slowed?" I started. "How much slower? What about you? Are you like, two hundred years old or something? How old is Eddie? How long have you and Eddie been together? Do you get tired of each other? What if I want to date a Normal? Do I have to stay under cover during daylight hours?"

"Wow! That's a whole head-full of questions. Some of your questions will have to wait, but they will be answered in time. Right now, we have to get you up and running with the basics. Sort of on-the-job-training.

"I was born to normal parents in 1972, and I was changed into a vampire in 2003. Look at me. I know that I still look the same age as when I was turned, not the forty-two years old that my birth certificate would show. My change was my choice. I selected the person that I wanted to help me make the change, and I chose the date."

"The person that helped change you. Are you now that person's slave, or are you tied to that person by some attraction to honor and obey?"

"Oooo, that is a good one," Amelia said. "The change can still be done by a vampire transferring some of their blood into the Normal that is going to be changed. It can also be initiated by swallowing one of those capsules I told you about, but ones that came from the filtered blood from an older vampire. Older like several hundreds of years old. I asked to have the change and have never regretted doing it. Not even for a minute.

"Eddie was created differently. I want him to tell you his story."

At that, Eddie opened the door and walked in, grinning.

"It's the better hearing," he said. "I am both younger and older than Amelia. Younger in that I was 27 when I was turned and older as my human birth date is 1920. I still look twenty-seven years old or pretty close. I didn't know vampires were real until I became one. It was during the war; I got mortally wounded and a vampire that was there bit me and got enough of his blood into my bloodstream to save me. It took a week for my body to accept the different or modified blood that was then coursing through my system. The vampire who changed me had a family and a daughter who was three at the time. She is here in Seattle, and she, too, voluntarily requested to be changed. You will meet Darja sometime soon as she is part of the Newmark family also.

"I digress… I spent a little more than two weeks with that family. The father was the only one who was a vampire. In the time I spent with them, the vampire taught me what I needed to know about being a vampire and how to get the special blood replacement I would need without biting anyone.

"Like you, one day, vampires were just a story, and the next, I had become one. The best thing that ever accidentally happened to me."

"So, there you have the accidental and the requested change stories from two people you now know," said Amelia.

"I'm hungry," I said. "I want something other than Jell-O if it is possible. Could one of you go over the daylight/sunlight thing? Will I burst into flames?"

Amelia took this one. "I just texted the cafeteria, and something will be up in fifteen minutes.

"Sunlight. You have to treat sunlight with respect. We all lose much of our skin coloring. When we go out, if the sun is shining bright, we wear long sleeves and pants and a hat, sunglasses, and PF-100 sunscreen. Seattle weather is perfect because there are 260 overcast days every year. London is another great place to work or visit."

Just then, a nurse brought my meal in. She also had the fun of drawing several vials of blood and took the rest of my vitals. When she was done torturing me, she patted my hand and said, "You have been the best accident case we have ever taken care of here. Just please, don't make it a habit."

Coffee, which I hadn't had for a month, milk also, garlic mashed potatoes with extra, extra butter, and steak. Well, Salisbury Steak, ground meat, hamburger. Something I could gum my way through, I had all my teeth, but my jaw was tender. It was just allowed back into the real world six hours ago. What do you expect? And for dessert, a strange-looking gel capsule. That must be my blood supplement.

Eddie and Amelia didn't talk while I was eating. That was good because I needed a lot of quiet time to digest everything I had been told this morning and this afternoon. No wonder I was hungry.

When I finished, I asked if it would be okay to watch the news on the TV.

Amelia came over and bent over and kissed my forehead. "I have to leave to take care of some company work. Eddie is going to be staying the night. Just keep in mind two things; he is a sucker for a pretty face and that he is very much spoken for."

Eddie handed me the remote, got a blanket to wrap himself up in, and sat in one of the padded chairs for my visitors.

"Eddie, are you really hundred years old?" I asked.

"Close to it, sister."

Sister, I was a little taken aback on that one. Was he considering that I was now kin?

I had a lot to learn about this sorority/fraternity. Friendly people though, great job too with good pay and excellent benefits. I couldn't go wrong joining, I hoped. I decided that I liked these people. It is a bizarre world that I was a part of now.

9 DECEMBER 2016 – 0730 HOURS

I got up, brushed my teeth which was pretty exciting, took a shower, and dressed in fresh clothes, including jeans, a colored T-shirt, and my converse sneakers. I also had my brown leather motorcycle jacket. I could tell it had gotten a lot colder while I had been in the hospital wing.

Discharge day. I was going to walk out of here soon. Out into a different life. Completely.

Amelia walked in with one of the nurses.

"Ride or walk on your own?" the nurse asked.

"I'll pack the things I am taking home on the wheelchair to get it all downstairs."

Nursie had me sign some papers, and then she handed me a gold foil-wrapped box with a blood-red ribbon, "That is a gift from the medical staff. We, every one of us, are so glad you have come into our lives. If you ever have questions that we might have the answers to, just call or stop in. No appointment needed for you."

Amelia helped me load up, and she pushed the baggage while I walked beside her.

"How am I getting home?" I asked.

"Eddie has your van downstairs with the bike trailer hooked on with your bike loaded. He will drive you home, and I will follow in the car," she said.

And I followed her to the elevator, where she did the eye scan and code entry. When the doors opened, we were on the ground floor of the hangar. The big jet was gone leaving the cavernous space cold and bare. You could build a whole city there. There was enough room.

I spotted the van with my motorcycle on the trailer behind it. Next to it was this stunningly restored Chevy Nomad.

"Is that yours? I asked her.

"No, that belongs to Zope. You will meet her Sunday at the Newmark Estate. Spartak and LaDoña are having a little welcome luncheon to present you to the household and the main officers with Newmark Industries. You are going to be a debutante."

"I just took a shower. Does this affair require me to take another shower just two days from now, on Sunday morning?"

"I'll get with Zope, and we will organize a mud run for earlier in the morning. Then everyone will look the same."

I didn't say anything. I didn't think she was serious, but I didn't want to encourage it either.

We loaded my things into the van and parked the wheelchair by the hangar wall.

"Can I ride in the Nomad?"

"Sure, hop in."

When she started the Nomad up, I could tell that there was nothing left that was stock under that hood.

"What is in there?" I said, pointing toward the front hood.

Zope just had a factory performance LT-1 with an Edelbrock supercharger.

Our little caravan pulled out and went north on Marginal till we got to the bridge that would get us over to the Alki Beach district where my studio was.

Eddie pulled the van with the trailer into the drive to the back of the property. Amelia parked the Nomad in front.

We both got out, and Amelia headed to the front door of the house.

"No, no, I live in the studio in the back," I told her.

"There has been a slight change," she said. "The property is now owned by a subsidiary of Newmark Industries. We moved your belongings into the front house, and we had weather covers built for the van and trailer. Your bike will park in the studio until we can figure where you want to house it. You do know that the rent is free—to you. Free for as long as you want to stay here and are an employee of Newmark."

That wasn't the only shock. The house had all new furniture except the one wing-back and desk that had been my dad's. Those were about the only pieces I had kept. Them and an odd collection of kitchen pots and pans and knives and mixing bowls and such. All that stowed away in the proper drawers. New paint, new carpets, new double-paned windows, and this queen-sized Sleep Comfort bed for me and a second one in the spare bedroom.

After several minutes of getting the tour, the show and tell in my new home, I sat in my dad's chair and curled into a ball. I was so overtaken with emotion that I couldn't move. My shoulders were shaking, and I knew tears were rolling down my face, but they were the happiest tears I have ever had.

Amelia got down on her knees next to the chair and reached around me. I was feeling like such a baby. Me, who had faced down an insane jihadist in the Afghanistan desert with only a pistol. I never so much as let a drop fall from my eyes.

"Paulie, you are safely home. You have a new job, new friends, and a whole new life. I need you to buck up because there are things I have to show you and someone I want to introduce to you."

"Introduce? To me?"

We went out back outside the studio, where Eddie and another guy were easing my motorcycle into the little studio.

"Nigel," Amelia called out. "Nigel, this is Paulette Zahn. And this is who you are to keep a watchful eye over so that she doesn't have any unsolicited surprises.

"Paulie, this is Nigel Parker. He is here to watch over this property. Both when you are away and also when you are home. He is here on loan from one of our subsidiaries in Canberra, Australia. He will be doing some security training with Larisa a couple of days a week. If you bring a date home, be sure to give him a fair warning. Don't want him tearing the arm off a friend."

Just then, her cell phone was growling at her. She pulled it out and said, "Yes."

I backed away to give her some privacy, which didn't work so well as my new acute hearing could hear both ends of the conversation even though I was probably ten feet away. I knew that Amelia knew that I could hear everything. If it had been confidential, she would have moved a lot further away.

"Eddie, that was Zope. They want us back right away. Paulie, there is a locked leather messenger's bag next to the dining table. That has all the information about your job, where to go, who are the others that work there, and the pecking order. Also, your financial documents, which our accountants have reviewed and put in order. There are also new company credit cards and some other papers that you should go through. We have to get back to the estate on Bainbridge Island. That is where you will come on Sunday morning. See you there at about nine a.m."

And they were gone, leaving me standing there flatfooted

with Nigel.

"It is a pleasure to meet you, Paulie. I think that you will want to go through how they have set your household up. That and reading through the other paperwork they left. So that you know, I am a vampire. I am a security specialist, and while I am learning new things, I will be here to protect you and your property."

He looked like Billy Gibbons. Even had on the dark sunglasses. I looked around him to see if there was a guitar anywhere nearby.

I was at a loss for words, so I told Nigel, "I'm just going to go into the house and get things put away" and with that, I just turned and up the stairs into the back door to the kitchen.

10 DECEMBER 2016 – 1245 HOURS

I had intended to open the pouch and read the documents and then go through every closet, cabinet, and drawer in the place to see where they had put everything. That didn't last for more than a few minutes before I was exhausted. I laid down on my new bed for what I thought a short rest.

The next thing I knew was that the sun was up, very up, up high in the sky. I had slept through the entire night and halfway through the next day.

I got up, showered, and went to get dressed. The underthings were new. Labels were still on. There was a brand new pair of jeans in the closet. There weren't any tags because someone had pulled them all off and washed the jeans a couple of times to get the stiffness out. I made coffee and a bowl of Lucky Charms. How did they even know what my first choice of cereal was? On the one hand, it felt spooky, and on the other, it was like I had a fairy godmother watching over me. You couldn't ask for anything more.

After eating, I opened the messenger bag with the key Amelia had given me.

The first thing on top was the deed to the property. It was titled Paulette Zahn or Newmark Industries. Having the name separated by the word 'or' meant that at any time, I could sell the entire property and keep all the proceeds. Then again, Newmark could sell it out from under me at any time.

Regardless, it showed that Newmark Industries trusted me,

so I should give them the same acceptance.

Next were my financial documents. My checking and savings account books and some other paperwork from a stock brokerage company.

My checking account balance had grown while I was laid up. A note inside the checkbook explained that I had been on the Newmark payroll since the moment I was carried into their hospital. The balance was more than I would need in the next year. My savings account had been changed so that some of the money from my dad's estate had been moved to CD's and there seemed to be some missing.

Next papers were accounts with a stock brokerage that the accountants must have opened on my behalf using some of my savings. The balance was quite a bit higher. I looked at the list of stocks held, and there were a couple of hundred shares of Newmark Industries.

Shit, I was rich. Well, I didn't know if I was wealthy, but I had more money than my dad or I had ever had at any time.

The last paper was a small 3 x 5 piece of card stock. It was all fancy and had my name across the front and on the back the words GOOD FOR 1 NEW VEHICLE. Wonder what that means?

I would have to ask.

Then I put on my leather jacket and went out back.

Nigel was out by the patio, wiping down his motorcycle. Twin Cam in a pretty tricked-out chopper. Red flames and ghosts were swirling around the gas tank. The motif went well with the beard, I must say.

"I think I want to go for a ride, shake the cobwebs out. You up for that?" I asked as I approached him.

"Are you sure you're up for it, missy?"

"Actually, I feel that I am in better shape than I have ever been."

"Okay, I'll help you get it out of my living room. We'll polish it up a little before we take off."

"*Your* living room?"

"My *borrowed* living room. That make you more comfortable, missy?" He grinned.

"I can see that we are going to get along just fine."

I can be snarky too. I might be a little out of practice considering what I have been through lately, but I AM the Queen of Snark, and I am ready to get out there and poke some pun at some illiterate chumps.

~ ~ ~ ~

I had been inside twenty-four hours a day for the past month or so, and I hadn't realized that winter was here with noticeably colder days. I had added on a new sweater in the drawer of the things someone from Newmark had purchased for me.

We both started our bikes up to get the engines up to temperature. I had my helmet and goggles on, and I was ready. I turned to Nigel, who gave me a nod, and we drove away from my house.

We crossed over to I-5 North and headed to the Lake Washington bridge that took us over toward Bellevue. We skipped the traffic light roulette of going through town. A little freeway cruising, and it was a great feeling. We went up 405 to the S20 back across the other bridge and back onto I-5 south at Lakewood.

Nigel was right next to me all the way. Every turn I made, he made the same turn at the same time. It was like we were joined at the hip.

I got off the freeway just before it crossed S99 onto Interurban Ave. There is a Starbucks right there, and it was time for a break.

Nigel got a triple espresso. I bet he was scary when he got all amped up.

When we finished, I said, "Nigel, I would like to ride up to Slim's Last Chance. I want to see if I can remember everything leading up to when I was attacked."

"Okay by me," he said. "But I want to make one thing very clear. At the first signs of any trouble, you are to get behind me and let me take the lead. Is that agreed?"

I thought about it for a few moments. I had always been one to fight my own fights. Now I was a different person with a different set of values. I could tell that Nigel was a heavyweight behind that beard and sunglasses. "I agree. I'm not looking for trouble. I just want to see if I can figure out how I had allowed myself to get trapped like that."

That was settled, and we cruised off and up to Slim's.

It was late afternoon to early evening and the Saturday night crowd hadn't made their appearance yet. That was good because we were able to park our bikes on the same side of the street as the bar was on. Just down toward the next cross street. We were along the wooden fence that walled off the outdoor tables and stage.

I didn't get any catcalls this time. They all must have thought I was with my 'ole man. I smiled to myself, thinking how funny it would be if they knew the truth. *Yeah, right, that will never happen.*

The bar chairs were full, but there were a few tables still open. We got the one farthest from the stage and dance floor.

The band didn't start till nine p.m.—two hours away. Neither one of us wanted to be too close to the stage if we were still here when nine p.m. came around.

I ordered my favorite, Texas red chili and a half-pint of lager, and Nigel got the burger and the same beer.

"What does Tillamook cheese taste like?" he asked the inked-everywhere waitress.

"I'll get your beers and bring you a piece of the cheese."

I was busy watching everyone in the crowd that I could see. I must have looked like a bobblehead as Nigel gave me THE look.

"Missy, I know you are trying to spot your attacker, but he isn't on this Earth any more."

"I'm trying to remember. I think I remember seeing the guy that attacked me here in the bar while I was eating. I think he was with two other scuzzballs. I am pretty sure I would recognize them."

"This is your first night out in a month. Don't turn it into a mission. Some eats, a few beers, do a little dedicated crowd watching, and back home and in bed at a decent hour. Something to make your mother proud."

No one sent me any drinks, and no one asked me to dance or even try to chat me up. Must be my companion.

Slim's had a photo gallery on the wall, and the real Gibbons had visited in the past. I noticed people around the room glancing our way, trying to decide if my bodyguard was the real Billy Gibbons or a look-alike. At first, I was a little uncomfortable with being on display, but after fifteen minutes of being under the magnifying glass, I realized that this was an opportunity.

They were looking at Nigel and me, it gave me the chance

to see every one of their faces without being obvious.

And there they were. At least, I thought they were the goons that were with my attacker that night.

Slowly, I started to remember. The three of them were at the far end of the bar when I came in for my chili and beer on that horrendous night. My attacker had separated from the two and came over and asked me to dance. I had blown him off. I mean, that's what a nice girl is expected to do.

I was absolutely sure they had been chum-up buddies with the rogue that had attacked me.

Before I could tell Nigel, he got up to go to the men's room.

As soon as he left our table, one of the stooges drifted over ever so casually. I stared him in the eyes all the way. If he thought his grimace was to scare me, he had a surprise coming. I was pretty sure he outgunned me, but I had two aces up my sleeve. One being Nigel, who would be returning soon, and the other was that this nut job didn't know that I had had some alterations to my body.

I had always been a strong, physically fit person, and now, because of the recent attack, I was a little stronger. More importantly, I was now trigger-quick.

I was sitting sideways to the cafe table with my feet facing the room. Mr. Stoogie walked right up and planted his cowboy boots on either side of my feet, and leaned down with one hand on the table.

"I want to talk to you about my missing friend. Just get up, and let's go out the back door nice and easy. Don't want harm to befall you," he said as I saw his hand start to move toward my arm.

My left foot shot up and re-located his gonads into his

lungs, and at the same time, I smashed my beer glass on the side of his temple. He crumpled to the floor like a pile of vomit.

I didn't waste time gloating over my handiwork as Mr. Stoogie #2 was on his feet and coming fast. My element of surprise was gone. I was pretty sure that this one was faster and stronger than I was. He wasted no time pinning me to the wall with his hand on my throat.

Besides cutting off my air supply, he was hurting me like nothing I had ever felt. Before anyone else in the bar could react, Nigel had shown up and put a vise-like grip on Stoogie #2's wrist, the one that was holding my neck, and I heard one or more bones crackle.

I was paying a lot of attention now, and I saw that #1 and #2 had enlarged canines. I knew them for what they were now. Two more rogues. Nigel had clipped #2 upside the head, and he was down with his buddy.

The bar crowd let us have some room. I saw the owner's wife on her way from behind the bar, baseball bat in hand.

"No! No! It's all over," I said, "We'll take the trash out for you, and we will be back in a few minutes to pay for the damages."

"You're the girl who was attacked out front a month ago, aren't you?" she asked. "The two people that rescued you are special friends here. I don't know you, so before you return, could you have one of those special friends vouch for you? I think you and your friend are capable of helping these gents out and on their way. I'll just get back to the bar now."

And she left us to take the trash out.

Dragging our friends by the scruff of their necks, we went out the back door that leads to the outside tables and bandstand that were vacant and dropped them.

"Go out the fence gate, and in my right saddlebag, there are some tie-wrap handcuffs. Bring me four pairs while I watch over our brood," Nigel said as he pulled out his cellphone.

I realized he probably was ratting me out and telling everyone that on my first day out of the hospital, I went right to the scene of the crime and got into a fight with two more rogues. Probably going to be dis-invited from the Sunday picnic.

It was less than five minutes when a white van with the Newmark logo on the side pulled into the alley that ran alongside the outside patio area.

Two guys dressed in old jungle camo got out and let themselves in through the gate and talked with Nigel. I wasn't listening. My thoughts were getting around to the fact that I had just been attacked—again—by a rogue vampire. Is it just me, or are there a whole lot of them around? Why are they so attracted to me?

I turned to see the two guys drag the two rats by their feet to the van. I watched as they loaded them in the back and chained them to some cargo rings set in the floor and sidewall of the van. It was as if Newmark had their own vampire paddy wagon.

After the van left, Nigel said, "That's enough fun for the night, missy. Let's kick our bikes and head home. Time to call it an evening."

11 DECEMBER 2016 – 0715 HOURS

I was awoken by someone banging on the back-kitchen door. With sweatpants, a T-shirt, and my bunny-eared muffies on my feet, I peeked around the curtain and immediately stepped back a half a step. Nigel was a little off-putting. I thought at first that there was some strange hobo knocking. Hobo? When was the last time anyone referred to bums as hobos?

"What is going on? Why are you beating on my door at this hour of the morning? Don't you know Sunday is for sleeping in?"

"Missy, we have to be at the Newmark Estate by nine a.m. We have to take the ferry. If we take your van, we might not get to be the firsts one. That will make YOU late for your induction. If we ride, we get to go to the head of all the car lanes."

"Induction? What are you rattling on about? I thought it was a normal get-together and that I could attend if I wanted to. Not that I must. Is there some ritual, you know, with alters and silver chalices full of blood?"

"Missy, you're quite the drama queen. I gave the poor recovering bar brawler the benefit of the doubt. Went out for a ride together to catch some fresh air figuring that your hospital stay had dulled your senses, and what do you give me? We stop for a bite to eat and a couple of beers, I leave the room for half a minute, and you are smashing glasses into some patron's head and going all postal on me.

"You have been invited to the boss's home for a BBQ. A

chance to meet many of the other people that are the backbone of the company. Maybe, just maybe, if you wipe your feet real clean and promise to keep your hands in your pockets, you will be given a tour of the mansion.

"I'm coming in to make us both some coffee while you get your leathers on."

"You're just going to waltz in? Like it is your place instead of mine? And the only leather (singular) is my brown motorcycle jacket."

"Call this intrusion a security check," he spoke as he walked right into my kitchen.

"There is a pair of new brown leather pants and brown engineer's boots in the closet. I know you aren't entirely aware yet, but your social status has moved up considerably. Once you get back to work, you will understand how important your position is.

"Now go and brush your teeth. Vampires are not dragons. Vampires keep their teeth shiny clean, and sparkling. You never can tell when you will have to bite someone."

"I'm not a vampire."

"Well, the jury is out on that. Just get dressed and brushed up, and we will take off for the ferry to Bainbridge Island."

~ ~ ~ ~

I brushed and dressed in my new togs. The pants were so soft and pliable, and they hugged every one of my curves. The boots put me over the 6' mark. They had to be custom handmade. My life had been one GOOD surprise after another since I presumably had become one of the Newmark gang.

Nigel handed me a cup of coffee, and I took a sip… and I

spit it out. That was the vilest coffee I had ever had.

"What is that? Army coffee was better."

"Sorry, I thought that you were a lot tougher."

"Piss off" was all I could come up with.

I walked out the back door and saw that Nigel had gotten our bikes out of his living room and next to each other in the driveway.

"Watch yourself going down the stairs, missy. Don't want you tripping and marring the fine delicate exterior."

I said nothing, mounted up, and started my bike. Nigel started his monster up. I got my helmet on so that I didn't have to listen to him any more. We sat for a few minutes letting our motors warm some.

It was a crisp day with breaks in the cloud cover for once. Little rays of sunshine danced around the atmosphere like fairies playing in the winds.

The path to the ferry staging area was an interesting one. What road you took one day was changed the next because of Seattle's version of The Big Dig. Same boondoggle, different city.

Nigel seemed to know the way, so I let him lead. As he said, the staging area for the vehicles that wanted to go on the ferry was in a large lot that leads to the loading ramp. Nigel wheeled past all the cars and to the head of the line.

At least two dozen motorcycles were waiting to get on. Most were a large gaggle of crotch rockets. Yuppie weekend devil riders. They weave in and out of traffic at all speeds, and they ride up the main road on one wheel. No fear. Young and invincible. And stupid.

I had to laugh, though. As Nigel and I rode up the ramp and onto the ferry, the rocketeers very smartly let us through to the head. We would be first off.

I guess when you are face to face with a 6'3" bearded biker dude and a 6' Amazon on her own Harley, you give them room. Bravado goes just so far.

The ferry takes about thirty-five minutes, and it was over before we even had a chance to look around. Just stay with the bikes because the terminal came up fast. We were the first ones off and up the ramp into the town of Winslow. Nigel led me through town and wound around some of the streets and lanes, with the trees becoming thicker until we ended up in front of a guard shack.

A guard came out, and he and Nigel had a fist bump bro moment.

"Nigel, you ole rascal, It has been some time since you visited. I will be up to the BBQ later. Hoist a few beer memories, *eh*!"

Then he turned to me and said, "And you are our new beer hall brawler. I can't wait to hear all about your adventures. I will see you up at the Manor in a little while."

I'm a brawler, eh? Only hit one guy upside the head with a beer tumbler and I get tagged as 'brawler' for life.

The gate swung open, and Nigel was already on the move. I followed as he wound his way on the street, no, not a street, just a sweeping driveway, and through a stand of fir trees. We burst out in front of this majestic building. Was this the house, the estate Manor?

I slowed, thinking we would be parking in front around the circular driveway that surrounded a fountain. No, Nigel kept going past the building and around to the back. You would have to think that it was an office building because it was so big. As we pulled around back, I saw all sorts of vehicles parked off the drive, which led to a fully paved courtyard, Well, it wasn't a courtyard because there were garages on both sides and what looked like apartments over and behind the garages on one side and the main building on the other. Maybe call it a paddock.

Several of the garage doors were open. Nigel pulled around in front of one that had two motorcycles already in the space. I think I knew them as the ones that Amelia and Eddie rode. Nigel stopped and shut his motor off and pushed his bike backward into that garage. He had stopped over to one side and waved for me to back in next to him.

Each garage stall was a car and a half wide and just as deep. Plenty of room.

The garages on the opposite side of the quad backed up to the building that was THE MANSION. That was the largest house I had ever seen, and I can genuinely say I have been around. It was larger than the castle that Lisa had taken me to in Italy. Not the same style, though. Now that I was looking at it with a little understanding of what it really was, I saw that this was an exquisite mansion. *This is where my boss lives. Hmmm!*

I heard a door open in the back of the garage and turned to see Amelia and Eddie walking through.

Eddie was wearing jeans and leather loafers without socks and a warm-looking sweatshirt with some band's picture on it. Amelia was in skinny jeans and a long-sleeved pullover shirt. Her shoes were a pair of converse sneakers in red. My kind of girl.

She was probably an inch taller than me, which I canceled out with the heels on my new boots.

"Paulie, come with me," Amelia said. "I'm going to show you our apartment, then I will take you out back and start the rounds of introductions."

~ ~ ~ ~

Their apartment was so, so, very comfortable. Oak beam ceilings, wood crown molding all throughout, even in the bathroom. Chair rails in the living room / dining area. And a deep stone fireplace that you could burn real wood logs to your heart's content without worrying about burning through a metal flue. All stone. It was roomy enough that they could have a dozen people over for a meal with ease.

Oh so domesticated they are, and lest I forget, they are both vampires. I had almost forgotten that I was now surrounded by vampires and that I may be one also. Or half vampire and half human, which apparently was a rare and unusual combination.

"Did you have breakfast?" she asked.

"Nah, Nigel made me come straight away. He banged on my door till I got up and let him in, then he dragged me out to our bikes, and I had to follow."

"Nigel can be a real tool at times, but I think you are embellishing what went on just a little bit," she said, grinning. "Come on, I'm taking you out to the party grounds."

We walked out through this ornately carved oaken front door and into a garden area slash party grounds. There were tables to eat at and tables covered with food and every drink imaginable. The party area was on the side of a small cottage. Out in front of the cottage was a vegetable garden, and beyond that was a hothouse and another larger building. I didn't know what the building was for, but I had a feeling I was going to find out someday.

Just then, an average-looking woman came out of the cottage. She smiled at me and came over.

"Hello," she said while holding out her hand. "My name is Lysbeth. I see you looking at my garden. All of the vegetables and some of the fruit you will get to eat today are all grown right here. I'm also the night cook, so if you are here overnight any time and want a snack, just come to the kitchen in the main house, and I will fix you up."

I shook her hand and said, "Thanks, my name is Paulette Zahn, just call me Paulie."

"You two will get to know one another better, but it will be a little later. I have to get Paulie introduced all around," Amelia said.

We started walking back to the tables where a few people were milling around. More people were walking across the lawn.

"This is Odie. He was in the guardhouse when you arrived. He has been with Newmark since 1973," Amelia told me.

I reached out and shook his hand, and then I stopped and stared. That meant he had worked here for forty-three years. He looked like he was somewhere in his early thirties.

Amelia saw the puzzled look on my face. "Go ahead and ask him the questions you are holding in. Remember, you are now on very hallowed and safe grounds. Everyone here knows what each other here is. Ask."

"How, *er*, *um*, I don't know how to ask. It seems just a little too personal," I said.

Odie seemed perfectly comfortable and also seemed to have an inkling of what I was wondering. "Paulie, those of us that are part of the inner circle have few secrets. When we are among our own, we talk freely just so there aren't any unaware Normals around. So, the answer you haven't asked is, yes, I am a vampire. My DOC [Date of Conversion] was 1973, and I was born in 1940."

This was the first time I knew both DOB and DOC of the vampire I was talking to.

"How long will you live?"

"Wow, hasn't anyone gone through all this with you?" he asked.

"Hey, you two are going to have to excuse me. I'm wanted in the house," Amelia said, and she left me there with Odie.

"I have no idea what all I have to learn, but I have the feeling that I have a lot to go through before I have a good grasp on this lifestyle."

"Don't worry, we will all make sure you are guided properly. The learning curve, though, is a steep one. I will always be available to answer any questions. I may not know all the answers, but I will always know who to send you to."

"Does one grow after their turning?" I asked. "I mean, Amelia is taller than me, and so is Lisa. Do you know Lisa Conner?"

"No, we never grow taller. We can put on muscle or even get fat if we want to, but we never grow another inch. You think about what an eighty-year-old man would look like to you. A little unsteady, a little stooped, and needs a little help while walking far. Then put that picture on a vampire, and you will have one that is between 800 and 900 years old."

I was stunned. I mean, really, I was just standing there trying to absorb what I had just been told without looking too stupid. Needed a stiff drink if I was going to hang around here all day and listen to this shit. I was reasonably sure he and everyone else was telling me the straight truth, but that didn't ease the incredulity of it all. I was definitely the only one at the party that was standing around naked. That's what I felt like. At least I was a little bit like them. I looked around and realized that everyone looked perfectly normal. Some tall, thin, whoops no, no, no, none of these people were too thin, some fat, again no, no, one here was overweight, Some short. No, wait on that.

I looked at everyone. I only had met a few of them, but the ones that I knew, Eddie, for instance, was 5'10". While Amelia and Lisa were taller than me. My new buddy here, Odie, was also my height.

Lisbeth was the opposite of what I thought was the norm. She had to be only 5'3" or 5'4". Definitely under the norm for most people.

"What about Lysbeth?" I asked. "She must have been converted when she was very young."

"Oh, Lysbeth," Odie said, "she isn't a vampire."

"I thought everyone here was a vampire."

"No, there are Vampires, damphires, and Norms here."

"Damphireeeee? What is a damphireeeee? No one told me about a damphireeeee."

"Slow down, Paulie. We didn't intend to cram all this down your gaping maw at once, but you are our surprise child of the century. No, let me change that; of the last five centuries. We are all a little in awe of your presence. So much so that we have forgotten our manners. I will tell you that we all love you to the moon and back, but there are so many things about our lifestyles that are the norm for us that we lose sight of the fact that you are new to this. Please don't take offense, but I will start referring to you as our Demi-V girl.

Like in demi-god. A god that is the product of a god and a human. Half-human, half-god. You are half human still and also half vampire. A Demi-V. And you are the only one in the world."

"Okay, I get it. I am a half-breed. Really excited about that. Again, what is a damphireeeee.?"

"There are two other regular guards for the Manor. Riley and Chuck. Chuck relieved me at the gate this morning, but Riley is over by the bucket for the cold beers. Come, and I'll introduce you."

"Why?"

"I will let him tell you and expand your education."

With that, we walked the few steps to where the drinks were. I got a beer and poured some Jack Daniels into the bottle. I was not going to take all this sober.

Odie made the introductions with Chuck and to another person standing there, Pete.

Chuck looked like he was ex-military Special Forces or something. He was wearing what looked like a custom pair of fatigues. Dark pants and dark, long-sleeved blouse with his name and the Newmark emblem over the breast pocket. He had on black tennis-type shoes, and he had a pistol on his waist. I saw the spare magazines, .45 Cal. Serious.

Pete was dressed in nice dark blue slacks and a white dress shirt. He was tall, well above me, and he moved with the grace of a ballet dancer. I could see that he kept his body in tip-top shape. Well, that wasn't so surprising as it seemed that everyone here and everyone I had met during my hospital stay were all in peak shape. Maybe it was the water.

Chuck said, "Let's go sit nearer the grill where there is a little more heat."

We sat at the table closest to the Chuck wagon-sized charcoal grill, which was just getting its bed of coals started.

"I am going to try to explain the three different types of species that are here today. It will be the same three that you will meet in everyday life, though two of the types are rare.

I came to work for the family here at the mansion when I was just thirteen years old. My parents had been working for the family when they were killed in an accident. The Newmarks took me in, and I started working in the kitchen as pot scrubber and general gofer."

"That's too young to be put to work, isn't it? I mean, child labor laws would be all over that?"

"I couldn't be put in foster care or put up for adoption because I am a damphire."

"Stop a minute, will you?" I asked. "I have some ideas on what vampires are, but what is a damphireeeee? Is this one of the three species you are talking about?"

"Humans—or the term we use, Norms—damphires, and vampires.

"Damphires are those that have some unique ability to enhance things that grow or to stimulate healing in an injured person, read tea leaves, and tell fortunes. Yes, fortunes like the gypsies do. As a matter of fact, damphires are usually called gypsies, and they still travel in small family bands throughout Eastern and Middle Europe. The average lifespan for a damphire is 250 years. A damphire can breed with all of the species. In fact, a damphire/vampire union is quite common as a pair can easily create children. Their children always resemble a Norm till they reach maturity, at which time they will start to show their abilities with nature, and that identifies that child as a damphire. The ones that show no unique talents are Norms and will remain that way throughout life unless...

"Unless they are turned into a vampire by another vampire or, like what can be done here at Newmark, turned into a vampire by ingesting the unique capsules from elder vampires.

This method applies to both the Norm children and damphire children. You will meet one such person that was borne of a vampire–damphire pair, turned into a damphire naturally, and when she was in her early 20s, asked for and received the change from a damphire to a vampire.

When you meet a Norm or a vampire, you have a relatively good idea of what you are dealing with. Damphires, on the other hand, aren't that easy since they can have a wide range of abilities and some have multiple talents."

"So, what is your talent?" I asked.

"I get particular feelings when someone is getting ready to make some move, like to punch me, and literally beat him to the punch. I also can tell with a fair degree of accuracy when someone is lying. Believe me, this gift is what makes me such a good guard."

"And Lisbeth grows vegetables and fruits, and probably flowers and such. Is that right?" I asked.

"That's right. So that you know, Riley—another household guard—Leigh, and Marisa—lead cooks on different shifts—and the housekeeper Stephanie are all damphires."

"So, which category am I in?" I asked.

~~~~

He didn't get time to answer as a group had just come out of the house and was headed straight to where I was sitting.

Karan Newmark, Lisa Connor, Amelia, Larisa, an older woman who looked to be a rather sour person and at least a half a dozen more in the group that I didn't know yet.

A moment later, they were followed by a garden tractor driven by Lisbeth, towing a trailer that carried Eddie and Pete,
~~~~

who were steadying a real large TV. That was the day that I became a Seattle Seahawks fan. It was either that or lose my job.

I bet there were enough vampires here that we could form our own team, and it would be a mix of boys and girls, and we could scrimmage the Seahawks. Great thought, but a bad idea. I mean, what would it look like, a team of yuppies that should be playing a friendly backyard game of flag football, facing off with a former Super Bowl Championship team and beating them soundly. Maybe satisfy my long-lost dream of beating the boys at their own game.

Everyone helped move the tables and chairs into a horseshoe arrangement in front of the TV.

Lisa came up to me and gave me a much-needed hug. I almost didn't want her to let go. For some reason, it felt like I owed all this to her. I had known her longer than anyone else in all of Seattle. I knew that she would remain my closest friend in my new world.

"Here, put these clothes on before you are designated the enemy," Lisa said to me, handing me a bag that had a Seahawks hooded sweater and a woolen Seahawks hat.

This wasn't some weekend beer and football TV crowd. This was a gathering of seriously dedicated hometown football fans.

"Do we all ever go out together to a local bar to watch the games on someone else's TV?" I asked her.

"NO, no, no. Could you see all of these vampire-Seahawk fans watching the game and in walks some Norm with an Indiana Colts cap or shirt on? He or she would be eaten alive, LITERALLY."

That visual struck home. I shuddered at the thought. Guess

that idea is NOT something that was ever going to happen.

Just then, Karan came up. "Paulie, We are all glad to have you here. I would introduce you to the ones you haven't met, but my dad wants to speak with you first. I will lead you, and if there is time after he is done, I will give you a guided tour of the Manor."

She led me past the garage paddock/quadrangle into the kitchen through the back door.

"This is the most common door used by everyone here, even my mom and dad. The front door is for guests or business agents coming for a meeting with myself or my dad."

The kitchen was huge. I mean huge. It was an open room with separate sections. There was the primary food prep and cooking area, an open-faced butler's pantry, a walk-in fireplace with a small smoldering fire going in it. Then there were a couple of eating tables with bench chairs. It looked like a dozen or more could have a meal here in the kitchen at the same time.

"Everyone that works here at the Manor and any other company employees that are visiting usually take their meals here. It is here where the daily staff meeting is conducted. We want to invite you to stay the night so that you can have the rush of sitting down in a room full of paranormals who are all your friends. I have made arrangements for you to stay with Zope in her apartment over the garages if that is all right with you."

"I haven't met Zope, have I?"

"Not yet, but you will meet her after you talk with my dad. Follow me now."

She led me through some rooms that were more luxurious than anything I had ever seen in the Reno Casinos or any of the places Lisa had taken me to in Italy. I went through a dining room that could easily seat twenty people or more, then across the main entry hall. It was perfect for a grand reception area with this double opposed circular stairway that went up to the upper floors. I had no idea how many floors there could be. From my memory as I pulled up, I knew there were two floors, but this house was so large that a third floor could be there without anyone realizing it.

Then we walked through the living room; I think that is the correct term. At the far end of the room were double doors that were standing open.

It was a den or private office. Dark wood, bookshelves, and a beamed ceiling with wallpapered sections between the beams. Some bookshelves and a fireplace to the left side of the desk. Warm and inviting, thought the fly about the spider.

There was a middle-aged couple sitting in the room. A man sat behind the prominent leather-covered desk, and the woman, of apparently the same age, sitting on a leather wing-back just to the side.

Karan said, "Mom and Dad, I want to introduce Paulette Zahn, the newest member of our family. Paulette, this is my mother, LaDoña Newmark, and my father, Spartak Newmark."

We shook hands all around. Karan's parents looked to be in their mid to late 40s at the most. The one thing that stood out was their grooming. Those clothes were NOT off the rack from Nordstrom. Mrs. Newmark only had an engagement and wedding band on and a small pair of pearl earring studs. The only jewelry I saw on Mr. Newmark was a plain gold wedding band. Neither one had a watch on that I saw. They were so elegant in their simplicity.

"You three have a nice talk," said Mrs. Newmark, "I have to tend to some details for today's party, so I will see you later. I especially would like a few minutes with you, Paulie. Maybe later this afternoon."

"Am I to understand that your knowledge of vampires is limited and about damphires is far less than that?" Mr. Newmark started. "Karan and I will tell you some of the more important parts now, and I believe the best teachers you could have are all going to be here today for you to meet."

Karan jumped in, "A lot of this information will come at you pretty heavily, initially. We will overwhelm you at times, but we want you to learn as much as possible in the shortest possible time.

"To start you off, my dad, 'Sparky' as we all address him privately, is a vampire. He started Newmark Industries before the First World War.

"My mother, LaDoña, is a Norm. That's right, she is 100 percent human. I was their best surprise. I was born twenty-three years ago, and I am an unknown."

"Unknown, what do you mean you're an unknown? I think that is what everyone is calling me, an unknown. Does that mean that you and I are the same?"

"Let me take it from here, hun," Mr. Newmark said to Karan.

"I am a vampire," he started, "LaDoña, Karan's mother, is a Normal human, and Karan, well, Karan has not shown a particularly strong signal that she is turning into a damphire. I have had some tests run, and there are indications that she may automatically make the change into a full damphire with the ability to absorb large amounts of numbers and make sense of what they mean. She has demonstrated strong management skills. She is in full control of all the everyday tasks required in running a business as large as this one is.

"If she does, she will have 250 years left in her life to enjoy. If, on the other hand, she turns into a vampire, the only significant change will be the length of her life. She can even, at any time, ask to be changed into a vampire, which can be done with the special flash-frozen platelets from a vampire elder." He paused before continuing.

"Then there is you, Paulie. You have already shown us that you have acquired some traits of a vampire. Faster healing, more strength, improved eyesight and hearing, and faster metabolism. When I said some, I didn't mean that you missed out on something. No, that isn't what sets you apart. Your abilities in all areas are much greater than a Norm of the same stature. Your abilities fall just short of what I would expect a full vampire to have. We've already determined that you don't need as much of the human platelets as a full vampire would need. We also don't know what your life expectancy is. That one will just take time.

"You may lose the vampire's abilities and revert to being a Norm, or you could eventually change into a full vampire. We have never seen anyone such as you. We are pretty sure that if you want to make the full change, that it can be accomplished with the old vamp pills. Not something you should worry about now.

"If you have any questions about being a vampire or any questions at all, as an employee of Newmark Industries, I will be available, but I think you would be better served by talking to those you have met and will get to meet today. I think it is time that Karan takes you back outside. Everyone must be wondering where the new child is hiding."

~ ~ ~ ~

"Come on, and I will show you around a little of the Manor," Karan said.

"Do you live here?"

"Yes, I have a small suite of rooms up on the third floor. My parents are on the second floor and have their own separate living room with my mom's study. There are two more guest bedrooms on the second floor and one more on the first floor. Whenever you want to stay here, it is arranged that you will be in with Zope. She has one of the apartments over the garages. And if you are uncomfortable with that, you can always use the guest room here in the Manor."

We were going down the hall past that room and into the kitchen.

"The apartments over or behind the garages all have some cooking facilities. For the most part, though, everyone that lives here and most times the people that live off-site will congregate in the kitchen.

"It's sort of the daily ritual for everyone to break fast together. Great real country breakfasts with an amazing assortment of food. It is also when the list of activities and statements of new changes affects Newmark Industries. Since you are living off-campus, so to say, you will receive the daily notices on your laptop."

The kitchen, which I had seen when I first set foot inside the Manor, looked even more immense. There were five or six people working, slicing, dicing, frying, boiling. I was hungry, and the sight of all that food reminded me just how hungry.

Karan led me through the kitchen and into the room that had food and utensil storage. It also had elevator doors.

"Is that for getting food up to the second floor?"

"It is used for that sometimes, but it is also how we get to the greater food storage in the cellar, which is also the wine cave. I'll take you on a more complete tour at another time. It is time to get you back to the party first of all, so you can get something to eat and drink and, secondly, to get you introduced around."

Back outside we went.

~~~~

It looked like there were two dozen people here at the Manor now.

I had met several of them and knew what they were. The shocker was that it was a mixed-species group. I had been in the army for almost eight years, where we all were in mixed racial or ethnic groups but never was I in a mixed-species group. This new group was like having different species of animals all together at the same cook-out. I mean, think about lions and zebras sitting down at the same table to chat and suck down a few beers.

I could also tell that each species didn't clump together. It seemed that they were mixing it up. To me, the humans (Norms) and the damphires seemed so similar that I could understand them sitting together and showing each other family pictures. They weren't ones to take a bite out of one another.

The vampires, on the other hand, were fabled to be biters. Like the dangerous dog down the street no one worried about until it was loose in the streets. Not here, though. Everyone got along.

Eventually, I was introduced around. First, it was Karan, then Amelia, and then Zope took over.
~~~~

Zope was the most impressive of all the girls I had met so far. Instead, of the vampire girls I had met. She was at least 6" tall. Her face had its own beauty. Germanic or Norse features. Through the attractiveness, you could see and sense strength and determination that you just did not want to tangle with. I would learn that she was an absolute master at all forms of hand-to-hand combat.

Eddie showed up with a woman in tow.

"Paulette Zahn, I want you to meet my sister, Darja Strykula," he said. "Darja, this is our very special new girl."

"Ignore my brother," she said. "He has a speech impediment in addition to having brain freezes on a regular basis. I live here at the Manor. I have one of the apartments above the garages."

"Are you really brother and sister? I mean, I don't see any similarities in your appearances."

"My natural father, Jurik Strykula, is Eddie's creator. Jurick's blood runs through both of our veins.

"I was born a Normal and changed naturally into a damphire when I was in my early 20s. Shortly after, I had a talk with my father and one of his best friends and my godfather, Leon Krupnick, about changing, and it was agreed to and arranged that Leon would be the one to convert me."

Having met so many vampires lately, I noticed that they all tend to be taller and broader than the average Normal. Clear skin, beautiful hair. *Amazon Island,* I thought.

There were so many more vampires and damphires and Normals that I got to meet that day.

Comrades all. I had a lot of 'comrades' when I was in the army, but when I was off duty, there weren't many of my 'comrades' who I was really chummy with. Maybe one, but that was because I felt sorry for the girl.

Here though, this was a cohesive group. It was made up of the strangest collection of different species one could ever imagine, but they were all close. So far, I hadn't met anyone that I wouldn't want to pal around with.

I had never been like that in my whole life.

The Seahawks game started at eleven a.m. and was over by two p.m. Sounds early, but winters in Seattle brought on early sundowns and late sunrises. Before I knew it, it was starting to get colder, and sunlight was fading fast. It was just a little after four p.m.

Everyone was helping to break down the party setup. I was helping, but if someone spotted me trying to pick up too much at one time, they came over and took some of the load off. I didn't even have to ask.

I thought the party was over, so I started looking for Nigel to see when he wanted to leave.

"Excuse me, have you seen Nigel?" I asked Nicole, who was one of the special security guards attached permanently to Darja.

"Oh, I can't tell you how much my twin, Irene, and I have enjoyed getting to meet you. Nigel was carrying things into the kitchen. You do know that this party isn't over till they close the kitchen, don't you?"

"If I eat and drink much more, I am going to pass out."

"No, you won't. I know that everyone hasn't quite decided what species you are now, but Darja has already told my sister and me that she has gotten or sensed that you will turn out as a full vampire and possibly something more. It doesn't make much difference anyway since you are completely one of us now."

That made me feel warm and fuzzy. Strange, but it really did. Through the day, I had learned a little about everyone here. Nicole and Irene were like the meanest, baddest ninjas ever. I had initially thought that they were unapproachable but quickly realized that was not true. At least not for me.

~ ~ ~ ~

The kitchen was jam-packed. More food and a whole lot more to drink.

Everyone was having a good time.

I never thought that I would find a group as varied as the group I lived with the past eight years in the army. I was wrong. There were only fifteen to twenty people in the kitchen, and I would never describe the differences from one to the other. They were just too great. People with uncanny reaction times, some with the ability to tell when someone was going to attack them as if they read their minds, a girl with this amazing Green Thumb, but they all had a few things in common. Everyone, regardless of species or type, were all in superb physical condition, They all had an excellent outlook on life, and they all worked together as one mind. And you know what, I was one of them. I felt like the luckiest person in the world to have ended up here, working with these people for the best company in the world.

"Hi, Paulie, are you enjoying yourself?" It was Zope.

I hadn't had an opportunity to spend any time with her, and I was curious about her opinion of me.

"Hi, Zope!" I said. "I would like to get a night out with you and some of the others to get to know everyone better. Do you think you would have time for something like that?"

"Well now, youngster, we have already been planning a girls' night out where you are sworn into our club."

"Club? What club?"

"You will have to wait and find out. In the meantime, I want you to follow me."

"Where to?'

"We are going to meet down in the wine cellar. There is a small lounge area where we can sit, talk, and taste some excellent wines."

"All of us?" I queried.

"Yes. We need to go over what happened to you. We need to get a handle on this sudden surge of rogue activities. You see, you aren't the only victim of these attacks."

We rode the elevator from the kitchen down to the wine cellar. And what a cellar it was! Exiting the elevator, I saw shelving on one side that held bulk food storage, and in the other direction was THE cellar.

It was huge. It had to be bigger than the footprint of the Manor above. There was more wine here than in the largest liquor store I had ever been in. We walked down the rows and rows of stacked wine bottles and kegs until we came across an open space that had couches and single chairs, a few coffee tables, and a sturdy bench that held several cork extractors and different styles of glasses.

Many of the seats were occupied.

Karan, Lisa, Amelia, Pete, Larisa, Eddie, and Mr. Newmark were all seated and had glasses of wine in their hands. Mr. Newmark stood up and approached me.

"Paulette Zahn," he started, "I want to welcome you to this, your first official meeting, with the very heart and soul of my security team. You are now on this team. Your clearance has been upgraded to the highest level the company uses. You are one of the eight members that make up this squad. It took a unanimous vote from the others, and everyone approved you. Outside of this room, no one knows of this group. Some guess, but no one really knows for sure who is a member and what the function is.

"You have been promoted to this position partially because of your military background but most importantly because of how you have acted since your first attack. You are resourceful and quick to take the initiative. The last two or three months of your life have been ones of rapid changes in your life. We all see how well you have come through and adapted to this new world you have been dropped into.

"For clarity, everyone here is a vampire except my daughter, Karan, and you. I'm sure you have some apprehension because we have been unable to confirm your change into a full vampire, but you have acquired some level of each and every aspect of a vampire, and so here you are, possibly a new species.

"Don't ever feel like you are alone in this world because everyone here, except for Karan, has had bits and pieces of their person altered, modified, or changed in some manner. All of us are here to talk with you if you are ever feeling like the odd man out.

"You are now a full member of the most exclusive investigative and security specialists on the face of this planet."

I had to be beet red from head to foot. I clearly understood this honor. I also had never been a follower, more of an independent type. This group, however, was so special, and I was awed that they had chosen me to join.

I was GLAD. Glad and excited because I already knew that this was my home, my place in life, amidst others that were like me and had my same core values.

The others all stood, and one by one, they came up to me, shook my hand, and hugged me like I had never been hugged before.

I looked up and was sure that I saw a tear in Lisa's eyes, and in fact, there were a few others that were the same.

Karan said, "Let's all get fresh glasses of wine and take seats. We have a serious situation that we have to devote all our energies to right now.

"Three rogues in less than two months. The two that attacked Paulie did give us some information. Most of them were recently made. They gave us a vague location of a private farm type of compound where it happened. One of them told us that there are fifteen to eighteen recently changed, just like himself. All of them were picked up from the street. Street bums, all of them. They were encouraged to get their blood needs by biting humans. He was less than a month old when an older one, the one that was assigned the task of taking the two of them out into the world to learn how to live and, more importantly, how to stalk, capture, and kill their victims, took him and the other one to the bar where Paulie was attacked the first time. He didn't give us an exact address, but we think we can locate the breeding farm without too much difficulty.

"We are going to send search parties of two of us at a time. Larisa is exempted as we have to have her running the Security Unit. So are you, Paulie."

"Why can't I go?" I asked. "I'm physically in better shape now than I ever was in my whole life."

Mr. Newmark stepped in, "Paulie, you are our little princess, and we don't want anything to happen to you. Look around at all of us sitting here. Except for Karan, you are surrounded by vampires that have been what they are for many years. Most of them were vampires before you were born as a human.

"You have acquired many of the traits that only a vampire has. We don't know the extent of your change because there is no yardstick to measure you against another like you. Until you have had training in several forms of hand-to-hand combat, you are going to be in protective custody. Not really that strict, but no fieldwork for you either, with or without a partner.

"Here is an example of what I mean; my daughter Karan here started hand-to-hand combat training before her 12th birthday. She is all human at the moment, and even with your new enhancements, I am sure she could wipe the floor with you. To have you go out and face a vampire that has been around for a while, well, that would be the death of you. Besides, I need you to learn the workings of the hangar that is connected to the security offices.

"You will be responsible for the maintenance schedules on all of the aircraft, making sure they are on time. See that the training for all the mechanics is on schedule. Our aircraft have some unusual components in several areas. Those are our designs and are not available to the public or even the U.S. Government. You will have to familiarize yourself with their capabilities. You will be responsible for ensuring that all of the aircraft are ready to go anywhere at a moment's notice.

"Our pilots keep their rating current at the flight school across the main runway from our building. Go make yourself known to them and talk to them about you getting your license. I eventually want you to be rated to fly everything we own.

"I have to leave everyone for a few days. Larisa and Karan know where I will be and contact me if there is any upsurge in the rogue activities. Now, I want to turn this meeting over to Eddie. He is the lead investigator for such matters as this."

During that talk, I went from depressed to elated beyond belief. My job description was everything I had ever wanted. I would be too busy to go play hide and seek with the nasty elements that had shown up. Now, it was Eddie's turn.

~ ~ ~ ~

Eddie took center stage and spoke up, "The rogue that attacked Paulie last month was not new. We believe that he was at least ten vampire years old. From what we learned from the other two, they had only been turned a few months before Paulie beat them up. There is farm-like property south-west of here. They talked about the toll bridge, so we believe that this breeding farm is in Gig Harbor or some town nearby. Pete and Zope are going to scout around there to see what they can find out. Next to go, later in the week, will be myself and Amelia. Amelia has some friends who live there, so we are going to drop in for a few days.

"That doesn't sound like much of a plan, and that is because we don't have any specific routine. We are just winging it, that and keeping our ears to the ground.

I had been invited to stay at the Manor overnight but it had been a real big day for me. I decided that I would rather sleep in my own bed so I told Nigel and he agreed.

I borrowed a heavier coat from Amelia. The temperature had dropped considerably since the sun had gone down. Then Nigel and I rode our bikes and caught the midnight ferry to Seattle. We were back at my house by one a.m.

NEW JOB AND A FEELING
13 DECEMBER 2016 – 0800 HOURS

It was still dark when I woke up. You only get 8½ hours of sunshine in December in Washington. Short days. It had gotten a lot colder, so I decided to drive the Ford van into work. I knocked on the door to Nigel's studio a few times and was going to leave when he came to the door.

"I don't have anything to do where you are going. So long as you go straight to work and straight home afterward, I think you will be safe," he said. Whoops! "Let me clarify that so we don't have any misunderstandings. When work is over, you come straight home here. If you think about going somewhere else after work, you call and I will either go with you or follow you. And I will not be seen, so I won't interfere with all your carousing."

"I'll be sure to do that, Dick."

"The name is Nigel."

"That may be your name, but you are still a dick."

"For the life of me, I cannot see why they want to keep you around."

"It's my fashion sense, and being seen standing next to you just proves my point that I am the new debutante."

"I'm serious now. If you would rather, I can ride with you and find something to do while working. Then I will be there to ride home with you when your workday is over."

"No, I promise to come straight home after work. Not

because you want it to be that way, but because I have to get back and straighten up my household."

"Just pretend that you are driving a Humvee off-base in Afghanistan. I mean, keep your eyes and ears open and watch your mirrors constantly. I don't want you ambushed."

Before I got in, I turned and gave him a hug and said, "Thanks."

And I pulled out and headed to my first day at my new job. New life, new future, and a bright outlook it was at that.

~ ~ ~ ~

The distance to work wasn't that far, but rush hour traffic made it seem interminable. I had driven this route on my motorcycle, but for some reason, I hadn't ever driven the van. The van was a Ford F-350 4X4 with an extended body. On top of wrestling this monster through the congestion, there was steady rain making the drive even more difficult. Drivers in Seattle do pretty well in the rain or even when there is some snow mixed in. But mix the rain with rush hour and add in the big clumsy tank I was driving, and you have a cranky driver, me, as well as anyone trying to negotiate around me. You had to set up for a turn three to four blocks in advance because if you waited to change to the proper lane until the last minute, you had better be ready to go around the block to try again. No one would ever let you in during the rush hour.

Common courtesy disperses when you are in a rush to get to work or home afterward.

When I finally arrived at the new job, I first had to stop at the security guard shack. I was fumbling around for my company pass when the guard came out and said, "Good morning, Ms. Zahn. Go right on through."

Wow, that was pleasant. When I was at Bagram Airbase, the MPs were living in the same barracks where I was billeted. We ate our meals together, we all knew each other, but whenever I had to go through a checkpoint, I never got instant recognition. In fact, they were so thorough that I was three threads short of a strip search most times.

There were other guard shacks through which one could access the main building that housed the security staff and the medical unit that I knew so intimately. The gate I went through was the vehicle and personnel entrance to the Newmark Industries Air Force. That wasn't the official title, just the name I gave my new home away from home. I would change that name later on after I got my feet on the ground. That and knowing what I could and couldn't get away with.

I drove alongside the building. I passed a typical door and a little further on a much larger door that would allow a semi to drive through. Both were closed, so I continued around the corner expecting that the monstrous sliding hangar doors would be open.

Nope, that wasn't the proper choice. I even drove north past all the hangar doors, and there were more than just one set. When I reached the end of the hangar, I slowed and looked to my left. One other regular-sized door, but that was also closed. I decided to go back to the first door I passed and try it.

I parked, got out, and went to the door. It had an alcove to the side that had a keyboard and retina scanner. I should have expected that. Security is number one here. It would become the standard routine after a while, but today it was just a nuisance.

I punched my security code in and stared into the hole for the retinal scan. Nothing happened. I looked back at the readout above the keyboard, and it said invalid code. Shit, now what?

I pulled my cell phone out and looked up the daily code, and verified I had typed it in correctly. Then I realized there was a date beside the code. It was from last week when I was first given this unit with all my 'stuff' in it. Larisa had told me to check for a new code any time after 0001 hours (one minute past midnight).

I pulled up the new code and ran my personal decryption password, and received the 'numbers of the day'. A minute later, I had executed the keypad and retinal scan, and I heard the lock on the door click.

The first impression was that the whole place was spotless. Second, it was jammed with aircraft.

The largest was 737-700. Your eyes went right to it. There were two other smaller commuter jets, a single-engine turboprop, a helicopter, and a biplane, And that is where I stopped and gaped. They had a Boeing AH-64, an Apache military aircraft.

That wasn't supposed to be available to the public, only to the military of select countries. I was more than shocked. I headed straight toward it. It was sans chain guns and Hellfire missiles, but it seemed to have all the mounting hardware and electronic sockets, meaning that it could be fully armed in less than an hour if you had the right personnel, oh, and the right hardware. What the fuck was this here for?

I climbed the steps and looked into the cockpit. Everything was there. When I mean everything, I mean that the electronics were the full array of a combat-ready Apache.

"Excuse me, ma'am, can I help you?"

Crack—Ouch, shit! I was startled and bashed my head against the canopy. I never said I was graceful. "Hi, what, who's that, who's there?"

"Sorry, I didn't mean to startle you. Here, lemme help you down." A young man held out his hand.

"I'm Charlie. Are you the new head of the division?"

"Hello, Charlie, I'm Paulie Zahn. And to answer the question, yes, I am. I have some things in my van outside and want to bring them in. Do I get a locker or something to stash my belongings in?"

"Locker? No, you're the boss lady here. We have a Flight Operations Shack built right inside the hanger here. You have the office that is inside of the OS. That's short for Operations Shack. Inside, there is another smaller office that is yours to command from."

He was pointing toward the rear corner opposite where I came in. It was about a hundred yards away. The hangar area appeared to be a square making it hundred yards by hundred yards.

"You can bring your car in if you want. Then whatever you have, you won't have to carry it far, and it is a lot warmer in here than outside."

No brainer there. I turned and went to the delivery door that I opened with my code and went outside and got in the van. Drove it right in and headed toward the Operations Shack.

How can you have a shack inside a building? As I drove up, I understood. It looked like someone had pulled weather-worn boards off of an old barn somewhere and used them for the rustic exterior of this inside building. Other than the large windows looking out on the shop floor, it could be a real flight line operations hut for any old barnstorming airfield in rural America in the 1930s. It even had a windsock on the roof. I later found out that the windsock replicated the movement of a vane on the roof of the building, and it was good for wind direction.

The insides of the shack had an assortment of tables and chairs around the room. There was a raised platform at one end of the room with a whiteboard and a scheduling board. The scheduling board listed the aircraft that must be under my command. It contained flight schedules and maintenance schedules.

"That's your private office," Charlie said, pointing to the windowed office to one side of the room inside the shack.

The inside of the 'inner' office was bordering on the plush. Functionally plush. Several straight back chairs, a couple of leather-covered wing-backs in front of 'MY' desk that held a full complement of electronic equipment.

The main room in the Shack had a back door, and my new office had one also.

"Where do these doors lead?" I asked Charlie, pointing first to the rear door in the main room of the shack and then to the one behind my desk, figuring they both probably led to the same room or hallway. I had already noticed that both of them had the universal iris scan eyeball and keypad.

"The one in shack's lounge area goes into the building's main entry and comes out next to the reception/security counter. I have no idea on door number two, never saw anyone going through that door."

It was now 0830 hours, and Charlie and I were the only ones at the hanger. "Where are all the other personnel?" I asked Charlie.

"There is always someone on duty 24-7. My normal shift is 2400 to 0800, but today I am staying later because the crew that is supposed to come in at 0800 was on a special project. I did hear from the team leader, and she said they would all be landing at 0900 hours."

I got the rest of my personal things from my van and dropped them on the floor next to my desk. I was shuffling through the desk drawers to see what prizes I might find when I heard the whine of a turbine and familiar whop, whop, whop of a helicopter. Charlie took off across the floor of the main hangar, waving a remote in his hand. There must have been a dozen electric motors that started up, and the gigantic hangar doors slowly moved aside. Outside, hovering just off the ground, was a beautiful slick helicopter. It was a French Dauphine.

The pilot popped the landing gear down and then rolled forward into the hangar. In Afghanistan, the helos landed far away from the repair hangars and get towed in to avoid having the oversized rotors blow everything all over the place. This hangar was so spotless that there wasn't anything loose to get blown around. Plus, unlike Afghanistan, there was no sand for the helo to kick up.

This helicopter was magnificent. Beautiful Delft blue and white paint with the Newmark logo on the side. No camo paint or bullet hole patches. A real smooth civilian passenger helicopter. In the coming days, I would learn just how great it was. It had things like a lavatory and galley—*in a helicopter!*

An Apache combat helicopter, this stunning Dauphine, a 737 passenger jet, and one or two other smaller jets and winged aircraft in this hangar. Were all of these my responsibility? This was just too ungodly to believe.

And I thought of my dad. He would be proud.

Three suits got out, and without even a howdy-do to me, they headed to the interior door that leads to the main reception room. Then two other guys got off, and they started going around, chocking the wheels and doing some inspections of exterior gear. And then Lisa Connor stepped off.

I went over to her right away and gave her a hug. "Is this your private chariot?" I asked.

"I wish. Well, actually, I am not wishing. Not since I found out how much the maintenance and pilots cost. I have some money put away, but this is way too much for even me. Besides, this all belongs to you now. Let's go to your new office. I need to sit without the noise and vibrations for a few minutes. Get my land legs back."

We started toward 'The Shack,' and just as we got to the door, I realized two people following us. Both had on relaxed or casual uniforms, and the stripes on their shoulders indicated that they were both pilots. They followed us into The Shack.

In unison, they said, "Morning, boss."

"I'm Carol, and this is my partner, Sue. We have heard snippets and look forward to working with you."

"I'm Sue and welcome to Sparky's Flying Circus. We have to file our flight report and check the schedule to see when our next flight is."

As they were talking to me, more people were showing up to work. About a dozen were in the hangar. I hadn't been given a job description or roster of the people working in my, 'MY,' department. I had an idea.

"Who's in charge when I'm not here?"

Sue spoke up first, "The senior-most pilot that is in the house at the moment takes the reins. That would be Carol. She is my senior by only 230 hours of flying time."

"You're limping, Sue," I said. "Did you bang your shin so something"?

"No, my lower left leg is a prosthetic. I left my foot behind in Iraq so that I would have a toe hold there for when I return."

And the two of them chuckled.

"Lisa and I are going to be busy for maybe an hour. Could one of you get everyone together for a general meeting at 10.30? In the office here or if everyone can't fit, we will have it just outside The Shack."

With that, I headed to my office with Lisa in tow.

~ ~ ~ ~

"How do you like my new office?" I asked Lisa.

"Honestly, it is nice, but it isn't you. Just needs some re-decoration to make it more personal. I'm thinking of some posters of UFM fights and one of Rhonda Rousey. You know, because you are getting a reputation for rumbling."

"That is not me, and you know it."

I didn't snap that back because I was secretly a little proud of the reputation I was being mantled with. I was too tall and buffed out to be dainty and demure, but to represent that, I was looking for a physical confrontation, well that was not how I pictured myself. At least, not until now.

"It isn't how we think of you, but look at everything for the tease factor. No one will leave it alone for some time, or unless you acquire the crown in a different venue.

"You hadn't even gotten our job offer when you ended up in our very private hospital. Think of what happened to get you here. Then, you are out of the hospital less than twenty-four hours and you are assisting in taking down two more rogues. You have a crew here that have already proven their worth to Newmark Industries, and I just want you to play nice."

I decided to let it go. She was just goading me anyway. I had to find out what I was supposed to do and quick.

"I know that no one has gone over your duties here. I will give you a quick breakdown. This section is for the dispatch of all flights, including pilot and crew assignments. It can become a little hectic when someone calls for a surprise flight, and you have to round up a crew because it is the weekend. And you make sure all maintenance items are handled on time. Most minor repairs and replacements can be handled here, but for any major electrical or mechanical repairs, we send the aircraft out to an independent repair facility.

"You are lucky that Boeing still has major repair, retrofit, and upgrade facilities at this field. Your aircraft will never be very far out of sight, and your Ace in the hole is Charlie. He knows how everything is run here and can be your number one assistant. Keep him close in the early months on the job. How do you like how your private room is outfitted?"

"What private room?"

"That's right, you haven't seen everything yet. Through that door behind your desk," she said.

The door had a keypad but no eye-spy receptacle. I tried my code, and the lock clicked, and I opened the door.

The room was bigger than my bedroom. It had a love-seat in front of a 60" TV screen, a day bed along one wall, and a kitchenette all in one room, and I saw a bathroom with a shower and lots of storage cabinets and two closets.

Lisa came in and turned on the TV. "This is your hidey-hole. This TV is also the screen for surveillance cameras in your office, around the inside, and outside of the hangar area.

"In the cabinets are assorted canned goods and food pouches. Cans of portable water. All this is set up like a fortress for you if trouble finds its way inside the hangar area. Or you can use it to catch a short nap, or you can even stay overnight when you don't want to make the drive home."

"Wow! You sure know a lot about this place," I said.

"I was the person in charge of the aviation section here until I received the European assignment in 2012. There are only two aircraft that are still here from when I was here. At the hangars back is a Stearman biplane that is Ms. Karan's and the antique Lear 70. That Lear was the company's first jet. Sparky still uses it for short jaunts.

"Now that you are in charge here, I hope you can get me aboard the 737 if it is going to Europe in the next two weeks. The luxury in that aircraft is the best anywhere. If you can't, then don't worry about me. I can catch a Greyhound to New York where I can get passage to Europe in a cargo plane."

"I don't see any tears, so, you must be putting me on."

"*Hmmm!* You may be catching on to me."

I got so busy looking through everything that I lost track of time.

"Paulie," Lisa said, "the crew is all in the outer room. It is almost 10.30—time for your meeting. I have to run inside to see Larisa. Don't worry, Charlie will be by your side to help get you through your first staff meeting."

Both of us went out to the main room.

People were not milling about or talking in groups. Instead, they were all sitting in the chairs in front of the mini-stage/podium, but every one of them was riveted on me. The stares were so intense that I looked down to see if my fly was unzipped.

Lisa walked with me to the podium, and she turned to them and said, "Good morning. It has been some time since I have stood here. I see a few faces in the crowd that was with me before. I want to introduce everyone to Paulette Zahn, who is now your new wing commander for want of a better title. She was selected by myself and Karan Newmark and was vetted by Mr. Newmark himself. She has never held a management position like this, but we know she is way and above being qualified to run this show. I just want one thing out of every one of you and that is to give respect to her title and help her out until she learns the ropes. I am expected inside for a meeting and will try to get back here to maybe get some time with all of you that worked with me before. Thank you, now give Ms. Zahn your attention and best support."

"Thank you, Ms. Connor."

I looked out over the group. Some were dressed in clothes similar to the army's camo fatigues, but these were colored blue and looked like they were all cotton instead of a synthetic mix. Some wore blue pants with white blouses.

The two-tone sets were the pilots. I was sure of that. Probably because they had epaulets with three and four stripes.

"I am new to working in the private sector. I will need everyone's patience and support," I started. "It will take a couple of weeks to learn the maintenance and flight schedules, so they will stay as they are for now. I will not be changing anything around until I am comfortable, and nothing will happen without input from all of you. The door to my office will always be open to anything that you want to talk to me about, well, *err*, of a sensitive nature or whatever.

"This is all I can think of for now, so unless one of you has a question, I will end this so that we can all get back to our jobs. Oh, one more thing. Would Charlie and Carol meet with me after this is over?"

Two hands waved. I pointed to the one that was dressed in all blue, so I assumed he was maintenance.

"Yes?"

"My name is Alex. I think that everyone here is in agreement when I say that we are glad that you are here. We all look forward to working with you. I do have a question, and that is about the attempted break-ins. Do you have any information on the status of the investigation?"

"Hello, Alex. I'm sorry, but I have had ZERO briefings on my role and any particulars about this unit. As soon as I get filled in on EVERYTHING, I will be in a better position to talk to you about that and anything else that is important to this section." I looked back at the crowd. "Anyone else?"

A blue and white raised his hand.

"Yes?"

"Morning, ma'am. I'm Demetrius, and I'm one of the helicopter pilots. Are you going to be Santa Claus this year?"

Oh! Shit! It was almost Christmas. I had no idea that it was this close.

"Santa Claus! I don't know anything about that. Does the company put on a party for the children?"

"Children? Well, you could say that. We were all given a short briefing on your background and know that you are new to the collection of souls that work at Newmark. Being the newbie on the block, we all believe that you are the proper choice for that role."

"Hold that thought, everyone. I'll have to find out what it is all about and let you know in the next few days. If there are no more questions, for now, go back to your routines. Carol and Charlie, come into my den."

~ ~ ~ ~

For the first time in my life, it was me, yes me, who got to sit behind 'the desk.' I didn't give it a second thought and wasn't in the least embarrassed for being in this position.

"Seat yourselves. Do you want anything before we start? I don't know why I offered because I don't even know if I have anything to offer."

"Allow me, Ms. Zahn. I know where everything is," Carol said.

She went to the refrigerator, which, by the way, was not a mini-fridge but a full-sized refrigerator. She opened the top drawer. It was loaded with white wine, champagne, and assorted cheeses. She looked and closed the drawer and opened one of the upper doors. Beers, sodas, sparkling water, assorted condiments, mustards, and salad fixings.

"Okay to make some coffee?" Charlie asked.

"Go ahead, Charlie, I think I want a cup too."

That's when I saw the coffee pot alongside a somewhat exotic Espresso machine.

"Will that machine make a latte?" I asked.

"One latte coming up," Charlie said.

"So, everyone will be coming into my office for refreshments?" I asked.

"No, we have a pretty complete kitchen in the meeting room," Carol said.

I rifled around in the desk drawers for a pen and something to write on. There were a spiral-bound notebook and pens galore.

"Carol, you have been a pilot her the longest, is that correct?" I asked.

"Yes, I am certified on the Lear, the Citation, the Bell, and the Dauphine. I am just finishing my check flight in the 737. Sue and I both hold the same level of qualifications. You have four other pilots. Those four are the regular pilots for the 737. Which, by the way, always leaves with a full double crew on board. One of those pilots, along with Sue and myself, is certified on the Dauphine. The other pilot for the helicopters is Carlos and he is our only Apache-qualified pilot at this time. How many of these aircraft are you certified to fly?" she asked.

"Me? None, no, I just fix them," I said.

"Charlie, weren't we told that she was a pilot?"

"That's right, our information says you" – he was looking at me – "have both an Air Medal and the Distinguished Flying Cross."

I told them the story about being shot out of the air in Afghanistan and how with the pilot injured, I had brought the damaged Apache to a safe landing. I didn't go into how I shot the Taliban ruffian with the pilot's .45.

"Some of the pilots at my base there had started a logbook for my times in the co-pilot's seat. The log has been signed off by the pilot of record for close to two hundred hours with me in control of the aircraft. I don't think the FAA will recognize any flight time toward a license of any type. I keep it as one of the pleasant memories of my time over there."

"As senior pilot, I am responsible for scheduling basic, advanced, or continuing flight schools for all the pilots in this section. I already have your name in my file with orders from Ms. Karan to get you through all the flight schools till you are qualified and checked out on all our aircraft."

"Mr. Newmark has mentioned that to me. I would love to get my license or licenses, but I don't know how I can fit that in or how to afford it," I said.

"Two of the 737 pilots have instructor licenses. You are going to start both fixed and rotary wing schools in January. They are two separate schools, but they are close to each other on the opposite side of the airfield. On your school days, Charlie and I will keep everything on track here. Classroom and flight trainer times will be in the evenings, and in-the-air times will have to be in the daytime in the beginning until you are ready for IFR classes and night flights. It is expected that by this time next year, you will be trained and certified in everything here except the 737 and the Apache. Those last two are going to take a lot more training, but we know that you will Ace all the classes and the in-air certifications."

I was getting red. So much praise before I had even done anything to deserve it. They were all running on blind faith.

"Thanks, both of you. I hardly deserve the praise that everyone is giving me. Where has it all come from? I have been part of this organization for maybe a month or a little more, and most of that time was spent in a hospital bed."

"Ms. Paulie, you are surrounded by vampires and damphires and Norms that know all about us. Some of us have been alive for 100 and 200 years and more. The older a vampire, or a damphire for that matter, is, the more they gain an insight into other people. Mr. Newmark is a person who has learned and acquired instincts on reading people. He has a fairly accurate picture of what kind of a person you are and what the limitations of your abilities are. I have had a discussion with Ms. Karan and Lisa. It is their opinion that this position that you are now holding is beneath you. Yes, that is correct. We are sure that you are destined for much, much more within Newmark. This current position is like your training wheels. Don't be looking around to see if you can figure out your next position. Remember, time is now on your side. You are not growing older nearly as much as you used to. Several years from now, when you still look the same, you will have learned to handle this job so easily that you will be running it in your sleep. That is when you will be ready for your next promotion."

"I hope I live up to all your expectations," I said.

I knew that my head must have swollen to twice normal with all this praise. *Maybe I should just put it away and concentrate on the present.*

"If neither of you has any concerns with the schedules and maintenance levels at this time, I want to ask about something that came up earlier. Something about an attempted break-in. Am I supposed to do the investigation?"

Charlie jumped in. "An investigation will be coordinated with Larisa downstairs, and as with all such cases, Eddie will be the actual lead investigator. You should contact one of them to find out what is going on."

I looked up at the clock. "It's noon so we should break for lunch. I'm going to see Larisa and find out if there is anything I or we should be doing. I think the three of us should schedule a regular meeting every Monday at nine a.m. Is that workable?"

So, the meeting was adjourned, and I headed for the security cellar as I had decided to call it.

~ ~ ~ ~

I rode the elevator down to the security section.

I saw that Eddie Vangh was in Larisa's office talking with her. I thought I would have to wait to see Larisa, but she saw me approach, and she keyed the sliding door open and waved me in.

"Paulie, I needed to see you, so I'm glad you came voluntarily. Saves me the hassle of getting the marshals to pick you up and drag you in by the scruff of your neck."

I was almost stunned. Almost, I say, because I saw Eddie trying his hardest to not break out laughing aloud. Hard to be the straight man in a room full of comics.

"Let me have your ID badge. I have a different one for you. Your clearance is now up to the highest level. Some things are on a special need-to-know, and you will eventually get read in on most of them. There are only three people that always have total access to anything and everything, and they are Spartak and Karan Newmark, and Leon Krupnick. Leon is the head of all of our business holdings in Europe and is Lisa's immediate boss. He is also a member of THE COUNCIL."

"Paulie," Eddie started, "we all poke fun at each other quite often. It does, in the end, take a lot of tension off. Just being what we are is a tightrope that we are balanced on twenty-four hours a day. We also know that you aren't averse to tossing a zinger or two out there yourself. How is your first day on the job? Is everyone behaving? Is there anything that you can think of in the short time you have had, to come up with any requirements for any new equipment or personnel you may want?"

"I haven't had time to make a full assessment of the operation. My first blush is that it is a cohesive group, and as for equipment, I will have to have more time with the crew and find out what needs they may have before I order any new aircraft…or such," I said. "I had a meeting with everyone and then a short private meeting with Carol and Charlie. Those two seem to have everything under control."

I turned toward Larisa. "The reason that I stopped in was to find out more about something that came up at my first meeting. Someone at the general meeting asked about an attempted breaking and entry of the security door on the north wall of the hangar. Anything either of you can tell me about that?"

"I'm already looking into it," Eddie said. "Over the past several months, there have been three attempted break-ins that we know about. Larisa and I have been reviewing the surveillance tapes. As near as we can tell, each time, it was a different person. The only thing that ties them together is that they only try the doors to the hangar and not the main building. That and the fact that it is always tried at nearly the same time, two a.m."

"Now that your credentials have been upgraded," Larisa was telling me, "you can access all the tapes any time you want to. You should take time to look at all of them. It might help you recognize one or more of the perpetrators. You know, like some night when you are out bar hopping."

Well, there it was again. You get into one bar brawl, and you are forever branded even though you weren't the instigator.

Just then, I noticed this guy walking through the pit full of the computer consoles operated by the security surveillance team. It isn't often that some guy grabs my attention, but this one was worth many a second look.

"Who is that?" I asked in general.

Larisa sat up straight and said, "Well, you two, this meeting is over, now both of you go back to work wherever it is that you work. And Ms. Zahn, that little item is spoken for."

"The first guy I look at in years, and you tell me that he is already collared?" I asked.

Larisa hit the button to unseal the door, and in walked the

stud muffin—correction, Larisa's stud muffin. He went right to Larisa, and he bent down, and they exchanged some lip gloss.

He looked up first at Eddie and then to me. "Hello, I'm Todd, and you must be Paulette."

I thought that he would extend his arm toward me for a handshake, but Larisa had a death grip on his right wrist.

I saw that Larisa wanted alone time with Mr. Hunky. Discretion was the order of the day, so I stood and excused myself, as did Eddie.

~ ~ ~ ~

Eddie caught up with me in the elevator.

"What floor, Eddie?" I asked.

"I'm following you. I need to schedule some flights, and since I will be walking into the flight shack with the, I mean with THE Boss Lady, I should be able to get preferential treatment."

"Good luck with that, pilgrim. No one can buy me. You want to garner favors, then you better bring a note from Ms. Karan or Sparky himself."

"Hey, I saved your life."

I was going to say that it was a momentary lapse in judgment on his part, but the elevator had stopped at the hangar floor.

"This is where I get off," I said and headed toward my office.

Eddie followed right behind and into the flight shack, where he headed toward the refrigerator.

Sue and Carol spotted us as we came in and shouted out in unison, "Eddie."

They both fast-walked over, and each one took an arm and were trying to move him off to the lounge area.

I stopped in my tracks. Was I back in high school? All that was missing were cheerleader uniforms for my two pilots.

"What are you two trying to do?" I asked them. "I need both of you healthy and not in the infirmary because you crossed Amelia."

"You must be the Grinch," Carol said.

"You're not Cupid," Sue said.

Eddie wasn't helping either. He was aglow with a deranged ego that could go to shit on him if he didn't take care. After the pleasant but not-to-be-ignored warning that Larisa gave me a short time ago, I deduced that cutting into the significant-others line could be a death wish around here.

"We are just helping him keep his options open," Sue declared.

"Please excuse me, ladies," Eddie said. "Paulie and I have some planning to do."

With that, he disengaged himself from Sue and Carol and re-engaged himself with me, and escorted me to my office.

I went right for the chair behind my desk, and Eddie took one of the chairs facing me.

"Am I being played for a fool here?" I asked. "I was told that you and Amelia are a solid thing. Is that wrong?"

"Amelia and I are definitely in a healthy relationship, and neither one of us would ever stray unless we both agreed that it was over.

"A few vampire couples have an open relationship. You will learn more about our lifestyle as you spend more time living among us. Your present feelings about monogamous relationships will change when you accept one significant factor, the longevity of your life. This does not mean that we all fool around at the drop of a hat. Me and my mate, Amelia, are devoted to each other. We are both very new to having a one-on-one relationship. Hell, we are both just having our first ever real relationship. Neither one of us have any interest in seeing anyone else. That could change, especially after fifty or hundred years have gone by. If you want to understand this better, you will have to sit down with Spartak. He can say a lot on this subject because of his real age."

"How old is he?" I asked

"Nay, nay, Nanette! Very un-hip to ask the age of a vampire that you work for or with. If he or I were to tell you how long we have been alive, it would be voluntary AND pretty spontaneous on our part. It isn't a big secret, just isn't something that we care to talk about."

"Do vampires become more powerful the older they are?"

"Not really. Once a person settles into their new persona as a vampire, they can get stronger after the conversion by working out in the gym. We do gain muscle much faster than a Norm would under rigorous workouts, but we do not lose the new muscle mass for a lot longer than a Norm would if both types were to quit the gym at the same time. There is the appearance of superior strength and stamina, but that is due to our exceptionally fast reaction times. The factors that set us apart whether we work to keep in shape or not are our reaction times. Our improved hearing and eyesight give us a huge edge in everything we do. You will have to start your physical training soon. Your primary teachers are Pete and Zope, and Amelia and I will sit in now and then."

"Whoa! The four of you are all real vampires. I don't stand a chance up against any of you."

"If you ever went to a regular gym and had a personal trainer, that 'trainer' was probably in a lot better shape than you were. Same here. The four of us are way ahead of you in all of the hand-to-hand combat training exercises. We continually train to stay fit and capable. You will also become fit and well-trained in many of the hand-to-hand techniques we are good at because of our special improvements. You may not have gained the full strength, agility, and reaction times we have, but you will be light years ahead of all Norms and many young vampires. Don't set your standards on what you see Pete, Zope, and Amelia do. It would be an unusual event to find another vampire that would want to go up against them just for the fun of it. I am saying that they are as good as the best. You are something new. We know that you have already taken on many special abilities that go with being a vampire, but we also know that your range is less than the average vampire. You, my dear, are a natural scrapper. That is why you prevailed in your skirmish with the last two rogues. Well, that and they hadn't been vampires for very long, and we don't think that they had been in perfect shape physically before they were turned. You will be working out with the four of us so that your abilities would put you on an equal basis with whatever you meet. It isn't going to become part of you for many months of training."

I must have let out a groan at that comment because Eddie jumped right on it.

"You are going to have to get one thing straight in your mind. You have to start thinking that you have a very, very long life ahead of you. For instance, if it were to take you ten years to learn the combat moves we want you to learn, it is only a moment in time against the length of time you have to live. And on the subject of how long you will live, we can only say that for you to live two hundred years or more is what we believe you can look forward to. Akin to a damphire. How much longer than that is not something we can estimate at this point. Remember, you are a discovery, and we don't have your answers yet. I may not have the final answers for a long time. If you want a chart, we can tell you this: a Norm lives between eighty and a hundred years, some damphires have been known to live as long as three hundred years. A vampire, well, we can't put a number on a vampire. There are a few vampires that are alive today that have passed the century mark.

"We, the group of people you are now a part of, believe, as do many from all the species, that there is another plane that the soul goes to after what everyone calls death.

"If you want to know how long you will live, all we can say is that the doctors upstairs believe that you fall somewhere between a damphire and a vampire. I didn't come here to give you instructions on your new life form. I need to schedule several flights."

I looked at the clock, and it had Minnie's little hand pointing at the five, and her big hand was near the number 3. I felt like I had been here for days instead of the few hours that were the real amount of time. I looked out into the meeting/scheduling area and saw Carol sitting there.

"Excuse me a minute. I want to get Carol in here to help me with the scheduling," I said.

I stood up and walked over to the window between my office and the flight shack meeting area. I tapped on the window to get Carol's attention. She looked up, and I waved her to come into my office. As I walked back to my seat, I thought that was a little presumptive on my part. I mean, I just crook a finger, and everyone comes a-running to my every beck and call.

As soon as she came into the office, I said, "I'm sorry. That was rude of me to wave you in. Just give me a little time to get my feet under me. I have a whole lot to learn about how things work around here."

"Hey, it's all right. I was just sitting there trying to figure a way to wrangle my way in so that I could cozy up to hunky pants here."

"Now, just stop that. I do not want anyone here hitting on someone that is already involved in a relationship."

Eddie… blank stare.

Carol… blank stare.

Then they looked at each other and burst into gales of laughter. I mean, they were falling out of their chairs. For no reason at all, my ears were starting to glow. What had I just said that caused me to be embarrassed?

"I'm sorry, I haven't had anything to eat since… *er*… I forget if I had anything for breakfast or not. Anyway, I am a little peckish, and that is my excuse."

"She is as cute as an elf," Carol said.

"She does sort of act like one," Eddie said.

"Elves. There are real elves?" I said.

Their mouths were agape. What now was all I could think.

"Well, are there really elves?"

Evidently, Eddie decided to save me and said, "Paulie, we are just teasing. We are teasing about hitting on another person's mate, on telling you that there are elves when there aren't."

Carol decided to step up and said, "Paulie, this teasing goes on all the time. Because we will be living for a long, long time, we have learned that though many things in life are serious and in our particular arena much is deadly serious, we, or rather most of us, have a seriously flawed sense of humor. We probably shouldn't be tossing around all these gaffs and gags until you are a little more used to all of us. I will talk to some of the others and see if we can't tone it down a little."

"At least until you have come to accept our level of jocularity," Eddie said. "Wow, where did that big word come from? I should say it three times quickly before I forget it. Bet it will be in tomorrow's crossword puzzle. Remember your first duty station? You had just completed six months of advanced training, and you thought you were pretty hot stuff. That was until you realized that being low man on the totem pole ensures that you got all the dirty jobs and your new best buddies in your unit rode you for a while. Well, this 'unit' is not that much different. You would think that I was beyond that but, the truth is that a day doesn't go by without someone making me the brunt of a joke. I know enough about you to fear already that you will become the head joker of our family once you have settled in."

That made me feel a lot better. It gave me confidence in being part of such a powerful and large company with the bonus of becoming part of a group or family of people with some amazing skill sets.

"You didn't come here to give me a pep talk, which I appreciate you're taking the time to explain so many things, but you have another reason to be here. So, what do you need?"

"Couple of flight schedules we need to get on the board. Sue and Tracy to fly Lisa in the Citation to JFK to catch an overseas commercial to Bern—that flight goes out tomorrow evening. Get the Stearman readied and up to the front of the hangar for an early departure tomorrow morning. Karan and Pete are taking it over to the Gig Harbor area to do some recon. They may stay over there for a few days. That is all the schedules I am responsible for getting set up. Now I would like to use your computer system to take another close look at the surveillance tapes of the attempts at breaking in through your side door."

After Eddie finished talking, I realized that it was already dark outside, and the wall clock showed that it was already five thirty p.m. Time for me to go home.

13 DECEMBER 2016 – 0500 HOURS

I got home last night at 6.15. I had intended to do some organization around the house but ended up laying down for just a minute, and the next thing I knew, it was after 4.15 in the morning. I took a shower and changed all my clothes, and drove to work. That impromptu sleep had been a real godsend. I felt awake, alert, and totally revitalized.

I was ready for the day. I was ready for the world.

I was feeling different all over. Everything was clicking along smooth as can be. I was mentally and physically accepting the changes in my body. And I was emboldened with this new ME.

The day was clear and cold. The traffic was light, probably because of the hour.

As I turned off Marginal Way, I headed toward the security shack. I saw more people there than I had expected, considering the hour.

I pulled up and lowered my window. "Good morning, Chuck," I said to the man sitting inside. I recognized him from the seahawks party at the big house. Two others were dressed in what I call urban camo.

"Morning, ma'am," was his reply. "These two here have been assigned to you for your security. Paulie, this is Irene and Nichole LaFarge. Girls, this is Paulette Zahn."

At first, I didn't recognize them, and then, as my mind filtered out the full combat wear and armament they had on, I remembered seeing them at the Newmark's Manor this past weekend, too.

"In case you hadn't figured it out, they are twins. Nicole has her purple hair in a single braid while Irene has blue hair in pigtails."

"Personal security? But I have Nigel. Why are you here?"

"Ms. Karan is in the hangar. She will bring you up to speed. I was brought in because of the increased threat to you and the company. Karan will explain everything."

I was learning there was a very fluid playing field within Newmark. *Just roll with the changes,* I told myself.

The twins were getting in from the passenger's side, one up front with me and the other in the back, sitting on one of the packing boxes of my things that I had yet to sort out.

I pulled around to the freight door that I used to bring my vehicle into the hangar through. Nichole jumped up, went to the security keypad, and entered her codes to get the door up.

When the door was open enough for her to duck under, she did just that and went into the hangar area. Once the door was close to all the way up, I drove forward and headed toward where I had parked last Friday.

The first thing I noticed was that the hangar door was all the way open, and some of the aircraft were out on the tarmac. The Stearman, the Citation, and the Apache.

My mind was drooling over the Apache. I really, really wanted to go up in it.

I parked the van by the back wall. Irene and I got out and headed to the flight shack. It was a packed house. It seemed that my entire staff was already here, plus half a dozen others.

Karan was on the podium when I walked in. She waved me to follow, and she got down and headed toward my office with the twins and Lisa in tow. Lisa went directly to the Espresso machine. The twins each pulled to either side of my chair behind the desk.

Karan sat and started in.

"There have been some security changes. This came about from a couple of incidents that happened last night, about 4–5 hours ago. The first incident was near your house, Paulie.

"Nigel was taking a walk when he saw a blacked-out SUV drive past the front of the house. He hid behind the shrubs on the property across the street. Shortly after that, the SUV came driving by again, very slowly. In fact, it went extra slow when it was right in front of the house. After it passed and had gone into the next block, it stopped, and someone got out. The foot soldier kept close to any cover available as he worked this way back to your house. He walked onto the property and went around the side, up the driveway toward either the back of the house or to the cottage in the back. Nigel followed on his little cat's paws and knocked the person out, bundled him up, and stashed him in his studio. Nigel and his new buddy are getting acquainted at this very moment." She paused for a moment before continuing. "Then, two hours later, a blacked-out SUV comes speeding up to our building here. It got access to the unguarded portion of the hangar by coming at it from the runways. When it got here, a passenger got out with a satchel of what we believe to be electronic hacking equipment. We know this because he went immediately to the keypad access panels and tried to hook some wires into our system. After getting nowhere at two different doors, he apparently got frustrated and waved the SUV over. He got in, and they drove off. The vital thing to note is that the SUV went back the same way it had come from, toward the northern part of the airfield. Eddie and Larisa believe that the

SUV is from one of the aircraft-related businesses located on the northeastern side of the airport.

Pete knocked and walked in.

"I just heard from Nigel. He told me that the night skulker was a vampire. A vampire with long canines, very long and mature canines. He was another rogue vampire. He regrets to say that his friend with the oversized canines passed away during questioning. I spoke with Eddie before I called, and we both agree that this rogue situation is a lot larger and deeper embedded in the Seattle area than we believed."

"That is a lot more than we knew yesterday," Karan said. "Pete and I are going on air recon of the Purdy-Port Orchard area. We will be staying at the Maritime Inn in downtown Gig Harbor and using the Tacoma Narrows Airport as our flying base. We plan on being able to locate the rogue's base of operations in two or three days. We should finish up on Thursday, Friday latest."

Karan continued, "Now to Paulie's security situation. Nigel has some pressing situations back in Australia and will be flying back later this afternoon. Nicole and Irene are now her personal protection until this is resolved. One of the twins will accompany her at all times. Paulie, your belongings are being moved out of the house in Alki Beach and into the Manor on Bainbridge Island. Everything will be transferred to one of the apartments over the garages. You will have a two-bedroom unit, and one of the LaFarge girls will be staying in the second bedroom. The other twin will be staying in Darja's second bedroom. You can work it out with them as to which will be staying where. They can rotate any way that all of you agree on. No matter what you thought, you will not go anywhere without one of them accompanying you. The only places where you will be without a bodyguard are on the Manor grounds or here inside this facility. If you go outside, even if it is just in front of the hangar when the doors are open, you will not cross the threshold without accompaniment."

"Thanks," I said to Lisa, who brought over freshly made cappuccinos for everyone. "Why am I singled out for this extra layer of protection? Is anyone else being this closely cared for?"

"You haven't been with the company very long, and it would seem overkill. The difference is your lack of experience in the paranormal world. You are very special to everyone that is part of the upper echelon with Newmark. The vampire side of you still has its training wheels attached. The human or Normal side of you still has a lot to learn about your other side. It's what makes you unique. You are still in touch with your Human side, which all the other vampires in the world lost the moment they were changed. It is a trait that we hope you keep for the rest of your life. It is believed that this will allow you to be more Normal naturally, without having to consciously and continuously watch your P's and Q's while you are out in everyday society."

One moment they seemed to be putting a cage around me, and the other, they seemed to be praising me for what I had become. Which wasn't all that reassuring because of the limitations they tried to enforce on me.

I looked Lisa in the eyes. She was my first contact with this world, even though I didn't know that it existed at the time. I met many people in the past two months that had been giving me guidance and love like I never had in my life. Of all of them, though, Lisa was my favorite.

No one had told me officially, but I could sense that Lisa was leaving.

Sue and another pilot, Mark, were flying Lisa to JFK in New York, where she would be taking a commercial flight to Switzerland. I had seen the schedule on the flight board in the other room. I also saw that the Citation and the Stearman were out on the tarmac being given their pre-flight checks.

A month or so in the past, I would have been feeling very insecure. But now, well now, it was very different. In the short time since this wild bunch adopted me, I felt like I was a very integral part of an extraordinary family. I was already proud to be a member. I would have to relish this feeling at a later time, though, because the level of activity around me had increased to an almost fevered pitch.

The short meeting was closing up, and we all were getting up to get to our various assignments.

"Walk with me as I board the plane," Lisa said.

I walked with her and realized that Nicole was moving right with us but on my other side.

Nicole and Irene were tall and attractive. Not model beauty, but more of a Lindsay Vaughn buff body. They were a lot taller than Lindsay, though. I was just short of six feet myself, and I was sure that they were possibly slightly taller. They both walked silently and with feline grace. Ever alert and ready to punch someone in the face. My type of friends, that was for sure.

I was going to get to know them close up and personal since they would be glued to my hip.

Sue was ahead of us and was boarding as we walked up. Lisa stopped at the bottom of the ladder, turned, and drew me in for a warm hug.

"Please keep someone by your side for the near future. You mean a lot to me and even more to the company. I have a backlog of work waiting for me in Switzerland and don't know when I will be back. Hopefully, in the spring. There is a gym / training facility at the Manor. Get Pete, Amelia, and Zope to start training you in hand-to-hand combat. You will be living there for a time, so use it to your advantage to get trained by the best. The twins are equally as good, so be sure to include them in your exercise routine."

Another hug, and she was up the ladder and into the plane.

Nichole and I moved back into the hangar's shelter as the Citation rolled off toward the taxi runway.

"She is very fond of you," Nicole said.

"Yeah, well, it is all her fault that I am here. She brought me in and introduced me to a world that I never knew existed. I don't know how I will ever show her how much I appreciate everything she has done for me. What about you and Irene? How well do you know Lisa?"

She didn't answer right away. She wasn't even looking at me as we talked. Her eyes were always looking past me, continually sweeping the surrounding area. I would come to learn that she and her sister never relaxed their perpetual alertness.

"She is our immediate boss within the European Division of Newmark. She answers only to Leon Krupnick, who is the head of the European division. My sister and I have gone on many missions with her. The three of us have been working closely together for over fifty years." She continued scanning the surroundings as she talked. "Another item, one you haven't asked; Darja was also number two under Leon when she was in Europe. Darja was head of engineering, design, and production while Lisa was in charge of human resources, security and special operations."

That was a lot of information since I had the feeling that the twins weren't exactly the chatty type.

Nicole and I were standing just inside the hangar's doors, and I heard someone walking up behind us. I turned and was greeted by The Michelin Man and The Pillsbury Girl. It was Ms. Karan and Pete. They were either sausage packers or arctic explorers.

Of course, they were bundled up; it was, after all, winter, and they were going flying in an open cockpit, unheated aircraft.

"Wow, you two are very Retro in those outfits," I said.

Pete got up and into the forward cockpit, but before Ms. Karan climbed in, she turned to Nicole and me.

"Paulie, I have given Nicole instructions to take you to a car dealership to get a new vehicle. That is what the card, ONE NEW VEHICLE, is for. You should turn your van in so that you won't have to find a storage spot for it. I'm sure it has served you well, but you have to have something easier to get around in traffic with. If you have any questions, Nicole can help you there. One of the radio sets in the flight shack is keyed to my radios in the Stearman. I won't be flying very high anyway, so our cell phones should always be in the range of a cell tower."

She climbed up to the rear cockpit and buckled in. She re-checked several things, especially the aileron and rudder chocks. She hit the electric (modification) starter, and the Wasp engine fired up.

It was beautiful watching this restored bi-plane come to life and extra special because it was owned by the company I now worked for.

She cracked the throttle, and the aircraft rolled forward and down the taxi strip. She was quickly out of sight. I didn't move.

I wanted to see it flying past just off the runway. It was about four minutes later when I heard the engine race up, and suddenly it was flying past the hangar already a hundred feet in the air.

After it passed, I turned to go back into the hanger and realized that almost everyone had come to the open hangar doors to watch Ms. Karan pilot the plane up and out on a recon mission. I envisioned standing on a dirt airfield somewhere near the front in France during WWI.

I headed toward my office. I wanted to see if I had brought the 'Free Auto' card in from home. Guess it was my former home now. I found it in the satchel I was starting to carry around like a dispatch bag.

The company had given me the bag. It was in brown leather to match my leather motorcycle pants and jacket.

"Nicole," I said, "what can you tell me about this card?"

"Irene and I both got them when we moved in here. We got a pair of BMW motorcycles. You can get anything you want. Well, there may be a few exceptions like a million-dollar Ferrari might be somewhat presumptive."

"Well, how does this work?"

"You find a vehicle you want, you give the card to the sales manager of that dealership, and they will take care of it from there. If it is in stock, you drive it home right then."

"Price limit?"

"No limit, but don't go too radical."

"I have to get my things from the Alki beach house and move it all to Bainbridge. We'll try to get time tomorrow to look for a car."

"Irene has taken care of your belongings. They are already being packed right now, so all we have to do is find your new car and drive home to the Manor on Bainbridge Island. As soon as you have everything done here, we will go shopping."

~~~~

Charlie and Carol stepped in and helped me through the paperwork and scheduling for the day, and I was pretty much up to snuff here, so it was time to go kick some tires.

I started walking toward the van, and Nicole was right beside me.

"Where do you think we should start looking?" I asked Nicole as we got in.

"Let's go to the BMW dealership first. I called while I was waiting for you, and they have something special that you might like."

She had the directions up on her cell phone. I drove, and she was the navigator. Just before we got to the dealership, she told me to turn into an alley and stop. I didn't question her, and with good reason. As soon as I had stopped, I saw a dark-tinted SUV turn in and also stop.

I put the van into reverse and started to back up toward my tail. The SUV backed right into the main street without bothering to check for other cars and lit out down the road.

Nicole was on her cell, probably to Larisa, describing the incident and anything that would stand out about the SUV. She reached my right forearm and clamped hold.

"No, we aren't going to chase them. This van is great for bashing through the jungles of Africa, but it is not any good for high-speed chases on the streets of a major city. Let's just pull into the BMW dealership and get a cup of their coffee."
~~~~

~~~~

The showroom was very modern and obviously, upscale. With all the young yuppie techies in this town, this dealership must be Beemer Heaven for them. I was in jeans, a T-shirt, converse sneakers, and my brown motorcycle jacket, and Nicole was in her camo fatigues with suspicious lumps in her jacket around her waist.

Most car dealerships have what could be called the bullpen, where the salespersons wait for their turn at a new prospective client. I could see that they weren't excited about losing their place in the queue because of our poor street vagrant lookie-loos.

Nicole went over to them. "We want to speak with the dealership manager. Would one of you be so kind as to point us in the right direction?"

"He's in a meeting, is there something I can help you with?"

"Tell him that Nicole is here."

"If you want to wait, I think he will be out in the next hour."

Nicole turned and looked around at the layout. I realized what she was doing when she walked straight off toward a set of stairs that came down from the offices on the second floor.

"Come on, Paulie. We'll just go see him on our own."

"Hey, you two can't just walk in on a private meeting. Come back down here, or I will call security."

We didn't even hesitate. We just marched right up the stairs and headed to the door marked PRIVATE. Nicole looked back over her shoulder and saw the overweight, out-of-shape salesperson huffing and puffing his way up the stairs. She put
~~~~

one hand on my shoulder, stopping me from going anywhere, and the other rested on the doorknob to the private room. *I think I love this woman.* She was baiting him. He came huffing down the hallway, and when he was ten feet away, she turned the knob and walked in.

The one person in the room was the man in a nice suit and tie, sitting behind the big desk. He looked up, not like he was startled but out of curiosity. "Hello, is there something I can help you ladies with?"

"Sorry, boss, they just walked right up, I tried to stop them, but they are deaf and dumb. I did call security, and they will be here momentarily." He was sneering at the both of us.

"Good afternoon, Mr. Markham. I'm Nicole from Newmark. I spoke to you a short while ago. We want to take a look at the new 6XM that you just got in."

Bang! He shot out of his chair and came around to the front of his desk. "Good afternoon, Ms. Nicole. I will be taking care of you personally. Skipper, go down and tell the lot boy to get the 6XM out of the new car storage garage where we keep the special edition vehicles. Have it brought to the wash rack and have them wipe it down, interior and exterior."

"Mr. Markham, this is Paulette Zahn. If she likes it, it will be her car."

Skippy, with a very red face, turned and ran. Markham turned and held out his hand, which I took and shook. I had expected the dead fish grip, but instead, it was firm and warm. His smile was also warm and appeared to be very sincere. He held my hand for a moment longer and gave me a knowing nod. I suddenly realized he was a vampire. I was sure he was. I was also sure that he knew that I was special also.

"Nicole," I said with great trepidation.

"It's okay, Paulie. You have now met the first one like us that doesn't work for Newmark. There are many more in the Seattle area that follows what Spartak Newmark has preached for many years. This, Mr. Markham, is the first and only person you should ever talk to at this dealership. He understands our special needs and also that we have the money available to satisfy any purchase request."

"Nicole didn't tell me who was coming to look at the vehicle. It could have been any of the Newmark employees with their cross-section of types. You, my dear, are a rare and unexpected treat."

I was fumbling around for some level of intelligent discussion. It was obvious that he knew more about me than I would ever know about him. I didn't like being on the outside trying to break in.

"Paulie," Nicole said, "Markham is an elder. He has been what he is longer than Seattle has existed. He is a close friend of the family."

"What family?" I asked.

"Our family," was all she said.

"It is so refreshing to meet a truly new face," he said.

I was so taken that I curtsied. I had never genuflected to anyone, ever. He took my hand and pulled me up.

"Paulette Zahn," he said, "you are new to our world, but you are a fresh breath on the scene. I am here for you if you ever need someone to talk to outside your primary arena. Please ask Sparky or Karan to make sure that I am part of the elders' inside ring. I want you to come by anytime, be it for repairs to your car or just to sit and chat. Remember, please remember that at one time in the far past, I too was a neophyte on the block, and if it weren't for some special people, I would have never have lived this long."

It was getting a little embarrassing, all these people coming up and praising me like I was someone special. I wasn't. I mean, they were the special ones.

"I'm pleased to meet you, sir," I said to him. "So, Nicole wants me to drive a soccer mom's SUV. I don't think that's my style."

Mr. Markham grinned and looked over at Nicole. "Come along, you two. I'm going to show you the vehicle and send you out for a test drive."

He walked out of his office and over to an elevator that took us back to the main showroom. We trailed behind him as we walked past the salesperson's bullpen. The three or four salespeople there all suddenly seemed to have something to keep them occupied. We may be a curiosity, but to get caught staring was not going to happen. They may have spoken to Skippy, but he wasn't there.

He was in the delivery lounge wiping down this new dark blue BMW SUV.

BMW dealerships don't sell you a car. Hand you the keys and point you to where your new car is parked, outside at the curb. This lounge had a Starbucks coffee dispenser. This is Seattle, after all. There were leather chairs around a couple of round tables and a display case full of accessories like BMW hats and socks and other things you didn't need.

"Are the dealer plates on the car?" Mr. Markham asked Skippy.

"Yes, sir," he responded. "And the tank is full. Do you want me to start any paperwork?"

"No, I'll have the office girl take care of whatever is needed. You can go back out to the salesroom now."

He led me around to the driver's door and asked me to get in.

The instant I sat down, the seat seemed to hug me. It was so comfortable. The dashboard was a close second to the panel in front of the pilot in his aircraft.

He handed me the key and said, "This is an electronic key. Keep it with you, or you won't be able to unlock the doors or start the engine. Go ahead and take it out and give it a good drive. I know that you will love all the features. If you like it and want to keep it, just call, and we will take care of all the paperwork and have it couriered to your office."

The overhead bay door opened up, and we were facing the street that fronted the dealership. I hit the 'Start' button, and the engine roared. Yes, it *roared* to life. It was not the four-cylinder model or even the six-cylinder model. I trod on the accelerator pedal very softly and eased the car out into the Seattle traffic.

"Head over to Interstate 5," Nicole said. "When you get to 5, head north to hopefully be rid of enough traffic so that you can unleash some of those ponies trapped under the hood."

"That will take us pretty far from the dealership, won't it?" I asked.

"You are keeping it for at least an overnight. Want you to think about this being yours and to make sure you are comfortable driving it."

"What if I don't like it?"

"You'll take it back, and we will look for something else. I know that you liked your truck mostly for its utility value. This vehicle is just as utile but with a lot more positive points, such as a great heater and AC, both of which cover not only the driver's area but all the way to the back. A fully integrated guidance and communications center and, well, dozens and dozens of other perks that are only available with a vehicle of this class. We are coming to the interstate on-ramp. Punch it, and let's see what this baby can do."

I glanced over at her. She was chafing at the bit. Seriously, she was almost foaming at the mouth with the expectation of blinding acceleration and speed.

This vehicle was heavy. I could feel it when I was braking. Don't get me wrong, the car wasn't going to have a brake failure or anything, and I knew that I could get this rig stopped at the same distance as most of the autos around me. That wasn't because it was a lightweight car but because of the massive brake rotors and multi-piston calipers. That and the P Zero tires that were glued to the road surfaces. Nicole wanted me to let it run. Well, I wasn't afraid, so I was willing to drop the hammer. I had had the reins handed over to me in a fully armed Apache helicopter traveling at 175 miles per hour while only 50 to 100 feet off the deck. Speed didn't faze me at all.

I nailed it, and guess what, I was slammed, not pressed but squashed back into my seat. I had not expected anything like the power this monster had. I started up the ramp and checked my outside mirror to see if any cars were coming up in the lanes behind me.

I realized my error quite quickly. It wasn't that many cars already on the freeway would possibly be cut off by my sudden appearance. It was the cars that had already passed that I was now closing on at well over 100 mph. I throttled back to a saner speed and looked down at the dashboard. Paddle shifters *never* had them on anything I had ever driven. The driver's seat was like sitting in the pilot's seat in an airplane. And that was the big selling point. "How much is this car?"

"Don't concern yourself with the price. Newmark

Industries is buying. You just put this vehicle through the wringer. You will have to get a solid understanding of its capabilities because you never know when you will have to rely on everything it has to get you out of a tight situation. Your life may depend on it."

"How much is this car?"

"Something north of $125,000, I think," she said. "Your comfort level is what counts. If you want something faster, we will have to switch to some of the more exotic sports models. It all depends on what you picture yourself driving today and next year. I notice that you have no qualms about passing every car on the road. Let's see how this Corvette takes it when you blow by him."

I was probably going twenty miles an hour faster when I passed him in the right lane. Sure enough, the moment I was in front of him, I saw that he was no longer receding in my mirrors but instead was closing the gap. What's a lady to do in this situation? That's right, I'm no lady, so my right foot went to the floorboards, and it was game on.

Either the Corvette hadn't expected me to try to stay ahead, or this vehicle had a lot more to it than anyone would expect. As soon as I hit the throttle, I could see that he was not gaining on me any more. It appeared that we were increasing the distance between us.

The Corvette suddenly dropped out of the little challenge, and I took note of my speed on the windshield as part of the heads-up display that is part of the vehicle's equipment.

The display indicated that we had gone past the 160 mph mark, so I decided to back off a bit.

"Atta, girl," Nicole said. "Now stay in this right-hand lane as we are going to get off at State Road 140 and head west."

Oh, lucky me. There was a Washington State Police car partially blocking the exit road. Christmassy with all its blinking and flashing lights going.

I pulled up and stopped. I was rooting around for my wallet with my California driver's license, which I hadn't gotten around to changing, mostly because I hadn't even thought about it. That and because I didn't have a permanent address yet. As I hit the button to open the driver's window, I noticed that Nicole was also getting her license out. She had a grin on her face. I don't know what could be funny about this.

"License and registration and proof of insurance, please, ma'am," said the Trooper.

It was Trooper Durite. I got that from his name badge, being the observant person that I was. What would one bet that his first name was Dudley. This was probably not the best time to ask. I handed him my license and said, "This is a dealer car, and we are just trying it out, Officer."

Nicole reached across and was trying to hand him her ID or driver's license.

"Ma'am, please step out of the vehicle."

Shit, how much trouble was I in? After I climbed out, he directed me to stand behind the vehicle and off the pavement. He was looking at the dealer plate and putting information into his PDA. Just then, another state trooper vehicle, lights a-flashing, roared up.

As the second trooper got out of his vehicle, Nicole got out of the BMW.

"Ma'am, please get back into the car," the new trooper said to Nicole.

Instead, she opened her wallet, which was already in her hand. I thought I glimpsed a shiny gold badge.

Officer number two went up to Nicole, looked at the badge, and asked her to step over to his vehicle. She complied without a word.

My designated police officer stopped what he was doing to watch what transpired between Nicole and officer number two.

Even with all the interstate traffic noise and the two-plus car distances away, I could hear everything number two was saying to his radio.

"Her ID is for a Nicole LaFarge of Newmark Industries. She is accompanying another woman clocked by our surveillance aircraft who reported the vehicle traveling in excess of 130 miles per hour. Does her presence make any difference?"

I heard the dispatcher tell him to standby while the ID was run through the system.

A few minutes went by, and then the speaker came to life. "Return all of their IDs and make sure you have no record of their names or information on the vehicle. They have consul credentials and are exempt unless they have caused property or bodily harm to others."

Number two put his microphone back and got out of his vehicle, and headed to where I was standing with Officer *Doooright*. He related what dispatch had told him, and he gave me a nod. Then he headed over to Nicole to give her credentials back and tell her that everything was okay.

"Here you are, ma'am. You're free to go. But in the future, could you please not test your race car on the public highways?"

~ ~ ~ ~

"*Phew*, that was lucky. What is that badge you showed the cop?"

"I didn't know that you hadn't gotten your full set of credentials yet. I will get that taken care of tomorrow morning. Now let's head to the ferry."

"Ferry? Where are you taking me now? It is getting late."

"If you don't want this car, we can return it tomorrow. Right now, we are going to Edmonds to catch the Edmonds-Kingston ferry. From there, we will go down the peninsula to the bridge on the north end of Bainbridge Island. We are going to the Manor."

~ ~ ~ ~

I kept the car closer to the speed limit after that. Closer but not at or below, mind you. I enjoyed the car's feel so much that before I knew it, we were crossing the bridge near the Indian Casino and onto Bainbridge proper. Nicole had already put our destination into the GPS in the car's system.

The active map in the car was a lot better than Nicole's directions. She had a habit of telling me to turn *just* as we entered an intersection. The map gave a verbal countdown to the next turn. It also told you which direction to turn.

Then there I was, pulling up to the guard shack at the entrance to the Newmark Manor.

Riley was in the guard shack this time.

"Good Evening Ms. Paulie, and to you too, Ms. Nicole."

"What's for dinner, Riley?" Nicole asked.

"Ms. K. has some baked Ziti with sausages, minestrone soup, shepherd's pie, and fresh garden salad from Lysbeth. Oh, and there's meatloaf. The meatloaf is everyone's favorite, so you better hurry if you expect to have any."

And in we drove.

Nicole led me around the mansion to the back where the parking garages / apartments were.

"Where should I park?"

"Drive into the courtyard and back into the third parking stall on your left."

We parked, and I followed Nicole into the apartment area. Up the stairs to the third apartment on the floor. The door was open, and Irene was inside. She was putting my things away in dressers, closets, and in the kitchen. There were still several boxes that hadn't been started on yet. I was surprised that anyone had gotten this much done already.

The place was comfortably furnished, and the layout was full of nooks and crannies that made it so much homier than a regular apartment would be.

Irene said, "I'm your roommate now. Nicole is going to be staying with Darja in her apartment, which is right next door. I've gotten much of your things put away. Over time, you will want to put everything in your own order. I will help you any way you need. I think you need to get some food in you."

"Now that you mention it, I am starved. I have had very little to eat today. It has been a very long and eventful day. Just let me freshen up, and I will be ready to go."

A few minutes later, the two of us were headed toward the kitchen.

A lot of people were there.

I turned to Irene and asked, "Isn't this rather late for everyone to be in for supper?"

"No, everyone is here waiting to see you."

"*Gaah!*" was about all I could say. I was glad to see

everyone but not to be put on display again. That was starting to wear thin. I just gave little nods and sometimes a little wave of my hand as I made my way to an empty spot at the dining table. I saw one lone piece of meatloaf on the serving platter, and I snagged it before I missed out. Added some of the very fresh salad and looked for a glass of water or something to drink.

"What does everyone drink at the dinner meal?" I asked the general population.

Zope, who was next to me, said, "I usually will have a flagon or two of red wine or some Perrier sparkling water."

Flagon? who uses that word. The last time I believe it was used was back in the late 50s by The Kingston Trio. Flagon?

She had a half-liter beer stein full of red wine. Vampires and their metabolism, I mean wine by the pint. Then I thought of my own body. I could probably down two, maybe three of those steins down and hardly feel it. Tonight, though, was not the time to test the waters.

Eddie and Amelia came in and sat with the rest of us.

"We saw your new car. It fits your persona perfectly," Eddie said.

"What do you mean by that?" I asked. "Besides, I haven't decided yet. I still don't know if I can afford it."

Whatever I said must have struck everyone's funny bone because everyone was chortling and grinning.

"Paulie," Amelia said, "you will never have to pay for your car as long as you work here."

"But this car is really expensive, like over $120,000, that's what Nicole said."

"I have worked for Newmark since 2003 and never had anyone go over any budget amount. We have all speculated, but so far, no one has had their pick rejected. There is a pool on what the outer limit is, and you can buy in any time you want. The person that picks an amount that is closest to the limit without going over. I know of one bet at one million dollars," Amelia said.

"If I want that car, the one I just drove here in, all I have to do is say okay? And it becomes mine without any strings or payments from me?"

"Nothing from you, but your loyalty to Newmark Industries," Amelia said.

I ate my meatloaf and salad quietly while I let everything rattle around in my skull. Every minute of every day that I spend with this company, I learn something new. Not little things like making sure I had enough paperclips. No, it is big things like being under siege by a band of rebel vampires.

Zope and Amelia had finished eating, and as they got up, they came over and said, "We're stopping at the gym for a short session. This would be a good time to show you where everything is. We are on a shortened training schedule for the Christmas—New Year's season, but you should see where it is and what equipment we have."

After learning that all I had to do to take possession of that car was to just 'yes.' So, what I wanted to do right now was to go out and take a much closer look at what just might become my car.

Zope said, "I'm sorry! I forgot that you just had your household relocated to the apartments today. You go on get situated and your things put away. Amelia and I will give you the full tour maybe this weekend or some evening early next week. After New Year's is over, we will get you on a regular workout and training schedule.

As I got up to go back to my new digs, I realized that my

shadow was moving in concert with my every move.

~ ~ ~ ~

I snagged a bottle of red wine on my way out of the kitchen and strolled over to *my new car*.

I walked around it, opening all the doors, and lifted the tailgate. The fit and finish were excellent. I got behind the wheel again and just sat there looking over the instruments and buttons and switches. I swear the car hugged me back. After about twenty minutes of enjoying my little dream, I shut all the doors and headed up to my new apartment.

Irene was there. She was in her bedroom putting her things away. Living with another person, even one that I didn't know, wasn't that new for me. Over the past eight years, I had lived in large open dormitories or barracks with a real cross-section of characters, many of which had nothing in common with anyone else. Sometimes, I had a room that I shared with one to three other girls. We all wore similar uniforms and worked for the same company. This was different, though.

Irene and her twin sister Nicole were vampires. Either one of them could physically match any guy I had ever known while I was in the army. Either one was a guy magnet, as was almost every female vampire I had met so far. If vampires were physically weak or had bad skin, or were generally ugly, I certainly hadn't come across any since I had become aware of their presence and in my life. Every one of them by themselves would bring a hush to any restaurant they walked into.

I'm not modest, and I know that I am an attractive woman, and add to that my height, I knew that I was on equal footing with the rest of the women of Newmark. It felt very, very good.

Irene came out of her shower wearing Baby Doll pajamas. She sat on the couch and was brushing her long thick, blue hair out. I thought she looked relaxed, but I knew she was also on trigger's edge, ever on the alert for danger. After what has happened to me in the past two months, I found that my body had become less relaxed, ever on the alert for anything out of the ordinary.

In this beautiful apartment on this beautiful island and working in a dream job meant more than ever that I had to relax without dropping my guard.

"I want to get an early start tomorrow, so I think I should get a good night's sleep. You also."

"Here is item #14 on being a vampire," Irene started, "you will realize over time that you can get by on less and less sleep. As a Norm, you were probably used to eight hours a night. You are young, but you already would be perfectly rested with five hours of sleep. I, as an example of an older vampire, can comfortably get by with three to four hours. Understand that the amount of sleep also depends on what physical activity we are involved in or, worse, if we are injured beyond a few cuts and scrapes, like multiple broken bones and lots of stitches. Then we need lots of rest and sleep to give our bodies the time to repair everything. We don't want to test the latter part of that until you have become more accustomed to your new body."

14 DECEMBER 2016 – 0500 HOURS

The alarm went off, and I was up and dressed in minutes. I was looking forward to today. I was going to be driving to work in my beautiful new car. And I almost forgot Irene was supposed to be with me today. Well, I was dressed and ready, so I figured to get some Starbucks and a scone on the way to work. I should have woken Irene before getting myself ready. Now I would have to wait till she got up and dressed.

"Irene, Irene, I'm ready to go. Come on, shake a leg."

I knocked on her door. "Irene, come on. We have to get going."

Not a sound, so I tried the doorknob. It wasn't locked and opened up wide.

No one was in the room. The bed was made, and everything was straight and neat as a pin. I figured that if I went down to the kitchen, maybe someone would know what happened to Irene.

I grabbed my leather jacket and headed down to the kitchen in the main house.

Zope, Eddie, Amelia, and Irene were all there having a real sit-down breakfast. The dining table was piled high with a dozen of the world's favorite breakfasts.

"Paulie, grab yourself a mug of fresh coffee and load up your break fast plate. We do this almost every morning. It is time to fill up on a good meal as we go over the orders for the day," Irene said.

Break fast. There it was, broken into two separate words instead of saying 'breakfast.' What was with that? I got myself some scrambled eggs, sausages, hash browns, and an English muffin with orange marmalade.

Eddie started with the daily updates. "Karan and Pete checked in just before you got here. They covered a lot of territory yesterday and think they found something interesting north of Purdy at the Port Orchard airstrip. They were going to take a closer look today. When you get to the circus this morning, Paulie, there will be six or eight additional people dressed as line mechanics, but in reality, they are special guards. They will, if they haven't already, be bringing in tents that they will set up on the back wall of the hangar. They will be on duty twenty-four hours a day until this crisis is over. As soon as you are there, I want you to get together with Charlie. Have him go over the helicopters to make sure they can take off with very short notice. If our team in Gig Harbor gets positive location information, we will need to transport everyone that is combat trained at a moment's notice. Get the ground crews to pull all the plush seats out of the Bell and Dauphine helicopters and have the Dauphine set up with two outside liter carriers and two inside in the event there is any action where one of us is injured," he continued his briefing.

"Starting today, everyone will be carrying a sidearm. Paulie, Irene will get you outfitted before you leave this morning. Zope and Amelia will be riding in with you."

Eddie looked at us all seriously, which was uncharacteristic for him.

"We are now on full alert. Larisa has gotten some intel, and we are starting to build a picture of this group. We don't know who is behind them or what their objective is, but we have heard that the group may be as many as eighteen strong, which is a shit load of rogues in one place. Not a coincidence, not even remotely. We are sure now that Newmark Industries is the primary target. The re-cap is that we aren't sure who or why so be alert about your surroundings at all times." He paused and looked at the group. "That is all I have. Zope, Amelia, Irene, anything to add?"

"Nothing major. We have a few things, but we can go over them as we drive to work," Zope said.

I grabbed another English muffin with butter and marmalade wrapped in a napkin for the long drive to the hangar.

I was feeling the edge of excitement growing as I walked out of the kitchen. MY new car was waiting. Irene took a shotgun while Amelia and Zope got into the back seat. I got in and started the engine. I took some time before heading out. I was getting all strapped in while I played with the throttle. The exhaust on my car was set up to send a little thrill up your spine, and it worked perfectly.

"While we are on our way into the *office*, I want to go over some things with you," Zope said. "We all like to keep a low profile. Getting stopped for driving in excess of 150 mph is not keeping a low profile. Please just take this with a grain of salt. I mean, I do get stopped on a regular basis, especially when I am out in my Nomad. Our reaction time is so much faster than a Norm that we can rely on this to keep us from getting into accidents. We become fearless and push past speed limits practically every time we are driving. My words of caution are to remind us, all four of us, that keen eyesight and super reaction times will keep us from many accidents, but there is another side to this. To be seen driving with what appears to be reckless abandon doesn't go over well with the Norms. We don't want to call attention to ourselves.

"The other thing on this subject is your credentials, Paulie. Larisa has a set of items for you to pick up from her office sometime today. You will be getting your concealed carry permit and a badge that identifies you as a member of the Newmark Security team. Newmark Industries is the sole owner of the unit, and it is treated as a security sub-contractor to the government. We use that badge sparingly. It gets us into crime scenes and makes traffic tickets go away." Zope ticked the items off her list. The last thing; if you're going to keep this car, tell Larisa, and she will take care of the paperwork. That's all I have. Any one of you have any questions?"

None of us did.

~ ~ ~ ~

The drive into work was the best time of my life. I had an amazing new car, and I was surrounded by a group of people that viewed life in the same vein as I did. I lived in this apartment that was part of an estate with the finest wine collection in the United States. All that, and they handed me a paycheck every week. I was getting paid to do what I had always loved to do. And then there were the rogues.

I looked at them this way; Rogues 1, Paulie 2. And I planned on staying ahead.

The drive to work, or back, consisted of the Bainbridge Ferry and another fifteen minutes getting to the Newmark Security / hangar building. Under an hour one way. On that particular day, it seemed to have taken less than half that. It was a combination of the new car and the three people that I could call friends. I was enjoying the drive so much that I didn't want to arrive at the office. That's not how it works, though, so I pulled past the guard shack and through the overhead delivery door that I had used in my old van to get inside the hangar to park.

The main hangar doors were fully open, and I saw that two of the helicopters were out front on the tarmac, being re-fitted with the combat interiors. Must have half a dozen personnel on each one.

I pulled my brand new car next to the flight shack. Preferential parking for the boss, ya know.

Before I reached the door to the flight shack, I looked back and saw half a dozen of the crew looking over my new car. 'My?' Yes, I had decided that that was my car.

Irene and I walked into my office within the office. The phone rang, and I just stared at it.

"Aren't you going to answer?" Irene asked.

She's right. It was my phone after all! "Good morning, flight shack, this is Paulie Zahn. How can I help you?"

"This is the security basement, Admin Girl Larisa calling. I need you to come by later this morning. I have some papers for you, Ms. Zahn. At your convenience, ma'am."

"I'll be right there. Could I ask that you have a double cappuccino ready?"

I hung up before she could respond. She had almost gotten me. It crossed my mind that she was spending too much time in that dark, gloomy basement. And in a flash, I had a plan for her.

"Irene, I'm going to the dungeon for something. Do you have to come since I am within the security of the hangar and security building?"

"No, but make sure you come to find me before you leave the building."

That made sense, I thought as I headed for the elevator door.

~~~~

When I arrived, I knocked on Larisa's office door, which was transparent at the moment. The door slid open, and I stepped in and said, "Sgt Zahn reporting as directed, ma'am."

Darja and Nicole were there. They were smirking; that was a good sign.

"Paulie," Larisa said. "You are quite the sassy one. Please have a seat."

I noticed a whiteboard off to one side. On it was a list of names or titles, most of which had a red line through them. Some but not all. The list went:

Hangar Boss – it had a red line,

Schedule Master – another red line,

SFA Zahn – red line…

"What is an SFA?" I asked.

"Senior Flight Administrator," Darja said.

"We realized that you want a title," Larisa said in reclaiming the floor. "The subject is open for more input, and I have put out a questionnaire to everyone that lives at the Manor. There is even a prize for the best title.

"Here is a fresh hot double cappuccino to help relax you."

Nicole was stoic, but Darja was having difficulty to not laugh out loud.

Larisa pulled open a folder, a quite fat folder that had my name on the front. She pulled out a manila envelope and handed it to me.

"Those are the final credentials for you. The envelope
~~~~

contains your new passport, a Washington State driver's license, platinum AMEX, and Visa. A leather card case that has a badge and CCW licenses from several states. Your current name should be good for fifteen years, give or take.

"You also have a safety deposit box for personal papers and such, which is located in the basement of the building next to the Umpqua Bank branch on 3rd Avenue in downtown Seattle."

That was certainly a lot of paperwork and stuff. I was gathering it all together when I suddenly stopped and looked up.

"What do you mean, my name should be good for fifteen years? What is it going to do, wear out or something? I'm sort of used to it and wasn't thinking of changing it."

"Paulie," Darja said to me. "To look at me, you would think I was around twenty-five years old. That is what I look to be, but I was born seventy-four years ago. Similar to Eddie; he looks to be in his late 20s, but he was born ninety-six years ago in 1920. When it starts to become apparent that our appearance can no longer match what IDs and other documents state our DOB to be, we have to disappear for a while and come back with a new name and all-new ID documentation."

Larisa jumped in and said, "Larisa Sykora is my real name. I became a vampire fifteen years ago and would normally be due for a name change, but I am an exception. I have lived the past fifteen years within the Newmark shell with infrequent contact with Norms outside of work. The probability of a Norm realizing that I haven't aged a day in the past fifteen years is minimal. However, I will be getting a new name and ID in the next year or two. Your friend, Lisa Connor, will be going through this right after the first of the new year. You will be given her new name and new contact information as soon as it is done. Your contact or ability to contact her will not be interrupted."

It was like sitting on death row knowing that I will cease to exist in fifteen years. Thinking about it, though, I couldn't come up with the name of anyone that I expected to ever meet up with from my past. My Normal past, that is.

In addition to her business phone with lots of buttons, Larisa had another unit that looked like an aircraft radio. As I sat there digesting what I had just learned, the radio came to life.

"Larisa, this is Karan. Can I talk?"

"Darja, Irene, and Paulie are here with me. I just sealed the door. Go ahead."

"Pete and I are positive we have found the main nest of rogues. It is a building on the Port Orchard Airport property. We just took off from the Tacoma-Narrows field and are flying back there now. Our cover is that we are looking for a hangar for rent to store the Stearman in. Pete will be sending you a text shortly with the building address and the license plate numbers from several of the vehicles we saw parked nearby. Stearman out."

That reminded me of communications in a combat zone. No frills, on and off as quick as possible. It warmed the cockles of my heart.

"Paulie, take your papers and go back to your office. You can use the safe in your backroom until you get a chance to get some of them to the safety deposit box. I want you and Irene to stay close from now on, as the game may be heating up. Give me a status on the two helicopters that were being re-fitted and let me know if Mel has the Apache ready."

"The Apache," I said. "What was Mel supposed to be doing to it?"

"We need some hardware to test the armament mounts."

"I'll get right back to you on that." And I headed back to the circus.

~~~~

I almost forgot everything else as I went back to my office. My mind was salivating at the thought of having an armed Apache under my control. If that punk lieutenant in Afghanistan could see me now.

The scene that greeted me when the elevator door opened was a shocker.

As far as I could tell, everyone was in front of the hangar doing calisthenics. When I was in the army, I avoided calisthenics. I did use the weight rooms but running around and doing jumping jacks in the 120-degree heat of Afghanistan was something I avoided. Whenever some sergeant or an officer came around to get everyone out for a trot, I would waive a 'critical' repair order and tell them that I would come out as soon as I finished—which was always never.

On closer look, I saw that the usual footwear of gym shoes was absent, and everyone was wearing combat boots.

It looked like we were going to war.

"Paulie!"

It was Eddie Vangh coming up to me. He had a pair of nice slacks, a broadcloth button-down shirt, and a Bombardier's jacket. A step up from jeans-n-t's for him.

"Where are you going all dressed up like that?" I asked.

"Amelia and I are going over to Gig Harbor this evening. The whole project has been stepped up. Ms. Karan and Pete will be the eyes in the sky, and Amelia and I will be knocking on doors and kicking tires.
~~~~

"We will be staying at the Maritime Inn in Gig Harbor, where Pete and Ms. Karan stay. I will also be taking some communications trinkets to allow our cell phones to act more like earwigs. Cell phone signals in that general area are five bars everywhere, so this setup should keep us in close contact as soon as things get lively. Amelia and I will be renting a car from one of the rental agencies at Sea-Tac. Want something that is as plain Jane as possible. We are just going to be tourists to the rest of the world."

Eddie headed outside, and I went to my office, where I went through all the papers that Larisa had given me.

The badge case or cardholder was big enough to hold the badge, which, for all the world, appeared to be for an official U.S. Government agency of some sort. It did have the great seal of the United States on it, but I couldn't remember ever seeing that particular agency's name before. I put the CCWs, my new driver's license, and the credit cards in the different slots and flipped it closed. It was still relatively flat, badge and all. That went in my hip pocket, and the rest of the papers and my new U.S. passport into the safe Lisa had told me about.

The passport was black instead of the standard dark blue. It also had the word 'DIPLOMATIC' on the front. I wondered what special treatment that would get me at any international border crossing.

Just as I was putting the papers into the safe, one item fell out. It was the registration for the BMW. It was already in my name. If I weren't so busy, I think I would want to take a break and have a nice cold beer.

As I closed the safe, No-Knock-Irene walked in and sat in a chair in front of my desk.

"I haven't had anything to eat since breakfast. It is too late for lunch and too early for dinner, so how about we take off early and stop for a bite on the way back to the Manor?" Irene suggested.

"That sounds like a great idea. Give me a few minutes to check on everything, and we will go somewhere," I said.

~~~~

I went out the door of the shack and looked around the hangar space. They had moved the Boeing back to the rear wall as far as it could be moved, and the three helicopters were lined up across the front, facing the runways. No more equipment was out on the tarmac, and the huge hangar doors were slowly sliding across the opening until they boomed as they locked home.

Alongside two of the helicopters were packing containers I recognized from the service. They were designed to carry small arms and ammunition, medical supplies, MRE field rations, and other war zone necessities. This was serious preparation, and I was a part of it too. I was in charge of it while it was here in the hangar. I was wondering who was the real commander once this gang took to the skies.

Which aircraft was I going in? I was sure that someone would clue me in before the entire machine set into motion.

I pulled out my cell phone and dialed up Zope as I walked toward my BMW. I even had the registration in my ID case that showed my name as the owner.

"Hello, Paulie," Zope said in my ear. "Irene called me a moment ago and said you two were heading out. I am done here and will be up in two minutes. What I mean is wait for me. I want to ride back with you two. Amelia won't be going back
~~~~

with us. She is going out with Eddie, and they will be getting packed and ready to leave early tomorrow morning to drive over to Gig Harbor. I am extra hungry, so you and Irene had better have some great plans."

With that, she hung up, and I headed toward the BMW. As I neared it, I saw that it already had regular license plates on it. There must be invisible gnomes working tirelessly behind the scenes. Everything was taken care of around here without any obvious effort. It was the most harmonious group of people that I had ever been around in my whole life.

With Irene riding shotgun and Zope in the back seat, I pulled onto Marginal Way and headed toward downtown Seattle and the ferry terminal.

"Let's stop for some chili," I said.

"NO!" they both said in unison.

"Definitely not today," Zope said. "We don't have time for a trip to the ER room. We are on standby alert in case Ms. Karan and Pete get a good locate on the rogue nest."

"I just called Mrs. K., and she will have some fresh homemade pizzas for us in an hour," Irene said. "Besides, I want to see if we can get around behind the black Escalade that just got on our tail."

I looked in the mirror, and sure enough, there was an Escalade SUV about two cars back. It stood out because of the very blacked-out windows.

I got this tingling feeling and knew that there were vampires in the vehicle on top of that vehicle looking very similar to the one that followed me yesterday when I went to the BMW dealership.

"I can feel them," I said.

Zope's face popped up in the rearview mirror as she leaned

close to my head. Irene was also staring at me. What was it that I did that caused this attention?

"What's wrong, guys?" I asked.

Zope spoke first. "What do you mean, you can feel them?"

"Yeah, give us a little explanation on that one," Irene said.

"I don't know. I have been getting a funny feeling every time there is another vampire near. Sort of a tingling sensation."

Irene said, "Head for the ferry terminal."

"Wait, don't you get a certain feeling when you are approached by another vampire? Isn't that how you recognize that another person is a vampire? You must have something that tips you off to their species. I mean, how do you know?"

"Ferry terminal," was the unanimous response.

The seat belt warning image and buzzer came on. Both of them had unbuckled and were squirming around in their seats.

"What are you two doing?" I asked.

"Ferry terminal," was the only response.

It was about four p.m., and the daylight was starting to wane. The darkening was more pronounced because of the heavy overcast. Nothing abnormal for Seattle at this time of year.

When we got to the ferry staging area, it was half full. We would make it onto the ship with the next group. Probably two-thirds of the way back from the prow.

I had lost track of the tail. I didn't know if it was on this trip or if it had even followed us all the way so far.

As soon as we stopped after loading, Zope and Irene opened their doors and got out. Before Irene closed her door, she said, "Lock the doors and call ahead to the Manor. Get Odie if you can. Tell him what is going on and to try to meet us at the ferry landing. And get your earwigs on. We are now in stealth mode."

They disappeared in the mass of parked cars. Zope had gone one way and Irene another. I think Zope was trying to pass the tail without being seen, whereas Irene was boldly and slowly walking between the cars toward the ship's stern.

Crackle. "Same lane, four back. Two in front, can't see into the back."

Nothing for about a minute, then *crackle*. "Pound the hood. Distraction. Ten seconds."

Then nothing more. Two minutes they were both standing outside the BMW's doors.

"What did you do?" I asked as they got in.

"Zope placed a magnetic GPS transponder on the underside of their vehicle. I banged their hood to do two things. One, to cover the magnet's noise catching on to the car frame and second, to let them know we are aware of them. I also couldn't be sure of how many bodies were in the vehicle as they have something between the front seat and the back."

Zope's turn. "When we arrive at the docks, we are going straight to the Manor."

"What about us following their car?" I asked.

"Odie is going to be there to take up their tail," Zope said.

"So, we just go home, eat pizza, drink some wine, and watch old movies on the TV?" I asked.

When I pulled into my parking stall, Eddie and Amelia were standing there. I thought they were waiting for us. Zope got out before I had killed the engine and went off with both of them. I looked at Irene, and she just gave me a shrug and followed me into our apartment.

The two of us washed up and went over to the kitchen and had the homemade pizza. And it was a surprise. One of the better or possibly the best I had ever had.

After we ate, we went back to the apartment.

Irene went to the fridge and pulled out a small container. She opened it and showed me the contents. There were fifteen or twenty gel capsules inside. She took out four and handed me two.

"I'm going to wash mine down with some beer, but you can use anything you want; beer, water, wine, whiskey. It doesn't make any difference," Irene said. "This is our blood replacement. I was due, and I thought I noticed you getting a little gray pallor to your skin."

I did as I was told and decided to turn in. I was feeling a little run down. The last few days, no, make that the last two months had been a whirling dervish. I would welcome a night to rest and ruminate everything.

15 DECEMBER 2016 – 0600 HOURS

I practically flew out of bed. I must have gotten a good night's sleep as I felt like I had not just gotten my energy back but that and a whole lot more.

I was also the last one up, it seemed. Again, Irene was already up and gone. So, I headed to the kitchen myself for one of those scrumptious break…*er* break fasts. I still didn't understand that, but that's what it was.

Eddie and Amelia were there dressed in tourist casual. Most of the rest in the room were in combat fatigues and holding travel cups for their coffee. Even Darja was 'geared up.'

Irene said, "Grab a coffee for the road and let's get on our way. The entire operation timetable has been ratcheted up about ten points. You don't need to change, Paulie. If we need you changing into combat gear, there is a full set for you in your locker at the circus."

"What about food?" I asked.

"It's in those boxes on the kitchen island table. We're taking the food with us and will be eating with everyone in the flight shack. There were several developments that came to our attention in the middle of the night. Zope, Amelia, and Eddie are riding with us, and one of them will start briefing you while we are in transit. You will get more at the full staff briefing at the hangar."

~ ~ ~ ~

Everyone was stone quiet on the ride-in. I remembered from Afghanistan that the chatty ones were the guys who were scared shitless. The quiet ones were going through everything in their mind and were ready. The only noise was the deep thrummm of the fire-breather that was under the hood of my car.

When I pulled into the hangar, I saw that there were a lot more vehicles. Spartak Newmark's limo was parked next to my space. Backed in military-style, as were every other vehicle both inside and outside.

The flight shack was bursting at the seams. Well, that was an exaggeration, but it was full of people. Most I knew or had seen, but there were a few new faces. I parked, and everyone helped carry the boxes of food in.

Mr. Newmark was near the podium talking to Mel, one of the pilots. As soon as I walked in, he separated and headed right at me.

"Good morning, Paulie," he said. "Could we go to your office where we can have a little privacy?"

"Yes, sir, Mr. Newmark," I said and headed directly there with only my cold coffee mug in hand.

Irene got to the door first and held it for the both of us. Once in, she closed the door and stayed outside in front of it. Shit, this was freaky. Like she knew or had a good idea of what he wanted this private meeting for.

I demurred to him to sit behind the desk, but he just grinned at me and took a seat in one of the two wing-backs in front of the desk. I sat in the other. Did NOT want to be looking down at him over MY desk. *Maybe I should sit on the floor at his feet…little too pretentious that.*

"Paulie," he started, "in the privacy of this office or in any other private place such as when we are at the Manor, you use my name, Sparky. You and I are on a first-name basis. And relax. I love the vehicle you picked out. I hope that you will take me on one of your death-defying rides someday."

Choke!

"I see you aren't quite used to the never-ending pokes that we all give each other. It's all right. In a private setting like in this office or at the Manor in my office, we are equals. Oh, there is a big gap in our social standing, but when we are together, and away from the maddening crowds, we are all the same." He leaned back in his chair. "I wanted to talk with you about a few subjects. First and most important is, are you comfortable with this position? Are you comfortable living at the Manor? Is there anything in your private life or your job that you want to change?"

He paused, so I answered.

"I love this position. I have only been on the job a few days, but I can't think of anywhere I would rather be working. Living at the Manor in that luxury apartment is living in a dream, a really good dream. Right now, I couldn't want anything else. My private life. Well, right now, I don't think that I have any private life at all. The companionship I feel with everyone I have met is making my life full. I had a rough patch there for a while, but the past month or two have been a dream or at least a dream for me. I wouldn't want it any other way. Maybe someday, I would like to meet a nice guy, a nice, completely single guy to date. Not right now, though. I think I almost made a mistake when I verbalized my thoughts to Larisa when her boyfriend came in. I did not know he was taken, or I wouldn't have said or even thought anything along that line."

Sparky let out a little chuckle at that.

"I heard about that. No offense was taken by Larisa. A little secret between the two of us; that is her very first boyfriend. She is, whether you see it or not, a very shy person. She has been with me for fifteen years and never ever dated anyone. Never even danced with anyone before he came into her life. Even at the annual Christmas party, she would have one small glass of champagne and sit quietly in a corner out of the way. The quintessential wallflower. You should get the full story of her meeting Todd from Amelia or Zope." His voice became more serious. "Well, I think you are settling in nicely, and I need to go, but there is one more thing. Irene and Zope talked to me last night. It was about your 'feeling' that there was a vampire or more than one in the car behind you. You never saw the vehicle until it was mentioned that there was a tail on you. Whenever I meet someone new, I always know if that person is one of us. I don't get a sensation, but I can tell from how they speak, how they posture themselves, just their persona that tells me. Remember, I have been around for a very long time, and it becomes second nature to me. Many of the people you are working with or live with now don't or aren't capable of identifying another vampire right away. The way it was explained to me, you were pretty sure what species were in the car behind you without you seeing them face to face. We are on a war footing at the moment, but when it eases up, I want you to spend some time with Pete Ozmosky. He may be able to figure out how you were able to get that 'feeling.' What I would hope for is that it is some manifestation that has developed because of your unusual conversion.

"Before you think about it too much, understand that we all think this may be a great thing. One last thing before I leave, if you plan on going out, even if it is just to the local Starbucks, I would prefer that you take Darja with you because that way, both Nicole and Irene will be with you. They are real-life ninjas of the highest level and will be your best protection. Be sure you do get out to the costume store for your Santa suit."

And with that, he stood up, and I did too. He pulled me in and hugged me. It was a hug like my father used to give me, and remembering that I teared up.

I honestly felt like the luckiest person in the world. I had things and a job that I never imagined myself having. And friends, yes, real honest friends that I felt a true blood bond with. Blood bond. Did I think that?

Before I go all melancholy and forget, SANTA SUIT?

After Mr. Newmark left, I looked out on the scheduling room and saw that the number of people there when I came into work had greatly diminished. I supposed the only ones still there were all part of the hard core cadre of Newmark.

When I walked out of my office, Eddie was at the front of the room, but he wasn't at the podium. He was sitting in a chair that was turned to face everyone.

"Well, here comes our ray of sunshine," Eddie said. "Come and have a seat. I have a lot to tell everyone."

As I sat, he started right in.

"I just had a short meeting with Larisa. She has been here all night trying to unravel the leaseholders or owners of the vehicles and the hangar that Ms. Karan and Pete have spotted and what they suspect to be the main base of operations for the rogues.

"Almost everything is held in corporation names, and she has been stripping the layers away to see who is the root of all of this. If the information is right, the primary holder is Stern Enterprises."

There was an outburst of comments ranging from; "Shit," to "Damn" to "Aha! I knew it."

"Hold up. There is something more. One of the vehicles, a new Escalade still on temp tags, is registered to an Iskenderian Industries of Mannyunk, PA. If anyone here doesn't know about my history with Vic, it is one of intense hatred. There was a meeting with Maxmillian Stern of Stern Enterprises at the Manor earlier this year. Stern is Iskenderian's boss, and they had come to the Manor in an attempt to disavow anything to do with the theft of the major portion of the blood capsules. Also, to try to have us believe that the kidnapping of my sister, Darja Strykula, was not at their direction and without their knowledge. The meeting was additionally tense as Ms. Karan had been dating Mr. Stern.

"During the meeting, Ms. Karan made it very clear that she held him in extreme disdain. It was at that meeting that Mr. Newmark announced her promotion to President of Newmark Industries and my appointment as the head of security.

"When Stern and Iskenderian started posturing and trying to get us to believe that they had nothing to do with either of the accusations, I let anger get the best of me. That brought the attention of Stern and Iskenderian onto me. I had pounded one of my knives right down through the dial and out the back of the 18Kt gold case during the ball downtown after Darja was kidnapped. The watch was forever and a day destroyed beyond repair. I understand that that watch was like a totem of his family's clan. Their anger and hatred were overshadowed by the two elders present.

"Mr. Newmark and Mr. Krupnick, both members of the Council of Elders, gave the ultimatum to both Iskenderian and Stern that they were to leave the northwestern part of the United States, including any businesses that they may have established in this area. They did not take it well. We did not expect them to try to reappear in this area for a long time. We would not have known that they were here until much later except for the attack on Paulette Zahn. It is the decision of Mr. Newmark and Karan Newmark that the following personnel are to be excluded from any raiding or attack parties: Karan Newmark, Paulie Zahn, Darja Strykula, and Todd Haswell."

I raised my hand.

"Yes, Paulie, you have a question?" Eddie asked.

"Why me and why Todd, and why not you?" I asked.

"I will start with you. We think they know that the rogue that attacked you did bite and give you some of the sera that would cause your change to a vampire. They deem you to be one of theirs. They aren't interested in making you one of their minions, but they want you to experiment on."

I realized what he had said, and it gave me a chill like I didn't believe I had ever had.

"Ms. Karan is on their prime list because of her new status in Newmark and the timing of her terse dismissal of the budding relationship with Mr. Stern. Darja. We are still trying to put that piece of the puzzle together, not from the present but from back in the spring when they kidnapped her. We have recently discovered that Stern Enterprises has a presence in Europe, where she was from. She was the second in command for all of Newmark's holdings in Europe.

"Todd Haswell had been one of Maximilian Stern's major thugs, and when they kidnapped Darja, he was also bundled up and held as they had become suspicious of his loyalties. Todd was, at the time, working undercover for the Council of Elders because they were looking into Stern's activities. If anyone is curious about how he and Larisa became a couple, you will have to ask them. It is their story."

I raised my hand again.

"Yes, Paulie?"

"It seems to me that they hate you just as much if not more than the rest of the people that are barred from the action."

"It is my responsibility to protect everyone and all property of Newmark, and yes, I am sure that I am in their crosshairs, but as physical security is my main responsibility, I will be out front directing the operation. More questions, anyone?"

One of the other pilots raised their hand. "Do we have a scheduled time to leave for their den?"

"Ms. Karan and Pete are flying back and should be landing any minute now. Amelia and I are leaving as soon as the plane is back in the hangar and will be setting up an observation post at the Port Orchard airfield. I expect the outpost to be live before noon today. If and when any raid will start will be determined by what I find when I have watched their operation for a while. It may happen tomorrow or Saturday at the latest. More questions?"

My hand went up. Again.

"Yes, Paulie?"

"I'm sorry to ask so many questions, but this is so new to me. I just want to be sure I have a full concept of what is going on."

"Paulie, to use an overworked adage, 'The only bad questions are the ones that weren't asked.'"

"Twice now, it has been alluded to that I am supposedly playing Santa on Christmas. Is that so, and if it is, why?"

"New kid on the block? Youngest vampire? You weren't present for the drawing, but your name won the prize."

Just then, I heard the putter, putter, putter of the Stearman's motor, and that was the break that everyone was hoping for as there were no more questions.

~~~~
~~~~

Ms. Karan was giving instructions to the ground crew for things that had to be done to the aircraft before putting it away.

Pete was already in discussions with Eddie, Amelia, and Zope. Everyone else was re-checking their battle packs and other equipment canisters that would be with the first wave.

The meeting didn't last long, and afterward, Pete and Zope headed toward me.

"Good morning, Paulie," Pete said. "Zope and I want to talk with you for a minute if you have the time?"

"Plenty of time since I am grounded. Or am I wrong? I think that is how it was explained a few minutes ago."

Pete had on his regular grim face. I don't think anything got him upset or excited. He didn't exude any emotion at all. I almost wanted to poke him to see if he was awake at all. Zope was smirking, but she put her arm around me.

"Paulie, you have to trust us. We have been in combat with these types before. We have the experience that only comes with time. Some of the rogues we will come in contact with may have been a vampire for longer than you have been alive. If this foray does turn into open conflict, we won't have any time to pay attention to the younger warriors in our group."

"Which brings up another point," Pete said. "We were going to have a training session in the gym at the Manor on Sunday. That has been moved to Saturday. It will start after we break fast, say 8.15 Saturday morning. Zope, would you please make sure she has her own outfit. Paulie, there is something I want to talk to you about. I want to do it while we are at the gym Saturday."

"Okay," was all I said.

~~~~

It had been quite a morning. Most normal people would be in
~~~~

information overwhelm. A few months ago, I would have been too. Except I was no longer a normal person.

Now I was asking myself questions and answering them with no one else in the room. Maybe my brain was deteriorating. Definitely no longer a normal person.

Minnie's little hand was already half way to the number IV. Where had the day gone? All I did was some meetings. One here, one there, all on the run. That must be what ate up the day. Then my stomach knotted up to say, 'I'm hungry, feed me.'

I turned and saw Irene standing near the flight shack's door.

"Where's Zope?" I asked her. "I want to get home for dinner."

"Pete and Zope are riding with us. I will get them and if they are ready, I will bring them to the car."

Ten minutes later, I was pulling Fang (the name I decided to give my car) out of the hangar and headed for the ferry terminal. Felt good to have other people with me as I drove. These people. My people. This really was my family now, and what a family it was.

"How is Ms. Karan getting home?" I asked in general.

"She left with her dad about an hour ago. I think they went down to meet with Larisa," Pete told me.

The rest of the drive home was silent. We were all thinking of the action that could break out at any moment.

17 DECEMBER 2016

Friday was a day of wait. SOP for the military "Hurry up and wait." The only event of note was the return of the Citation which gave us two more pilots in Carol and Charlie.

The ground crews were moving the helicopters to the side to get the jet into the hangar. It was really just busy work. Gave everyone something to take their minds off of the impending live action.

Most of us just sat in the flight shack trying to burn the espresso machine out.

Sturdy little item, that. I may have to order coffee beans in the 35 lb. bags like dog food.

The only really senior member of the team I talked to was Pete. He was in and out of the security basement mostly. When he surfaced, it was to re-check the readiness of the helios' status, to be airborne at a moment's notice.

I hadn't heard from Eddie or Amelia and Pete didn't have any information on what they were doing or what they had found.

Early in the afternoon, Larisa called my cell.

"Paulie, start sending most of the crew home for the night. No parties, no bar hopping. Tell them to go straight home and keep their phones on and close by. You will be staying in your private room behind your office. You will be the first one notified if and when Eddie or Amelia call for air support. You will be first on up to make sure that the two groups get to their respective assignments and into the air as fast as possible."

~ ~ ~ ~

That was Friday. It was now Saturday and I had slept in fits and starts. Everyone was on their toes.

Drink more coffee and pee a lot.

A little after nine a.m., Pete appeared and said, "Paulie, grab Zope and let's head for the gym at the Manor."

I had sort of put that appointment out of my mind. I knew that the gym thing was where the primary vampires who lived at the Manor trained. I hadn't been inside the gym yet, but I guessed that was where I was headed now.

On the drive home, Pete was his usual self. If you didn't see him in the mirror, sitting in the back seat, you wouldn't even know he was there. Stone faced.

Zope and Irene on the other side of the coin were animated and chatting on about nothing important. They seemed a little relieved to have something to do other than the sit-n-wait party at the hangar.

I drove into the compound and around back to my parking slot under the apartments.

"I'll see everyone in the gym in ten minutes," Pete said as he got out.

"As soon as I have changed," Zope said. "I will come to your apartment, Paulie. I have a set of gym clothes for you."

Several minutes later, she was knocking at the door. Irene opened the door even though it was my place. Security, personal bodyguard. It was going to take me a lot more time to get used to this personal protection.

Zope brought several packages with her. She set them

down on the coffee table and she and Irene started pulling things out and holding them up like I was in Nordstrom's picking out a new blouse.

I was interested, but Irene and Zope were opening everything like it was their birthday presents. They opened up two different outfits. One was dark blue, and the other was a reddish-pink set. I immediately picked up the dark blue set.

They were changing, so I did too.

"You should have worn the pink outfit," Zope said. "Opponents will always underestimate an opponent in pink over one in the more traditional blue or black. It won't make much difference in the beginning, but six months from now, you will want every advantage you can get."

"Why is that?"

"We expect you to have gotten far beyond the basics by then. You will be expected to give a fair accounting of yourself against any one of us. When we have decided that you have attained a certain level of defensive and offensive moves, the gloves will come off, and you will have to be ready to use every trick we have taught you to protect yourself during our training sessions."

Just when I thought that I was assimilating into this new culture and with all these new friends, I was being told that my initiation had only just begun.

All suited up and wearing flip-flops, we headed down and out toward the gym.

The gym was a good-sized building behind the apartments and Lisbeth's vegetable gardens. Actually, I didn't know if it was a large or small building. It was a gym. I guess that was the correct size for a gym. Or maybe it was oversized because it was a vampire's gym.

The interior was partially what one would expect a regular gym to look like with muscle machines and a free-weight area. No roped sparing ring, but there was a matted area for wrestling or Judo contests, and there were what looked like tackling dummies off to one end and a locked cage that contained an assortment of knives, bows, swords, and more knives for the most discriminating ninja.

Darja and Nicole were already there. We all headed toward the floor mats by the dummies.

"We only have a few people here today," Pete said. "We won't do any planned workouts. I just want to take this time to have Paulie see what those of us that have been trained to the highest level can do.

"Zope and I will show you some of our knife skills. None of us are as good as Amelia with knives. She is the very best."

I went over near the dummies while Zope and Pete opened the weapons cage, and each selected several knives. Everyone else gathered around a table that was about thirty feet away from the dummies.

When they, Pete and Zope, came over, they laid the knives on the table, and Pete picked up a three-inch square of paper.

"Paulie, would you please take this paper and pin I have and go pin it to the chest of one of the dummies over where the heart would be."

"Sure." And I took the 'target' down and pinned it right where the heart should be. As I stood back slightly, I felt the air move as something flew past my right side.

Thunk!

The knife was buried to the hilt right through the center of my target, and I was trying to get my balance. I had jumped when the knife flew past. What the fuck was that?

"Hey, I'm down here. Could you wait till I'm off the range next time?"

I was standing between the two dummies, and Pete and Zope were standing with their hands at their sides. Motionless. No expression. I couldn't tell who had thrown the knife.

"Stand there very still," Zope said. "Just watch. And whatever you do, do not move, not one inch, okay?"

"*Err!* Okay!"

And in the blink of an eye, there was a knife sticking out of the chests of both of the dummies.

I had barely registered any movement by either one of them. Barely, I said, but I did see some hands or arms movement. I also saw the paths of the two knives as they flew the thirty or so feet into the dummies.

I don't remember moving at all but found myself crouched down on my haunches and both arms extended out with hands splayed as if I could stop or catch the knife before it hit me.

Zope was walking toward me. She extended her hand to help me up.

"You have some exceptional reflexes," she said. "It usually takes a young vampire months to be able to react that fast. I am going to show you what we expect you to do in a few months."

She motioned for me to go back to the firing line… the throwing line may be more correct.

She then stood at a 45-degree angle to one of the dummies. I watched Pete suddenly throw a knife at the dummy next to her. It never got there. It never fucking got there. It happened so fast that I didn't even see her move, but there she was, standing next to the target dummy with the knife that Pete had just thrown, clasped in her fist.

I also saw blood dripping out of her fist. She had grabbed

the flying knife by the blade with her *bare fist.*

"I am NOT ever going to try that," I said. "That is just stupid insane. Do you need help bandaging your hand, Zope?"

"Paulie, the cuts are superficial and will heal over in a day or two," Zope said. "We were just showing you what a carefully trained vampire can do in particular situations. We aren't going to have you trying to learn knife offense and defense today. Today, we will demonstrate several of the forms of physical combat that we train in and what you will be learning for as long as you are part of Newmark. Let's go over to the mats."

And she walked off in their direction.

Darja and Irene were out in the center, facing each other. Zope had sat on the floor at the edge of the mats and patted the spot next to her. She wanted me to sit next to her.

Nicole sat on my other side. Pete was back in the weapons cage putting the knives away.

Darja and Nicole bowed to each other and took the stance. You know the en-guard stance, or is that for sword fights? Then there was a flurry of flying feet and swinging arms, and *WHAM*, Darja was flat on her back.

She bounced up and went right back into the stance. They went right back at it, and it ended the same way as before. Darja looking up at the ceiling.

She got up a little slower than the first time and bowed to Nicole as Nicole bowed to her.

"Paulie," Darja said, "come out here, and I will go through a few of the basics."

She didn't add any adjectives that would emphasize which move might end in my turning into an old mattress-back. She didn't, but I already had this distinct feeling that I was about to be handed my hat.

She didn't square off. Instead, she came up beside me and took hold of my wrist.

"For the beginning, you will be trained mostly in defensive moves. If you are approached or attacked by anyone, be they Norm or vampire, we want you to be able to keep them at bay long enough for one of us to step in and save your bacon. Don't take offense at how I say this. I went through it myself a long time ago and have always trained regularly to keep a keen edge. Now just hold your arm out, slightly bent at the elbow and your hand up, palm facing your opponent. That establishes a do-not-cross line in the sand. Even against an older and experienced vampire, that position will let them know that you may be more of an opponent than they first thought. That also gives you space and few moments to further ready yourself for what may happen. Hold your other arm back, cocked with your hand, palm outward just like your first hand. The type of hand-to-hand combat we train with does not wholly fall within any of the several types of karate, Judo, etc. They are adaptations to our superior reaction speed.

"I was going to do a few takedowns, but we don't have much time today. You will be starting combat workouts three times a week, and your instructors will be either one of the twins or Amelia or Zope. They are all masters at hand to hand with or without hardware. Come, let's sit while the twins go through a practice set."

Nicole and Irene stepped onto the mat and went through the bowing routine. I watched as carefully as I could, but their speed was blinding. They weren't fooling around. Each gave as good as they got. After several minutes, they stopped, stood back, and did the bow thing again.

There had been some whacks that had me cringing. Some

punches or hits that would have broken a lot of bones on other people. Either one of them would bring shame to Jackie Chan.

Just then, Pete materialized next to me. "All of you but Paulie, run through some exercises. I want to talk to her for a few minutes."

As we walked toward a secluded corner with a table and a few chairs, I noticed that Zope and Nicole were sparring while Irene and Darja watched.

"What do you think about all this, Paulie?"

"I don't see how I could ever get as good as any of them. When I was in the army, every base I had always had the karate and boxers in contests. In the past five minutes, I saw several people that could beat every one of them in a fight. And they are all girls. I just don't know how I will ever be able to achieve these standards."

"Practice, practice, and train with the best. It will take time, but you have to step back for a moment and remember that you have a lot of time to learn. You have a very long life ahead of you. I have you here because I need to ask you a few questions about yourself. The other day when you were leaving the circus to go back to the Manor, you sensed that there were vampires in the vehicle that was shadowing you. I need you to describe in as much detail everything that you were seeing, everything you were feeling, everything you were hearing. Tell me every sensation that you were aware of at the time."

"Why?"

"I have been a vampire for several hundred years. That's right, I am, according to your perception, ancient. Trust me, I am still a child in the world of vampires. A couple of hundred years, though, establishes me as one of the resilient ones. Many of the elders recognize that I am wiser than my years would indicate. You have to trust me when I say that I need to know more about your 'feelings,' that it is crucial."

"Why?"

"In my lifetime, I have met hundreds or possibly thousands of other vampires. I had only recognized that another person was a vampire when that person was in my presence. Their inflections, the way they carry themselves, their attitudes, and what and how they speak are traits that help me identify another vampire without them telling me that they are one. The other day you may have sensed the presence of a vampire. That SUV was in your vicinity, but you couldn't have seen them in person before they were tailing you. Without direct confrontation, you knew that they were vampires. Ms. Karan is presently in the library, researching to see if there was ever anyone with this ability. Later tonight or tomorrow, she will show you how to access the library in the Manor basement. Right now, I am trying to learn everything you were feeling at the time you identified them. It could be a singular sensation or several from different parts of your body. A tic in your eye, an itching sensation on the back of your neck, a fluttering in your stomach. Something that made you think, 'that person is a vampire.'"

"I can't think of anything in particular. One moment I was just driving toward the ferry landing and a voice in my head said, 'There's one behind you.' I can't remember any particular sensation at all. Just one minute, I am driving, and the next minute I knew the person in the SUV behind me was a vampire. I didn't think about it much until everyone started making a fuss over it. In the little time I have spent thinking back, I have not been able to single out some particular instance that I could tag so that the next time I would know right away what it was that I had sensed."

"*Hummm!* That is interesting," he said. "There were three of us in the car with you. We are all vampires. Didn't you sense us?"

"No, I know that. I already know what the three of you feel like. I'm used to having you around. What I felt at the moment back then was a new feeling, someone that I didn't already know. Someone with, well, like an invisible signature or emanation that was different from the ones that I feel or felt from the three of you. Someone that didn't fit what I come to expect when I am around anyone from our entire group. For example; to describe it as best that I can, if I were in my rooms at the Manor and someone knocked at the door or was just passing outside for that matter, I would know who it was as long as it is someone, a vampire, that I had already met. Talking about this with you has made me realize that this is something that I just sort of grew into without belaboring or practicing it. I hadn't ever separated this out as something unusual. It didn't come on in a rush. It was a gradual thing. Now that you have me talking about it, I realize that it was so gradual that I didn't even know it was happening. I took it as something to be expected now that I am what I am. I remember back when I was in the hospital. After the first week or so, I would know which nurse or doctor was coming to see me long before I could see them. It is like you know who someone is by the lilt or tone of their voice. With me, it is just something I know."

"For now, I want you to limit this information to myself and the four here and Eddie, Amelia, Ms. Karan, Pete, and Sparky. I am going to change your protection team to always have one of the twins and one of the other persons that are from the core cadre. I am not trying to stifle your life, but this may be the unique trait you have gained during your very abnormal conversion. This must be the item in your DNA that has had the doctors figure out if you are a vampire or what. Just so you know, I believe that you may be a new breed of vampire. I believe that you are a full vampire with all the rewards that come with becoming one, plus a new and unique ability that makes you, well, I don't know how to put this any other way but that you are special, a good special.

"The next time you have one of these feelings, I want you to immediately tell anyone of the core cadre. Try to remember what you were doing at the time, where you were, and who was nearby.

"To try to get you to understand the importance of this particular trait, I have to recall some experiences from my past. Like many of the vampires here at the Manor, I have, at one time or another, been faced with a bad vampire. The people you have met at Newmark who are vampires have lived because they won the day. There are others that we have lost to a bad vampire that got the upper hand with them. None of us were aware that the person challenging us, for whatever reason, was a vampire. Those of us that are still alive were lucky. It was a fight that could have gone either way.

"Luck doesn't always land in our favor. That is evident in the ones who died at the hands of a vampire that got the jump on them. An unusual sensation that would alert us that the goof standing in front of us is a vampire would give us the edge needed to win. A word of caution. Even if you know the person you are in front of is a vampire, it doesn't mean that it's throw-down-time. Especially if that vampire is superior to you in strength and agility. Discretion is the rule. Back out of the situation if you can, alert whoever is near that is part of our team.

"Let the elders handle the situation. You are a feisty person. Naturally aggressive beyond your capabilities. Don't get upset at this. Open your eyes. Do you think feisty would get you a win in combat with anyone in this gym? We are all well-trained, and in the best shape anyone could be in, but we could lose a fight for our life at any time. None of us want to die. None of us want you to die. I will say that again in hopes that you hear and understand it to the depths of your heart. None of us here want you to die. Think about this carefully.

"You are only a few weeks old, that's all, only a few weeks. Almost everyone around you has been a vampire longer than you have been alive since your natural birth. I am not demeaning you in any way. You are already so much further in your development as a vampire that if someone didn't know your history, they would think that you have been what you are for quite a few years. I can't put a specific number on it, but I would guess that were a vampire to meet you for the first time now, they would think you are more than a recently converted. No, not an ancient and not even one that has settled in at around forty or sixty years as a vampire, but they would think of believing that you have been a vampire for some time now. You are an elder before your time.

"Thanks for talking with me about this item. I'm going to leave you to watch the others spar, and they would be glad to start you with some of the basic moves for the hand-to-hand combat training. I have to be elsewhere right now but hope to see you at dinner."

Pete walked away, leaving me with my thoughts. I went back over what had been discussed, and I was getting a real happy feeling from it. The crux of my glee was the probability that I wasn't a half-breed. Maybe I was a full vampire just like all the others, well, with the one exception that I may have an ability that no other vampire had. Today, right now, I felt like I fit in. The idea gave me a warm feeling as I walked over to the mat area where everyone was going through full-body contact bouts with one another.

I squatted at the edge of the mats, and instead of concentration on the action in front of me, an action that I could learn a lot by watching, my thoughts went off to a happy place. It was a private place in my head that had its fill of good and bad times. Now, a good month into my new life, my new persona, I was starting to appreciate what I had become, and the topper was the significant number of people that I could call my best friends that surrounded my life now.

Then I almost jumped out of my skin when this screaming banshee of a klaxon horn drowned out all other sounds and shattered my thoughts. I hardly had a chance to blink when the four girls who had been tossing each other a moment ago were now racing to gather up their gear and were running out the door.

Zope called out to me, "Shake a leg, Paulie. Head right to your car. We will all change at the airfield."

No one had to tell me anything. I knew the raid was on.

My bonus was that now I had a car full of stinky, sweaty gym rats sitting on my brand new leather seats. *The sacrifices I make for this company.*

Zope was riding shotgun and was sitting on the front edge of her seat. She wanted to be the first one there. Well, not really, but she was in high anxiety, and this was not the time to tell her to sit back and buckle up.

As I neared the ferry terminal, I pulled into the lineup of vehicles waiting for the next ferry.

"Go around, go around," Zope was practically yelling.

I was almost at a stop when I turned to look at her. Go around, now how was I going to pull that off?

"Go, go, go" was what she was saying rather loudly. "Paulie, just pull out of this line and head to the front of the line where the police car was sitting off to the side of the ramp. Come on, come on, step on it."

She must know what she was doing because there weren't any objections from anyone in the back seats. In fact, I got the feeling that they were waiting for me to follow Zope's lead.

What's a girl to do? So, I pulled out and headed toward the loading gate where a local policeman stood. As I pulled around up in front of him, I saw that he was giving me the stink eye.

"Jack, it's me, Zope," she yelled out the window. "We are on an emergency."

"Hello, Ms. Zope," he said as he reached for the gate release.

I pulled through and was then first in line to get onboard.

~~~~

Once we got off the ferry at the Seattle dock, I took off as fast as I thought I could get away with. Weaving in and out of traffic and pressing my luck on the traffic lights, I got to the hangar in record time.

Irene, Nicole, and Zope headed directly to their assigned helicopter. Both of the choppers were already fired up, with the main rotors slowly revolving. I suddenly realized that we didn't have Pete with us. Shit, I must have driven off without him. That is not good, not good at all. He was one of the raiding team leaders, with Zope being the other one.
~~~~

There was the screech of tires, and I turned to see Pete leaping out of Ms. Karan's Audi R8 Spider. Ms. Karan was right behind him, leaving her car right there. They went to separate helicopters and dove in, and both craft throttled up and lifted just off the ground and headed down the taxiway toward the end of the field.

Then they were up and out of sight.

Riley, one of the Manor guards, was walking over with Todd—Larisa's Todd.

Todd said, "Let's get into the flight shack so we can listen to the radio chatter."

I used to listen to the chatter from the attack Apaches while they were on a mission in Afghanistan.

There were still quite a few pilots and ground crews left. They had done their job in making sure everything was prepared, and it appeared that they had done a crackerjack job of it. A few of them followed the four of us—Todd, Riley, Darja, and myself—into the shack. Then I noticed that one of the guards that normally worked at this building was standing outside the shack door. Full body armor, Kevlar helmet, and all the combat webbing you could imagine. Sidearm, but what got my attention was the AR he had. Not a .223 but 7.62x51… for knockdown power.

"Why are you here, Riley?" I asked. "Aren't you usually at the Manor?"

"While the twins are off on this excursion, I have been assigned to watch over you and Ms. Darja. We are not expecting that the rogues would risk attacking this building. Too much firepower and a whole lot of highly trained personnel."

I took Darja with me to my private studio apartment behind the wall of my office in the shack. We both showered and changed into clothes she had brought and me into things that were already in the drawers of the little unit's closet. Jeans, black Converse high tops, a rock band T-shirt with Pink's picture, and a brown leather flight jacket with real sheepskin fur on the inside.

Once we were all clean-looking, we went back to the main room of the shack to listen to the chatter coming from the two choppers. There were also several TV screens on the walls that had feeds from body cameras. The body cam signals bounced in and out because of poor signal strength. The cameras mounted on the helicopters though, gave a strong, steady streaming view.

The Bell, piloted by Mel, was just skimming the treetops toward the building where the suspected rogue nest was supposed to be. He was coming in from the south.

Charlie, the Dauphine pilot, was flying in from the north end of the Port Orchard airfield. He had further to go before setting down because the destination building was located on the south end of the airstrip.

We saw Zope, Irene, and two others from our security team hit the ground. They were running to get as close to the object building before anyone knew they were there.

A moment later, the Dauphine, piloted by Charlie, touched down just on the north rear corner of the building. Neither helicopter could see the other as they were at opposite ends of the building. This did, however, leave no blind spots that anyone could use to leave the building unseen.

There were three vehicles, two SUVs and an Audi Sedan outside the open, overhead doors that faced the runway. Those vehicles and that entrance to the building were the responsibility of Zope and Irene's group.

There were windows and another overhead door that was

also open, on the backside of the building under the control of Pete and Nicole and their team of four other security personnel.

Two of the RIBs (Rogues in Black) came out the back doorway. They were both armed with double-barrel shotguns whose barrels couldn't have been more than twelve inches long.

Back in the flight shack, there were several noticeable gasps from some of the gang that was watching the live feed. Someone said, "Shit, I hate shotguns."

Almost immediately, both the RIBs went down. I was pretty sure I saw a knife sticking out of the eye socket of one and out the neck of the other. They were certainly out of commission.

Nicole and Pete were now right to either side of the doorway, each with two of the members of the security team. The sound was intermittent and scratchy, so I couldn't be sure of what was being said. The important thing was that they were safe.

The door where Zope and Irene and their team were approaching was large. Wide enough to allow most single-winged aircraft to enter. That area also seemed more important because of the presence of three vehicles. Their only cover was going to be behind the vehicles out front.

"Everyone, this is Amelia. Eddie and I are just leaving the airfield lunch hut and will be driving down the runway taxi strip and should be there in one minute. For your information, the Audi Sedan is in Iskenderian's name, and the two SUVs are titled in the name of some obscure corporation that seems to be a wholly-owned subsidiary of Stern Enterprises."

Suddenly, several RIBs appeared in the hangar door and were firing at the six members of the south team who were seeking cover behind the vehicles.

Zope broke in, "Pete, Nicole, can you get in the back door and start clearing the nest out? Right at the moment, we are pinned down and can't give you any support. We won't be firing into the building if you are coming in behind them."

"We are entering now," Pete responded.

The sounds of a lot more gunfire broke out. A lot of the fire was going out the hangar door and was obviously directed at the team out there.

"Pete…*Pete…*" was all we heard for a moment.

I grabbed the mic and keyed it for transmission. "Pete, who was calling your name?" I asked.

"That was Zope's voice," he said.

"She's down, she's down." It was Irene.

"Where is she?" came the frantic call from Amelia.

"She is behind the front of the vehicle that is parked the farthest north. Close to you," Irene called out. "I'll try to get over to her, but there is a lot of heat coming out of the hangar door."

Suddenly, a Honda sedan came tearing down the taxiway and slewed to a stop on the far side of the first SUV. It was still rocking from side to side when the passenger side door flew open, and Amelia dove out right where Zope was lying face down behind the front tire of the RIB's SUV.

I was standing. Something had happened to me at the same moment that Irene reported that Zope was down. I had felt a sharp, searing pain go through my chest. My hand had come up and was pressed to the upper right side of my body. I had to sit down for a moment. I did, and the feeling went away after a minute.

"She's awake," Amelia called out. "Eddie, we have to get her up and away from the action."

While that was taking place, half a dozen RIBs came out the hangar door. Irene and the four other troopers on her squad were up and firing. Believe me, the RIBs would rue the day that they had to go up against this highly trained squad. Three of them fell on their backs as they were shot by Irene's group. Another two fell forward as they were shot from the team that was now inside the building and behind them.

"I have two that I captured inside. And this one you have here makes three," Pete related.

Amelia was on the communications channel. "Charlie, get airborne and over here by the hangar door. We have, we have, *choke*. Zope is down. You have to get her back right now."

My hand hurt, and I looked down at it. Darja was holding it and squeezing the bejesus out of it.

Charlie brought the Dauphine around as close as possible to where Zope was lying.

Luckily, this was the rainy season for this area. The moisture cut way down on the dirt, dust, and sand that the helicopter rotor would churn up.

Amelia and Irene got Zope into the helicopter and strapped her into the stretcher. Three of the security team jumped in, and Charlie lifted off with the turbine screaming for every ounce of power it could get out.

Somehow, the hospital unit on the upper floors of the building the circus' hangar was attached to knew that there were wounded inbound. A full-on surgical team was exiting the elevator door that let out into the hangar to wait for the helicopter's arrival.

I wasn't listening or watching the action in Port Orchard. Darja and I were headed, along with the medical team and their equipment, toward the hangar's open door.

The flight time back was not very long.

Then I heard it. The rotors were chewing their way through the atmosphere at full tilt. Charlie brought the ship in directly over the top of our building, spun around, and dropped right in front of the open hangar bay.

No one waited for the rotors to stop or even slow. Everyone, including me, was running right out to the cargo door. Darja got there first and yanked it open. Amelia was up, lying on the stretcher and holding Zope tightly. I could see that she was seriously distraught over this incident.

I had spent quite a few years on the front of a combat zone. It was a helicopter unit too. I had seen it hundreds of times. Helicopters returning to base flat out, coming in hot, we would call it. That was when they had injured aboard. Occasionally, it was the pilot that had been injured, and he or she was the only one on board that knew how to fly the machine. Those were the worst because so many of them were hurt so badly that they couldn't set down once they reached the airfield.

I had learned in my first tour overseas that you just don't make close friends. Every time you did, they went out and got killed the next day. The injured pilots 'coming in hot' had about a 50/50 chance of landing safely and living. There was a pilot that had taken a liking to me and had taken me up in his Apache while I checked a new piece of equipment I had just installed. He was the first one that had allowed me to take the controls, something that saved my life and the life of another pilot later on. One real bad day, he had received ground fire and was wounded. He was trying to make it back and probably passed out just as he came in over the field border. Right into a parked fuel truck. I was standing in the hangar doorway and saw it all. I was pretty bad off for about a week.

It was then that I decided that I was committed to this life and this work and dove back in with a vengeance.

The medical team was unwinding Amelia from Zope and getting her out and onto the hospital gurney. They put on one of those tubes that fed oxygen to the patient's nostrils and plugged in a bottle of… blood?

I took another look. That is right, they were using a glass pint bottle of whole blood. I had never seen blood in a glass bottle in my life, and I had seen a lot of blood bags hooked up to wounded warriors. Never a glass bottle. I put that away for another time.

The medics tried to get Amelia away, but they were fooling with a woman possessed. Darja and I could see that she was not going to be separated.

Irene came up to me and said, "She lost a lot of blood. I think the bullet or bullets shattered her right scapula."

I gave her a puzzled look.

"That is your right-wing," she said.

"Why is Amelia so upset?" I asked.

"Amelia and Zope are very close, very special friends."

"Are they like related?"

"Leave it," Irene snapped. "If you want more, you will have to ask them."

Everyone was walking back inside the hangar except Charlie and a couple of the ground crew. They were cleaning the inside of the helicopter and replacing the used medical supplies. They weren't changing the configuration back to a passenger transport with the cushy seats yet.

Irene's comments had stung me, and I didn't want to talk to anyone right then.

I also didn't want to go back inside yet. I started walking

without any particular destination in mind. I had forgotten that my walk pace now that I was a vampire was about the same speed as a Norm at a fast jog. Anyway, I realized that I had walked almost to the north end of the field. More than a mile from the Newmark flying circus. I was also getting chilled. Lucky me, I had the nice fur-lined leather aviator's jacket. I zipped up and turned to head back when I heard a vehicle behind me.

It was an aircraft service tug that backs the large planes in and out of their slots or tows them around the airfield. I turned and had a split second to jump out of the way. That dick had almost run right over the top of me. Mr. Dick smashed the brake pedal down so hard that the wheels locked up, and that is almost impossible as the brakes are not very large and the thing weighs a ton. Guess he was going to apologize… or not. He had gotten off and was headed toward me with a very angry face on. And he had a Taser unit in his hand. WTF was going on?

I wasn't going to even think of engaging him in conversation. Obviously, he had some other agenda on his mind. I did not have time for this shit, and I started backing away. He was closing the distance, and when he was about twenty-five feet away, he fired the Taser barbs at me. After having to jump out of the way, my body had shifted gears. As he fired the Taser, I could see the electrode barbs headed my way in slow motion. As they arrived at where I stood, I batted one of the barbs aside. The other one buried itself in my thigh. No shock, though. It takes two to Tango. Just one makes it a dud. He realized what I had been able to do, and he hauled back and threw the Taser gun at me. I side-stepped, and it flew past. Now he was starting to run at me. Who was this dildo? What was his problem?

And I noticed that there was an alarm bell going off in my head.

He was a vampire. He was an un-nice vampire. He was one of the bad people. Holy shit, I had to get the hell outta there, so I turned to the right and ran. Ran at top vampire speed. I was headed to the buildings that were on the west side of the airstrip.

I was almost to the nearest hangar when I took a moment to glance over my shoulder to see how far back he was. A good forty feet now. Well, I guessed that little miss newbie, miss hybrid was in pretty good shape after all. I also saw that he was pulling at the butt of a pistol sticking out of his belt top. That in itself made the forty feet look like it was now only ten feet. I didn't have time to mull things over. I turned left and headed south toward my hangar, which was probably close to two miles away. What the fuck had I been thinking to go this far off the reservation? I concentrated on picking them up and putting them down, 1, 2; 1, 2; 1, 2. I was pretty sure I was increasing the distance between us but didn't bother to stop for a lookie-see. That guy wanted me dead; I was sure of it.

I padded the pocket of my jacket and whoo, whoo! I did have my cell phone with me. Before you could say Candy Crush, I had it out and was speed-dialing the one number that I knew would respond right away.

"Paulie, what do you need?" It was Larisa. Larisa, in her security cellar; Larisa who had the means to alert and engage the entire Newmark Security forces.

"I'm a mile or more north of the hangar on the taxi strip. I am being chased by a rogue. We are both on foot, and he has pulled out a gun. I might be fifty feet in front of him and juking back and forth just in case he pulls the trigger. I can't stop since

I think he already knows that I'm not armed."

Larisa said, "The team is on the way. Don't talk; just run as fast as you can until we get there."

I stood tall with my head back, and I ran for my life.

My Converse sneakers were a godsend. If I had on boots or, worse, high heels, I would not have a chance.

I thought I saw something pulling out of the circus hangar. It was a motorcycle, and it turned toward me, and the front wheel came up off the ground about a foot or so. No helmet, so I could see the rider's hair. Sky Blue. It was Irene on her R1200.

I turned my head to see how close he was. I still had a good forty yards on him. Still, not the time to do anything silly, so I just kept on truckin'.

I saw that Irene was closing fast and had started slowing. She pulled just past me and turned around, and came back up beside me.

"Jump on," she screamed, and I grabbed her arm and swung myself onto the little pillion seat behind her. As soon as she felt my arms around her waist, she took off for the hangar.

I looked toward the hangar and saw several additional vehicles pulling out onto the taxiway, heading for where we were at an accelerated pace. Two of the vehicles roared past, and the third slowed and swung around in front of us. Irene slowed and pulled up beside the van. It was one of the utility vans that we used mostly for deliveries. This time, however, the back was filled with armed personnel.

Irene shouted for me to get off and into the van. So that was what I did. As soon as I was in, she took off toward the last place anyone had seen my jerky new buddy. I didn't see him anywhere, and the two other vans were crisscrossing and going around to the other side of all the buildings I had just run past.

Irene was also going over all the ground between where I had gotten off her motorcycle and all the way to the north end of the airfield. Then the van I was in started out back to our home hangar.

As soon as I got out of the van, inside the hangar, Charlie came running up.

"Paulie, Larisa called and said you have to come down to security immediately."

When the Evil Queen calls you to go.

~~~~

When I got to the security section, I saw that Larisa's office was crowded.

Larisa, Todd, Eddie, Mr. Newmark, and Pete. I suddenly had an image flash into my mind: I pictured Larisa's condo set up to be a mirror of her office where she sits behind a big desk, and her boyfriend has to take a seat opposite her.

I shook my head to clear the image.

I hadn't even known that Pete had gotten back.

There wasn't a smiley face in the crowd.

"Take a seat, would you, please," said Mr. Newmark.

Oh! Shit. I must be in some BIG trouble.

"Paulie," Eddie started, "we had wanted to sit down with everyone that was on the raid this morning to wring it out to see what could have been done better. However, your little stunt will now absorb a lot of time and resources. Your excursion outside has caused us to have new concerns. We now are certain that this group has a base of operations somewhere at this airfield. The hornet's nest from the Port Orchard airport has been cleaned out. We obtained two prisoners that we will be
~~~~

chatting it up with and a lot of documentation to sort through. The biggest thing, though, was that Zope was brought down during the action. She is now upstairs. We are all praying that she holds on long enough for the doctors to rebuild the damage. It will be touch and go for several days. Now we come to your reckless excursion. Paulie, I want you to be looking into my eyes. NOW!"

Shit! He was really pissed at me. I think that everyone was pissed… at me. I froze in my chair and looked straight at him.

"You disobeyed a direct order from none other than the boss and owner of this organization, Mr. Spartak Newmark. There is no higher authority at this company. I was made completely aware of that order. I, Eddie Vangh, am the one officially in charge of your personal security and the personal security of everyone that works for this company. Your recklessness falls on my shoulders. You have one of the two best personal bodyguards on the face of this planet. You live in a luxurious apartment that is located at a site that is triply enveloped with security. You were able to purchase an extremely fine vehicle. You were put in charge of the main aviation hub for Newmark Industries, a well-known and prominent company with holdings worldwide. Your little stroll 'alone' in a place that you have never walked before, WITHOUT your assigned bodyguard, has put EVERYTHING at extreme risk. EVERYTHING means, in case you have gone stupid on us, every person, and all the business holdings of this company. Effective immediately, your security clearances have been suspended. You will turn over the keys, including the spares, to your car, and it is to remain here, locked up. Todd will drive you back to the Manor, where you are to remain on the grounds for the time being. Irene will be going with you and staying with you, but there will not be any rotation exchange with Nicole. We will be having a general staff meeting about the middle of next week to decide your fate."

I couldn't move. My whole life was falling down in shambles. I couldn't move at all. I was frozen in place.

I saw Todd walk out and head toward the elevator.

"Why are you sitting here? Was there something I said that wasn't clear?" Eddie said in a large commanding voice.

"Get out of that chair and go catch up with Todd." That was from Larisa.

~ ~ ~ ~

I ran out of Larisa's office and was able to catch up with Todd at the elevator he was holding for me. I thought that I would crumble and fall into a little pity ball on the floor at any moment.

We rode up in complete silence. When we got off in the hangar, there was a van waiting, and Irene was in the passenger seat, and the back door was open, waiting for me, I assumed. I got in and buckled up. All my clothes and personal things were piled in the back.

Todd got in, started the van, and we drove out.

"I'm so sorry—"

"SHUT THE FUCK UP, YOU IGNORANT LITTLE SHIT FOR BRAINS! KEEP YOUR FUCKING MOUTH CLOSED!" Irene vented.

~ ~ ~ ~

When we arrived at the Manor garages, Todd got out right away and headed into the main house. Irene got out and went upstairs. I thought that she would be coming back down to help me carry all my stuff in. I grabbed some items up and headed upstairs.

The door to my apartment was closed and locked. *Where has Irene gone,* I wondered. I tried my key in the door and thank the heavens that my key was still good. I walked in and headed to my bedroom to drop what I was carrying on my bed. I went back through the living room to go for another load when I noticed that the spare bedroom door was ajar and the light was on inside.

I went over and stuck my head in. "Irene…"

CRASH! A half-full wine glass crashed into my forehead and shattered.

"The ONLY time you can knock on my door is when you are leaving the apartment because I have to get up and follow you around. I have had my clearance level put on limited accesses, and they took my bike keys away. I am not allowed to go anywhere unless I am with you. I am not to leave your side when you are outside of this apartment. You are NOT one of the people that I want anything to do with right now. There are a few places you can go without me. Going down to get the rest of your belongings out of the van in the portico below, the kitchen in the main house, and the gym. If you ever go outside of those locations without me, you will wish that you were dead. My sister and I have been vampires for longer than twice of your lifetimes. We have spent our entire lives working, training, and learning the job we perform. In a moment of extreme stupidity, you have done what no other person has ever been able to do, and that is to have my status and job put into question. Now go make busy getting your crap up and put away. I do not want to come out of this room and have to move or stumble over something of yours."

I was almost unable to move. I felt numb from head to toe. My face and probably my whole body was beet red with embarrassment.

It took me several minutes before I could move at all. Eventually, I regained awareness of my surroundings, and I eased back out of her doorway and out the front door of the apartment. I didn't close the front door because that would call for me touching something that would cause Irene or anyone getting upset… more upset with me.

Who could I be angry with? Not the most difficult question; it was me. I understood that my airstrip walk could have resulted in untold complications for the firm and probably the lives of some of my friends. That error in judgment coupled with everyone's concern for Zope's condition had everyone on a razor's edge emotional ride.

I stood there for easily half an hour. To move at all was a struggle. One foot in front of the other, step, step, step.

All of my things were stuffed into large plastic garbage bags. I thought that whoever packed my things up might have cut holes in all the clothes or poured some foul-smelling goo on everything. I didn't want to look there in the portico. I didn't want to face anyone right at the moment. It took four trips to lug all the bags up to my room. Not just to my apartment but all the way into my bedroom.

As soon as I had everything up, I closed myself into my bedroom and laid down. I don't know how long I laid there, but it must have been quite a while. It was one of those heavily overcast nights with stray lights bouncing around. I got up because I really had to pee, and on the way back from the toilet, I looked at the window to make sure it wasn't covered with anything. Just a really dark night.

Day, night didn't make any difference to me right now. I pulled the shades down and the drapes across my bedroom windows.

Time passed. I must have nodded off and was not sure of the time, or what day it was. I had taken my watch off and the clock radio toward the wall. I wasn't interested at the time. I was no longer on any schedule. I no longer had a schedule, any schedule at all. I wasn't on any work roster, anywhere.

The last time I wasn't on any schedule had been after I mustered out of the army and was waiting to hear back from the places I applied to. That had only lasted two days before the Boeing Museum hired me.

Now my life was so different. Now I wasn't even allowed out to look for a job, not that I had any idea of where I could look. I was not the same person that I was two months ago. I didn't have any idea that someone of my species could look for work.

I rooted around and located my laptop. I didn't know if it would work since it was given to me by Newmark, and maybe they had turned off the ability to boot up, let alone have any Internet access. I opened the lid and hit the on-off button. Twenty seconds or so went by, and the homepage showed up, but it wanted a password to enter the local Wi-Fi network. I typed in my password and got the big red ACCESS DENIED.

I went back and into the settings. Looking for Wi-Fi connections. There were several, but I knew they were Newmark ports and that my password would not work with any of them. I scrolled down and then saw 'Log-in as a Guest.' I clicked on that one and was rewarded with my desktop screen again. I tried Google, and that came up right away. I tried several searches for sites I already knew should be available, and they all were. No restrictions on public Internet access.

I typed in 'Vampire Help Wanted.' Nothing came up. I guess, vampires aren't in big demand, that or businesses that were willing or wanted to hire vampires. That or there was a special secret site maybe somewhere on the dark web. A place for which I had no idea how to get there.

My mind was in a fog. I couldn't think of anything I wanted to look up, so I just closed the lid and set it on the shelf over my little desk to charge up.

The only thing I had learned from the computer was that it was 9.45, Tuesday morning. I hadn't eaten a thing for three days or more. I noticed when I stood up. I felt a little unsteady and had a little dizzy spell.

When I was overseas, we took these dizzy spells as a warning that we were low on sodium and dehydrated. I couldn't remember when I even had a drink of water.

I sat back on my bed, crossed my legs under me, and thought about my plight. That's right, my plight. Not anyone else's worry. I said to myself, "Get your ass up and start reintegrating with society by going over to the kitchen and getting some nourishment."

And that is what I did. I didn't see or pass anyone on my way to the kitchen. When I let myself in, only the kitchen staff and Ms. K. were there.

No one seemed to acknowledge my presence for at least ten to fifteen minutes. I just stood there not knowing what I should do when Ms. K spoke up.

"Ms. Zahn, there is a table set for two that is in the far corner of the food prep room. That is for you and Ms. Irene should she wish to dine with you."

She pointed, and it was evident that she had nothing further to say.

I went into the kitchen and saw a small plain wood table with stiff-backed wooden chairs. Silverware was wrapped in a napkin and stuck in a water glass, salt and pepper shakers, and a bowl of assorted sweeteners in paper pouches. That was all, not even a tablecloth.

I sat down and decided that I was sorry for what I did but that I am a proud person and not ashamed of how I had been conducting myself. So, I held my head up while I figured out how I would get food to the table.

Guess it was self-serve because not one person working the kitchen acknowledged my presence. So, I got up and found a plate, and went around to the different items on the stove. There was pasta, and a good dose of carbs might be what the doctor ordered. The sauce had choices. Plain, with meatballs, and with sausage. Kielbasa... perfect. There were vegetables and fresh salad. Salad with Italian dressing. A couple of slices of fresh bread and I went back and sat down. Still, I must have become a ghost as no one seemed to notice me.

No one except Lisbeth. She brought me a whole freshly opened bottle of Cabernet from Nickle and Nickle winery in Napa.

"Keep your head up, ma'am. I know you don't believe it now, but everyone here is pulling for you to get fully reinstated. We all really love you and don't want you making the mistake of leaving. I made mistakes myself. One of them had caused the Newmarks a lot of grief and problems. They never stopped supporting me. This is my forever home, and I am so thankful for it. Just don't give up because as the little girl sings, 'The sun'll come out tomorrow...' It will all be behind you soon."

She was a slight girl, but when she bent over and gave me a hug, it was the hug of my life. Many may think that she was just a simple farm girl because of her garden and all, but this woman was overflowing with warmth and love.

That started the waterfall that I had been holding in since Saturday, three days ago.

It was self-pity, and that wasn't me, but I couldn't stop. A few minutes must have passed before I got enough control to look up. My plates and the wine were gone. In their place were a couple of paper bags.

"I've packed your dinner and some dessert so that you can take everything back to your room. I know you want to be alone for a while. I was the same way after my problem was known to everyone. If you want any more food, call me on the number to my cottage, and I will see that it is prepared and sent over to your apartment."

The greatest love and compassion always seem to come from the lowest person on the totem pole.

That is how things went for the next few days. I would only go to the kitchen when I knew that the fewest people would be there. I even took to eating between ten p.m. and six a.m., the hours that Lisbeth was the head cook. We had some time to get to know each other better. She had quite a story.

22 DECEMBER 2016 – 0230 HOURS

I walked into the kitchen, and Lisbeth was there just like always, the wee hours. I went and sat at the regular table since no one else was around. Lisbeth brought two cups of coffee. We had been having our little middle-of-the-night chats. Tonight was a little different. I was usually the one talking, but this time Lisbeth looked like she had something on her mind, so I didn't say a word. I let her start on her own.

"I had met this guy, Tommy Doyle, and I thought I was in love with him. No, that isn't true… I was in love with him. I talked with Ms. Karan, and she gave me the family's blessing and supported my desire to marry him. I did, and I moved into his apartment in Winslow. Then he changed. He started coming home late and was pushing me around. Chuck or Riley had noticed my change of attitude and that I had bruises on my arms. When I showed up with a black eye, they moved me back, and Ms. Karan arranged for the attorney to rid me of the shackles that bound me to him. About that time, someone had broken into a special vault that is in the basement of this Manor and stolen some things that were very valuable to the Newmarks. That's when we all met Eddie Vangh for the first time. He is a real detective, and he was hired to solve the mystery and recover the stolen items. He was real good. I found out later that Tommy was involved. He had used our relationship to gain access to the entire Manor.

"Because Eddie was closing in on the mastermind behind

the robbery, someone must have gotten a little nervous, so they murdered Tommy. The way he met his end was horrible. Tommy and I were done for good, but he had been my first love, and I would never have wished something like that to happen to anyone.

"A lot of good came from the entire mess anyway. Eddie and Amelia met and became a couple, Larisa met Todd, and they are now a solid couple. The best thing, though, was that Maxmillian Stern, who had been dating Ms. Karan, was found out for what he really is, and that ended any further involvement with the two of them." She looked at me kindly.

"I'm trying to point out that though I brought a threat into this household, everyone stood by me and supported me, and welcomed me back into the fold. I want you to remember my story and know the lesson from it. The lesson that should show you that you are still living here because this family, everyone, has faith in you and know that this will all work out eventually, and before you know it, it will be back to how it was just a week ago."

"Thanks, Lisbeth. That will go a long way to lift my head out of my butt. It's time for me to get a grip on my future."

"That's the spirit, ma'am. There is another subject I would like to talk about."

"Sure, whatever you want to talk about. I will do my best to give you a sensible response."

"Please don't be upset with us for talking about you behind your back, but I have had some discussions with Charlie and Chuck. We three are damphires. You haven't been around us very long, and I'm sure that you haven't been told very much about our 'special' abilities."

"I talked with someone at the party a week and a half ago,

one of the guards. He told me that you have a green thumb and can work magic with growing plants. He said that he, I think that is who he identified, has like a sixth sense about the intentions of people near him. There were other abilities, but I was in awe of everything and everyone and missed keeping close attention to everything said. Is there something more?"

"The types of special talents are vast. I suppose that there is a list of known damphires and each of that individual's talents. Some of us have more than one talent. There are a very few vampires that converted from a damphire that retained some or all of their damphire talent. They are extremely rare, though. An example is Darja Strykula. She is pure Romani, a gypsy. Before she converted, she had the uncanny ability to see into the souls of inanimate mechanical and electronic devices. That passed through during her conversion, and that is part of the reason that she became head of the European Research and Development facility for Newmark Industries."

"Why isn't she still there?"

"During the investigation of the purloined blood products, Eddie found some documents indicating that there was a faction that was going to attempt a takeover of the R&D unit in Europe. She had come over to meet and discuss the options with Mr. Newmark and Ms. Karan. The first evening she was here, she was kidnapped by a group under the control and direction of Maxmillian Stern. I'm sorry. I have gotten off the reason I wanted to talk to you. Some reports have filtered back to the three of us. It was noted that when Zope got shot, you, who were miles away, complained of a sharp pain in your right shoulder, the same place Zope was shot. Tapes of the entire incident have been reviewed over and over, and it is noted that when you reacted to the pain, it was exactly the same moment that Zope got shot. I believe that someone is going to sit down with you and talk it through."

"Is this like a curse or something?"

"No! No! No. The addition of a special talent of any type to a vampire increases their value tenfold. Don't be ashamed. Believe me that it is a blessing."

Before I could comment, Eddie walked into the kitchen.

"Paulie, we need to go to the security building. I already alerted Irene, and she will be waiting in your car."

And he headed out the back door of the kitchen.

Lisbeth told me to go ahead that she would clean up our break fast dishes.

~ ~ ~ ~

When I arrived at the BMW, I saw that it was pretty full. Darja, Eddie, and Nicole were in the back seat, and Irene was upfront in the passenger seat. The only door that was still open was the driver's door. I didn't see anyone else in the garage area, so I believe that they intended for me to drive.

The euphoric feeling I got just being surrounded by the people I wanted so badly to be accepted by was pretty great. I got a little giddy-up in my step and a lump in my throat.

I got in and said the words, "Everyone, please buckle up. It is for your safety as well as the law."

Darja was the only one to comment, "Ouch! We may have created an iron maiden here. The next thing she will do is have us stand at attention while she inspects our fingernails to see if they are clean."

I sensed the twins trying to not smile.

I would have all of them making me the brunt of some joke

rather than giving me the cold shoulder.

When I stopped at the guard shack at the security/hangar building, I was given a badge with a big red 'V' on it.

That hurt. 'V' for 'Visitor.' I couldn't look at anyone in the car right then. No place to hide.

I parked, and everyone got out and headed toward the elevator door. When the doors opened, they all got in and advisably arranged themselves to have obvious space for another passenger.

I didn't think that I had any options, so I got in, and off we went down into the torture chamber in the basement.

When I walked into the general security area, I saw that things had been moved around in the central area. There was a curtain dividing the surveillance monitor desks and an area that held a conference table surrounded by a dozen chairs. People were already occupying some seats. It started with their importance to the company and me; Spartak Newmark, Karan Newmark, Todd, Larisa, Riley, Pete, and the five of us. Everyone sat but me.

I didn't know if I should be sitting in a chair for the accused or, looking around, if I would be put in a pillory. I didn't see a brazier with pokers warming from red to white-hot. Walls had pictures but no implements of torture hanging up.

"Take a seat anywhere you like," Mr. Newmark said to me. "In fact, I would like it if you came around and took the seat to my left."

~~~~

"Paulette, this is a formal inquisition into the events of last Saturday. You are not a defendant in this. You are here because
~~~~

you were in the flight shack during the entire ground encounter at the field in Port Orchard. I am going to open a screen that will have every camera that was turned on at the fight location, showing in parallel time along with all the radio chatter and comments from those in the flight shack at the time."

"What are we looking for?" I asked.

"Every one of us that are the core of this unit take weight training to keep our bodies healthy and fit, and everyone partakes of the hand to hand combat, firearms, and knife training.

"The teams that went to that arena were the best of the people that we have. The actual action appears to have surprised the rogues. Still, our top lieutenant sustained a life-threatening wound. It shouldn't have happened. Someone missed their assignment. It is the purpose of this panel to figure out who missed their cue causing this injury."

The room darkened, and the screen came alive. It commenced with the helicopters just arriving at the scene. Most of the cameras were showing scenes of everyone while they were still airborne. Only the cameras on the helios had any worthwhile footage, and I couldn't spot anything out of kilter.

Both copters landed and disgorged the fighting teams. That's when someone in the room would raise their hand to stop the motion and go back several minutes in time. We got to match everyone's progress in the arena of action.

I hadn't seen the full coverage I saw now. After the first run-through, the recording was reset, and it started again. No one was asking to do short re-winds of a portion. They were letting it run.

We all heard someone say, "*Oh shit!*" and that was all for several seconds. Then Zope appeared to have tripped and fallen right by the right front tire of one of the rogue's vehicles. There was another audible '*gasp*' heard just as she went down.

Sparky stopped the tapes and rewound them back about thirty seconds worth of action.

"I want to identify who said '*Oh shit!*' and who let out the '*gasp*.'"

Both of those comments or exclamations were not from anyone at the scene of the action. They were from someone present in the flight shack.

Sparky turned off all voice and visual tapes from the battle site. He started the tape of any sounds from the floor of the flight shack. When we heard the first comment, the tape was stopped.

Mr. Newmark looked around the room. "Anyone know who that was?"

Todd spoke up, "It was Darja, I think. I was standing right next to her during the start of the action."

"Darja, do you remember saying that?" Mr. Newmark asked.

"I remember," she responded. "There was something that I saw that felt out of place."

"What was that?" Mr. Newmark asked.

"Back up just the tapes that show the field of action that started from the Bell," Darja said.

The tapes were rewound to the moment everyone exited the Bell helicopter. Sparky set all of them in slow motion.

"There, hold the scene right there."

The tapes stopped.

"Just ease it forward, frame by frame for a minute," Darja said.

"That's it, just a few frames more and… STOP."

"Look, see that guy behind Zope? He was supposed to be providing covering fire while Zope advanced. Instead, he is sitting behind the rear tire of the RIBs van. He was half looking at her, and he had his rifle laying on the ground next to him. He was in no position to be covering her. He had pulled himself out of the action with inaction. The person from inside the RIBs hangar must have seen that Zope was moving closer, out in the open, or not shielded very well, and that made it possible to get that shot off. I knew she was now at the full risk of getting shot, and that is when I said something. I forgot about it after Zope went down. Almost all of my attention was on Zope. I do want to add one other thing. Finding out who dropped the ball is very important, and I think we know who it is now. There is a secondary and possibly a more important issue before us this morning. If we slowly advance the tape of Zope's movements just before and to the time she was shot. That is the outbreak by Paulette."

I shot her a glare. How dare she try to make me responsible for Zope's getting hit. I was half rising out of my seat when Mr. Newmark took hold, a very strong hold of my arm. He, in a very soft voice that only I could probably hear, said, "Calm down, dear. She isn't accusing you of being involved with the incident. Quite the contrary. Your reaction to Zope's being shot is possibly the most important discovery we have ever uncovered in recent history. Stay calm as everything will become apparent in the next several minutes."

He continued but with his voice at normal room temperature. "As of this minute, everything that has transpired or is still to happen at this meeting is classified as TOP SECRET with a need to know by my authorization and only my authorization. Anyone here have any questions about the Top

Secret label?

"Everyone clear on this?"

Everyone, including me, nodded our heads in agreement.

"Anyone have any thoughts on this?"

Darja raised her hand.

"Yes, Darja."

"Years ago, long before I became a vampire, when I was a gypsy damphire, I met one very ancient damphire. She spent many hours teaching me about what I was and what I could expect to do with my gift. There was one time she told me about another damphire she had known. That person would be somehow connected to another person when that person would sustain some damage. He would feel the same pain in the same spot as his 'connection' did at the same time. She told me that he was what is called an empathetic damphire. Paulie, would you be kind enough to remove your coat and shirt so we can look at the upper right area of your torso?"

I stared at her. Was she crazy? I was never very shy about covering my body but to do a little striptease. Just how far had I fallen from the graces of these people?

Again, in a soft voice that I knew was only audible to me, Mr. Newmark whispered to me, "It's okay. Please show us the area around your right shoulder."

This was weird at the same time that it was awkward. I felt a little silly taking off some of my clothes when no one else was ripping their clothes off at the same time.

As soon as I had pulled my T-shirt over my head, there was a collective intake of air, a gasp, so to speak. What had they seen?

I looked down and saw that the whole upper right quadrant of my torso was an angry red. How I hadn't noticed that earlier was beyond me. I think my brain had closed its eyes on what I saw now.

"It's okay to put your shirt back on, so please do and take a seat," Mr. Newmark said. "Paulie, there is an excellent possibility that you are a vampire empath. I cannot remember ever hearing of one, and I will have Karan research this from the files in our research vault in the Manor's basement. After this meeting, I want you to go upstairs and visit with Zope for a bit. She was asking after you. Then our psychic team will want to interview you. Todd, I am giving you the task of locating Mr. Cooper. I want you to bring him for some questioning. Once you find him, you will have to move very fast to make sure he doesn't get away or kill himself. We need some answers. This meeting is adjourned. I want everyone but Paulie to clear the room."

Once the room was clear, he turned to me and handed me several packages.

One envelope contains all your IDs, keys to your car, and your full access security card. You are off any probation with a few exceptions."

"What are they, sir?"

"You will NOT go outside this building or the Manor without either Irene or Nicole at your side. There will be one exception on Christmas morning, but that is a surprise I have for you later. For clarity, you don't get out of your car to run into a store, even just to pick up one small thing without your bodyguard tagging along. Not even for the blink of an eye.

"The next two packages are handguns. An HK-45 and a Smith and Wesson snub-nosed revolver. You will not go anywhere without at least one of those two pistols on your person. Everyone at the Manor goes to the shooting range for practice. You will start flight school next Tuesday at the Flight Academy across the airstrip from this building. You will use the gym to get better trained in the various forms of hand-to-hand combat, both armed with sharp pointy weapons and unarmed. A minimum of twice a week. That raid only cleaned out one nest of hornets. We know that there is another and it may be located at one of the many buildings at this airport. After that, only with time and careful surveillance will the presence of other locations become apparent. Now, Paulie, you go and see Zope. She has been asking for you."

I had spent eight years in the U.S. Army and had seen action. I had scars to prove it. Beginning with high school, there was never an instance or event that would make me cry. Suddenly, in just the past few months, it seemed that I was getting weepy at the drop of a hat. This was one of those times.

Mr. Newmark had given me my life back. He also had revealed something that could be why the doctors upstairs were having trouble quantifying me as a full vampire. Maybe I wasn't a half-breed after all, but a rare and superior vampire. Just the thought caused my chest to fill out to twice normal size.

As I walked out of the meeting space, the entire security room staff was up and clapping. It was led by Larisa, who was down in front and the first to come up and give me a hug, a hug that I realized I had been starving for in the past few days.

The tears were flowing, and I had to work hard at getting enough control to make it to the elevators without trying to find a place to sit for a moment.

When the elevator door opened again, I saw that I was on the top floor. I didn't even remember selecting any particular floor button when I got in. I think that it was preselected for me. The top floor is the general recovery area, whereas the floor below is where the operating rooms and intensive care units are located. The top floor means that the patient's condition had improved to the stage that required less intensive care and maintenance.

The door was directly across from the nurse's station for the third floor. There were two nurses on duty when I walked up. One, who I sort of remembered, said, "Hello Ms. Zahn, happy to see you are here, NOT as a patient. Zope is down the hall in room 303."

"Thanks. And thanks for remembering me. It is a little better, walking into this ward under my own propulsion. Anything I need to know before visiting her?"

"Nope, she is fully stabilized now and just needs some downtime to rebuild, replace, and mend. She has been asking about you."

I knocked at the open doorway to room 303 and walked in. Amelia was sitting in the leather chair, and it looked like she was reading a book to Zope. Zope herself was sitting up but had an IV from a glass pint blood bottle running into her arm, and her upper right shoulder was bandaged over.

"Hi, Paulie!" they both said at the same time.

"It's good to see you sitting up," I said to Zope. "It's good to see you too, Amelia. I heard that you have been here the whole time."

"I'll be going home tonight," Amelia said. "I would appreciate a ride when you go."

"Sure, not a problem. When are you going to be able to leave?" I asked Zope.

"Doctor Smyth says that if the wound is closed and my blood panel is clean, I will be going back to the Manor tomorrow afternoon."

Amelia spoke up, "We would like to ask you some questions if that would be all right?"

"Ask away."

"Could I please take a look at your right shoulder?" Zope asked.

"I'll show you mine if you show me yours," I said. "Then you will have to answer one of my questions; fair enough?"

They both grinned, and Amelia got up to help Zope undo the bandages covering her shoulder.

This was definitely strange. Everyone was trying to get me undressed. I decided to let it go and went through the strip session like I just did in the basement.

Zope's scar tissue matched the redness that I had in the identical areas of my shoulder.

"What do you remember from that day?" Amelia asked.

"I haven't tried to analyze that moment. At least not yet. It seems that this may be important to the community. It is hard for me to get my head around any of this as I hardly know what a normal vampire would think if this happened to them." 'Normal vampire' that was the apex of stupidity.

Vampires are NOT an everyday occurrence. A month ago, vampires were something you saw only in B movies, according to my outlook on life back then.

"We were all in the flight shack watching and listening to the Port Orchard action as we were calling it. We watched multiple views of the action, some from the primary feed from the two helicopters and several body cameras. I saw you, Zope, leave the helicopter as soon as it touched down. I watched what was coming from the camera in the helicopter and the scene in front of you as you advanced toward the shelter of the van's wheels. I felt a sharp pain that seemed to match the instant you were hit. I was just told that I am possibly an empath. Someone who is connected to another person and feels any pains that the other person incurs. It's like we were both hit by the same projectile and at the same time and in the same place. My flesh wasn't torn open, and I wasn't bleeding, but the pain I felt was severe enough to practically cause me to faint. In an earlier meeting, I was told that I may have some unusual psychic ability to sense when another person is a vampire or have some paranormal abilities. This was something that had to be tested further." I finished my monologue and looked at them. "It's my turn for a question," I said. "I see that you have a pint, glass bottle of blood attached to your IV tube. I can't remember ever seeing one of those. When I was in the service, we all gave blood once every eight to ten weeks. It was always collected in plastic pouches. I also have been to the emergency ORs, and anyone receiving a blood transfusion was from a plastic sack. Never once have I seen actual glass bottles of whole blood."

Amelia had my answer. "When you see a glass bottle of whole blood, you can believe that the blood in that pint is true, pure blood from a vampire. Every one of us has to give a blood donation once every five or six months. You are supposed to have been alerted to your date in the rotation. If no one has told you already, you can expect to get your draw schedule soon."

"I thought we ate capsules for our blood requirements?"

"When our injuries are serious, we can't wait for our bodies to digest and assimilate the contents of the capsules. We need fresh whole blood to replace what we lost. In Zope's case, she had not only lost way too much blood, but the organs that make new blood had gone into shock and weren't making any new red blood cells."

"That makes a lot of sense. That information, along with

some things Lisbeth had told me, fits together. Funny thing, that. I am pretty sure I had heard someone mention Eddie Vangh's involvement with 'The Purloined Pint.'"

Zope and Amelia looked at each other and smiled.

At that moment, Dr. Smyth walked in.

"Good afternoon, everyone. How are you feeling today, Ms. Zope?"

"Good enough to go home. Have you come to discharge me?"

"Not today. Tomorrow though looks like the one to plan your escape for. Right now, I need to draw some blood and take you off the IVs. I'm pretty sure you are going to be well enough tomorrow to finish up healing at home."

She started setting out a needle and half a dozen test tubes. I started to leave the room when the good doctor said, "Hold on there for a few minutes, Paulie. I need to get some samples from you also."

When she was done with Zope, she put the filled vials in a plastic case with Zope's name on the lid. That done, she reached into the box of test tubes and pulled out at least thirty vials.

"She's going to run out of blood if you need that many more," I said.

"These are for you," said the nice doctor.

She was looking at me. I looked at the pile of empty test tubes, and I swear, it grew.

"Are half of those for me and the other half for Amelia?"

"Nope, they're all yours."

"That'll drain me dry. Won't it? I'm sure I don't have that much blood."

"Your body will naturally replace this amount in a few days."

"Yeah! Don't be a wimp. Here, you can sit in my chair," said Amelia as she got up.

As I sat there with my life's blood dripping out into little glass tubes, I talked with Zope.

"I'm sorry I haven't been up to see you before this, but I was pretty much in solitary confinement since you were injured. It was easier now because I was ordered to come up."

Dr. Smyth was packing up, but before she left, she turned back to me and said, "I will see you next Wednesday at nine a.m. Please be on time."

"Why, what for?"

"I will be doing your medical clearance for your pilot's license. There may be some other items that I want to cover with you, but I want to have a chance to review the blood test results before we meet."

And with that, she left.

"Everyone's been telling me that you felt the bullets that got me, at the same instance when I got shot. Did you see me get shot on the battlefield screen and imagine the feeling?" Zope asked.

"I was watching other screens at the moment you were hit. I felt the bullets hitting my body, and it was then that I turned to the screen that you were focused on. I knew that you weren't dead, but I also knew that you needed immediate medical help. I didn't relax until you had been wheeled into the elevator to the OR. I knew better than anyone that your wound was very close to you losing your life. I also knew that you would make it."

"How can you say that?" asked Amelia. "I was with her every minute since she landed back here. I have not left her side for the past five days. Zope was supercritical for the first forty-eight hours. The doctor kept telling me that I should be prepared to lose her. And you are standing here saying that you knew she would make it."

"No! No! No! Please just hold on. I'm just telling you what I was feeling then and now. Her, excuse me, Zope, your condition I knew to be overly critical. Once you hit the emergency ward and received the whole blood transfers, something in my mind realized you were going to make it.

"I just knew it. Something happened to me. A switch flipped, and everything in my body and mind was feeling parallel to what was happening to you, Zope. It never happened to me before.

"I have to go. I didn't mean to offend anyone. I just wanted to see how you were doing, Zope, and say that I want to see you back soon."

~ ~ ~ ~

I went back to the hangar. At that moment, I didn't even want to be here. I didn't want to see anyone I knew. I wanted some alone time to think things through. Just thinking about all the things I wanted to think about gave me this intense sharp pain behind my eyeballs.

Alone time was not in my future. Not with the limitations of my movements.

When the elevator doors opened onto the hangar floor, I saw activity. A lot of activity! Was there another raid being organized?

"Charlie, CHARLIE, where are you?"

"Right here, Ms. Paulie."

"Shit, you startled me. What is going on?"

"Maintenance and pilots are going through full pre-flight

checks of each and every aircraft here."

"Are all the aircraft going someplace?"

"No, we are making sure every bird is ready to fly at a moment's notice. We are getting ready for this weekend when this building will be on a very shortened crew. This is true for everyone from every unit in this building."

"Who has to be here all weekend? How were those that have this weekend duty picked? Seniority? Age? Single? In a relationship? The person has children? Whatever it is, I want on that list. I'm not up for celebrating Christmas right now. Staying here would be peaceful with only a few people around. Gimme me a chance to sort some things out alone."

"No such luck," Charlie said. "You are on Santa duty."

"Santa duty? I have no idea what that means."

"Every Christmas, one of us dresses up as Santa and gives out gifts at the Christmas party at the Manor. The duty always goes to the newest person here. Look around. Do you see anyone who has started here since you did?"

"No. Do I ride in a sleigh? And now that this has come up, I realize that I don't have any gifts for anyone. My life for the past few weeks has been on the fireball roller coaster."

"You get a pass on the presents this year. No one will expect anything because they are very aware of what your life has been since you first came to us after that fateful bite. This whole building will be on total lockdown at 1800 hours today, and that won't be lifted until noon on Monday. You are the one exception. You have to report here at 0600 hours Sunday morning, Christmas day."

"Why? What for?"

"Sorry, that is all I have been told."

Humph! That is just weird as hell. I turned and went to my office in the flight shack.

The main room in the flight shack was devoid of anyone. My personal office had no people in it, but there was a box and garment bag hanging from the coat hook and a good-sized box on the floor at its feet.

I suddenly thought that this office might belong to someone else now. I looked around to see if I could see any other changes that would give me some idea of who was in charge now.

There was a new name placard on the desk, so I picked it up. It had etched into the brass front,

PAULETTE ZAHN

VP of Air Operations

Maybe they were keeping me after all. So, what was in the bag? And in the box?

I unzipped the garment bag and saw that it contained a Santa suit. They must be serious. They all thought I was playing Santa on Sunday. The box held white whiskers and wig, a Santa hat, a big black belt, and black boots.

Then I heard Charlie's voice booming over the PA system.

"Attention. Attention, everyone. We have completed our readiness checks and are ready to go home to enjoy Christmas. This building will go on high-security lockdown in forty-five minutes. Now all of you get out of here except for the skeleton crew."

I was not one of the 'stay behind' crew, so I grabbed my jacket and headed toward my car.

My regulars; Irene, Darja, and Nicole, and Eddie, were already there. As I was about to get in, I stopped and thought that I should go back and bring the Santa suit and box of Santa accessories.

"Give me a minute. I forgot something" and I turned to

head back to my office.

“You don’t need to bring the suit. You are going to be coming here to put it on,” said Irene.

I shut the car door and started it up. I didn’t say anything until I had pulled into the traffic.

“I wish that someday I wouldn’t be the last person to know what is going on.”

Not one comment from the peanut gallery. Silence all the way home.

23 DECEMBER 2016

The sun was shining through my bedroom window when I woke up. That meant it was after eight a.m. I had slept over fourteen hours. And it felt really good. My mind had calmed down, and I had stopped thinking and worrying about stuff that I had no control over. I got up and did my bathroom beauty treatment before heading to the kitchen for breakfast, oops, break fast. What red neck got everyone started saying it that way?

I was surprised to see so many people in the kitchen at that hour.

"Paulie, welcome back."

"Hi!"

"Paulie, good to see you!" from just about everyone in the kitchen.

I looked around, and there was Christmas decoration everywhere. The tables were all decked out with green table cloths and red napkins. Multi-colored candles. The smell of balsam pine boughs and cinnamon, and other spices. It was warm and cozy, and best of all, it appeared that everyone was speaking to me. It was infectious. I WAS getting into the Christmas spirit.

After getting some food in me, I walked outside. Irene was right with me. She didn't have to be attached to my hip while we were on the Manor grounds. I had gotten used to her being so close and actually welcomed the… re… I didn't know what to call it. Not up to thinking of it as friendship. A special association that sounded safe.

"Would you want to see the preparations?" she asked.

"What preparations?

"Just follow me," she said and led me around the apartment/garage building to the space where the Bar-B-Q party had been held a few weeks earlier.

There was a half-circle of small tent-booths around a little stage that faced them. Each of the booths was set up to look like a village of shops that only sold items associated with Christmas. Toy store, doll store, electronics store, and several tent/storefronts had various food items.

There was a huge, fat, and tall pole with its base centered between the stage and the village. Lots of ropes and bodies hustling around it. Right then, they were all pulling on ropes pulling the pole erect. It must have stood fifty feet tall.

"What is that going to do or be?" I asked Irene.

"There is a huge big-top tent that can be erected in a matter of minutes in case it rains or snows on Sunday," Irene informed me.

"This can hold a lot of people. Far more than I know about even including everyone from work."

"This is the first Christmas here for both Nicole and me. I don't know what to expect either. It really looks festive. I don't know how many are planned for, but I agree, it does look like it can accommodate a lot of people."

"Could we go into the town here, the one on the island? I think I need to find a gift store."

"I think that is a great idea. What would you think about asking Darja and Nicole to come with us?"

And that is what we did.

I didn't think of what our entourage looked like until we had gotten a parking space right in the middle of the main street through Winslow. After we were out standing on the sidewalk in front of one of the shops that I got to see what we looked like, as a group, in the store's window.

I mean, picture this: four women all close or at six feet tall, hardly an ounce of fat between us.

Nicole, Irene, and I had jeans, running shoes, and light jackets over various colorful T-shirts.

Darja was dressier. A denim swing jacket by Balenciaga over a paisley print silk blouse with a peasant skirt with doeskin boots.

We were HOT, and we knew it.

Then there was our hair. I was plain honey blonde, Irene was dyed electric blue in pigtails, Nicole's hair was a rich purple in a single braid that hung down her back to her waist, and last, Darja. Her thick plaits were a deep auburn.

We walked 2 x 2, so we wouldn't take up the whole sidewalk. We received a lot of curious looks as we walked by. Most of the men would look down or away. I think they may have been intimidated.

Men! That was the last thing on my mind.

I was still coping with my short time in solitary for my stupid actions. I still didn't know if Irene had eased off. She had carried the responsibility for my actions, and it isn't easy to forgive and forget something that affected one's reputation. She seemed fine, I decided to give her some extra special space. She wasn't even walking next to me. It was Darja.

After a few hours of pawing through piles of 'stuff' in the various shops in town, we ended up at the Bainbridge Thai Restaurant for lunch.

We got a table overlooking the harbor and ordered right away. We were hungrier than we had expected because collectively, we must have had one of everything on their menu.

The twins and Darja were carrying on a discussion, much of which I missed because they would change languages probably to fit the subject of their discussion. I didn't mind. I was using the time to clear my mind.

"Paulie, Paulie, earth to Paulie," Nicole was saying.

"Oops, sorry, I was daydreaming. What did I miss?"

"Wherever you have been, you missed our discussing Christmas presents. We need to discuss this before we spend any money," said Darja.

Then Irene came in with a change of subject. I started to get nervous when she started in on ME. Her subject was ME.

"Paulie," she started, "I want there to be peace in our relationship. What happened last week had gotten me very angry. I was angry with you, but I was even angrier with myself. I let, in the order of importance, the company down, you down, and finally, I let myself down. It caused not just you and my pain, but others took what happened personally. No one knows how long you, and Darja for that matter, will be considered to be 'at risk.' Right now, I am your primary bodyguard. We, you and I, are sharing the apartment. I don't want us to have a personality strain. I want to bury the whole thing and go back to how the two of us got along in the beginning."

"Thanks, I would like it all back to normal also. I could not forgive that easily, so thanks."

"You need to understand us because that is what you are now," Darja said. "We, and I am talking about" – she hesitated and looked around at the other diners to see how far away from our table they were – "those of us, that is what we are now, don't like to carry grudges. It is just baggage that we don't need in our lives now. There are exceptions, but this is not one. You are a special part of our family. So, we've buried the hatchet on that subject and now on to the next problem."

"Yes," Nicole said. "Christmas presents. Irene, Darja, and I haven't been here long enough to know what would be a great gift to give anyone. The group at the Manor alone is pretty daunting. I don't know what the rest of you are thinking, but I would only have three people with a good idea of what they would like. I know everyone now, but not all that well. I would like to find something that would fit everyone. While you were off dreaming of getting a ride on one of those sailboats in the marina, we were working on answers. The strange thing is we believe we have figured out the perfect gift for you to give everyone. But we haven't figured out what we should be getting."

"If you give me this idea, then you will know what I am getting you. Or is there some trick to this?"

"We, the three of us, decided that what you should be doing for Christmas is getting some really nice cards and envelopes, not Christmas cards, but ones are used for wedding gift thank you notes. A hundred percent rag bond with maybe a gold leaf initial on the paper and envelope. You could just give each one of us that you have met so far a short handwritten note telling of your appreciation of having that person as a friend and fellow member of the Newmark family."

They were all looking at me for a reaction.

"You're going to handwrite the messages. That way, the cards will be from you on a personal level. What do you think?"

"Sounds like a good idea," I said. "How can I get cards and

envelopes printed up before tomorrow afternoon?"

"Oh, ye of little faith," Nicole said. "It is time you learn the power of the Newmark name."

We went up to the main drag and crossed over to the other side. Down the block, and we turned in a small side street, and when I say small, it was an alley with room for only one car at a time.

Partway into the alley, we came upon a store that caters to weddings and such. It had a selection of small gifts that the bride and groom give to their wedding party. Irene guided me over to a chair in front of a desk with sample books on top of sample books.

As I sat, I had a tingly feeling, raising the hair on my arms. My head snapped up and toward the curtain that covered the doorway leading to the storage area or back room for whatever it was used for. Pushing the curtain aside and walking into the showroom was a striking woman. She was tall with a full head of silver hair, fair-skinned with delicate facial features.

I knew two things about her immediately. The first was that this was a woman that many people my age would want for a mother. The second, that she was a vampire. I had known that she was a vampire before she had appeared. My mouth was hanging open.

I felt like I was in the presence of a goddess.

She seemed to float across the shop floor, and she came right to me and took my hand to shake, or maybe just to hold in her hand, softly and warmly.

"Hello, Paulette Zahn. I'm pleased to have you visit my shop. My name is Danielle Nollan. I want you to call me Danny. That name is very private, and there are only a few people that I allow to use it."

"How did you know my name?"

"Your life's secrets are safe with me. I am on the Council of Elders. I was made aware of your presence the moment you popped up on the radar. That was when you were injured and taken to the Newmark Medical Facility. I had even stopped by to see you when you were still in a coma. When I entered the room, your monitors all took a slight uptick. Your heartbeat increased, which triggered the blood pressure cuff to start up to get a reading. Your blood pressure had also moved up some. The nurse looked at the readings and told me that you had not had any reactions like that before. It was part of the puzzle we have been trying to put together to understand the range of the very rare and unusual abilities you have been exhibiting. Before we start helping you pick some things out, I want to say that you are always welcome to stop by to talk any time of night or day, seven days a week. If the door is locked and the 'Closed' sign is up, reach up to the top of the door frame, and there is a small button that will alert me that someone is here. Now, what are you looking for?"

I told her about the personal memos for my presents to everyone. She led me through several sample books, and we picked out something elegant. She used an iPad to bring my initials and name onto the screen and adjusted the positioning until it felt right. That was when I told her that I needed them by tomorrow.

"They will be delivered to the mansion in two hours. Now, what else can I help you with?"

"I would like to find a small gift that is suitable for either sex. I was thinking about some small jewelry item. I was thinking along the lines of a friendship ring, but that has drawbacks. I notice that no one wears any ring jewelry at all.

Hoop earnings seemed like a good idea, but then when the guys put theirs on, we would look like a gang of pirates. So, that won't work."

"I have an idea. Could you give me a list of names of all those that are close to you?"

"What's your idea?"

"You just send me that list within the next two hours, and I will have everything taken care of for you and delivered to your apartment on Christmas Eve."

I used my new credit card for the first time. The other three had picked out some gift items, and after we were all paid up, we headed back to the main street shops.

Darja and the twins picked up a few more trinkets at different stores until it started to grow dark. It was after four p.m., and we decided to call it a day and headed back to the Manor.

I pulled into my parking space, and we all got out and headed for our apartments to put our packages away, and I wanted to see if anything had come for me.

Sure enough, there was a box outside my apartment door. It was not your standard delivery box. It was wrapped in white paper with green and red ribbons and a note attached. I lifted it and took it inside to the small kitchen table.

The note said:

Dear Paulie

This gift you have chosen for your new friends and family is perfect. Have a Merry Christmas, and I hope to see you soon.

In addition to the notepaper and envelopes, there are enough blue silk pouches with drawstrings and large gold foil seals to attach the bags to the envelopes with.

Your friend,
Danny

I made myself a cappuccino and sat down to write a short note of thanks to everyone I expected to see at the company Christmas party on Sunday.

It was dawn before I finished penning comments that were particular to the person I was giving that envelope. I had each individual's name on the envelopes. I finished sealing all the envelopes and got up and stretched. I wasn't tired, but I was stiff from sitting in the kitchen chair for the entire night.

I got up to take a shower when the doorbell rang. That was my first doorbell ring at this apartment.

It was Al, the Manor guard.

"Morning, Ms. Paulie. This package was just delivered to the front gate. The messenger said that you had to get it straight away."

"Thanks, Al. Will you be here on Christmas day?"

"A special set of guards are brought in every holiday so that all the Manor personnel can attend without sacrificing security. Yes, I will be there."

The box wasn't very large, but it was weighty. A note also accompanied it.

I took it back to the kitchen table and opened it up.

Inside was a rectangular box about 6" x 12" and 1" deep covered in black velvet. Inside there were four rows of slots and ten slots to each row. Each slot held a wide banded gold ring in a size that would probably be too small to fit any intended recipients.

Each ring had my name engraved on the inside, and the outside was plain. I sorted the envelopes into alphabetical order and started putting a ring in the silk bag, and glued them down with the round gold foil stick-on.

I was ready for Christmas, probably for the first time in my life. First time where I didn't use any gift credit cards. I had gotten a real gift for each member of my new family.

Now I had to go through my wardrobe to pick out an outfit for tomorrow. Whoops! What was I thinking? I was wearing a Santa suit.

Irene came out of her bedroom and said, "Just on the phone with my sister. She says that everyone is going to gather in the wine cellar for drinks."

Well, now that just settled everything for my plans. That was just what I was hoping to do. With that, we headed out to the kitchen, where we could ride the freight elevator down to the tasting room.

~ ~ ~ ~

It must have been close to midnight when the wine and cheese party broke up. All I had been told about vampire metabolism was slightly overrated because I felt the alcohol's effects.

I didn't even get all my clothes off before I lay down and went right to sleep. A wonderfully deep, restful sleep.

CHRISTMAS DAY
25 DECEMBER 2016

Irene awoke me.

"Wakey, wakey, princess. Your chariot awaits you."

"Already? Can I just have a few more minutes? What time is it?"

"4.30 a.m. and Mel is downstairs waiting to take you to the hangar."

"Mel. Why Mel?"

"Get up and go. All will be revealed in time, grasshopper."

I brushed my teeth, ran a brush through my hair, and put on my normal outfit of black Converse jeans, a Gene Simmons T-shirt, and my brown bomber jacket. Down the stairs to the garages.

Mel was waiting in his Jeep with the motor idling. There was a good chill in the air, and I didn't see any stars. It was overcast. It almost felt like it was going to snow. That would be great if it did, and on Christmas Day too.

I jumped in and said, "Merry Christmas, Mel."

"Merry Christmas to you too. Are you ready for this trip?"

"I have no idea of what or where I am going. All I know is that I am to get into the Santa suit in my office, and after that, I know nothing. I bet you know, so are you going to tell me?"

We were already driving out through the Manor's front gates. Mel didn't say anything till we got into the queue for the ferry.

"I will reveal all once you are suited up. I'm itching to tell you but have a strict guideline that I have to follow, and that includes not telling you anything until you are ready to go in the suit."

Conversation killer. It was real early, and there was no traffic to speak of, so we arrived at the hangar in record time.

Mel drove into the hangar and parked by the back wall.

"Go get your suit. I will come and get you in fifteen minutes."

When he came for me, I was Santa.

And holy shit, he was dressed up as an elf. A very, very large elf. Striped tights and shoes with long toes and a bell on the tips. And they told me that there were no elves. When I followed him out of the flight shack, I heard the whine of a turbine. I stopped and looked around the hangar.

"The Apache is missing. Where is the Apache?"

He took my hand and led me out the side door, and there it was. Santa's sleigh.

It was the Apache, and it had been painted red and had some decorative panels fastened on the sides to make it look more like Santa's sleigh. Christmas tree lights were running all around the landing gear, and they were on. The radar dome on the front had a red light on it. Rudolph flies again.

"You painted the Apache red?"

"It's only watercolor paint. It will wash right off. Now you hop up in front, and we will run through the preflight check. Now you will learn about your destinations. The first stop will be at the sports field at the Lewis-McCord Joint Base. There will be a lot of bleary-eyed moms and dads with their wide-eyed children. I will land on the field, and you will get out and be swarmed over when the children are released. There will be two dozen GIs dressed in elf costumes that will be handing out the gifts. We will be there for an hour, and then we will take off for our next and last stop."

"Last stop, where is last stop?" I asked.

"I'll tell you after we leave the base."

We were airborne fifteen minutes later.

It didn't take me long to notice that we were flying quite slowly; 60 mph ground speed at best. I keyed my mic and asked, "Why so slow?"

"I don't want to blow the decorations off. I've been testing different panels and decorations and picked the ones that held up to the buffeting the best. I also found out that the fastest I could go before shredding everything was seventy-five knots."

Well, that gave me a chance to look down on the lights of the houses. They were all lit up with decorations. It was peaceful and beautiful.

It was just after eight a.m. when we came in over the sports field. Mel took us in a wide-sweeping circle around the field two or three times before he hovered over the center and slowly settled onto the grass.

I barely had time to get my feet planted on the ground when the swarm of kids was coming for me. There were hundreds of them, and they all wanted to hug Santa. It made me feel good for them. Many of these children had a parent stationed overseas. My presence gave them something to enjoy for a few hours, at least.

I waded through them, hoping to give each child a chance to get a hug from Santa or at least to let them hold my hand or grab hold of my pants. I had never seen so many sparkling eyes at one time in my life. And they were looking at me. I tried to get to each of the stations where my cadre of elves was handing out gifts.

Then Mel was at my side. "It's eleven o'clock. We have to wind this up and head to our next party."

He helped run a light interference to clear a path back to the Apache. My cadre of elves formed a perimeter around the helicopter so that we could take off safely.

I was in the Christmas spirit. The last Christmas I had ever enjoyed was the one during my senior year in high school, the last one that I spent with my dad. That thought gave me a small moment to remember the good days I had with him.

My daydream was interrupted by Mel.

"We are going to the Manor. Every year, the Newmarks open up the grounds for orphaned children in foster homes or from a poor home with a single parent. They are being bussed in right now. There will be around 150 kids there. You are going to make a lot of children happy today. You're going to bring some much-needed sunshine into their lives."

I remembered that we held a Christmas party for the local children the first year I was in Afghanistan. That was the one, and only time we ever did that. Days later, we learned that many of the children were beaten half to death for going to a Christian affair.

I looked down and saw that we were over the Puget Sound and near Bainbridge Island. Sixty miles per hour sounds slow, but traveling in a straight line made it seem like ninety.

As we crossed onto land, he increased altitude a lot. Looking down, I thought I saw the Manor and grounds that we were passing over. As we did, I heard a pop and looked back as far as I could. Mel had fired the flare set that was used to confuse heat-seeking missile. From the ground, it would look like white sparkly angel wings. He then slowed, dropped altitude, and circled the grounds a few times before heading for the landing pad behind the gym.

There was something else to see. When you are in the air, you can hardly tell if it is raining or snowing because it is blown away by the rotor downwash. As we were nearing the ground, I saw that it was spotting with snow. What had started to be my perfect day just got better?

Two elves were running toward me. It was the twins. They were the last people I expected. Elves had to smile and be silly fun. These two were deadly ninja warriors. Warriors that kept the 'serious' face on at all times. If they were to smile, their faces would crack.

They were smiling. Real genuine warm smiles. They came up, and with one on either side, they took my arms and led me to the party.

I saw a peak of blue hair and knew which one was which.

"We will be with you the whole time. Every one of the children has a prize bag that holds the toys they were given. The bags have extra space so they can take as much food as they can carry. We have Santa's chair set up in front of the podium."

"When will I be able to give my envelopes out?"

"I have put the box of envelopes on a shelf in the garage. We will be exchanging our gifts after the last of the children are gone."

I was led to the Santa chair with wild shouts of glee when the children saw me. There was a row of snow fences keeping them at bay. I sat, and there was a space in the fence that was guarded by two more of my elves. They started letting the kids through in small groups. I gave them all a greeting befitting Santa. I never asked if they had been bad or good. I figured that was taken care of at the local department stores or mall wherever Santa had set up for photoshoots. Those Santas were just some of my elves dressed as Santas while the real Santa was right here. It was me.

Now and then, one of my elves would bring me a sugar cookie and some hot spiced cider. The big tent had been half put up with the coverage over the Santa workshops set up facing the Santa chair I was in. The snow had stopped, leaving just a few traces on the ground. Just enough to make it festive.

Then there were no more children waiting to say hello to Santa. I saw that the horde was thinning out. The festivities were tapering off as they were bussed or driven off to their homes. I took a moment and remembered the happiness I had brought them and felt proud.

An elf was bringing me another hot cider. I thanked him, and he left. I wouldn't have thought anything about it, but when he approached me, I got a bad feeling about something. Someone near me had bad intentions.

"Irene, who was that elf? I know that I have seen him before, but I can't remember his name."

"That, I believe, is Cooper, John Cooper. Why?"

"That is how I recognized him from the raid. The 'why' is that I felt something was wrong when he came up to me. It is like the feeling when I realize or sense that someone is a vampire. The strangeness is that I am here at the Manor, surrounded by all types, including a lot of vampires. I already know every vampire here, and none of them would set my alarms off. When he came up, I got the feeling. I have a bad feeling about him."

"One thing you are right about, he isn't one of the inner group of Newmark employees that are Manor staff. I didn't think that anyone outside of this core group was supposed to be here."

I spilled my cider onto the ground. I looked up at Irene, and she was staring at the ground. Right at the spot where the cider spilled. I looked down, and there was a foam boiling up at the site of the spill.

"POISON." We both said it at the same time.

I was stunned. I was staring wide-eyed at Irene. She reached into her elf tunic and pulled out a fob, and she was pressing the button. The air around me became charged with electricity. I looked up to see if Cooper was still nearby. I didn't see him, but I saw everyone else standing at alert and looking toward the twins and me.

"John Cooper," Nicole shouted. "John Cooper was just here, and we need to catch him. He just tried to poison one of us. Use any force necessary to detain him, but it would be nice to talk with him."

"Come with us, Paulie," Irene said.

How had he gotten away so quickly? He was here. Then he was gone. My neck muscles were tightening up. I tried to relax them as the three of us headed toward my apartment. I wanted to shake off the tenseness in hopes of getting contact with the side of me that gets these intuitive feelings. I didn't feel anything until I entered the apartment/garage building.

All the hallway lights were off. I reached out and tried the switch. Power was off, and the three of us knew that it was intentional. Irene got behind me, and Nicole stayed in front. They were slowly easing me back out of the darkened hallway.

I was walking backward when I heard Irene let out an "oof," and she slammed into my back.

Nicole was around me and down on the floor, holding Irene propped up. "Where are you hit?" she asked Irene.

“He must be using a silencer. Not sure if I saw a flash. I just felt this battering ram slam into my chest. The bullet didn’t go through my Kevlar, but I’m going to have one hell of a bruise. Assface may have broken a rib or two, also.”

The lights came back on, and people were running over to see if we needed any help.

“We’re all okay,” Nicole told them. “Does anyone know where Larisa is?”

“She went with Ms. Karan. I think they went up to her parents’ room to help protect them,” said Odie. “We can reach her on our phones now.”

Nicole was on her cell phone immediately, “Larisa, have they pulled up all the security camera footage of the last fifteen minutes at this party?”

We waited while Larisa talked with the duty personnel at the hangar. Ten minutes passed before we heard anything. Larisa must have come back on the phone with Nicole since she was grunting at whatever was being said by Larisa. She hung up and turned to the rest of us.

“He is off the property. He went out over the rear gate. There was a black van waiting for him. We were going to be exchanging gifts in the living room. We are still going to be doing that, but it will also serve as a general meeting with Spartak Newmark overseeing everything. Paulie, let’s go upstairs and change out of our costumes. We can get our gift boxes or bags and head for the living room.”

~~~~

There must be twenty-five people in the room, which was large enough to be far from crowded. Everyone who worked at the
~~~~

Manor was present. From housekeeping to the dishwasher to the three Newmarks, everyone was there.

Sundown had come and gone. Outside, it was dark and wintery, but inside, the fire was crackling away, and we were all getting ourselves drinks. Quite a diverse collection of drinks; wine, beer, champagne, hot buttered rums, and I even saw a couple of martinis in regular martini glasses with cranberries instead of olives. Everyone was getting rosy cheeks. We were all getting warm and fuzzy.

"Welcome to our annual Christmas gathering," Sparky said. "The one little incident won't put a dent into the joy and happiness we are all feeling today. None of the children saw any of it, and they are all home or on their way with bags full of presents and a lot of food. It was a success. A complete success. I have to thank and compliment every one of you for the parts each of you played. Special thanks to Santa."

He raised his glass in a toast to me.

"Paulie, would you please come over here and sit with Karan, LaDoña, and myself? You are the star of the show today, and you did yourself and all of us proud. It will be hard to come up with a replacement for next year. Let's all start the gift exchange."

Everyone started going through their boxes and bags, trying to find the gift they intended for the person next to them. There were shrieks and gales of laughter as presents were being unwrapped.

Everyone took turns coming up to me to give me a present. I, in turn, pulled out the personalized envelope for them.

Time passed, drinks were refreshed, and everyone looked comfortable and pleased with what they had given and what they had received. I was opening packages also.

I got everything from a black evening gown to throwing knives. Dress up Jimmy Choo heels, a pair of goggles for wearing while riding my motorcycle, or maybe an open cockpit airplane as the lenses were split-pane lenses, and a 1940s fighter pilot helmet. Several pairs of earrings that I could wear on any occasion. Girls gave me wearables while the men gave me hardware. Nothing wrong with that.

LaDoña reached over and took my hand. She was seated next to me, so neither one of us had to stand.

"Thank you for your beautiful card. And the friendship ring. I would never think of something like that. You have a beautiful mind, young lady. You are the only vampire here that is younger than me. However, to me, you are wise beyond your years. I know that you aren't aware of it, but you have brought a fresh breath to this entire group. I would like to have you up to my den for tea or coffee sometime. Just the two of us."

"Thank you. I don't know what to say other than I look forward to sitting with you some afternoon."

Karan and her dad came up to me with a box in their hands.

"Paulie, those cards were amazing, and the engraved friendship rings are over the top. Everyone is trying to decide how they are going to wear them. No one has ever done anything quite like it. Thank you. This present is from my father and me."

And she handed me the box which, like a little kid, I shredded the paper off.

The box was labeled 'BOSE.'

What? Stereo speakers? Or the Wave radio for my bedroom?

I lifted the lid, and it was the Bose aviation headset with a microphone. I had seen a few of these sets before. Some of the army pilots had gotten them on their own. There was a reason that they were so sought after.

"You will be the envy of every pilot you come across," Sparky said.

"Thank you, both. I will be the best pilot you ever had."

I ended up standing in front of the couch as everyone came up to me and hugged me, and thanked me for the notes, especially for the rings.

After everyone had thanked me, and there was no more line, Karan asked, "Would you please come to my father's den?"

So, I followed her and her mother into the den, which was at one end of the living room.

Karan shut the door and motioned for me to take one of the red leather wingback chairs in front of Mr. Newmark.

"Well, youngster, you certainly have had an action-packed introduction to our world. I know that your entire world was turned upside down when you were told what you might have become. Your change was involuntary, and to put that in perspective, only ten percent of the people that were turned that way live very long. Then there is you. It appears that you have adapted quite well. There are other things about you that we are still learning about and wondering if there are any more surprise abilities to learn about. That isn't why we are meeting, though. LaDoña rarely, if ever, is present at any meetings, be they formal or informal. Before I tell you why she is here, I want to explain some family secrets, and you must remember that they are just that. If any part of this meeting leaves this room, your life is forfeit. Stern and dire words, but I want to make sure you understand."

"Thank you, sir. I have no reserve on telling you that I will protect anything and everything you tell or teach me."

"I believe you know that my wife here, LaDoña, is a Normal and that my daughter Karan is, well, she and I know that she is not a full Normal. She and I think that she may be turning into a damphire, but what her special trait is, we haven't any clear idea.

"All of that has nothing to do with why you are here. There is a different reason, and it does have to do with both of them. I had always hoped that LaDoña would choose to be changed and, well, I will let Karan speak for herself and explain the reason you are here."

"Paulie, when I was old enough to understand the different species and that my father was a senior elder in the Council of Vampires, I knew that there would come a day when I would want to be changed. You are here because we want your blood to be the blood we use to obtain our changes. It isn't today or next week, but it will be sometime in the future. The best possible way is to receive a transfusion of whole blood that we got from you. It only takes about 250 CCs to cause the change safely. We want to take 500 CCs of blood from you once every six months. The old blood will be treated, freeze-dried, and stored in capsules in cryogenic vats till needed. Your blood capsules could be used to help other vampires that have received some grave injuries, similar to what happened to Zope. Only the blood of another vampire can boost the regenerative process of an injured vampire."

"I would be honored. But why me?"

"I just received a fresh report from Renee on your blood sample you just gave."

"Who is Renee?"

"Sorry, Dr. Smyth, Doctor Renee Smyth. Your latest blood

panel has brought up some unusual indicators. There is an unknown marker in your DNA. There are three we can't identify. We suspect that one is responsible for your ability to sense that another person is a vampire without actually staring him in the face. Another may be the cause of your empath ability. The third may only be a subpart of one or both of the others, or it could be some ability that is yet to surface. That is only a part of what she has discovered in your blood. The blood that is now part of your system has some highlights present in a very ancient vampire. We don't know anything about the person that attacked you, but either he was several hundred years old, or he was the product of another ancient vampire. Having the blood of a true ancient coursing through your system gives you a special layer of strength and protection. You won't get much more muscle strength, but your reaction time maybe even faster than it is now. Your hearing and eyesight will further improve beyond what's common for other vampires. There is a downside to all this, though. Many vampires in this world would kill to get some of your blood. I'm stressing this point because even some of the inner cadres of this household team would consider killing you for your blood. There is no one that you can trust with this secret. Whether you give Karan and my wife the blood we want for their conversion, you are being brought into a very tight special circle. Your security resume will now include the codes that will allow you access to the vault where the blood is stored and processed and access to our library, which holds records and histories of vampires going back to the beginning of our species. It is the largest and most complete library of its kind in the world. You will be able to go in and read anything you want any time you want. Karan will give you a tour and orientation sometime in the next week or so. I don't need your decision to give your blood for the conversions right now. My last words to you are to tell you that I understand that you are being loaded up with many things, but you can rely on Charlie to run the entire flying circus on his own. That will give you peace of mind when you start flight school."

I just sort of stared at the three of them. I was sitting in the den of one of the more if not the most powerful vampires in the world, and he just asked me to provide the blood that could be used to convert his daughter and wife into vampires.

I closed my gaping mouth and said, "I have no reservations about giving you my blood. It will take me a long time to understand this honor. How many people have access to this vault?"

"Pete, Eddie, Amelia, Zope, Darja, Larisa, Leon Krupnick, Danielle Nollan, and Phil Markham, Karan, and myself."

"All of those people will know about me?

"No, only the four of us in this room will know."

"What about Lisa?"

"She had access, but she is going through a change of identity, and when we are sure it is a good ID, she will be added back in. That could be a year or two away, though. We know that the two of you are close, and she is one of the inner circle, but what we have agreed to just now is not for anyone but the four of us."

I stopped listening to any more. Not that anyone was saying anything, but I wanted to close the world out for a moment while I let everything sink in. It was a lot. I thought back over the things I had learned, the things that have changed in me, my new abilities, and to top it off, this honor that the Newmarks had bestowed on me.

"Paulie, Paulie, earth to Paulie," Karan was saying.

"Oh! Sorry, I was just going over the many things that have happened over the past weeks. If there isn't anything else, I think I would like to go back to my apartment to rest up. Again, thank you for the honor you have given me."

Ms. Newmark stood up and hugged me. I had thought that she wasn't the huggy type, but she had no reservations in hugging me. It felt good.

After she stood back, I excused myself, left the den, and went back to my apartment.

27 DECEMBER 2016 – 0430 HOURS

The alarm on my iPhone woke me up. I stretched and preened in my bed. Boll and Branch sheets and My-Pillows on a Sleep Comfort mattress and a goose down comforter. Total decadence. I had slept late yesterday morning and then just puttered around the apartment putting order to my few possessions. Ate an early dinner of meatloaf and mashed potatoes with gravy and glazed carrots.

Meatloaf Monday… feature of the day.

Don't take this wrong. I like meatloaf. I've had army meatloaf, and those cooks work hard to make it the ugly meal, but with enough catsup, it's all good.

I loved it. Now for the review of Ms. K's meatloaf; it is made with ground choice sirloin, a small number of breadcrumbs, Contadina tomato paste, and secret spices. Best meatloaf ever.

After I ate, I decided to walk the inside perimeter of the Manor's property. There was a footpath that went all the way around, and for the moment, it wasn't raining, and it wasn't as cold as it was on Christmas day.

I heard voices ahead of me. My vampire-enhanced hearing belied how far ahead of me that or those persons were. I picked up my pace, curious to see who it was. A few twists and turns in the path, and I overtook the source.

It was Amelia pushing Zope, who was in a wheelchair.

"Hi!"

That was all I could say. I was still a little unsure of my general acceptance with everyone. These two were very important to me, and I didn't want to be on their bad side. I knew that they treated me very nice when I went to see Zope in the hospital, but I also knew that my fame, or lack thereof, changed daily.

"Hello, sister," Zope said. "Would you walk with us for a while?"

"Sure. How are you feeling now?" I asked Zope.

"Pretty good now. I still will have some downtime while everything heals and builds itself back together, but I've come a long way from the moment I went down."

"It isn't talked about, or maybe I wasn't in the loop, but how bad was it?"

"The shooter got me with a 45-70. Very large and heavy bullet. It shattered everything in my right shoulder area, including most of the blood vessels. 99.99 percent fatal in a very short period every time. I was beyond lucky. Doc Smyth says that I will be in a sling for three to four more weeks. The bones were pretty smashed up, and even with our amazing healing speeds, that much damage takes time to rebuild everything fully."

"So, Amelia, you're staying close to help her until she is healed?"

Amelia didn't answer right away. She and Zope looked at each other, and they both nodded.

"Paulie," Zope started, "Amelia and I go back to 2003 when she came to work for Newmark. We have had a long relationship. I'm not sure of your level of tolerance for women who have a relationship with another woman. There isn't any way to ease into this discussion other than to tell you the full story.

"From 2003 until Eddie Vangh showed up last year, she and

I were together. Together as a couple. Soon after he started working here, he caught Amelia's eye, and they started dating. That developed into a really serious relationship, and before you wonder or ask, I was perfectly okay with it. In fact, I encouraged it because I had come to like Eddie as a person. He is perfect for her, isn't that right?"

"Zope and I will always and forever be special close friends," Amelia explained. "When Eddie started here, it stirred up feelings that I didn't think I had any more. It started with me vamping him a little. He was so new and fresh, even though he was a much older vampire than I was. He was like a little boy when it came to being around other vampires and no experience at all with women vampires."

They were both smiling as Amelia told the story.

"Are you serious about your relationship with him?" I asked.

"Eternally serious," she responded.

I was a little confused for a moment. Seeing how these two were since Zope got shot, I thought that maybe Eddie was out of the picture. But then I understood. Amelia knew that Eddie was safe and sound, and she went to care for her closest friend.

"I think that maybe I am a little jealous," I said. "I haven't ever been in a real relationship. Now, because of my change, I don't know how I would find anyone to date."

"I don't—" Amelia started, but Zope cut her short.

"Sorry, Amelia, I want to answer this one," said Zope.

Amelia smiled down at Zope and nodded.

"I have been what I am now for over fifty years. I have never lacked relationship choices. I have dated vamps, damphires, and Norms, men and women. You, Paulie, for all intents and purposes, are still in diapers. Don't rush life. Remember, you have a long, long life ahead of you, so don't try to force any relationship thinking it may be your last chance at happiness. If you get the chance, you should talk to Larisa or Darja. They both have been around for quite a long time, and until Larisa met up with Todd, neither one of them was ever in a romantic relationship."

"Zope's right, Paulie. You have forever time on your hands. Don't worry yourself into rushing a relationship before you have enough time to learn the other person completely."

The path we were on came out of the tree cover, and we were at a paved road. It looked like it went toward the Manor to the right, and almost immediately on the left was a gate with heavy stone turret guardhouses on each side of the gate.

Chuck, one of the damphire guards, was standing outside one of the mini-towers. He waved, and Amelia turned the wheelchair toward the gate and Chuck.

"Well, hello, you three. Good to see you up and about, Ms. Zope."

"No one is happier to be up than me, Chuck. It feels very peaceful out here in the back lot. Must be a restful break for you."

"Normally, it is calm. With this current heightened security level, we are doubled up. I have Al here with me, and at the moment, he is showing our newbie trainee around the perimeter."

"Who is that?" said Zope. "I haven't seen anyone new around."

"Scotty Barton is his name. He is a five-year-old vampire who came to us from New York. He was trained in security at the Newmark Electronics Lab near his home there." Chuck looked straight at me and continued, "Heee'sss ssingle. Just tossing that out. Not to anyone, in particular, mind you. I wouldn't want to gather the mantle of matchmaker. Hell, I can't even scare up a date for myself."

"Everyone is a matchmaker here at the Manor. Take Eddie

and Amelia here as an example. We all worked on making that relationship grow so carefully that they never knew we all engineered it right under their noses," Zope said.

Amelia must have slipped because the wheelchair hit the stone guardhouse.

"Oops, so sorry, Zope. Are you okay?"

Which caused Zope to respond, "You must have lost muscle tone since you have been sitting around keeping me company for the past week. Why don't you take a break and let Paulie push me around for a while?"

Just then, Al and the new kid on the block emerged from the path that continued around the perimeter. I knew immediately that he was a vampire.

"Hello, ladies. A special hello to Zope. Seeing you up is an inspiration to all of us. I want you to meet our newest guard, Scotty Barton. Scotty, meet Ms. Zope in the wheelchair, Ms. Paulie, who looks to be her pilot today, and lastly, Ms. Amelia. These three beauties are the core of our persona defense team."

Zope reached out and shook his hand. "Good to meet you, and welcome to the Manor. Just ignore his comment about 'beauties.' Mr. Al here doesn't get out much and has no experience to be able to make a comparison."

That got a big laugh out of Chuck.

He shook Amelia's hand and mine, and we exchanged 'welcomes' and 'good to meet you' comments.

Hum! Or maybe *Huummm!* He was about the same height as me. Dirty, unruly blond hair and a ruddy complexion. Physically, well, he was just another vampire with this athletic body. Not overly muscled like a fanatic bodybuilder, no, just a regular-looking guy. His face was definitely not ugly.

He was standing there looking from one of us girls to the other and back. I could see that he had questions, but if he didn't belly up and ask, none of the three would help him.

"He doesn't know," Chuck said. "He has a feeling but isn't sure. Are one of you going to tell him, or should I put him out of his pains?"

Scott stared wide-eyed at Chuck. He was also getting a nice sunburn red to his face without the sun shining. He turned to Zope. Probably thought that the injured person was the meekest. Chuck had said that Scott was turned five years ago. That made him a lot older, in vampire years, than I was. I had to think that his early years were sheltered. I also remembered that I could tell if someone was a vampire from a distance while most other vampires weren't sure until the other vampire was very close and talking to them. Well, he was directly in front of the three of us and had shaken our hands and spoken with us, and he still didn't know.

"All three of us are," Amelia said, hoping to put him out of his misery.

"Interesting!" That was all he said.

He didn't smile, and other than embarrassment, he displayed no emotion.

"Well, let's get going," Amelia said and started pushing the wheelchair with Zope in it.

"Oh, goody. Can't wait to sit down at the kitchen table across from Mr. Pouty Face. We have enough stress in our lives, and what better way to perpetuate it than to have a meal with a Glum Gus to help keep our spirits bottled up. I do not want to be left here around him tomorrow when everyone goes off to work."

"You can come to work with me tomorrow morning," I volunteered. "I have to go to my first flight school class, but I don't think they will go on all day long. Besides, you can visit Larisa or get your shoulder checked by Dr. Smyth. When I am finished with class, we could go shopping. I want some new clothes."

"That's a great idea," Amelia said. "I can't go with you, but I'm sure you can take care of her. You'll have Irene with you also, won't you?"

"Irene will be with me all the time. I am not here on the Manor grounds," I told them. "I haven't been told officially, but I believe that she will be with me even when I am in class. That means you will be left to your own pursuits while I'm in class," I told both of them.

~~~~

While the three of us continued following the path around the Manor's grounds, they asked me about my time in the military and my earlier years as a teenager and high school times. I think they were using my memories of my years as a teen to help jog the memory of their teenage years.

I hadn't dwelt on my past, my life before I became a vampire. The recall of my knowledge of car repairs that I learned from my dad and the intricacies of the mechanical and electronic innards of aircraft that the army had taught me was always there for immediate recall. I suddenly realized that many of the memories of the people I had known were already dimming.

As I walked along the path covered in pine needles with these two incredible women who were my friends, smelling the fresh forest air and generally feeling at peace for once, I realized that my past, my early years, were no longer important to hold onto. I would always remember my dad, but the rest was garbage, and I didn't need any of it.

Right at this moment, I felt more at peace than I had in many years. This was where I belonged.
~~~~

FLIGHT SCHOOL
27 DECEMBER 2016 – 0430 HOURS

Alarm! Ooookay, time to get up for school.

When I got out of the shower, I could hear Irene rattling around in the living room.

Jeans, T's, and my brown Bombardier jacket.

When I came out of the bedroom, Irene was standing there in a similar outfit.

"How did you know what I was going to wear?" I asked.

"We all know pretty much what you will wear on any given day. Do you have your sidearm?"

"Sidearm? I'm going to be in a schoolroom. Why the pistol? And we are going clothes shopping after class with Zope and maybe Amelia if she can make it."

"Go back into your room, put on your hip holster for the .45, make sure you have a round in the chamber, the safety on, and a full clip. You can bring the snub nose revolver. Load it with .357 hollow points, and you can drop it into the pocket of your jacket."

"Are you expecting trouble?"

"I always expect the worst. That is why Nicole and I are still alive. Now let's get something into our stomachs."

We went to the kitchen and had a hearty meal. When we were done, we got up and were leaving when Ms. K stopped us.

She handed Irene a Wonder Woman lunchbox and gave me a pink Hello Kitty lunch box.

"What is this?" I asked.

"You are in school. There is a midmorning snack and an apple and sandwich for your lunch. Please bring the lunch pails back and without any bullet holes in them."

Irene grabbed my hand and said, "Don't say anything. Just take the lunch bucket, and let's head to the car. We have to get Zope and her wheelchair in."

When we got to my car, Zope and her chair were there. Amelia and Eddie were there also.

"Are you all coming?" I asked.

"No, we are just making sure Zope gets buckled in properly. Amelia and I have some things we have to take care of."

Zope was able to get up and into the car without any help. She did need someone to help her buckle the seat belt on. Eddie folded the wheelchair and got it into the back of the car.

Fifty minutes later, we were pulling into the Newmark security building lot.

The three of us got out, and I got the wheelchair out of the back and made Zope sit in it. She would have walked off without it. I probably would have walked off if it was me with just a shoulder brace on, too. We are sometimes just too proud to let anyone think we are hurting. I pushed her over to the elevator doors and headed toward my office.

Charlie was in the operations room, making sure all schedules were on time. "Good morning, Charlie," I said. "Anything urgent?"

"Tracy and Sue are flying Mr. Newmark to Chicago in the Lear. After that, there is nothing else scheduled."

Irene popped her head in and said, "Shake a leg, Paulie. We need to get to class. You know what Mum would say if we were late."

She had our aircraft tug waiting. We both got on with her driving. As she pulled out of the hangar, she turned left toward the north end of the runway. These tugs weren't very fast and had to stay in contact with the tower. She announced our entry onto the taxiways, giving our departure and destination sites. I heard the 'roger' from the tower, and she picked up the not-breakneck speed.

"Why are we going this way? I thought the school was directly across from our building, and the quickest way would be around the south end," I asked her.

"We're in civies and could be any two people working for any company that is located here at the field. If you noticed, this tug doesn't have any special markings or logos that would signal that it is from Newmark Industries."

"Why the stealth?"

"We have a little time before we have to report in to class. I thought we could cruise past some of the buildings on the other side of the runway. The ones on the northern end. That guy who chased you last week wasn't here on a random search. We think that he is working or stationed with one of the businesses here. We also believe that the attempted break-ins were carried on by persons from one of the businesses that ring the airport. Keep your eyes on the alert for signs of anything that could be a base for this rogue operation. I want you to keep your vampire senses on the alert. We may not see anyone, but you may sense unknown vampires nearby."

That made sense, except I wasn't confident enough in this very untested talent I was supposed to have.

We drove past all the buildings on the west side of the runway, but as soon as we crossed over to the east side, Irene slowed us to a crawl.

We wandered off the taxiway and close to each of the buildings, hangars, and office structures. Some structures were deeper than wide, and we drove into those alleyways and back out.

I didn't pick up on anything for a while. We came around a building with signage that said 'Signature Flight Support,' and as we headed toward the access road, I got an intense tingling sensation on the back of my neck.

Irene slowed and picked her way through the parking area and turned left to go behind the building. As soon as she turned, the tingling on my neck moved to my right side. I put my hand on her arm, and she brought us to a stop.

Over to the right was where Perimeter Road South bent through an 'S' curve that turned it in toward the field away from the railroad yard. It gave way to additional building sites behind the hangars. Across the road from where we were sitting was a one-story block building. I saw three black Escalade SUVs. The rogues' vehicle of choice.

"Paulie, pictures of the license plates. Shoot from the hip so that no one notices us taking pictures."

And with that, she drove across the street and slowly, ever so slowly, past the building and vehicles. After we had made our pass, she picked up speed, and we headed south on Perimeter Road till we were almost across from Newmark's building.

HELICOPTERS N.W. It was the sign on the building we stopped at. She had pulled into a parking slot directly in front of the door. She shut the tug off and pulled out her phone.

She called Larisa and gave her the information of what we thought we found. Her last words were, "Paulie has pictures that she will send for license plate IDs."

Irene got out and said, "Grab our lunches and let's get into the classroom."

"*Whoah!* You can carry your own lunch," I said.

"I can't protect you if I have my hands full."

"That is so lame." I grabbed both of the lunch buckets and headed into the school.

Right inside the front door was a reception / waiting area in front of a 30" high divider fence with one of those 1940s era gates that swing two ways. The area had several cushioned chairs, a table with stiff back chairs, and endless literature pinned to the wall. Two other people were sitting in the chairs, and one person at the table filling out forms of some type.

Behind the dividing fence, space was outfitted as an open space office with three desks, file cabinets, copiers, printers, and computers. A regular office that, at the moment, had three women running everything.

"Welcome to flight school," said the woman seated at the desk that was butted up against the divider and facing the reception area.

"I'm Paulette Zahn, and this is Irene LaFarge. We're here to start flight training."

"Oh yes. I already have all your paperwork and medical clearance papers. Thank you so much for sending them in advance. Here is your school schedule, your initial study books, and materials. You can go right through the doors to my left, and it is the third classroom down the hall. The bathrooms are at this end of the hall. Glad to have both of you and good luck."

And she handed both of us backpacks with the schools' logo on them. They were pretty hefty, and soon I would find out just how many books there were. I led the way.

There were three doors on both sides of the hallway. The three on the left were close together, and the first was labeled 'MEN' and the second was named 'WOMEN.' The third, well, I had no idea what was behind door number 3. The three on the right were about 25 feet apart, and they were all standing open. They were all classrooms.

Each classroom held display models or mockups of different hand tools used to calculate navigational problems. The dash panel mockups were basic generic layouts.

The third classroom had six rectangular tables, 6' x 30", with two chairs behind each table. There were eight or nine other students that were already seated. They were all men. Irene and I made our way down the center aisle to the last tables, both of which were vacant.

I already heard whispered comments that pertained to Irene and my presence. Some comments were negative about women pilots, and others were discussing, no, they were choosing which one of us girls that particular talker was selected for his own.

One of the men got up and came back and took the seat at the table in front of us. The seat in front of Irene. Here it comes. This shit never ends well for the guy.

He turned his chair around and faced Irene and said, "Hello, doll, my name is Ray."

"Is that a stage name there, Ray Boy?" Irene responded. "Rule number one; you and all of the other *boys* here should NOT speak to either of us unless we speak to you first."

"Wow, a real tigress. You shouldn't turn your back because you might miss out on something special."

And he reached over the desk and took Irene's hand… for about half a second.

One of her hands shot out and grabbed his wrist, and the other grabbed his fingers and bent them backward until he was frozen with the pain.

"No one ever touches either one of us without our invitation. Am I clear there, Ray Boy?"

"Okay, I got the message," he said.

She released his hand, and he pulled it back, but his eyes were on fire. He was pissed, and I knew this was a person that would carry a deep grudge. Totally embarrassed he was.

"You made a big mistake," he said.

She leaned over to me and whispered, "Tear a page out of your notebook, fold it in half and take it to the back of the room and hold it up in front of the cork-board that is in the center of the wall."

Then she got up and went to the front of the room.

"Gentlemen and Ray, give me your attention for just one minute. I want to make sure all of you clearly understand the boundaries."

Then before they could respond, she moved lightning quick. One second she was standing there addressing them, and next, she was in a partial crouch with her right hand and arm straight out. It was too fast to follow, but the loud thunk from the back of the room had them turning their heads.

The paper I was holding out had a knife sticking through it and into the cork-board.

Silence.

Irene walked back and took her seat, and opened her new backpack to see what she had been saddled with.

In walked what appeared to be our instructor. It was a he, and I thought he must be the flight instructor's version of Dukie Howser, M.D. I swear he couldn't be twenty-one years old yet.

"Good morning, ladies and gentlemen. My name is Jake Martin, and I will be your instructor for both classroom and aircraft time. Please read the rules pamphlet that is in your school packages.

"This portion of your training consists of forty hours of classroom instruction, and you should all devote an equal amount of time studying outside of class. This class is scheduled to meet twice a week which would typically mean that you will be in aircraft by mid-January. I will only have four hours of classroom each time we meet, which will push our first flights into early February.

Now I would like to have everyone take a turn to tell the rest of us your name and a little about yourself if you will.

When it was Irene's turn, she stood and said, "My name is Irene LaFarge, and I am from Europe. I am here to get my pilot's license that will provide me an opportunity to raise my standing with my employer."

Improve her standing? What is that about? Irene and her twin sister Nicole were at the top of the employee pyramid at Newmark now.

It was my turn, and I stood and said, "My name is Paulette Zahn, and I, like Irene, work for Newmark Industries."

"I have read your file," Jake said. "You have had a very impressive military career. I also saw that you have had some time at the controls of helicopters. Would you care to tell everyone about those experiences?"

"I don't have that many hours at the controls. I was aircraft maintenance in Afghanistan. Occasionally, after I had repaired, re-calibrated, or installed new hardware, I tried my best to go on the shakedown flight just to see if everything was right. Many of the pilots in my group would have me take control of the aircraft once we were airborne."

"That is a very modest declaration. Would you mind if I expounded on your career?"

"I don't think anyone wants to hear about my past."

"Gentlemen, your classmate was a sergeant in the army. She has a Purple Heart, the Air Medal with a V for valor, and a Distinguished Flying Cross. I thank you for your service, ma'am. My dad is over there right now."

I sat. Everyone was looking at me. I just looked down at all the items that I had taken out of the backpack.

Jake went over some of the basic guidelines for the flow of our studies. He was just finishing up as noon approached, and I suddenly reached out and dug my nails into Irene's arm.

"What?"

"I think we have company. I can't tell if it is friendly or not, and it feels like more than one."

She stood and went over to the window.

"Nothing outside this window. Grab your bag, and let's go out front."

The front windows were mirrored. Either for privacy or to keep the afternoon sun out during the summers. The best part is that we could look out over the parking lot without anyone knowing they were being watched.

A black Escalade was parked at the curb on the street, and the back doors were open. Two grunts were looking over the tug right in front of the front door to this office. One of them walked around to the front of the tug and just stood there looking at the door behind us. He stood there for about a minute, then turned, collected his partner, and returned to the Escalade, and they drove off.

"What was that about?" I asked.

"I think the other guy may have fooled with the tug. Those tugs do not have any exotic controls or electronics. They are about as basic as a Model A. I'm calling Larisa for instructions.

"Okay… okay… okay."

She turned and went over to the receptionist/secretary. "Excuse me, but do you have a PA system for announcements?"

"Yes, why?"

"I need to make an announcement to everyone in the building. Don't let anyone out the door till they check with me first."

"I'm sorry, ma'am, but that is highly irregular. I don't think I can let you do that," said the, er, whatever she was.

"Here, this should get your attention," and she pulled out her badge. "This is a police matter. Our transportation may have a large fuel leak and could explode if anyone smokes or there is a spark near the tug."

"Oh my God. Here is the microphone. Should we evacuate everyone out the back?"

"No, a HazMat team will be here in a few moments. Just everyone stays inside, and this will get checked, and we should be released soon."

Three minutes later, a van pulled up in front of the building, between the building and the tug. Several people got out, one in bomb squad padded and armored protection. I couldn't see the suited person's face, but I recognized the other two. They were aircraft mechanics from my hangar crew.

One of the response team came into the school office.

"Hello, boss!" he said to me. "The tug is being checked for explosives and incendiary items. When he gives us the 'all clear,' we will go over the tug to see if there are any other surprises they may have left."

Irene's phone rang. "Yes?" and then she listened. After a minute, she hung up and turned to me. "Larisa said that they have clear footage of the SUV pulled up and of the guy that got out. When the SUV left, it continued down on the taxiway and around the south end of the runway, then up past our building. Nicole went out on her motorcycle to follow them. We are to stay here for the rest of the class."

After a short but tense few minutes, the Pillsbury Doughboy waddled around from the front of the Newmark van and conferred with the driver of the van. He pulled off the padded helmet and gave the thumbs-up signal toward the building.

Irene turned to the receptionist and told her that it was all clear. "Ms. Zahn and I are going back to the classroom. The parking lot is safe now, and the crew outside will be finishing up and leaving."

She headed through the double doors entering the hallway to the classrooms. I followed to find that Mr. Suave and Debonaire had taken a seat in the front row, as far from us as he could. Then he surprised me by getting up and heading for us as we sat down.

"I want to apologize for my actions earlier. I'm originally from Louisiana, and sometimes the redneck in me seeps out. There isn't any excuse for what I said. I just ended my enlistment in the army. I served two tours in Iraq and have been stationed at Lewis-McChord for the past four years in a training unit. Please forgive my intrusion. I was curious about what the instructor said about your awards. I called my commander at the base, and he went on and on about how much everyone who had heard your story and he has unlimited respect for what you did in Afghanistan. I, myself, received two Purple Heart medals, but they didn't involve anything heroic. I just forgot to duck."

"Apology accepted, and thanks for giving service to this country," I responded.

"I would like to buy the two of you a drink sometime if that isn't over the bounds."

"Thank you for the invitation and maybe someday, but right now, both of us are on a very tight work schedule that includes these classes," I told him.

"Well, we can pencil you in as a 'possible' on our dance card, so don't give up hope," Irene said. "My name is Irene, and you know my friend's name—Paulie Zahn."

"Thank you. My name is Buddy, Buddy Donaldson," he said, then he backed, turned, and went back to his seat upfront.

When the instructor came in, he informed us that due to the disturbance, this class was ended for the day. We were given instructions on which chapters in which book to study before Thursday's class.

Irene and I left and rode back to the hangar in the company van, leaving the tug for the HazMat crew to bring in. So much for the disguise of two chicks riding around the airfield in a tug.

~ ~ ~ ~

When we got back to the hangar, we both headed to the security basement.

There are a dozen workstations in the pit surrounding Larisa's soundproof office. Some had two screens, and some had as many as four screens. The views were not just of this building and the mansion grounds but also the Newmark Industries complexes worldwide.

As soon as we entered Larisa's office, she sealed the

privacy door, but she didn't opaque the glass that surrounded the office.

"Have a seat," Larisa said to us. "Your surveillance on the way to class this morning has, we are sure, ferreted out the location of the rogues that have recently been scratching around our doors late at night. I have a team installing cameras on the buildings' roofs across the street from their office building. We should be able to get good visual IDs on everyone entering or leaving that building.

The fact that they sent a van to follow you to the school says that they are keeping a very keen eye on our operation and possibly more specifically on you, Paulie."

"Why me?" I asked. "I mean, I have only been in Seattle what, a total of four or five months maybe. And much of that time, I was in the hospital here. I haven't met many people outside of Newmark. How is it that I have garnered this much attention? Almost makes me want to go knock on their door and ask."

Larisa and Irene both rolled their eyes in unison.

"We believe that all of these people are ultimately working for Stern Enterprises in Maryland. I think you were told about the theft of the blood supplies from the mansion basement and how Stern's plans all fell apart thanks to Eddie. Stern was run out of town by Karan and Spartak Newmark. The rogue that attacked you outside of Slim's was an upper-level lieutenant in the team we believe Stern has sent to disrupt all operations of Newmark Industries. Paulie, you are of particular interest to them because they think that you may have been turned into a vampire from his bite and believe that this makes you their property.

"Their interest is also increased because of the second

incident at Slim's, where we grabbed two more of their clique."

"Why is the second incident so interesting?" I asked.

"The two you captured were not newborn vampires. Not very old, but they had been vampires long enough that they should have been able to gather you up in one hand without breaking a sweat. Instead, you bested both of them. A brand new vampire as young as you were, or still are for that matter, should never be able to react as well as you did. Simply put, someone at Stern thinks there may be something special about you. A newly converted vampire with the abilities of one that is a hundred years old. We don't think they know of the other special abilities you are displaying, and we hope to keep them a secret."

"Why?" I asked.

"They would like to ask you a lot of questions about our operations and to see if your accelerated conversion time was done by some enhancements that are a secret of Newmark's. There is the secondary thought that if they can't get any information out of you, they would then start draining you of your blood for them to use for their conversions in the belief that your blood will create a super race of vampires for them."

"Shit." Yeah, that was my comment. 'Shit.'

"You aren't the only high-value target. Stern wants to get his hands on Darja just as badly. She slipped his grasp after he had kidnapped her from the gala at the art museum. Her status within Newmark, namely her position in the R & D unit in Europe, identified her as a valuable Newmark asset. To them, she was trading goods. Her rescue, coupled with the revelation that Todd had been a spy inserted into the Stern operations for over four years, had or rather has him screwed up through the ceiling. After we rescued Darja and Todd and the final meeting face to face of Stern and the Newmarks, we had thought that Stern would take his game and leave town, never to return. Or at least for a long time. We were, it appears, very wrong. He is the force behind all the rogues appearing in and around Seattle. I believe that we can wipe out all of the ones here, but that won't stop Stern from sending another group in. We have to shorten his leash or outright eliminate him and his top generals so this won't happen again. His senior field general is Victor Iskenderian. We believe he is here somewhere overseeing this operation. He has a very special personal vendetta against our Eddie Vangh. At the gala, Eddie Vangh realized that Darja was his blood sister from 1945. Her father, the vampire that converted Eddie, was her biological father, which meant that Eddie and Darja share some familiar genes. When she disappeared from the gala, we knew she was taken out of there against her will. Eddie went a little berserk and put his knife down through the center of an ancient Patek Phillippe Repeater pocket watch that was a family heirloom of Iskenderians and of substantial personal value to him, something like a tribe totem. More background for you. Maxmillian Stern is not a member of the Council of Elders. We don't think he has any friends on the council, based in Europe, Switzerland in particular. There are only thirteen members of the Council of Elders. You, Paulie, have the honor of working for one, Spartak Newmark, and you have been introduced to two more, Phil Markham and Danielle Nollan. Nowhere else on Earth are there three council elders living this close to each other. The council is closely following your life. It is a good thing because they have jointly, at the request of the three elders from Seattle, proclaimed that you are to be given extraordinary protection and security. I have already discussed this with the council members that are here, and we all agree that we will do our best to keep the protection as light as possible so that you have a normal life. I wanted to increase your security detail from one to two, but that was nixed, and we are just going to continue as things have been. Please do not leave this building or the Manor grounds without Nicole or Irene with you."

I had nothing to say. This was a whole lot to take in. It had cleared up some questions I had, no, I think it may have cleared up most of the questions I had about my new persona.

"Wait, excuse me, I was lost in thought, so I missed part of what you were saying," I said to Larisa.

"I was going through the surveillance plan. There are four two-person teams, and each team has a vehicle assigned to them. I have talked to the operators of businesses that are in the buildings across from the rogues. Our teams will keep their vehicles in those buildings, and the teams will be there 24/7. The team leaders are Amelia, Eddie, Todd, and Pete. Each one of them will have a company guard that has been through anti-terrorist training. We will follow anyone leaving their building. Procedure calls for one team to always remain in observation, so if more than three vehicles leave their place, we won't be able to follow the fourth car out. We must locate where the leader of this local group is. We have to cut off the head of this beast before it gains more traction in this area.

"The second but no less critical is tying this group back to Stern Enterprises."

"What do you want me to do?" I asked.

"You, Darja, and the twins are to stay away from the hot spots. If you and whoever is your protector of the day are confronted by an equal or greater number of these rogues, you are to extricate yourself from that arena as fast as possible. We need you not to get captured, which is their object."

Hummm! I wasn't known to be a shrinking violet, but I figured that I would take those directions well. I mean, I wasn't thinking about going over to their little den, smashing my way in, and beating them all up. Well, maybe a little bit, but giving it a sober second thought, considering that it was a covey of rogue vampires that wanted to eat me, well, sitting in the background may be a wiser choice.

"Without fear of repeating myself, what am I supposed to be doing now?"

"Go back to your office and conduct operations as you would normally. Darja and Nicole will either already be there or will show up soon. For the time being, you and Darja and your twin protectors are together as a traveling troupe, not to be separated until this threat is eliminated.

"That is everything I have at the moment. I have to get to some projects that need my attention, so if there isn't anything else, let's get back to our jobs."

With that, I left and went back to my office in the flight shack.

~ ~ ~ ~

Darja was already in my office when Irene and I got there. I wasn't too chipper at the moment because I was feeling a little caged. I was free to go anywhere I wanted—as long as it wasn't anywhere that could be dangerous, like downtown Seattle to shop for clothes. I also had to have this security gaggle surrounding me at every turn.

I dropped my new book bag on my desk and pulled everything out. I flipped the pages of two or three of the instruction manuals. My impression was that the text was written for someone that was a couple of grades behind me. If all the class materials were this simple, Irene and I should be done with the classroom portion without a worry.

"Darja, do you fly?" I asked.

"I have a basic fixed-wing and a glider pilot's license. Gliding is a popular sport in Europe. I have been flying sailplanes for fifteen years in the Alps that run through Switzerland. The scenery is breathtaking when you are soaring with the eagles. I've looked at some of the glider clubs in and around Seattle and haven't gone to any of their meets yet. I could lease one of the powered gliders, and we could explore the mountains and valleys east of here."

"I would like that. Do you think they will let just the two of us up together? Won't be able to take the twins along, too much weight, and the cabin is only set for two."

"Bucket list. Put it in your bucket list, and when we get the rats nests cleared out, we can go for a flight."

Irene came into my office, "Nicole just returned from her snoopy trip. Having the de-briefing here in your office. Larisa will telecommute in to be present."

Nicole was in her black leathers, and if I were a guy, I would be drooling. Her boot heels have 1 ½", bringing her close to 6' 2", and with that neon purple hair, a single braid down her back to her waist, she stood out.

I envisioned the twins, Darja and I, all riding motorcycles. Now, if we could talk Eddie into letting Amelia take his Harley, the five of us would be one hell of a motorcycle gang.

"Earth to Paulie, hello, where did you go just then?" Nicole asked.

"Sorry, dreaming about something I want to do with

everyone after this mess is taken care of," I said.

Nicole turned toward the screen that had Larisa on, live. "Good afternoon, Larisa. I want to bring you and these three up to speed on what I was doing while I was out enjoying a ride. I wasn't far when I heard the radio talk about the possible locations of the RIB's den and then the chatter about a van pulling up in front of the school. I was coming down Airport Way South and nearing the RIB's clubhouse when I saw a black Audi S8 pulling out of the lot, so I turned and followed it. I followed the car onto Interstate 90 East over the bridge to Mercer Island. I got hemmed in by a redneck in a pick-up and lost sight of the car. I believe that it may have gotten off the interstate at the first Mercer Island exit. Could we get a team sitting on that exit so the next time that car gets off there, we will have a tail in place waiting for them?"

"I can get that put together," Larisa said. "Audi S8, black with heavily tinted windows?"

"Yeah. I never got the license plate, though."

"Not a big problem," Larisa said. "There aren't that many Audi S8s around, especially with the heavily tinted windows. It would be wonderful to pick up the trail of that car and follow it wherever that person is living, and bets are that it is Iskenderian himself.

"Now I want everyone to go quiet. Go home and hunker down until we get enough intel to make a move."

Irene and Darja rode with me, and Nicole rode her bike back to the Manor.

~~~~

Just driving onto the Manor grounds was enough to pull the
~~~~

stress bands right off your back. Furrowed brows would go calm. One's mind would automatically know that you were now in your safe zone.

Irene and I dumped the contents of our backpacks out on our dining table. We pushed the table back against the wall under some shelves, perfectly situated to hold all the books and study materials.

"All this studying has made me hungry, and I want some wine," Irene said.

"Studying? What are you talking about? I even carried your book bag in for you."

"Have to keep my hands free in case we are attacked."

"You're such a load of crap. It's a wonder you have been able to live this long. Are you going to be serious about this course?"

"Of course, I'm serious. I'm looking forward to getting my private pilot's license, and I intend to get qualified on many different aircraft. We didn't get an assignment for Thursday, so let us go over to the kitchen, get some dinner, and visit the cellar."

"Cellar? Do you mean the wine vault under the Manor?

"Of course, you do. Free drinks for those of us on scholarship."

We went to the kitchen to fill up on some amazing home-cooked creations from Ms. K, which included fresh vegetables right out of Lisbeth's garden. Most of the regulars were there, and the comradeship felt amazing.

None of the groups I had ever been part of in my life—even in the army—were as cohesive as the one in that kitchen. Vampires, damphires, and Norms made up this group, but no one felt different or excluded. Everyone has each other's back. It didn't get any better than that.

When Irene and I finished eating, we headed toward the cellar. We weren't the only ones headed down for a drink. Pete, Eddie, Amelia, Darja, Nicole, and the new guy, Scotty Barton, all followed us.

I waved Scotty over to sit by me. I was going to explain how the wine cellar works, what you could and couldn't drink. He was gushing with 'wows' and 'holy shits' at what he was seeing. Cute watching a newbie to the clan. And, it seemed like I was taking the lead in showing him the ropes.

I was taken by his innocence and probably his looks. He was older than me in both Norm and vampire years, but only by a little. I was considered the baby of the group, but what I had been through in the last two months put me far ahead of many vampires much older than me. He was the same height as me, and I was attracted to that fact. Most of the other male vampires were in the six feet plus height except Eddie, who was also the same height as me. It occurred to me that Eddie was very taken. Scotty wasn't.

Whoa, Nellie! Where had that thought come from? I wasn't boy crazy, and romantic relationships hadn't been a priority for me since I had high school. I wasn't sterile, though. A small infatuation and a romp in the hay every so often, but nothing ever became serious.

And I wondered what sex with a vampire would be like.

"Hello, Paulie," Amelia was saying. Or teasing.

I panicked for a moment. She couldn't read minds? Could she? Shit, if she knew what I thought, there would be no end to the teasing.

I turned my Plain Jane faced toward her and asked, "What were you saying? I was thinking about school."

She was sitting at the end of the table. She put her elbow on the table, and rested her face on her fist, and looked at me with a smirk.

"What?" was all I could say.

"*Uh-huh*, so that is your story." *Or should that comment end in a question mark?* I thought to myself.

To add to it, she turned her head a little to look directly at Scott's face and rolled her eyes.

The room temperature must have gone up fifteen degrees because I felt extremely warm all of a sudden. I tried to appear nonchalant over her words and actions, but it appeared that everyone else in the room was suddenly all ears.

"Can I get you another glass of wine, ma'am?" Scotty said loud enough for everyone to hear.

Oh, fuck! was all I could think. "Sure, thanks," I said.

"*Whoee!* She has him trained already?" Pete wondered.

He said it *out loud*. Pete was the staidest and reserved of everyone here.

"Wait, have I done something wrong? I know that I'm new here and I don't know all the proper etiquette. Paulie, please pardon me if I have violated your space or sump-thing," Scotty said.

"Don't worry about it," I said. "All of the people here are socially challenged and starved for recognition. Just ignore what they say. You should talk to Eddie. I understand he went through a ream of teasing when he started here."

Thank god for Eddie. He broke in with a change of direction in the subject matter.

"Depending on the weather, I'm thinking of going out for a New Year's day ride on my Harley. Any of you others want to go?"

"Are you taking me?" Amelia asked with a little sharpness in her voice.

"Nicole, Irene, either of you want to go?" Eddie asked.

"What about me?" I asked.

"I want to go too," said Darja.

"We can do this. We just have to make sure you, Darja, and you, Paulie, are covered within a security blanket. How about you, Irene, and you, Nicole? You want to go for a ride on New Year's day?"

We took some time and several glasses of wine before we finalized who was driving and who was riding. Eddie was alone as he had no pillion seat. Amelia had recently gotten a BMW R1200 Adventure similar to the ones Nicole and Irene rode. Darja would ride with Nicole, and I was going on my Harley.

"What about you?" I asked Scotty. "Want to go? You can ride behind me."

His face lit up with a huge smile. "Thanks, I would love to go."

With that all arranged, everyone settled in, telling tales about each other's past and drinking more wine.

Then we had just one more glass of wine before we stumbled off to our apartments.

~ ~ ~ ~

Other than struggling to get out of bed, Wednesday was a regular workday. Nothing to report from the observers over at the rogue den and no one had attempted any break in at the hangar overnight.

Thursday, Irene and I were up and out together early as it was a school day. We rode in my SUV and went straight to the school building instead of driving a tug from the hangar.

There was a beat-up old Dodge Power Wagon parked on the street across from the school. Two guys in what could be aircraft mechanic's coveralls. They had the hood up and some parts from the engine sitting on the fenders.

They were members of the Newmark security team. They or another team with a different vehicle would be sitting there every day that Irene and I were in classes; eight a.m. to five p.m. with an hour break at noontime. This was a change in the times. With this schedule, the classroom portion of our instructions would now finish on Tuesday, 10 January.

That was Thursday. On Friday, it was back to managing the hangar. The Boeing was out. It had left early with Mr. Spartak and eight of the managers from the local facilities. They were flying to Rome and wouldn't return till late January.

Before departure, Mr. Newmark came into my office and asked how everything was going.

"It couldn't be better. Things seemed to have quieted down with the rogues, but no one is letting their guard down. If you see Lisa, tell her hello for me."

He reached out for my hand and held it softly.

"I will see the person formerly known as Lisa. I want you to forget that name. I know you two are close, and I will have an update and personal words from her to you when I return. I'm taking four pilots and Bumbo as the ride-along mechanic."

"Four Pilots? Why so many?" I asked.

"Only stopping for fuel, and we would exceed the amount of time a pilot can fly as a crew member without a break. Crew change over in Newark. Everyone and all our gear are loaded up, and it is time to go. Take care of this place and especially take care of yourself. Please don't go anywhere without one of the personal guards going with you."

"Yes, sir. Have a safe trip."

That night, we—Darja, Nicole, Irene, and I—went out to dinner at the Hitchcock on the main drag in downtown Winslow. Amelia had told us to use her name for fast seating and the best service. She said that was where she took Eddie on their first date.

~~~~
~~~~

Friday night's dinner started very relaxedly. I was starting to get spoiled on the quality of the food that Ms. K at the Manor prepared for us, but Hitchcock's was exquisite.

On Saturday, Irene and I studied our lessons. And when evening rolled around, we went over to the kitchen in the Manor for our New Year's Eve dinner. The celebration of New Year's wasn't anything important to me, and it appeared that no one else was all Ga Ga over it either. I was in bed before midnight, and I heard Irene come in just as I was nodding off.

Sunday, New Year's day was spent studying some more and going through the apartment, arranging and re-arranging everything, until I finally felt that I was settled in comfortably.

MOTORCYCLE GANG RIDE
2 JANUARY 2017

The newly formed VMC motorcycle gang all met in the kitchen for coffee and juice and hot croissants. The sun wouldn't be up until eight a.m., but we could already tell that it would be a clear day. Cold, but clear.

Everyone but Scotty was picking up their continental break-fast selections and sitting down at the long table. The Scotty exception was due to the number of used cups and plates in front of him. He must have been here for hours. His face was slightly flushed, probably from the anticipation of going with six of the core cadre of Newmark Industries on a ride.

No, I knew what it was. He was looking forward to riding behind me. I mean, what guy wouldn't want to be snuggled up behind me as the wind blew through our hair?

"Paulie," Amelia was saying. "Where did you go?"

BLINK!

"Oops! Sorry," I said. "I was going over one of the lessons from flight school."

"You are such a liar," Amelia said. "You were staring at Scotty there at the end of the table. With eyes wide and your mouth was hanging open a little."

"I was not."

I looked around the table, and everyone was looking at me with little smirks on their faces.

"Maybe it would be best if Scotty rode with Irene," I said.

“No, no, no,” was the chorus from the other five.

I certainly wasn’t pleased with that vote of non-confidence. I noticed that Darja, Nicole, and Irene were huddled up and having a little laugh. It was definitely at my expense.

I only had two other contacts with Scotty. For just a few moments when we were introduced by the rear gate and our little wine party in the cellar last night. He had poured me a glass of wine, that’s all.

I didn’t care. Whatever they were saying, they were not going to arrange a situation between Scotty and myself. Twenty-eight years old, and I hadn’t needed a boyfriend before, which wasn’t changing anytime soon. I mean, I barely had my feet on the ground about the new person I had recently and unwillingly become. That and flight school and the management of the flight crews had my dance card over-full. I didn’t have time for any romantic relationships.

Chitter, chitter, chitter was all I allowed myself to hear for the rest of the meal. Sounded like a pack of raccoons fighting over a piece of fish.

As soon as I finished eating, I dropped my plates and such at the sink and went out to the garages to uncover my bike. Wasn’t even dusty. The last time I had her out was when Nigel and I captured the two rogues in the Last Chance. It was more than a memory. It would always stand out as the first time I ever flexed my new abilities.

The others in the gang were coming out of the kitchen door and headed to their apartments for their gloves, scarves, and heavy jackets. Scotty already had his stuff and came over to me and my bike.

“Look, I’m sorry for whatever it was that I might have caused in there,” Scotty said to me. “I don’t think I gave anyone any impression that I was hitting on you."

"Don't worry about it. I haven't been here much longer than you have, and I know that teasing is S.O.P. around here, especially at meals."

When I said that, I looked up at him. He was embarrassed. His cherubic face was pink-tinged, and it wasn't sunburned.

It was a moment that I could have done some teasing myself but chose not to since he would be cuddled up behind me once we got riding.

'Cuddled up?' I hadn't said that out loud but just the thought or the vision of him behind me on my Harley had me thinking that I should have spoken up when we were all deciding who would be riding with whom.

My bike only had a small pillion cushion for a rider. I showed Scotty the footpegs for the rider and then gave him my rules for riders.

"No unnecessary talking. Don't lean into turns thinking it would help. It won't and could cause me to lose balance. If you feel the need to hang on, either put your hands on my shoulders or on my sides just above my hips. How do you carry your sidearm? Shoulder or hip holster?"

"Sidearm? I'm not carrying any pistols."

Just then, Irene showed up and heard his statement.

"This is a pleasure ride, Scotty," she started in. "However, we are on a war footing and are never to be without our sidearms. I'm talking about it all the time, even when you are off duty here on the Manor grounds. Go back inside and get armed up."

His face suddenly got a darker shade of red.

Eddie and I had our respective machines out in the center of the garage quadrangle warming up. The other three machines didn't need a lot of idyll time, but the Harleys require several minutes of warm-up before taking off down the road. Warming up may not be needed on newer machines, but my bike, in particular, was an old classic, and I treated it with soft fuzzy gloves.

Finally, all the bikes were started, and we were all mounted up to go except Scotty.

He was stepping out of the kitchen door with all his togs, including crash helmet, on. When he came up to me, I looked at him and asked, "What holster do you have?"

"Why?" he asked.

"Because I want to know what side and which hand will be in play if something comes up. If something happens where we get into a shoot-out, I want to know which side of my head the report from your gun will be coming from. I don't want to be startled while rolling down the highway at 115 miles per hour. I could lose control, and I'm sure you don't want that to happen. As soon as I am on and ready, you climb on behind me. Sit up straight and let me do all the leaning. Remember what I said about where you can put your hands. Are you ready?"

He didn't say anything, but I felt his helmet go up and down with a 'Yes.'

Eddie and Amelia took the lead, followed by the two ups, me with Scotty and Nicole with Darja, followed by our tail gunner, Irene.

We rode through Winslow and turned north-west when we came to State 305, headed off the island by the Indian casino.

It was 2 January, but it was recognized as the official New Year's Day, and traffic was light because so few people were working. I had never driven or ridden these roads, so it was all new to me. It was all gorgeous too. Green fir trees abounded, creating not only beautiful scenery but also a natural fresh pine smell.

For much of the ride, we were two up, side by side. No lane splitting or doing wheelies down the freeways. Just a slow cruise.

I memorized the routes which took us to Route Number 3, where we turned right. The next turn was onto the bridge and Rte 104 toward Port Townsend and a ferry ride to Whidbey Island.

We toured Whidbey Island for a few hours and ended up in Clinton, where we got the ferry to Mukilteo on the mainland. We stopped in Mukilteo at the Diamond Knot brewery for a late lunch.

It was already three in the afternoon when we finished eating, and since sundown was at four thirty, we decided to head back into Seattle to catch the ferry back to Bainbridge.

~ ~ ~ ~

We queued up for the ferry, which was just unloading when we arrived. Ten minutes later, we were loading. Motorcycles go to the head of the line, so we got on and parked and pulled off our helmets to shake off the tension you get when you ride any distance, and we had ridden quite far today. I had gotten to see a lot of beautiful country sides. It is amazing that you could be deep into a major U.S. city and moments later, so far into the wooded countryside that you forget that a big city is just a short drive away.

I was completely relaxed for probably the first time in two months. It would feel great if it wasn't for that itch in the back of my neck.

"What's wrong?" Irene, who had just come over to me, asked. "Your head is swinging back and forth like a radar antenna."

I stared at her for only a split second when I realized the signs.

"We have company," I said to Irene, and then I motioned everyone over for a huddle. "There one or more vamps nearby."

Nicole and Darja closed the space between us, and we lined up so that we were looking at the autos behind us on the ferry.

"What is everyone doing?" Scott asked.

He was the perfect little cherub. Scrubbed, shinning innocent face.

It was then that I first noticed that Scotty had little or no facial hair. Was he a transvestite, or maybe he had not reached puberty yet? Just one of those observations one folds up and puts in their pocket for later review.

There was a passageway on both sides of the ferry separated from the vehicles by a bulkhead with a doorway at intervals. Eddie had gone through one to get to the outer side of the ferry, and Amelia went out the other side. They were going to go toward the rear and then come back through the line of cars and amble up past each vehicle, trying to get sight of the occupants.

We were almost to the ferry dock on Bainbridge Island when they came up to where the rest of us were.

"There is an Audi RS3 three rows back on the starboard side," Amelia told me.

Scotty had heard her and was shuffling off in that direction, maybe to get a better look.

"SCOTTY," I said. I said it loud so that he wouldn't miss it.

"What the fuck are you doing, dipwad? Want to make sure

they know that we are on to them? We aren't setting up for a Tiddly Winks tournament."

He turned toward me, and he had a bad face on. Like I didn't have the right to call him out on anything.

Irene grabbed his arm and told him, "You are riding the rest of the way behind me, so get over by my Adventure."

Then Nicole came up behind him and put one hand on the back of his neck. She was squeezing also because his face screwed up with pain, but he didn't jerk away.

"Don't say or do anything other than what I instruct you to do. Am I clear?" Nicole said.

He nodded, acknowledging that he understood.

"Go over to Irene's bike and stand there or get on if you want, but keep your eyes forward toward the ferry landing. There are six of us here, and we will tear your heart out if you dare do anything stupid again. Is there anything you don't understand?"

"No, ma'am. Perfectly clear," he replied and went forward to where Irene's bike stood.

"Were you able to see how many were in the car?" I asked Amelia.

"There is a driver and a passenger in the front seats. I couldn't see into the back due to the dark tint covering the windows."

Eddie came over and told us, "When we get off in Winslow, we go through town to Madison, where we will all turn left, heading toward the harbor. At the first street, Amelia and I will turn to double back around while the rest of you go down to the Harbor Public House Restaurant and pull into their parking lot. When you stop, line the bikes up facing the entrance to the lot for a fast exit."

We docked a moment later, and we all mounted our bikes and were among the first vehicles off the ferry. We rode slowly through town till we came to Madison, where we all turned. It was about a hundred feet to the next turn. I was right behind Eddie and Amelia then and watched my mirrors to see if we were being followed. Didn't see them, so we cruised very slowly to the parking for the Public House.

We pulled in and rounded the wagons, and I was starting to think that we may have lost them when I saw the Audi slowly poking its nose around the corner and pointing toward the parking lot where we were.

The sun was approaching sundown, but our location was masked by the hills of Bainbridge Island, putting us into twilight early. Because of what type of species all of us were, our night or twilight vision was excellent, as was the eyesight of those in the car following us if what my senses were telling me was accurate.

The car stopped in the parking lot entryway. As I watched from the cover of the other cars already here, I saw the interior light in the Audi come on.

AMATEURS!

The light to the car door remained on longer than necessary for one individual to get out. There had to be one or more in the back seat, which required the front seat-back to be folded to get out. As I heard the car door slam shut, the headlights were turned off.

That was considerate of them. I mean, when the headlights were on, we were slightly blinded in the glare, and now, thanks to the AMATEUR driving, we were back on an equal footing to see our adversaries.

I saw one figure run to the right and the other one moved to the left. My eyes were going back and forth on the two. When I swept my vision to the left, I realized that the first one had disappeared. That wasn't good.

We hadn't expected to get into a situation such as this, and none of us had put earwig com units in. We all had our cell phones, but I wasn't about to take mine out and have the light from the screen put me into the crosshairs of the enemy.

I started to stand so that I could see over the hood of the car I was hiding behind when I realized that one of the enemy had come up on the other side of the very car I was behind. I heard the soft chuf, chuf of a silenced pistol firing followed by two tings as the spent casings hit the pavement.

I dropped to the ground and mentally ran a physical check of my body. I determined that I wasn't hit, so where were the shots going? Suddenly, all hell broke loose.

I heard someone calling out that he was hit. It sounded like Scotty Barton. It must be as he was the only male in my group that was in the parking lot.

Taking a chance to see my adversary, I rose again. He was in a high crouch and was looking to his left, which was the direction he had shot in.

KABLUEY!

A pistol went off right next to my temple. Vampires are no different than a Norm, and hearing goes to shit when there is an explosion only inches from your ear. My head snapped to the right… it was Irene. I hadn't heard her come up to my hiding place. I looked back toward the RV (Rogue Vampire), and he was lying on the ground with half his face missing. He was NOT going to get up ever again.

Scotty was calling for help, but Irene grabbed my arm and held me down.

"If we go to help Scotty, we will be sitting ducks. There are at least two others out there. One on foot, and one is still in the car. Pretty sure the one on the loose will be focusing on Scotty, hoping that one of us would be stupid enough to go over to him. Stay out of the line of sight from the Audi, and we will try to work our way around behind the other foot soldier.

Just as Irene and I were getting set to dash to the cover of a different car, two motorcycles pulled in behind the Audi. It was Eddie and Amelia. Amelia had LED high-intensity running lights on her bike, and it was like the sun had just jumped overhead. I could see through all the tinted windows, and there was only the driver in the car. No other passengers.

That was enough to startle the rogue that was on foot. He stood and was starting to head toward the Audi when I heard a soft 'pop.' That wasn't a silenced pistol. That was a stun gun. Darja carried one as well as her .45. At the same time as this went on, there were sounds of scuffling back by the Audi. Eddie and Amelia had captured the driver. And Nicole and Darja had tied up the other foot soldier.

We got together quickly. We had to mop up and get out of there before a crowd of Normals formed. The dead body went into the Audi trunk, and the two captured and well-bound thugs were cast into the back seat. We got Scotty into the passenger's seat, and Darja was assigned to drive back to the Manor.

We rode and drove off just as some patrons were coming out of the restaurant. We were almost back to the Manor grounds when we heard sirens in the distance. They weren't getting louder, so it was assumed that they were going to the restaurant and not after us.

When we rode into the garage quadrangle, Karan and Odie were waiting for us. Karan asked Amelia if she thought Scotty should go to the medical facility.

It was a through and through wound in his right thigh. Blood was seeping from the wound, so maybe no arteries were hit. To be on the safe side, though, Karan had Scotty get into the back seat of my SUV, and she told me to take Irene and get us to the vampire hospital.

As I was helping Scotty into my car, I glanced back at the Audi where Odie and Eddie were helping the two survivors out of the back seat of the Audi. I realized that I looked because my internal vampire radar was singing loudly in my head. This sensation goes off when a vampire is nearing me that I didn't know. This time, I knew the person. It was emanating from the driver of the Audi. It was *the* John Cooper that had tried to poison us at the Christmas party. John Cooper was the person that was supposed to be back-up for Zope when we raided the compound in the Port Orchard airport. I started toward him.

"Paulie," Ms. Karan was saying. "We have this one. Your mission is to get Scotty to the hospital. We'll try to leave a few pieces for when you get back."

I had an idea, and there was something I wanted to try.

"Ms. Karan. Just let me look him in the eye. That, and could I touch him with my bare hand?"

"No, er wait, why do you want to do that?" Karan asked.

"I don't know. Something tells me that I should do it."

"Okay, but make it short. I want Scotty looked at and at least you and Irene back as fast as you can."

Ten minutes later, Irene and I were sitting in the queue for the ferry back to Seattle. Scotty was in the back seat babying himself.

After the ferry crossed the sound and we were off and pulling into traffic, Scotty said, "Stop, I have to puke."

I pulled over and stopped the car. Scotty let himself out and was on his hands and knees alongside the road emptying his stomach of lunch.

As he climbed back in, I asked him, "Is your wound that painful? Is it causing your stomach to be upset?"

"Later," was all he said.

When the elevator door opened on the hospital floor, Dr. Smyth was waiting with two attendants and a gurney. They took over from there, so Irene and I went to the waiting area.

Twenty minutes went by before Dr. Smyth came into the waiting area.

"Scotty Barton is going to be just fine. Gave him a blood booster transfusion and gave the openings a few stitches. I want to keep him overnight. Just want to make sure there isn't any infection before I release him. You all can go back and see him if you want."

So that is what we did, visit.

We both said our hellos as we walked into the room. He was quite flushed.

"Are you in any pain?" I asked.

He looked down as if he hadn't heard me.

"Scotty, talk to me. I asked if you were in any pain?"

"No, ma'am. I'm okay."

"I was asking because I thought there was something about your wound that I didn't see at first. You know, with your stomach emptying its self."

Scotty looked very uncomfortable. He was scrunching himself down under the bedding.

"Scotty, what's up?" I asked.

"Sorry, ma'am. It's just, well, it is just that I never saw anyone get killed before. And to see their face blown off like that. I'm still a little off, but I will be all right by morning."

"We are going to go back to the Manor now. One of us will bring you a change of clothes from your room. Is there anything special you would like us to get?" Nicole said.

He gave me a short list, and Irene and I left to return to Bainbridge.

~~~~

When we arrived back at the Manor's garage area, we saw Amelia pushing Zope in a wheelchair, toward the kitchen.

"Suppertime?" I asked.

"No, we're going to talk to our newest captives," Amelia said.

"Where are you keeping them?" I asked.

I thought I had seen most of the Manor's insides and couldn't think of a place to keep prisoners such as these two. So, I just kept quiet and followed.

I followed everyone through the house to Sparky's den. Karan was waiting there, and as soon as we were all in the room, she had Irene close the door, which automatically locked. Then she went over to the floor-to-ceiling bookcase and touched something. I heard some mechanical equipment moving a section that opened onto a hallway that looked right out of a Victorian house or a bordello. Crushed red velvet with sconces on the walls with fake flickering candles in them for illumination. Short hall, dead-ended at elevator doors.

"Paulie, as this is your first time in this area of the Manor, I want you to use your access codes on the elevator. Once we are all in, you go to the back and open the iris scan port with its keypad for the password. I want you to use your eye and your
~~~~

passwords to get us to the floor we want," Karan said to me.

After we were all in and I was poised over the scan port and keyboard, I hesitated.

"What are you waiting for? Go ahead and log in."

"Don't I have to push a button for the floor I want?"

"This elevator has stops at the level under the kitchen and is where all the food and household supplies are kept. The next button down takes us to the wine cellar. When you went there before, you had entered this same elevator but through the back door facing into the kitchen's back hallway. This time, because you are triggering your codes into the keypad attached to the scanner, the elevator will stop half a floor before the wine cellar. When the car stops, the back door will open onto a secret section of the Manor. This is your first trip here, and hopefully, you will come here when you are off work."

"What is here that I would want to see?"

"There are three security doors that lead off this hallway. The one straight ahead is our private library that holds a collection of books from modern to very ancient that have anything to do with vampires. It is the greatest collection of documents, papers, and books that memorialize our history starting a few thousand years ago. But we aren't going there today.

"The two doors opposite each other used to be to the processing and storage rooms of human and vampire blood that we process into the capsule replacement for whole blood. After the robbery, we moved this entire processing plant to another location. These two rooms are now temporary quarters for your guests," Karan told me.

It had to be me that all the explanations were directed to. Everyone else standing there must have had been given this tour way before I got here.

"Let's go into this room," Karan said. She unlocked the door, and we all walked or were wheeled in.

The room was full of medical supplies. But it appeared more suited for autopsies than operate and save. There were two gurneys in the room, and the two latest captures were tied down on them. I didn't recognize one, but the other one had my alarm bells going off loudly.

It was John Cooper, the local poisoner. I went over and loomed. Loomed and stared into his eyes.

They were unflinching, and he stared right back. It felt like he was straining to reach into my brain and take information out. As far as I knew, that wasn't possible. I had the time, and he certainly wasn't going anywhere soon, so I continued to stare directly into his eyes and imagined I could see what he was thinking, see right into his brain.

I couldn't hear anyone else in the room. My eyesight dimmed except my tunnel vision of my sight into Cooper's eyes. I could tell that I was making him very uncomfortable. He was moving his hands and legs to get away, but he never stopped looking directly into my eyes. I thought I heard something tearing or ripping. With each sound, Cooper winced, but his eyes never left mine.

The sounds I was hearing coincided with a matching needle prick at my brain. I stared harder, and I felt like I could see inside his brain. It was dark and crowded. It seemed like there were internal conflicts going on. Or was that a feeling that I was creating on my own…

"Paulie! Paulie, snap out of it."

I broke eye contact and had to shake my head to clear the slight dizziness that suddenly clouded my brain.

"Are you all right?" Darja asked.

"I'm fine."

"You need to talk to me about what just happened," Darja said.

It seemed that she was the lead person, in control of what went on in this room.

"Paulie, do you know how long you were staring into his face?" she asked.

"Two, maybe three minutes, why?"

"You were locked onto his eyes for over forty minutes," she said.

"I was not." I was emphatic. "I have only stared at him for a minute or two. Where did you come up with forty minutes?"

I took a quick look at everyone else. Or not, because only Zope in her wheelchair and Darja were still in the room.

"Where is everyone else? When did they leave?"

"I asked them to leave," Darja said.

"This is beyond weird. What is going on?"

"We need to go back upstairs. I want to sit with just you and me. Just trust me when I say that I think I know what is happening to you."

Suddenly, I had this vision of myself in a room with another person. A much older person was dressed in a black suit with a black silk shirt and black silk tie. He was slightly stooped but still had a commanding presence. He was talking to me. I wasn't there, but he seemed to think he was talking to someone.

Then with a shake of my head, the vision cleared, and I was back in the room with Darja and Zope.

I put my hand out and grabbed a hold of Zope's chair. I had a little attack of vertigo. I was not a person prone to dizzy spells.

"What is happening to me?"

Zope looked at Darja, and Darja looked at me.

"We need to go upstairs and get someplace private where I can talk to you, just the two of us, okay?" Darja asked gently.

"Okay." And the three of us locked up and rode the elevator back up to Sparky's den.

"Zope, could you ask Karan to meet me here?"

~ ~ ~ ~

I made myself comfortable in one of the leather wing-back chairs. I could relax in this room. Darja sat in the twin chair next to me. We were close enough to each other that we could touch. That is, if one or the other of us wanted to touch. I certainly didn't feel the urge to hold Darja's hand.

We didn't wait but for a nanosecond when Ms. Karan showed up. She went and sat in the boss' chair behind the desk. Well, actually, she was the boss.

"Paulie, I think you had a vision of something John Cooper had seen, heard, or done."

"I can't do that. I mean, that is like reading someone's mind, and that is not something I could ever do. Why are you saying that about me?"

"You haven't been among us for very long. Not enough time to hear and understand everyone's background and past life. It is important that you listen to me while I explain *my* past. My parents were an unusual couple for the times. My mother is a damphire, and my father is a vampire. I say, 'is' because I don't know for sure that they are not still alive. From an early age, I exhibited a talent for hearing people's thoughts. I was officially confirmed as a damphire when I was only six years old. When my mother and I were fleeing various regimes bent on eradicating all gypsies, I picked up a little income, reading minds. Nothing deep or too serious, but the difference was that it wasn't some cheap parlor trick. I could and still can read what someone is thinking. I lost a lot of the ability when I became a vampire, but I still get snippets every now and then. I recognized that was happening to you when you appeared to become comatose while staring at our buddy downstairs. You have to tell me if this has ever happened to you before."

"No, never anything like it ever. Is this part of where I can sense when a person is a vampire even if I couldn't touch or even see him directly, or my feeling someone else's pain in a sympathetic tie to that person?"

Karan was staring at me. She wasn't a starer. She was usually cool and aloof.

If she was stunned, then maybe I should also be stunned. I am sure this was just a freak happening and not something that we should make a big thing out of.

"Paulie, you and I have to spend some time together. It will be best if we can have these meetings right here in this den. It is just as secure as Larisa's glass chamber in the security section."

Karan added, "That is a great plan. I want to say a few things before we try to find normalcy. You cannot discuss this with anyone but Darja and me and my dad when he returns.

"This whole thing could be a quirk that happened because of the high amount of stress you have been put through lately. On the other hand, though, this could be another interesting ability that is evolving in you. Understand that if our foes get even a hint that you may have some unusual abilities, the price on your head will go way up. Just to put it into perspective, I think you would be worth easily a hundred million dollars—alive. And that is just openers. We will see what my dad thinks when he gets back. Another item is that I want you and Darja to share an apartment, and I want your apartment to have a joining door to the next duplex where the twins will move into. The four of you will move together as one person tied at the hips. The twins are two of the best ninja/assassins in the world. You two, you and Darja, are no slouches, as far as vampires in general go. The four of you together should be invincible. Just don't get the idea that you *are* invincible. Don't let your guard down. This has been the longest day we all have had in a while. You two should get something to eat and get back to your apartments to get started on moving your things in together.

Darja and I each snagged several bottles of wine on our way through the kitchen. When we got upstairs in the apartment area over the garages, we separated, with each of us going to our rooms. It was decided that since I was the new kid on the block and that I hadn't amassed very much in the way of personal belongings, it would be me that was moving. I started boxing up my possessions and hauling them down the hall to Darja's suite.

Nicole was there packing her things to move into my apartment with her sister, Irene. She didn't take them down the hallway as I did though, She had opened the door connecting the two suites and pushed her stuff through that way.

There were possessions of mine in storage, waiting for me to get a permanent place to live. No room for all that stuff here, so I stayed as a minimalist.

Zope had rolled in and helped drink some of the wine. I mean, that is a big personal sacrifice on her part. Her dent in the wine supply kept us from drinking too much ourselves.

We got everything squared away by one in the morning, and we all crashed.

NO SCHOOL TODAY
3 JANUARY 2017

The alarm went off at 0500 hours. I was looking forward to getting back to work. Or was it back to school?

I washed up and combed my hair and packed my book bag, and I was ready to go. The twins were up but not Darja. First thought was to let her sleep in.

Nicole and Irene came into my suite and looked approvingly at my state of readiness.

"You guys go on to break fast. I will work on the princess to get her motor started for the day," Nicole said.

Before I sat down at the kitchen table, I went to the stove and picked up a bowl of oatmeal with butter and brown sugar, a plate with hash-browns, three eggs over, and country sausages. Luckily, there was fresh coffee and an assortment of Danish pastries, and unlimited butter.

Darja and Nicole weren't far behind Irene and me.

I finished and went out to my BMW. I got in and started the motor to get the heat up because it was quite snappy outside. I was feeling warm and fuzzy all over. I was thinking that I finally fitted in around here better than your favorite old coat.

My cell phone went off. I looked at the screen and saw that Larisa was calling. "Hello, Larisa," I said, and then there were several other voices on the line. I heard both Nicole and Irene on the line at the same time. Conference call.

"Everyone, listen carefully," Larisa said. "The observation

team across from the rat's nest notified me that last night around 9.30, the rats nest building lit up like a freeway diner. Vehicles were rushing in and out, including the big black Audi S8. Iskenderian's personal car. Amelia, ride your bike and go directly to the building where the observers are posted. Don't leave your motorcycle. I want you ready to go the instant that big Audi leaves. It is assumed that he is living on Mercer Island. Better yet, after you check in at the observation post, and if Iskenderian hasn't left, you go on over to the first exit from the freeway that crosses Mercer Island. Sit there, ready to pick up the tail when that car is headed to wherever his home is. The rest of you, Darja and Paulie and the twins, are to head in just as if there wasn't anything going on. When you all get to the hangar, come down to security, and we will figure out the school schedule.

We were about to leave when Zope came wheeling out. "Hold it, load me in. I'm not going to just sit here. At least I can be in the security section where I will be on top of what is going on."

Finally ready to go, or almost. Before I could back out of my stall, Ms. Karan was pulling out in her Audi R8. Pete was with her. As soon as she was clear, I backed and started driving toward the front gate.

The street in front of the Manor was straight and clear in the direction of the ferry landing. It was empty. Karan must be in a big hurry.

My cell phone rang. It was Ms. Karan.

"Paulie, go around the waiting vehicles to the loading ramp. They are holding the ferry until you get on board."

True to her word, the emergency lane was opened by an officer from the Bainbridge P.D. I pulled onto the nearly empty ferry and parked behind Ms. Karan's sports car. We would be the first ones off.

When we arrived at the Seattle dock, Pete and Karan took off like a shot. I didn't even try to keep up. As it turns out, I arrived at the hangar five minutes later. I parked, and everyone got out, including Zope, who was being pushed toward the elevator doors.

All the elevator cars in this building were spacious enough to hold a gurney, medical equipment, and attending nurses and doctors if needed. That meant we all fit in with ease, and I punched in my access codes and destination; Larisa's crystal cave of security.

As soon as we entered her private office, the sliding door shut, and the glass walls went opaque.

Ms. Karan was standing behind Larisa's chair and waited until everyone was in, seated, and the glass wall in stealth opaque mode. "Okay, everyone, listen up. We have been counting noses over at the Bat Cave, and we think that all the rogues in this area are there at this moment. Including their local leader, Iskenderian. We have the personnel and hardware to raid their special union hall and obliterate it and everyone inside. Good thought, but a bad idea. We can't allow this to turn into open warfare where the Normal population would become too curious. The first priority is to follow and determine where Iskenderian is housed locally. I would like to capture Iskenderian alive. We are not interested in capturing the rogues—too many problems housing, feeding, and re-orienting them. Doubt if any of them could be rehabilitated anyway. I am not promoting the total destruction of them. If anyone of them surrenders, then capture, do not kill them. Let's not worry about this point now. We will take the results to task when we can count the number of survivors we end up with."

Then we were all dismissed, so most of us headed up to the flight center. Pete, Karan, and Larisa were the only ones who remained. I knew that Pete would not leave Ms. Karan's side while we were at this alert level.

Zope didn't get off when the lift stopped at the hangar floor. She said she was going up to see the doctor. The rest of us headed toward the flight shack. The huge hangar door was fully open, and the Bell and the Dauphine helios were out front on the tarmac.

Mel and Charlie were in the shack's operations room. They looked up at me with expectation in their eyes.

"Who ordered the two helios readied?" I asked.

"Ms. Karan gave the order, and we are designated to be the pilots," said Mel as he nodded toward Charlie as pilot no# 2.

"There are four separate squads of four men, each on their way. Each helio will have a four-person assault team, and the other two squads will be held here in reserve."

At that very moment, a large truck was pulling to the hangar area. It carried the sixteen assault team members along with cots, a camp kitchen, food, and weapons cases. They immediately got down and offloaded the equipment. The portable kitchen was set up outside the side door next to the vehicle doorway. Lockstep precision. These were not ordinary, everyday household or plant guards. These were highly trained offensive attack units. This was one of the times where I wondered where all these troops were staying or where did they work during non-emergency times.

I knew with fair certainty that I would someday know all the answers. I didn't want the answer to this one at the moment as I was still in mental overwhelm with all I had been shown or taught in just the last two months.

The air was electric with the anxiety over the impending action. It looked like the Four Horsewomen; Darja, Nicole, Irene, and myself, were going to be sitting this one out.

The large screens in the flight shack usually showed the flight and maintenance schedules of all the aircraft based out of this hangar and several screens of weather patterns in different parts of the world; everywhere we had an aircraft flying near or the destination of any of our aircraft. Not now. They were live cameras focused on the Pig Pen and from a helmet cam on Amelia out at the first Mercer Island exit.

A Klaxon horn sounded. Two of the assault teams immediately ran for the two helicopters, as did the two pilots.

Irene's cell rang.

"Yes, ma'am," she answered.

The conversation was muffled, but it was over shortly, and Irene turned to us and said, "Karan wants me to leave for Mercer Island. Paulie, take two of the assault teams with you. Eddy had called and notified us that the large Audi we believe is used by Vic Iskenderian and another SUV just left the Viper Pit. Karan wants to try to be as close behind those two vehicles as you possibly can by the time they reach the Mercer Island exit."

3 JANUARY 2017 – AAANNDD, CUE MUSIC!

There was nothing I could say that would adequately explain my excitement. I was being inserted into the heart of the action. Irene had her hard-to-read, hard-ass face on. The two in the back seat seemed to be right at home with the way I was driving.

I cut directly across the airstrip. Probably going to get written up over this, could have contacted ground control and gotten permission, but we were in a big hurry. I went through an alleyway, came out on Airport Way, and yanked the wheel over to head north. I didn't look at the speedometer, but when I made the sharp left onto Airport Way, my SUV was in a four-wheel drift. As soon as I was facing north, I smashed the gas pedal to the floor, and the thoroughbred that this car was came through for me. No, for all of us, because it was made to corner in one piece or go through the chain-link fence and end up on the railroad tracks.

I tore up the road. The object was to cut through some of the side streets to catch the north on-ramp for I-5. I finally got the on-ramp that crossed back over Airport Way and the railroad tracks and onto I-5 North. It was three miles to the junction with I-90 East. I glanced at the speedometer reading and immediately ignored it. I was over 130mph. I guessed that Iskenderian would be driving 80.

He didn't want to be stopped by any law enforcement right

now. He wanted to stay out of the limelight. I, on the other hand, wasn't concerned with the police. I had one objective, and that was to catch up with that limo and find out where it called home.

As I neared the I-90 cutoff, I slowed for the eastbound traffic. It wasn't excessive but passing other cars at 130+ miles per hour wasn't a healthy idea. My thoughts on slowing down meant to keep it under 100 and probably something closer to 80, which was what many of the other cars were traveling at. As I was driving around a long curve, which was the interchange from I-5 to I-90, I could see many of the cars in front of me.

"Irene," I said, "look up ahead. Can you see the two black vehicles just about to enter the tunnel that funneled the interstate down to the water's edge where it became a causeway over Lake Washington?"

"That's them," she said. "We have to pick up the pace again. Got to be a lot closer so that we can see which off-ramp exit they take on Mercer Island."

That was the excuse I needed to justify driving a little over the speed limit. I called Amelia on her cell.

"Amelia, the subject's car is nearing you. By the time we have crossed the bridge, we should be right on their tail. Get ready to follow them down the first exit, which is, what? Mercer Way? Or be ready to storm out onto I-90 if they don't turn off there."

"Ready," was her curt response.

I was within a hundred yards of them when they pulled off on the first exit.

"There's Amelia," Irene said. "She is back about twenty-five yards. I think this dead-ends at the bottom onto W. Mercer Way."

“How did you know that it’s Mercer Way at the bottom?” I asked.

“You need to get out more, dearie,” Irene said. “The live map is right there on your dash console. Isn’t modern technology great?”

Mutter, mutter, mutter. I was driving, so it is the co-pilot’s job to watch the gauges and dials and take the radio chatter. As I said, I was driving, and this vehicle wasn’t a featherweight go-kart. It weighed about as much as a charging rhino, and it took concentration at a buck twenty-five to keep everything under control. “Dammmmnn!” I thought out loud. I was closing on Amelia, and the two black cars in front of her a little too fast as all three of them were slowing for the stop sign at the end of the exit ramp.

THE MERCER ISLAND DUST UP

The black limo and tailing SUV only slowed enough to make sure there wasn't any cross-traffic near, and they blew past the stop sign and headed south.

Schools were out for the Christmas break, and this was a residential neighborhood. Bikes and trikes and prams were everywhere.

This predicated that we had to slow down the local pedestrian traffic. It was giving me great angst. I didn't want to lose them now that I had a good shot at locating the hidey-hole that held the head rat. Amelia had pulled ahead and was now out of sight. I had driven a mile since I turned onto Mercer Way. I was coming around a long curve when my cell phone had an incoming.

It was Amelia.

"I'm close to both of them. They have slowed up as of the last bend in the road. I believe they may be getting ready to turn into one of the homes along this street."

"We should be up with you in half a minute," I said back to her.

As I came around a long curve in the road, I saw Amelia less than a hundred yards in front of my car, and at the same moment, I saw the tail of the black SUV turning down one of the streets that led to the waterfront homes. It was a dead-end street, so this had to be their home base, that or they had just cornered themselves.

The way they blasted down the residential street, they had to be aware of our presence. The chase group had bunched up since we turned into this street, so I knew that we were visible to anyone looking back. We were almost to the waterfront when the limo and following SUV turned into the last property driveway on the right side of the street. The waterfront home had a guardhouse at the entrance to the driveway. As the RIB's SUV cleared the checkpoint, the iron gates started to swing shut.

Amelia, on her motorcycle, was right there. She almost laid the bike down when she swerved to a stop right in front of the door to the guard hut. Straddling the stopped motorcycle, she reached under her leather jacket and came up with her pistol with a massive hole at the end of the barrel. She didn't wait for any discussion, and we heard the twin bark of a double-tap into the guard's chest.

Shit was what I thought at first. Could this have been a private local guard company that did not know that their client was a vampire, a rogue vampire banned from being in this part of the United States? An innocent norm caught up in the conflict between a species that he wasn't even aware existed. Collateral damage was the term we used in Afghanistan or Iraq. To lose your life while defending the wrong side was the worst thing that could ever happen to some poor Joe that was just doing his job.

The thought only occupied a millisecond but, when you are a vampire, a millisecond could mean a lifetime. Amelia didn't hesitate after she shot the guard. She holstered her pistol and headed down the driveway flat out on her motorcycle.

I pulled up, but couldn't fit past the partially closed gate.

RAM THE GATE, Irene was shouting in my ear. GO! GO!

GO!

I did it.

Was I unlucky; I ram the gate, it stops me in place, or it breaks off and is now part of the radiator grill on the front of my BMW. Or am I lucky; the gate flies off to the side, leaving me unfettered access to the rogue's main campus. I had a flash thought that I must have a guardian angel sitting on my shoulder now. It couldn't have been just fate that I had gotten me through so much in the recent months of my new life. This couldn't happen to just anyone.

I had been lucky… Again. The gate flew off its hinges as I rammed through.

My assault team disgorged before I had come to a stop in front of the garages for this waterfront on Lake Washington.

Status check: my team consisted of Amelia, myself, Irene, and our two assault troopers. On the other side, well, I had no idea of how large a force we were opposing. All I could think was that this was our chance to eradicate the entire rogue forces entirely and finally.

I drove further into the estate. The driveway was paved with bricks and split into a 'Y' with one fork pulling up outside the garages, and the other looked like it wound around to the front of the property that faced the lake. The garage had four car stalls, but the doors were only open on two, and that was where the Limo and the SUV had parked.

Suddenly, my head felt like I had just eaten some ice cream too fast. Brain freeze.

No, not brain freeze. My head was telling me that I was missing something that was right in front of me. The cars in the garages. They were empty. I mean, they were only a minute in front of Amelia's motorcycle and my Beemer. Just doesn't seem like they would have parked and bailed out of their vehicles that quickly. Unless they knew we were right behind them, and they rushed in to make sure the household staff had a wonderful surprise readied just for us. Probably inside right now, heating a pot of boiling oil.

I stopped right where the drive split for access to the garage area and to be able to go around the front. *Front of what?* I thought. I had no idea what the layout was like. This area was heavily forested and landscaped. You couldn't see the houses on either side of this one because of the dense foliage. My two assault guys in the back seat were out of the car as soon as it stopped.

Taking advantage of the coverage, they wove back and forth from shrub to tree till they got close to the open garage doors.

I was getting anxious for their safety. I was sure that the rogues had driven into the garages, and they wouldn't just get out of the vehicles and walk into the house. No, I was sure they were in the process of setting up a trap of some sort. They knew the layout one hundred percent, and we were flying blind.

My two-man assault team was talking to each other using sign language as they approached the opening to the garage. The first one to the edge of the garages dropped down by the outside wall while the other got up ahead of steam running to cross in front of the garages. He made it to behind the first car, which was the limo.

He stopped and was waiting, I think, to see if anyone was lying in wait to get a shot at him or any of us for that matter.

Nothing. No gunshots, not even a peep. I was getting antsy to be involved. Irene and I had already disconnected our seat belts and had our handguns out and ready. I turned to let myself out of the car, but a steel talon grabbed my arm.

"Sit," Irene said.

She said it in a very quiet voice. That alone got my attention. It also put me on higher alert, if that was even possible. I mean, I had my combat antennae out and searched for the signs of anyone, anyone at all, though the only other person from our clan that I didn't have in sight was Amelia. Both Irene and I had our windows down and hadn't heard her motorcycle since we blasted through the main gate. I was just about to ask Irene what our next move would be, but she must have been working on this when she spoke.

She was on her cell phone. She relayed everything that had happened so far and waited for a response.

"Roger. Over." She ended the call and said, "We're to make sure that you and I and this vehicle are safely away from the main activities. The Bell is already in the air and on the way here with reinforcements. We should be hearing it within the next minute or two.

"I will get out and walk down the driveway branch that we can't see because it curves around, hugging the house's side. Keep your senses on high alert. At the first signs of anyone approaching you that you don't know, I want you to drive away as fast as you can. If someone approaches from the rear, you drive on down the drive extension till you come across either myself or Amelia or both of us. If you are approached from the front, drive backward until you have gotten out onto the street. Head the car toward our return route and keep watching and listening."

With that, she softly eased the passenger's door open.

No door buzzer, but the interior lights did come on. That made me aware that nighttime was creeping in on us. In a former life, that would be a bad thing, but with my new spidey senses, my vision was only slightly diminished at night, and my hearing was sharper than ever.

Just as Irene started off, I felt a pain in the back of my head. It rocked me forward so hard I banged my head on the steering wheel. I turned away from the door and lay back with my head going toward the passenger's side, and my pistol firmly gripped and pointing toward the driver's door. I didn't see anyone other than Irene. She must have heard me when I got hit in the head.

She was around to the driver's side and had my door open in an instant. She leaned in, grabbed my hand, and pulled me erect in the driver's seat. She gingerly felt around on the back of my head.

"You're not bleeding. I don't feel a bump or anything. Did you bump your head on the door frame?"

"No. I hadn't even moved out of position behind the wheel. It felt like someone had reached in through the window and rapped me on the back of my head with a lead pipe. There may not be a bump or any blood, but I still see stars."

That's when we heard the wop, wop, wop of a helicopter headed in all-out; weapons being discharged back by the garages, and where the hell was Amelia?

There was a motorcycle and other vehicles pouring in through the wrinkled gate. It was Eddie on his Harley, leading the charge, and Nicole on her motorcycle with Darja hanging on to her back, and two military HumVees full of Newmark security personnel. One went around my car on the grass and headed toward the shoreline, while the other one went past the garage opening and across the side lawn toward the shoreline on the opposite side of the house.

Our earwigs crackled to life, putting us online with everyone on the operation.

"This is Team 3 leader. We passed the south side of the house where the secondary driveway led. There is a BMW motorcycle lying here. No one else, and the house seems strangely quiet."

"This is Team 2 leader. We just cleared the north side of the house and are closing in on the boat dock. There are three people headed down the dock, and they are dragging a fourth person. Three are in black, and the unconscious person is in motorcycle leathers. There is a floatplane with its motor running at the end of the dock."

"This is Irene LaFarge. T2 and T3, back down. Do not approach the people leaving for the aircraft. T2, do you have a rifleman that could knock that engine out? If you have any doubt, just hold off, we can't risk harming their prisoner," Irene said.

"Irene to the Bell. Who is the pilot?"

"It's me, Mack."

"Mack, we believe they've taken Amelia."

"WHAT!"

That was Eddie. He had pulled up on the left side of my car and had just gotten off his motorcycle, and was at the driver's door when he heard Irene say that the person being kidnapped could be Amelia.

He didn't wait to chit-chat but tore out in the direction of the waterfront. The seaplane was being loaded up with a cargo item worth everything to Eddie and actually to all of us. We couldn't let the rogues get away with her. I was out of the car and running right behind Eddie when I realized that Irene hadn't chastised me for going off alone; well, that wasn't true, I looked to my side, and she was right there step for step as we raced for the dock.

As Eddie ran onto the dock, the last man on the rogue abduction team turned and aimed with a pistol.

CRACK! I heard the report of a large caliber rifle off to my right. I didn't take my eyes off the scene that was unfolding on the dock. The gunshot I had just heard must have been from a friendly as Eddie was still standing, and the rogue that had been rear guard had crumpled to the dock and was not moving any more.

The floatplane wasn't waiting and had turned on full power and was pulling away from the dock.

Eddie tore down the dock and launched himself off the end in an attempt to grab hold of one of the pontoons. It wasn't to be. He was too short, and the plane was already moving faster than Eddie could swim.

Out of the darkening sky appeared the Bell sans the required running lights. The Bell was faster than the de Havilland, and Mack flew it in front of the seaplane where he rotated the helicopter so that it was flying backward in front of the seaplane. The seaplane pilot was kicking the rudder back and forth in an attempt to get around the helicopter long enough to get airborne.

Mack turned on the landing lights which were a lot brighter than anything on the much older fixed-wing aircraft. They were blinding the seaplane's pilot, making him unsure of how close the helicopter was, and I think he knew that he wasn't going to get out of there. He cut the throttle, and the plane slowed in the water till it was just creeping along.

Meanwhile, back on the dock, Irene and I had jumped into a Riva speedboat that was tied up opposite from where the seaplane had been moored. I went immediately to the control panel and pried the ignition switch out of the dash panel with my combat knife. Easy as hot wiring a '55 Chevy. I got the speedboat's engine started, and Irene loosed the mooring lines, and I headed toward Eddie. He heard us and stopped trying to swim after the seaplane and waited for us to come alongside. Irene reached over the side and grabbed Eddie by his jacket, and hauled him aboard.

The seaplane was a good three to four hundred yards out by now, but it was not going anywhere. The prop was still churning slowly, but the blades were feathered, therefore no headway.

Mack had backed the Bell helicopter up and away from the seaplane, which had slowed and almost stopped. I headed directly for the seaplane. We were down to one hundred yards when I saw the cabin door on the pilot's side of the cabin open, and someone leaped into the water and disappeared below the surface.

"I see where he went in," Eddie said. "I have to get into the cabin of that plane and rescue Amelia before I worry about who is trying to swim away."

I eased the runabout alongside the right pontoon and passenger door. I was getting close enough so that Eddie or Irene could cross over to stand on the pontoon where they could access the aircraft's interior through the passenger side door. Eddie launched himself from the deck of the speedboat onto the pontoon.

His right arm shot out toward the door release, and he not only pulled the door open, he ripped it off its hinges and dropped it into the lake. An arm wearing the requisite rogue black was seen swinging around with a pistol in its hand. The rogue was turning to get a shot at Eddie while Eddie was reaching for the arm of the rogue.

The rogue's gun went off before he had Eddie in his sights. I watched intently and didn't think that the gun had been pointing in my direction when it went off. Something wasn't right because I felt a sharp pain in the upper part of my left arm. I let go of the throttle and rudder and reached around with my right hand to feel for the point of entry.

Eddie had the rogue's gun arm firmly in the grasp of both of his hands, and he was trying to pull the rogue out of the passenger seat. That was what I was seeing while Irene was shouting at me from the prow of our boat.

"Paulie, get around to the other side. Now, now, now."

I got ahold of the boat's controls and spun it around in front of the plane, and headed for the left float. Irene was crouching, readying herself for the leap from the boat to the plane. Just as I got close enough, I saw Irene leap across the gap. She landed on one foot as the other one slipped on the wet surface and saved herself from a water landing by grabbing one of the pontoon struts with her right hand. That was when I saw that her left arm was not holding up its side of the exercise. In a flash, it dawned on me as to what had happened. She had taken the wild shot in her upper left arm, and I was feeling the pain as it seemed that I had a connection with her pain. But where had the knock on my noggin come from?

Okay, so I knew now that Irene had taken a bullet to her arm. It didn't seem to slow her that much as she pulled the pilot's door wide open. She was working her way into the cabin. It seemed to take forever as I was feeling every bit of the pain she was experiencing. Then she disappeared into the plane's interior.

I heard two more gunshots, and then it might have been quiet except for the howl from the Bell's turbine and the battering from the helicopter's downwash that had the waters roiled into a froth. The downwash was also catching the wing surfaces of the seaplane, which had it doing its version of the Irish jig.

Over the turbine's howl, I heard a person yell and then a splash.

Mack pulled the Bell off and away to give us some calmer waters so that we could sort everything through. Me, not sure of what to do next, pulled the boat around the tail of the seaplane and up to the right pontoon. Then I saw Eddie; he no longer had ahold of the shooter's arm, and in fact, I didn't even see the shooter any more. Eddie was scrambling his way into the plane's cabin. Someone turned on the interior lights in the seaplane, and I could see Eddie and Irene working on something in the back seat.

As I pulled up alongside, Eddie's butt was backing out of the passenger's doorway. He was, with the help of Irene, pulling a bundle out with him. It was a person wrapped up in a blanket that was held closed by several regular pants belts. He undid the belts and let them fall into the water. The bundle he eased into the boat. I got up and eased his bundle into the wide bench seat to the aft of the boat. She or Amelia had a white or formerly white piece of a sheet wound around her head. She wasn't moving, but she was breathing. I had expected Eddie to have jumped in, but I turned to see him helping Irene out of the aircraft, and then both of them crossed over onto the boat.

Once they were aboard, Eddie went to Amelia's side, and Irene went to the boat's helm.

"Paulie," Irene started, "can you steer the plane back to the dock?"

I had been issued a Taxi License by the army. Those that held one could move aircraft around the airport under the aircraft's power. We just weren't allowed to lift off. The seaplane was just another fixed-wing aircraft, so I didn't think it would be a problem.

"I believe so," I said back.

I didn't wait for exact instructions. I just pulled myself onto the pontoon and then climbed up into the pilot's seat.

The pilot that had jumped into the lake water and disappeared must have been a big boy because at 5'11", I was just able to reach the rudder pedals. I located the throttle, which was where it instinctively should have been, the pitch control for the prop took a few moments longer, but once I found everything I thought I would need, I started steering back to the dock in front of the rogue's roach hotel.

8 JANUARY
THE CLOSE OF THE SECOND STORY IN *THE PURLOINED PINT* SERIES

The 'A' team was collected in the wine cellar.

Zope had come without any wheelchair or other walking aids, but her right arm was still in a sling. No cast, just a sling. Amelia and Irene were the walking wounded.

Amelia had received a concussion and several stitches and was on cautionary restricted activities. Irene's left arm was in a sling but gave the appearance that she was 99.9 percent.

For what we had accomplished, we had to give thanks that our losses were insanely minor in comparison. The rogues' nest at the airfield had been cleansed. There wasn't much there that would give us any information on their operation. The house on Mercer Island was a different thing, though.

It was clear that they, the rogues, did not expect us to unravel their plans so quickly. There were extensive paperwork and copies of correspondence between Max Stern and Vic Iskenderian.

Intel was always good, but something we could all use was the equipment we recovered. Loads of electronic equipment, firearms, the Audi Limo, and half a dozen already painted black SUVs and a nifty speedboat and best, as far as I was concerned, a seaplane that only needed a new passenger-side door to make it perfect again.

Karan Newmark stood and raised her hand.

"We are all here. We all made it through with only minor but fully repairable injuries. I would have preferred no injuries on our side, but this whole caper came out of the blue.

We did pretty good, considering that we were totally blindsided. If Paulie here hadn't become the sacrificial lamb a few months ago, we would not have been aware of their presence. I don't want any one of you, though, to allow yourself to be bitten by strangers to uncover some hereto unknown plot against our company and our people. In going over everything at the Mercer Island house, it has been determined beyond any doubt that Vic Iskenderian was the agent in charge of this attack. We also believe that it was Vic that was at the controls of the seaplane and that he had on a wet suit and other diving equipment with him when he bailed out and disappeared beneath the water. We don't know how he left this area, but we are sure that he is long gone. We are off the alert level back to the lowest level with one exception.

"This was a wake-up call. No matter how sure we are that the threat has been eliminated, it can arise again without our knowledge, and we find ourselves again fighting from behind. I do not want us to have to fight our way from a position of starting from the basement but rather looking down from the top. Just think about how quickly Stern and his minions recovered from their eviction from Seattle to a position of coming close to causing some serious harm to our corporate as well as our personal lives.

"Irene and Nicole, we are going to relax the personal security coverage of Paulie and Darja. However, I would ask that you, Paulie, and you, Darja, not do anything alone when you are away from this property or away from the security building.

"You can count on one thing, and it is that Stern and Iskenderian will be returning with another surprise. Still, this recent activity from them may have cost them in both material items as well as the loss of so many soldiers. They are wounded, but they are NOT out of business.

"I am asking that Irene, Amelia, and Zope become a traveling troupe of three very bad-ass wounded warriors until all three of you have final clearances from Dr. Smyth.

"Paulie, you are someone that we are all looking up to right now. You are the baby of the group, but you demonstrated the abilities, resolve, and attitude of a vampire whose age is numbered in the hundreds of years rather than the few weeks you have had to learn this life. We all, including my dad, have decided to give you the de Havilland seaplane. Well, it will have the pontoons removed and wheels installed for you to use as your plane to get your license. After that, you may want to get floatplane certified, at which time we put the floats back on.

"Now, with Sparky's blessing, we are going to the back of this cellar where the real good champagne is kept under lock and key.